THE DEBT

BOOK TWO: THE BRIDGE SERIES

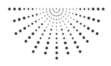

ANN HOWES

Whenever I'm alone with you
You make me feel like I am home again
Whenever I'm alone with you
You make me feel like I am whole again
~Love Song~The Cure~

Thank you for selecting this book. I hope you enjoy!

For updates on new releases, you can follow me at:

https://www.facebook.com/AuthorAnnHowes/
https://www.amazon.com/author/annhowes/
https://www.bookbub.com/authors/ann-howes

Cover design:
Taylor Sullivan at
https://www.facebook.com/ImaginationUnCOVERED/

Editing: Gillian Holmes
https://reedsy.com/gillian-holmes
&
Sue Seabury
https://thetechnopeasant.wordpress.com

❀ Created with Vellum

Buttercup and Pumpkin,
you are the bestest of the best!

&

The rest of the ladies of Casa Buttercup,
you know who you are.
Words cannot express how grateful I am to you for the laughs, love,
gallons of champagne and loads of support you have given me in this
writing thing. Here's to many more book signing parties.

This book is dedicated to all of you.

CHAPTER ONE

Friday afternoon

*D*ude *call me. It's a 911!!!*

Three exclamation points?

Terra Miller stared at her iPhone screen. Two missed calls from Lucas, and one text message.

The drummer from her ex-band was not known to be overly dramatic, but unless he'd been kidnapped by aliens or got married in Vegas, had second thoughts and needed help ditching his new bride, his text definitely smacked of drama.

Drama she was no longer a part of and hadn't been for two long, heart-crushing, soul-sucking months. She shouldn't care but seeing his message she realized she still did—a lot.

"I'm gonna take a quick break," she called across the sales floor to her coworker at Provocative, an exclusive, high-end lingerie store on California Street, downtown San Francisco. "While it's still slow."

Helen, who also happened to be her best friend, looked up from organizing a drawer of matching bra and panty sets after a particularly crazy Friday lunch-hour rush and flipped a shiny curtain of long auburn hair over her shoulder. As she took in Terra's expression, furrows formed on her smooth brow. "You okay?"

Was she?

She supposed she was.

Each day got a little better but there were some when she couldn't tell the difference between okay and not okay because she was just that numb. Today was one of those days.

She pinched the bridge of her nose, let out a long sigh and gave Helen her sales-floor smile. "Just need to return a call."

"Your mom finally call you back?" Helen's voice carried enough worry that Terra knew she wasn't buying the fake smile.

"No, this one's from Lucas," she said and pretended not to see her expression of mild concern turn to an expression of unhappy.

She couldn't fault her. It had been Helen who'd cried along with her when she gathered the pieces of her shattered heart—got her through the worst with her special brand of dork and bottles of cheap wine when all she wanted was to crawl into her guitar case and die.

The little brass bell jingled as she pushed the door and stepped into the mild afternoon air. Her thumb hovered over Lucas's number for several seconds before she pressed it.

"Dude, you're calling me back," he said after the second ring. "Been climbing out of my skin worried stupid you wouldn't."

"Why wouldn't I call *you* back, Lu?"

"Well, you didn't when I checked on you before."

Yeah.

That was true.

"Like ten times," he went on when she remained silent. And there was that drama again. "Since you didn't answer, I thought… we all thought we'd just give you space. Figured when you'd had some time to think you'd come back fighting. Grab that skinny skank by her bony ass and toss her into the bay."

The *skinny skank*—aka Ruby—was the reason she walked away —not just from her band, but her relationship as well. Her gaze roved to the red-brick building of St Mary's Cathedral. She could use a little serenity but hadn't been inside a church since her early childhood and she wondered if that was the reason she was on God's shit-list.

"Are you calling to lecture me?"

"No, that's…"

"Because if you are, I *really* don't want to hear it. I've got enough happening as it is."

"Listen Tee, I love your stubborn ass to the stage and back but I'm gonna give it to you straight. I know something bad went down between you, Dannie and Ruby, and it sucked hard for you. But if you've left the band, you need to let us know."

"I didn't technically leave, Lu. I got replaced."

"That's bullshit, and you know it. We had last-minute gigs, and you weren't answering your phone. What the fuck were we supposed to do? Ruby stepped in but it's not permanent unless you let it be. Don't let her do this to you."

Let her?

She felt a prickle move up her spine that quickly turned into angry heat. It spread up her chest, her neck and into her face.

"Jesus, Lu, I didn't *let* her do anything."

"Maybe *let* was the wrong word to use…"

"You have no idea what went down."

"Uh…"

"And I'm not going to fill you in, that's for Dannie to do, if he has the fucking balls to tell the truth. But all you need to know is they broke me, Lu. *They fucking broke me*. I needed space to deal with this thing with my mom, to get my head straight and I couldn't face them right then."

"Dude…you're right, I have no idea what happened. But you gotta know, whatever it was, we love you and we need you."

As she absorbed his words, she took a deep breath and felt her temper ease a bit. "I appreciate that, much more than you know, but…."

"We want you in the band."

"Lu," she whispered. "I'm not sharing the stage with her. Don't ask me to do that."

"We're not asking you to share. She's gone."

At that moment, a car honked loudly beside her, drowning out Lucas's voice, so she thought she'd misheard. "What?"

"Ruby's gone," he repeated.

"Gone? What do you mean gone?" *Is she dead?*

"She sent Dannie a text—said she hauled ass with someone to Seattle."

"I'm sure this is all very nice gossip and…yeah, I wouldn't be human if I didn't think Dannie deserved to get his ass dumped but I can't hear it."

She heard him take a deep breath, the stillness as he held it, then the blast of air as he let it out. "We have a gig tonight," he said finally.

Ah—a gig!

Now it made sense.

"So that's your 911? Wow…Lu. You're asking me back because Ruby left, and you need me to bail you out?"

"When you put it like that it sounds horrible."

"That's because it is horrible."

"But I'm not asking you back, because as far as I'm concerned you never left. Dannie wanted to cancel, but I thought I'd risk my neck and beg you to do it."

Again, she thought she'd misheard. They wanted her back?

Did she want to go back?

Then he pulled out the big guitars.

"The gig is at Chuck's."

Her breath caught, because, well…fucking Chuck's. The hottest bar in the Tenderloin where bands went to play their rock-and-roll pants off. They'd been trying for months to get a gig there, but the line-up was long, and no one gave up their spot. Not even when a band member died or were held at gunpoint and kidnapped. Which was the running joke because some of her crazies had threatened to do just that. Of course, they never followed through—thank the music gods, as it would've been left to her to bail them out. *Because Ruby sure wouldn't.*

"Chuck's, dude," Lucas said. "You're getting me now?"

"Damn—how the hell did that happen?"

"This is where it gets a little bit more horrible."

"Oh crap, do I want to hear this?"

"Ruby knows the owner. She got him to move things around and give us a slot."

Of course, she did. Terra stared into the distance, watching a pair of pigeons landing on the stairs of St Mary's and let out a long breath.

"Actually, gave us two slots."

"Two?"

"The first we played a week ago and it went well but not like it would have if you'd been there. Think of it this way: wouldn't it be the ultimate stick in her ass if you fronted us at a gig she'd begged for?"

Define 'beg.' More like 'blew someone,' but that was neither here nor there, because it would. She curled her lips in a salty smile. It so, *soo* fucking would.

"This is your chance. Take it."

"Lu…"

"Don't let whatever happened with Dannie mess with what you have with the rest of us. Fuck him. I mean, I love the man like a brother, but he never deserved you. So, show us who you are. That you're stronger than this."

"Lu…"

"Please, Tee. I'm begging you. Come back and help us out…"

"Lu…shut up for a minute."

He sighed. "Okay, I'm shutting up."

"If I do this, and I'm emphasizing *if*, I need to know that everybody's okay with it. I mean *everybody*. I can't be showing up ready to put myself out there again to have anybody give me crap."

"Will four out of five do?"

"Four meaning?"

"Me, Jeff, Jake and with you, that makes four. Dannie can either deal or go fuck himself."

"The others are cool?"

"They're more than cool. They're right here, listening on speaker."

"Ohmigod!"

Her boys were all right there? Suddenly she wanted nothing more than to show up and do her thing—stick the gig in Ruby's metaphorical

ass because they were *her* boys and she should be on stage with them.

"You guys are such assholes," she giggled.

"Will you do it?"

"Yes—fine—okay, I'll do it."

"Yeeoow!" One of the guys, probably Jeff, yelled in the background, making her giggle even harder. "She's back."

"I'm back." She leaned against the display window of Provocative grinning for the first time in a while. The cool glass felt good against her fitted, button-down blouse and she breathed a sigh of relief, like the burden of her mom's problems had lightened a bit. Tonight's gig money would go a long way towards tomorrow's payment. "Okay, uglies. I'll see you there."

After a chorus of "laters," she hung up, waiting for it to sink in, letting the glow ease the pain, loosen the tightness in her neck and shoulders that she hadn't realized was there until that second.

She was back!

Holy hell!

She had to avert her gaze from a man strolling by thinking she was flirting—which she definitely was not, because of the stupid smile on her face. And for a few minutes more, she enjoyed the early August sunshine then checked her messages again. Still no response from her mom. It had been several days—and longer than usual for them not to have communicated in some form.

Worry was a constant when it came to Rebecca Miller. Today, it felt a little more pervasive, but she wasn't going to let it get to her. The rehab facility limited access to phones and computers, so communication was sketchy at best. Therefore, she thumbed a new message.

Hey Mama. Call me when you can. Love you lots xx.

CHAPTER TWO

Friday evening

*Z*ander Milan lifted the lid of the dumpster in his alley, preparing to toss a bag into it when he heard it.

PAPOW!

Thanks to his instincts, still sharp from years of growing up in the surly Tenderloin, he ducked and took cover while his heart drummed a rhythm that couldn't be described as normal or healthy.

Was this it?

Was it over—at thirty-two? *Now?* After he'd made something of himself—like into the owner of one of the busiest bars in the city.

With his heart in his throat, he waited a few seconds before peering around the metal container. Red lights glowed at the entrance to his alley and he stepped further into the shadows— between the dumpsters and his carport.

His pulse pounded when a large vehicle—some kind of van,

reversed, stopped and turned, spotlighting the narrow lane. Then it moved towards him in a slow crawl.

Shit.

He looked around for an escape route, but he knew his alley and there wasn't one. He was an agile man, and could possibly pull a Spiderman, if he had a running start.

But he didn't.

He was trapped.

This neighborhood had been somewhat gentrified over the past few years, but the occasional drive-by shooting wasn't unheard of.

Then the vehicle came into the light and hit a pothole.

PAPOW.

Relief seeped through him as he got the cosmic joke the universe played on him. Not a gunshot—a backfiring relic from the Summer of Love.

"Very fucking funny," he muttered to the stars.

He scraped a hand through thick, overlong hair as the ancient Volkswagen bus, complete with camper shell, drove towards him. Who in their right mind would drive such a hideous piece of crap? The thing looked like it was held together with duct tape and paperclips.

The van whirred and veered left, pulling up outside the back door of his club before spluttering to a silent death.

He sighed when the headlights dimmed. "Oh no, you don't— that shit's not gonna fly."

He made a move to confront the illegally parked groupie but the garbage bag he carried bumped his leg, reminding him why he was out here in the first place.

After tossing the bag into the dumpster, he wiped his hands on the bar towel he'd stuck in the back pocket of his jeans, his body buzzing with adrenaline. Then he readied himself to face the overzealous loser obviously trying to skirt the cover charge at the main door.

A woman climbed out. One long-ass leg tipped with a motor-cycle boot at a time. Unexpected, but cool—not a dude, therefore chances of getting physical were minimal.

As he approached, she came into the light and caught a mass of reddish-blonde curls behind her head, twisting it into a coil and something odd happened to his heart. It seemed to stutter.

He examined her shape and he had to admit he liked what he saw—curvy yet slim with perky tits on which his eyes got stuck.

The woman shut the bus door then stood with her hands planted on her hips staring at the back entrance, as if she was contemplating entering.

"Yo, babe," he called, noting his voice had gone a tad hoarse.

She ignored him. Or perhaps she didn't hear since he was still a fair distance from her. Either way, and probably because he was amped on adrenaline, it annoyed him. He was not a man used to being ignored by anyone, especially an attractive woman.

"You need to move your van," he said a little more forcefully when he got within ten feet of her. "You can't park there."

"I know," the woman responded without looking at him. Her voice carried a husky note that reached inside and wrapped around everything about him that was male—made his dick sit up. "I need to unload my stuff first, then I'll move."

Zander focused on her profile. She looked to be younger than him, maybe twenty-fourish and really pretty. With a cute little upturned nose, plump lips that glistened and the aforementioned tits displaying a decent amount of cleavage. He couldn't see her ass since it was covered in a long, off-the-shoulder sweater, but he would hazard a guess it compared nicely.

"Stuff for what?" He asked, fascinated and a tiny bit jealous of the tooth that mauled her bottom lip.

"I'm with the band."

"The band?" He raised his eyebrows, trying to envision which lucky son-of-a-bitch member she had a fixation on. "Which one?"

"Which one what?"

"Which member of the band do you belong to?"

The eyebrow closest to him, the one he could see, arched. "None of them, I'm *in* the band."

Christ.

Like he initially thought—a groupie, and a delusional one at that. Nothing he wasn't familiar with, but disappointing and not what he needed.

"Babe, you're not," he said trying to keep his voice even. "The main entrance is around the corner. You have to pay the cover charge, just like everyone else."

"Look...buddy." She turned to face him, giving him a once over, starting at his feet. Normally that would make him happy, as most women, once having checked him out, liked what they saw. Sadly for him, considering her front was even prettier than her profile, he wasn't getting that vibe. Just the opposite, which turned out to be even more disappointing because he suddenly realized he *wanted* her to like what she saw.

"I'm not a groupie trying to sneak in for free," she continued. "Like I said, I'm with the band. Do I have to go up those to get to the stage?" Her chin pointed at the flight of concrete stairs that led up to his office and his apartment. The movement caused a tiny diamond stud in her nostril to catch the light and twinkle.

"Stage is to the left of the stairs, but that's not where you're going."

"Why not?"

"Because like *I* said, main entrance is around the corner."

"Hmm," she hummed, pursing her lips and considering him for a long second. "Good to know." Then she turned and instead of climbing back in her van, pulled the lever on the dented sliding door. When it opened, he saw it really *was* a camper with a sideways seat that probably doubled as a bed. He also saw a stage monitor, an acoustic guitar and a worn leather bag.

Huh!

She leaned in, bending at the waist. His vision filled with two round, perfect ass cheeks molded by tight skinny jeans and for a moment he completely forgot all about her illegally parked van.

He blew out air, then positioned himself at a respectable distance slightly behind and to her side, finding it hard enough to keep his eyes on what she did inside the car. Though not completely succeeding since she caught him looking.

"Maybe instead of staring at my ass," she shot over her shoulder, "you can help me with my monitor? The thing doesn't have wheels and it weighs fifty pounds."

Zander heard her voice but was having trouble focusing on the words.

"Who the fuck are you?" he managed at last, recognizing it should've been the first question he asked her.

"I'm Terra and I'm with the band." This time she said it slow, enunciating each word as if his IQ was below the triple digit mark.

Zander folded his arms across his chest. Clearly this was getting them nowhere. "You have the wrong night, babe. Because I know the band that's playing tonight, and you're not one of them."

She angled her head and stared at him, something flitting across her face. It was quick and he couldn't be sure, but it looked like pain.

"I suggest you stop what you're doing, get back in your van and move this piece of shit out of my alley."

That's when her head jerked a little and she tensed.

Good—the woman was finally getting it.

Careful to avoid bumping her head on the bus ceiling, she moved that delectable rear end backward and toward him, then straightened herself to her full height. Which, he now noted, was slightly above average yet a whole lot less than his. She blinked and trained, long-lashed eyes that flashed blue fire.

"First"—she swept a graceful hand indicating the van—"*this* is not a piece of shit. *This* is Iris. She's reliable and she's mine.

Second, and pay attention because I'm only going to say this once more. I'm. With. The band."

"Bullshit."

"Oh, for fuck's sake!" She threw her hands in the air. "I don't have time for this." Then she dug into her bra.

Zander's eyes widened, thinking she was about to flash herself then bit down his disappointment when the woman produced a phone, jabbing it a couple times with a thumb adorned with a silver ring. When it rang, she put it on speakerphone.

"Dannie," she said when he answered, keeping her gaze locked on Zander.

"Where the hell are you?" Dannie's voice smacking of panic was higher pitched than normal. "You're late."

"You can calm down now. I'm in the alley at the back door and definitely not late. The bouncer won't let me in. He thinks I've got the wrong night."

Bouncer?

That almost struck him as funny. It had been a while since anyone had mistaken him for one of his employees. He held out his hand, still holding her gaze. "Let me talk to him."

Terra slapped the phone into his palm. It was warm from her body and considering where it had been a few seconds earlier, made his fingers tingle.

He took it off speaker. "Dannie, this is Zander."

"Oh, shit," Dannie responded with a groan. "Sorry, man. Terra's mouthy but she is with us. She's covering for Rube."

"What do you mean *covering for Rube*? Where's Ruby?"

"She bailed on us. Went to Seattle. Or at least that's what she said."

Typical.

He knew he shouldn't have trusted her and now he was going to have to have words with her. He hated having words with women and avoided it as much as possible as it mostly ended with him feeling like a dick or them crying. Or both. "You should have told me. I could've replaced you."

"I know that, but we didn't want to get replaced. That's why Terra is here."

Great—a fucking surprise.

Another thing he hated.

"If you fuck this up, Dannie, you're not coming back."

"Trust me, man, we won't fuck this up."

Zander grunted, narrowing his eyes. "I'll guess we'll find out." Terra had resumed her earlier position with her tempting ass back on display, tugging the zip on the worn leather kitbag filled with small musical instruments. He caught a glimpse of a tambourine, the brass edges of a cowbell and several drumsticks.

As if feeling his eyes on her again she called out, "Can you tell Dannie I need help." She hooked both hands into the handle of her monitor and hefted it to the edge of the van floor. "Since you're not willing."

He'd already ended the call, but she was wrong. He was willing, all right—only not the way she thought. Especially as his eyes were riveted to the way her top slipped off her shoulder, exposing a red-and-black lacy bra.

His fingers felt warm as he cradled her phone in his hand, reluctant to give it back. Since her hands were unavailable, he shoved it in his jean's back pocket. "Give me your monitor. I'll carry it to the stage. Once you've unloaded you can park in the lot at the end of the alley with the rest of the band."

She smiled—a sweet parting of those juicy lips, showing off pretty teeth and making that teeny nose stud sparkle under his overhead lights.

It was a gut punch—and it took him a moment to recover.

He liked women but he hadn't yet tied himself to one. In his bar there was no shortage of females offering themselves. So far that had worked for him, but he had a sudden and odd feeling in his gut *this* woman would challenge that.

And despite that smile, she didn't look remotely interested.

She thanked him and turned her attention back to the leather bag.

He got as close as he dared and looped his hand around the monitor handle. "You're welcome," he muttered.

Christ—she smelled good too. His nostrils flared when he breathed in deep, catching her flowery scent that made him think of orchids in a rainforest. He didn't know why, because he'd never actually smelled orchids in a rainforest, but there you had it. It was light, yet intoxicating, like her, and he wanted to linger, but didn't want to come off as desperate.

Because he wasn't desperate.

Yet.

The monitor was as heavy as it looked as he carried it to the stage, ignoring the looks he got from the rest of the band when he lugged it up the stairs. They'd stopped unrolling guitar cords and arranging mic stands to stare. Jeff, the bass player, did a double-take.

Zander empathized.

He never touched the talent's equipment for liability reasons, and he wasn't a fucking roadie.

"Where do I put this?" he asked Jeff. The man's mouth hung open, exposing perfectly straight teeth—probably a result of years of Invisalign.

Jeff pointed at a gap between a mic stand and an amp. Zander placed the monitor in the designated spot and without looking back placed a hand on the edge of the stage and vaulted off. Then he sauntered across scuffed wooden floors towards the bar—because it wasn't like he had anything else to do other than help a woman who'd mindfucked him into helping her. He shook his head and suspected all she needed to do was crook a finger at the nearest chump, and he'd drop what he was doing. In his case, she hadn't even crooked a finger—he'd *volunteered.* Fucking hell—he was in danger of becoming a gentleman.

Though it was still early in the evening, several after-work regulars sat nursing half-full beers and colorful cocktails. He'd worked his ass off since receiving the deed from Chuck, the previous owner, to change the vibe from biker-dive to citizen-friendly and usually Friday nights were packed. The last time this band, Obsessed, had played, they had done decently enough—they had better tonight as well otherwise they *weren't* coming back. Though *she* could, if she wanted.

He greeted Barney, the silver-haired bartender he'd inherited with a chin nod. The ornery bastard carried a tray of clean glasses that needed organizing and Zander sidestepped to allow him to pass.

"Nicky's gonna be late," Barney said in his gravelly, two-packs-a-day voice. He'd given up smoking years ago, but the voice stayed. "Her kid is sick. She's waiting for the ex to show but you know how that can go."

"Call her, tell her not to stress. I'll cover for her until she gets here."

"*If* she gets here."

"Whatever—her ex is unreliable—that's not on her."

Which reminded Zander, why had Ruby disappeared? Not that he enjoyed dabbling in band politics but when it came to his bar and his bottom line, band politics by default became his business.

"Fucking scars on her forearm," Zander muttered to himself. "That's probably why." He'd seen needle marks when Ruby's sleeve had slipped up her arm and he doubted she'd suddenly become diabetic. The only reason he'd booked this band in the first place was because she'd asked, and their history went way back.

"What...Nicky?" Barney asked.

"Ruby."

"That skinny runt-junkie that fronts this band?" Barney asked.

Zander cut him a sideways glance.

"Can spot them a mile away, son," he said, changing the song playing over the bar speakers to Aerosmith's "Dude Looks Like A Lady".

Indeed, he could. Barney had been around long enough—since the bar had been a front for dealing heroin back in the nineties.

Zander hauled two cases of German beer from the back and began to unload them into the fridge then entered the quantity into the inventory list on the iPad he kept behind the bar. Glancing up, he caught a glimpse of the woman again.

Everything in him locked up tight—not one damn muscle in his body moved except the ones in his eye sockets as they followed her movements.

She claimed the stage like she'd been born on one, swinging that ass just enough to make him wonder what else she could with it. Or rather, what he wanted her to do with it and no doubt would fantasize about later.

Fuck.

He was fantasizing now.

CHAPTER THREE

Later Friday

"Hey, you bunch of ugly assholes." Terra's nerves skittered in her stomach like a crab on crack as she stepped onto the stage, dropping her kitbag next to her monitor.

"You're here." Lucas swaggered towards her, putting his toned drummer's shoulder to her stomach and lifting her in a fireman's hold. "Fuck, yeah!"

"Ohmigod...put me down, you big jerk," she squealed in between bursts of giggles as he twirled her. "You're gonna make me puke."

Lucas laughed, smacking her butt before he placed her back on her feet. "I knew you couldn't stay away—we're all too damn good-looking," he muttered, grinning and giving her a squeeze.

"Missed your chubby butt, Tee," Jeff, the bass guitarist said, kissing her cheek. "You look good—shit hasn't been the same without you."

"Missed you too, goofball, and my butt is not chubby. What is it with you guys and my butt? You all turned into bigger pervs than usual since I've been gone?"

"Compared to Ruby's, everybody's butt is chubby and from where I stand on stage, I'd rather look at yours."

She chuckled because she got his not so subtle dig at Dannie.

"Hey," Jake said, swinging his guitar behind his back to give her a hug. "Glad you're here. Give the prick hell," he said softly, so only she could hear. "Don't let his gruff fool or intimidate you— we've got your back."

She returned his hug, then stepped away to face the prick in question. Dannie—the former love of her life, now ex-boyfriend stood off to the side, thumbs hooked into his pockets in his usual *I'm so cool* pose. He was looking down, shaggy, brown hair falling over his face. Hair she used to love running her fingers through but now just seemed so *tainted*. The happy vibe the rest of the guys exuded did not extend to him.

Several seconds ticked past, and Terra sighed. "Hello, Dannie," she said, folding her arms, but trying hard not to get her bitch on. She didn't need a fight, just a simple apology so they could move on.

He looked up finally, an uncomfortable expression blanketing his handsome face. "Hey, Tee," he muttered.

"Are we going to do this all night—ignore each other?"

"Fuck, what do you want me to say?"

"You can start with an apology."

Dannie looked at the other members like he expected them to back him up but none of them were paying attention, or at least were pretending not to.

"Or you can thank me. Either one will go a long way."

"Which would you prefer?"

"Both."

"Shit." Dannie looked at his boots again.

"Look, I'm not going to rehash history in front of everyone but what you did was beyond a dick move."

"I know," he said softly. "But do we have to do this now…here?"

"Well," Jeff piped in, "since you refused to have a band meeting about whatever it is that happened, yeah we do. We're all here so let's just talk about it. Get it out in the open and over with. Otherwise this gig is gonna suck."

"Shut up, Jeff," Dannie uttered through clenched teeth. "Keep your voice down. This gig can't suck. If it does, we'll never come back here."

"Then just say you're sorry, man," Lucas said, attaching a cymbal to its stand and tightening it. "You screwed up. How hard is that?"

"Listen to him." Terra took a step closer to him. "Or I'm leaving. You can do this without me."

"Terra…"

"And FYI, I didn't come here for you. I came for them, because I didn't want *them* to lose out on this gig and I'm not asking for much, Dannie. Only what you owe me, which is an apology."

Dannie stared at her for about a year, something moving through his eyes. Then he closed them.

"Ah…fuck." He moved towards her and hooked an arm around her neck, pulling her into him. "I'm sorry," he said against her temple, then his other arm came around her waist. "You're right, I'm an asshole and a dick and every other name you called me. I deserve them all."

"Yeah, you are," she whispered into his neck.

His arms tightened around her, shaking a little. It made her realize he was probably just as nervous to face her as she was him. "Can you forgive me?"

"I'll have to think about that, but it's nice you're asking."

He slid his hands into her curls and gripped a handful, then moved his head away so he could look into her eyes.

"Thanks for doing this."

"You owe me a beer."

"I owe you more than that."

"Uh huh, but I'll start with a beer, and your portion of tonight's door take."

"I really am sorry." He tugged on her hair. "I don't know what the hell I was thinking—I was drunk, and she came on strong..."

"Dannie...don't. We can do this later after the gig but not now, not if you want me to be able to get through this."

He swallowed, then leaned in like he wanted to kiss her. Like he had a million times before—those million times when she'd wanted him to. But that door had shut. She angled her head, so his lips landed on her cheek instead.

"I mean it about your portion of the door."

"Okay." He nodded, looking chagrined she'd rebuffed him. Then letting her go, but she could feel his reluctance in the way his arm tensed.

"I need that money, Dannie."

"You got it."

"Okay."

"Okay," he agreed.

"Finally," Lucas said, making her jump. She'd forgotten they were there. He tapped out a *ting-ticka-tsshhh* on his cymbals. "Now we can all move the fuck on."

She caught her men's eyes. That's how she thought of them— her men, but they were mostly like brothers. They were all smiling, some, namely Lucas, in bigger degrees than others—but smiling.

She grinned back and shook her head. "Assholes."

With that, the rush she always got before performing—the combination of nerves and adrenaline she got happy on—began to move through her.

Then she caught that bouncer's eyes—the one who almost didn't let her in. He stood behind the bar leaning against the counter looking all badass and intense with those ridiculously sexy arms folded. Only he wasn't smiling—he was glowering —at her.

What the hell was his problem? It wasn't her fault he mistook her for a groupie and got proven wrong.

But she couldn't lie. The way he'd manhandled her monitor like it weighed less than her guitar case had made her stomach flutter. *And* she'd checked his ass out when he left her at Iris, and holy hell the man had an ass—the kind that belonged on an athlete. And he was big. So much bigger than Dannie she couldn't help wondering what it would be like to be manhandled by him—naked.

That glower carried an electric current and it moved through her, getting stronger the longer she held his eyes. When it became too much, she broke contact and bent to her kitbag before she stroked out.

Thankfully, her hair covered her face while she focused on finding her mic beneath her tambourine as she was pretty sure she glowed like ripe tomato gone nuclear.

She stayed down and organized her instruments, until her face cooled. When at last she looked up again, he was gone.

CHAPTER FOUR

Still Friday

ander ripped his eyes off her when Terra bent down to do whatever it was she did with that bag.

Again, with the gut punch. What the hell was it with this woman? He couldn't hear what they talked about but he sure as shit didn't like the possessive way Dannie held her. There was a familiarity in the way they acted that went beyond friendship, that didn't make sense in light of what Ruby had said. She'd called Dannie her man, but he wasn't getting that after what he'd just witnessed.

He dropped to his haunches and finished loading a third crate of beer into the fridge a little harder than necessary.

Barney eyed him. "Careful you don't bruise those bottles, son." Zander eyed him back, but kept his mouth shut because he was right. The old man knew more about running a bar than he ever would. Nobody needed the bottles exploding when their tops were popped. They had enough to clean up each night.

Leaving Barney to it, he gathered the empty cartons and

tossed them in the back storeroom, then headed upstairs to his office. Once he'd shut the door he reached into his pocket for his phone. But he didn't recognize the white plastic case with the dragonfly on the back. Took him a moment to remember it belonged to her. It shimmered as if in flight when you moved it, like one of those 3D images he had as a kid.

Terra—not Tara.

He rolled it around his tongue and liked how it sounded. Unusual name for an unusual woman—earthy and a little bit exotic. Those curls. Not tight ringlets, but loose and thick enough for a man to get a good grip and guide her head to wherever he wanted.

He groaned as the fantasy filled his brain. And since he still had her phone, he planned on keeping it until she came to him so he could get to know her a little better. He smiled at the thought, which was a miracle in itself as he rarely smiled lately.

Especially today—the fifth anniversary that spiteful bitch, cervical cancer took Ginny from him and he'd felt her presence more than usual. Like she'd chosen today to look down on him from above.

Fuck—he missed her.

He shoved his grief aside, took a deep breath and shoved Terra's phone back in his pocket. Then he found his own lying on a pile of invoices he still had to pay. He scrolled through his contacts and tapped on Ruby's number, letting it ring until it went to voicemail.

What do you want, bitch? Ruby's voice said.

Zander snorted, then shook his head. Charming—and so like her. The woman had been hardcore since high school. They'd run in the same circles, had some of the same friends, knew shit about each other but had never been close. In fact, he doubted anyone got close to Ruby because that's just the kind of woman she was.

"Rube, you've got some 'splaining to do. Where are you?"

After he ended the call, he tossed the phone back onto his desk then strode to the one-way mirror. From his viewpoint, he could see the stage and the bar though at the moment; he wasn't interested in either. He was interested in *her*. And weirdly, her eyes kept glancing upward as if she felt his gaze on her. It was disconcerting even though he knew she couldn't see him, but then again, everything about her he found disconcerting.

The band completed their sound and equipment check, and the guys headed to the bar. She headed in the direction of the woman's restroom.

It was almost starting time and most of the tables had been claimed. Looked like it was going to be a good night indeed.

He kept checking the restroom door, waiting for her to exit, which she did about five minutes later. She'd changed into a tight-fitting, white, V-necked tee-shirt with *Obsessed* written across her chest in sparkly bling. He also noted she'd darkened her makeup around her eyes, making it edgier but sexy as fuck with all those wild curls falling around her face.

Christ—the woman was hot.

If she performed half as good as she looked, he knew every single straight man in the house would go home with a stiff dick.

Himself included.

Some in the crowd greeted Terra like they knew her. Gave her hugs, and a couple of dudes flirted and bought her shots. He watched her tap glasses and toss them back, afterwards laughing and nodding at something one of them said.

By the time he headed back down to help Barney cover for Nicky, the bar was two deep and he was too busy to pay much attention. Until Dannie played the opening riff of Guns 'n Roses' "Sweet Child of Mine."

Zander stilled and looked up. They hadn't played that last time. He would know, as it was on his top ten all-time favorites. There was also something different in their energy—the way they came together and seemed to gel into a more cohesive unit.

Terra moved to the music while she waited for her cue. Then she grabbed the mic, opened that delicious mouth like she was gonna fellate the fucking thing and belted out the words.

Goosebumps erupted all over him.

Jesus.

Then he got it.

Terra wasn't filling in for Ruby. It was Ruby, that lying junkie bitch, who had filled in for Terra.

CHAPTER FIVE

Saturday morning

Terra lifted her head off her pillow and opened one eye. Something was definitely wrong. The sliver of light peeking through the curtain was much too bright. She bolted into a sitting position. "Ah!"

Her head.

She put pressure on her temples, hissing through her teeth until the sharp needles in her frontal lobe stopped sticking into her brain. Holy hell, she hadn't had that much alcohol…had she?

One shot of tequila…oh…wait, two before the gig to loosen up and two beers, one during each set break. Hardly overdoing it.

Nothing a couple of Tylenols, food and a pot of coffee couldn't cure. But why hadn't her phone alarm gone off? She was ninety percent sure she hadn't changed her settings. A one-eyed squint at her bedside table showed an empty space next to her lamp where it would usually be plugged into her charger.

Her eyebrows came together.

Where in hell was it? In Iris? Crap—think—she had it with

her when she left work and the last time she remembered using it was to call...

No.

Fuck.

That irritating bouncer had it. Groaning, she flopped back onto her bed and covered her eyes with her arms. She needed to check in on her mom. Now she would have to call the rehab center from work on her break. Then go back to Chuck's after work and track the dude down—if he was working. And he wasn't exactly friendly or approachable. The kind of man she made it her mission to avoid, not chase after for a phone. She could not afford a new one, if indeed the jerk had absconded with it.

She blew a loose curl off her face, swung a naked leg over the bed and padded to her kitchen to set the coffee she'd prepared late last night, or rather early this morning, to brew. While it gurgled and puffed, she hopped into the shower, shampooed and shaved her armpits, forgoing her legs as she'd be wearing her super-sexy stockings. Wearing them usually translated into higher sales. And higher sales translated into higher commissions —which she desperately needed. Her portion of last night's door-take combined with Dannie's and what she had left in the bank was enough to cover what she owed for this week's payment. The one that was due today.

One problem at a time and dealing with the Russian was up first. Her phone was gonna have to wait.

§&

"*D*o you have those in red?" Brooke, Terra's most lucrative customer, asked pointing at the new crotchless teddies Terra had wrapped in tissue paper.

"We do indeed," she answered.

"I want one in red too, then."

"Oooh, sorry." Helen turned from helping another customer, making a grimace face which on anyone else would be just a grimace, but on Helen was adorably cute. "I just sold the last one we had in inventory."

"Not to worry," Terra said quickly, noting Brooke's frown. "I'll order it for you and have it sent to your address. Shipping will be on us."

"That will be fine." Brooke smiled and handed over her credit card. "You always take care of me, Terra, that's why I come back."

Terra rang her up and bagged the teddies, a lacy bra-and-panty set and two pairs of silk stockings in their signature tissue paper. Then she walked her to the door of Provocative and watched Brooke climb into a black Tesla and drive away.

"God, my feet hurt," she said to Helen when she came back and collapsed into the red velvet French settee, trying not to think about her bank balance. She'd stopped at the ATM on her way to work, like she did every Saturday morning. Though this time was different. This time was alarming because technically there was no balance—according to the zeros on the ATM slip.

Five-hundred dollar withdrawals every week had also depleted her savings. She'd just paid rent but unless something drastic happened to change her circumstance, she wasn't sure she'd be able to pay it next month. She'd sell a kidney or half her liver before she'd screw her friend and landlady Shelley DeLuca.

Because of disclosure laws about a death in an apartment, it was often difficult for a landlord to rent a unit after a dead body had been discovered in one. This one in particular had been a doozie, though the facts were something she chose to ignore, considering Shelley's man, Gianni, had rented it to her at a huge discount. He'd insisted she did him a favor, instead of the other way around.

However, she had a much bigger problem than her rent. She glanced at the Provençal clock mounted behind the bustier display. It was approaching five-thirty and he still hadn't shown.

Each tick of the clock increased her anxiety. She'd skipped lunch since she found it impossible to eat until the exchange had been completed, but also to keep selling. The three-inch heels her aching feet were jammed into didn't help.

The bell on the front door tinkled and Terra glanced over from behind the counter.

Finally.

Both relief and trepidation swirled through her simultaneously as he loped towards her. She wasn't aware of his name as he'd never shared that with her, but she didn't need it to know he was Russian mafia. In his fifties, he had that rugged, *survived prison by the skin of his testicles* look, tall with a tattoo on his neck and he always stank like a week-old ashtray.

She rose, and he followed her to the counter, surveying the store while he waited for her to retrieve the envelope from beneath the register draw. The exchange was usually efficient, never taking more than a few seconds. This was fortunate due to her struggle to keep her lip from curling in disgust and her ability to hold her breath.

As always, after she'd handed the envelope over, he tapped the glass counter twice and said in a thick Russian accent, "Good girly. Next week, same time."

Which in itself was ludicrous—according to him, *same time* just meant *Saturday.* She nodded and waited for the door to shut behind him before she retrieved a can of linen-scented Febreze she kept under the counter. As she sprayed, she prayed another customer wouldn't enter until it had done its job and using a flattened box, she waved the air to facilitate it along.

She was straightening the cushions on the couch and about to take her break when a man in a light grey, button-down linen shirt and well-fitting jeans entered. He pushed designer sunglasses to the top of his head as he scanned the floor, stopping on Helen for a moment before continuing on. In the moment before his gaze landed on her, she stopped breathing.

Oh...*fuck*, why was *he* here?

She'd never seen him before—well, not in the flesh, but she didn't have to. Her mother had described him perfectly.

Wait till you see Vasily, honey. He's scary as hell but if your heart doesn't go flippety-flop, you aren't alive.

Her heart went flippety-flop all right but not for the reasons her mother had stated. For a moment she thought she might actually faint, the blood leaving her head at an alarming rate, and she gripped the backrest of the couch just in case.

Their eyes locked and his widened for a split second before he made his way towards her with a gait that would be considered graceful.

In another life she would have agreed with her mother. Vasily Melnikov *was* handsome—stunning even. Tall with thick blonde hair cut shortish and neat, and killer grey eyes, the kind that looked like polished pewter. Unfortunately "killer" was the appropriate word as he currently headed a faction of the Russian mafia. As he got closer, his heritage became more evident in sharp cheekbones and a strong, clean-shaven jaw with a little dent in the middle of his chin. It would be easy to make the mistake of thinking him a male model, only tougher, sharper and a lot deadlier.

"You're Terra."

It wasn't a question.

She nodded as it would be stupid to deny it. She looked just like her mom, the only difference being her hair color. Rebecca's was more auburn, and straighter.

He studied her for several long moments, his expression flat and almost cold. Probably assessing if she'd be a good fit for his brothels. Well, fuck him. She wasn't.

"What can I do for you, Mr. Melnikov?" She was proud her voice didn't shake, even if it did come out huskier than usual.

"Ah—so you know who I am." His tone though deep and

attractive, was as cool as his expression—almost bored. "That's good, it'll save us time."

"My mother mentioned you once or twice."

"I'm sure she did. You can call me Vasily."

"That's okay—I prefer to keep this formal. Though I have to admit it is a surprise."

"A good one?" His eyes flicked to hers.

Definitely not. She couldn't fathom what in the hell had brought him here as she'd literally minutes ago made the payment to his goon. Unless it was to notify her of an increase in the weekly amount she had to pay.

That would be terrifying. The way her heart seemed to have lodged into her throat confirmed that terror.

"I suppose that all depends on why you're here."

"Well, then, I hope I don't disappoint."

"Did you come to buy lingerie?" she asked in an attempt to lighten the tension, which had become as thick as butter. "For your girls?"

He seemed to consider that, holding her eyes while he did. Then he surprised her again. "Not unless you model it for me."

"Sorry?" she said, quickly realizing her mistake, her head jerking back. This was the last man on the planet she needed thinking she was flirting. "That would be against store policy."

"What about your policy?"

"Mine too."

His expression remained aloof as he leaned inward, tilting his head so his lips were close to her ear, in a move so brazen it smacked of confidence. He said softly, "Then I'm the one who's disappointed."

His breath against her skin sent an unexpected shiver racing across her skin, which much to her surprise could not be regarded as unpleasant, considering he didn't exactly project warm and fuzzies. But she wasn't getting an overwhelming evil overlord *you shall become my slave* vibe either like you would expect from a man like him, who was reputed to have done the things one read about in crime novels. Or heard about on the news.

"All right, that aside," she said, holding her ground and refusing to show fear, though probably failing miserably. "I'm guessing you're not here to recruit me because that would be ridiculous."

His eyes narrowed, and he waited a beat before he asked, "You *want* me to ask you if you want to be recruited?"

"Absolutely not!"

"Good." His lip twitched at her vehement denial. "Because that too would be disappointing."

Her brows snapped together while she took him in. Isn't that what he did—troll the city for women to cater to deviant men with disgusting sexual appetites and more money than sense or scruples? The man was a pimp after all. The silence between them grew, along with tension until she couldn't stand it anymore.

"Can I ask why are you here? Is there a problem with our agreement—has something changed?"

He seemed to bristle at her question and when he spoke again, his tone confirmed his annoyance. "Why would've anything have changed, Terra?"

Technically she had no agreement with *him* per se, as it had been the cigarette-stinking San Quentin look-alike who had presented it to her and explained in his thick Russian accent. *Five hundred dollars every week, or Mr. Melnikov make bad things happen.*

She did not want bad things to happen. And by virtue of his very presence, she was convinced bad things would.

"I can't seem to figure why you are here. Forget I said anything."

"Thing is, you have said something and now I'm interested in what you think has changed."

"I misunderstood, that's all," she answered, hating her voice was beginning to shake. Surely, he had other more important mafia-boss things to attend to, other than torturing her. Or perhaps that *was* his thing—getting off on making women squirm.

"I don't think so," he answered quietly, those cold eyes still boring into hers. "Lay it out for me."

"Lay what out?"

"Whatever our deal is that may or may not have changed."

Was he serious? She blinked and stared at him.

He raised his brows in an impatient gesture and she determined that yes, he was deadly serious.

She cleared the sudden obstruction in her throat. "Okay…um, the deal is I pay five hundred every week until mom's debt is clear. If I don't something bad will happen to us."

"And so we're clear, her debt was what again?"

"Twenty-five thousand dollars," she mumbled.

"For?"

"The heroin she stole."

Christ—why was he making her say it, like he thought she didn't quite understand the level of shit she was in. A darkness seemed to grow and surround him as he stared at her while she spoke, the air feeling heavier, much more oppressive.

"Of which you still owe…how much?"

"Five thousand," she whispered, praying he wasn't going to call it in. Not today.

He studied her for so long, she struggled to maintain what little poise she still had.

"You'll get your money."

He narrowed his eyes, contemplating her. Like he didn't believe her.

"You will," she said a little more forcefully. *Bad things happen.* "Ask your man, he was just here, literally minutes ago. If he says anything else, he's lying."

"Now I find it interesting you think he'd perhaps say something different. Is there a reason you believe that?"

"Do *you* have a reason to believe that?" she countered because she didn't know what else to say or where this was going.

"You're suggesting I shouldn't trust my man?" His tone carried an edge that sent shards of fear shooting through her and his eyes got harder.

"No, I'm not suggesting that. Please," she begged, "leave my mom alone." The back of her eyes began to burn. She blinked, remembering cigarette man using his knife and cleaning beneath his fingernails. *Be good girly...or fingers go missing.* "She's really trying, and she doesn't need any added stress. She may be nothing more than a" —her breath hitched—"a hooker to you, but she's my mother. She's all I have."

He reached over and caught her chin, which had begun to quiver. Her eyes widened, a tear rolled down onto his thumb. He ignored it and she made no attempt to jerk it away. His fingers were warm as he studied her, but those eyes were flat and cold, showing no emotion, just a hardness no doubt brought about by the horrible things he'd been reputed to have done.

"Good," he said in a tone that sent icicles shooting into her brain. "You asked why I came here today. Here's your answer. I came to look you in the eye, make sure you understood exactly who you're dealing with...just in case you didn't already know. I find the personal one-on-one goes a long way to prevent any future problems from arising."

Holy hell—did he really think for one second, she didn't know what he was capable of—that she'd think of fucking him over? She liked living and all her digits *attached* to her body, thank you very much.

"I understand," she said.

"Terra?"

Oh, fuck—she'd completely forgotten about Helen.

"Is everything all right?" her friend asked, staring at them. She held a letter opener in her hand like she was ready to use it in a way other than its intended purpose. Her pretty, russet-brown eyes were ferocious and ready for war.

Vasily, still holding Terra's gaze, took his time releasing her chin, like it was his to grab it in the first place. Then he turned slowly to Helen. "Everything is fine. We were just talking about Terra's mother."

Helen looked back at Terra, who nodded and wiped the tear from her cheek. "We were."

"Doesn't look fine to me. Why are you crying?"

God...Helen, stop! "It's fine, babe," she confirmed.

Helen had no notion of danger, and even if she had, she ignored it, charging in anyway, teeth bared and claws unsheathed. "I'm just worried about her. You know that, it's nothing new."

"You're sure?" The set of Helen's mouth told her she didn't believe her.

"I'm sure."

Her friend's gaze lingered a moment longer, then focused on Vasily again before she moved to the other side of the couch. She turned her back, but she stayed within earshot and pouncing distance.

"Is there anything else, Mr. Melnikov?"

"Vasily," he demanded, picking up one of the store's business cards from the little side table next to the couch and flipping it over. On the back, using one of the red-feathered pens their customers used to sign their credit card slips, he wrote something. "Now we understand each other, keep that." He handed it to her.

When she took it from between his fingers, his eyes flickered over her cleavage. Her black, button-down blouse was professional but clung to her and even though the top couple of buttons were undone, it wasn't revealing. His gaze didn't linger more than a second, but it contained a lot more heat than the rest of him.

"I'll be in touch," he said. "Our business is not yet concluded." Then he turned and left.

She watched him, her blood whooshing in her ears as he walked past a dude sitting astride a Harley whose head turned to follow Vasily's progress across the street—until he climbed into a sleek two-door luxury Mercedes.

Not a pimp car.

It was a strange thought to have as her glands squirted adrenaline into her bloodstream. Because that's exactly what he was— her mother's pimp.

"I'm taking a break," she said to Helen.

"You all right?" Helen asked again, stepping in front of her. She placed her hand on Terra's shoulder, stopping her. "Who is that man, Terra?"

"He's no one."

"No one, my ass." Helen stepped back and folded her arms. "Mr. No one is pretty damn intimidating and if Mr. No one *was* no one, you wouldn't be as pale as you are."

"He's just a friend of my mom's."

"Then why are you shaking?"

"I guess my blood sugar is a little low. I haven't eaten yet."

"You know I don't I believe you, right?"

"Helen, honey—stop. I appreciate your concern but you're gonna get on my nerves if you keep this up."

"As your BFF it's my job to get on your nerves, especially when I think you're lying. I love you more than most people, Miller and there's more to this thing with your mom than you're letting on. All I'm saying is I'm here for you if you need me."

"I know that, babe. That's why I love *you* more than most people."

"He gave you his number?"

"What?"

"That." Helen glanced at the little white rectangle in her hand. "It's his number?"

Terra flipped the card and blinked at the digits. It was indeed a phone number, but she doubted very much it had been a friendly gesture. It felt somehow like...something else. But what? The little bell tinkled again, and a regular customer walked in.

Helen sighed. "I'll get her, go eat. We'll talk later."

Terra nodded but said nothing. She considered tossing the card in the garbage, but something about his tone made her keep it. To that end, she dropped it into her purse. But talking later with Helen was *not* going to happen. She shared a lot with her—almost everything—but she couldn't share this.

In the break room, she sank into a plush lounge chair and bent double with her arms clasped around her waist. She sucked in a deep breath, then another, waiting for the shaking to stop.

What the hell was going on? What had happened that she warranted a one-on-one with him asking her *those* questions—today—when her money was all gone?

Did he know her money was gone and that was why he was here?

It wouldn't surprise her. Everyone knew the Russians specialized in identity theft and hacking. So maybe he'd been monitoring her bank account, and this was his not so subtle message to ensure she continued paying.

Ashtray man scared her, but this Vasily dude with those silver-grey eyes that sliced through a person like an icy bayonet scared her far, far more. You don't get to be a big dude in the Russian mob if you haven't left bodies along the way.

Rebecca could never be considered a normal mother with her wild, gypsy ways, but holy hell, she had to go and do something stupid like steal heroin from *that* particular Russian?

What the holy fuck?

Five thousand dollars!

She could do this—she had to—or both of them were probably going to get very tortured or very dead.

She ate the grapes and cheese she'd brought for lunch, which helped with the shaking, but not her unease. As she sucked the last dregs of her chocolate milk Helen walked into the break room. Her pretty long lashes fluttering.

Oh, lord—now what?

"I don't want to hear it, Resnick," she said, holding up a hand. Except at second glance, Helen looked kind of funny, all flushed and holding her auburn hair off her neck. Eyes so wide, Terra thought they may fall out of her head. Not the reaction she'd had earlier to Vasily.

"Um…" Helen held up a French-manicured finger and pointed to the sales floor.

"Yes?"

"Have you been holding out on me?" she stage-whispered.

"What are you talking about?"

"OMG, Tee! There's a freaking hot-as-sin biker dude out there."

"So?"

"He's looking for you."

Oh fuck—was this *another* intimidation tactic by Vasily's crew?

"He says he's got your phone?"

"Oh!" She chuffed in relief and closed her eyes. *Phew.*

"And he's not looking happy."

Yeah—she had a feeling that was just his normal.

"What did you do?"

"I'm not exactly sure."

"Who is he?"

"I think it's the bouncer I had an interaction with last night." Wait—how the hell did he know where she worked?

"And this was where?"

"Uh…Chuck's."

"You went to Chuck's?" Helen's pitch got higher, her head cocking to the side.

"Last-minute emergency gig. They asked me back and I said yes."

"Wait, I'm confused. Dannie asked you back?"

"The rest of the guys asked me back, not Dannie."

"My little bro, Petey, just got a bouncer gig there. Why didn't you tell me? I would have gone with you and helped pummel that prick's ass."

"I know you would, but I also knew you had to work today. Only one of us needs to be exhausted."

"That's a crap explanation but never mind that...excellent, you're still single. Did I tell you this dude is *sizzling*?" Helen touched a finger to her tongue and made a hissing sound.

Terra snorted. "You're exaggerating. He's hot but not *that* hot."

Was he? He looked pretty damn good in the muted bar lights, but experience told her no one who looked as good as he did in the semi-dark fared quite as well in the harsh light of day.

"Girl, your blood sugar must be all the way down somewhere in the vicinity of *Australia*, 'cause that man is fine. Now, get your butt out there before he gets tired of waiting and leaves."

"Jeez—I'm going already," Terra answered, waving her hand and popping a spearmint Tic Tac into her mouth. She did need her phone back and if it was that dude, it would save her a trip after work.

Bonus.

She pushed herself up, pausing for a moment to allow the needles in her feet to dissipate. Normally she wouldn't wear heels this high to work, but due to her money problems she needed every advantage. She really ought to get some of those gel thingies to put in her shoes. Why she hadn't already was a major oversight.

He had his back to her when she entered. Either looking out the window or checking out the display mannequins. *Her* gaze, however, got glued to his ass and not on the worn, black leather jacket, or the full-face helmet he dangled from one hand. Holy hell, it was less than twenty-four hours since she'd seen it last, but she had forgotten how nice it was. What did he do to get it that firm?

There were no patches on his jacket, which was a relief. So, he didn't belong to one of those outlaw, one-percenter motorcycle clubs. But regardless of the absence of patches, he was no less formidable-looking. There was a wild and dangerous quality to the way he stood.

The plush red carpet hushed any sound her shoes made yet as she approached, he tensed. First his head, then the rest of him turned with an onslaught of testosterone that came at her like a frigging tsunami.

Okay.

Yeah.

He was hot.

Then she caught his ridiculously pretty brown eyes, framed by long, curly lashes and for the second time that day almost fainted.

Hotter-than-fuck grumpy biker dudes and cold-as-ice mobster pimps were the two things she really should be avoiding.

Funny how that was working out for her.

His eyes started a journey. Beginning at her shoes, then her black stockings, her red-plaid schoolgirl skirt then, when they hit her breasts, they took a *vacation*. A tingle moved through her spine. And she wasn't sure if it was because he looked so damn feral or because of how in-your-face, drop-dead gorgeous he really was.

But when they finally made it to her eyes, Terra realized Helen was right.

He wasn't happy.

He took a few steps until he was close enough that she could

smell him. A sultry mix of leather and soap layered with something all man and—*oh boy*—all sex.

But no matter how alpha, she would not be intimidated and
digging deep, summoned her sales face. Then he opened his
mouth and made her almost choke on her Tic Tac.

"What's your deal with Vasily Melnikov?"

Her eyebrows sky-rocketed and a snicker escaped before she
could stop it. "Usually most people start a conversation with *hello*.
Or *hey*"—she dipped a shoulder—"nice to see you again."

"Right." He pulled his lips in as he considered her, then let
them out, making a popping sound. "Excuse the fuck out of my
bad manners. Nice to see you again."

"See? That wasn't so hard."

"Yeah," he grunted. "Well, now we got that out the way, what's
your deal with Melnikov?"

Okay, so the dude was serious and the rude was persistent.
Like she thought—his normal.

"Hmm." She put the tip of her index finger to her lip and
pretended to think about it. "I'm wondering what business it is
of yours?"

There was a pause while his eyes wandered over her face.
Before they settled on her mouth, some of the hardness softened
and she would have sworn the gold in them flashed, like it got
caught in the sun. Except there wasn't any sun.

It made her lips feel dry and her tongue darted out, flicking
them with moisture.

He blinked. "I'm interested in everything that he does, but I'm
especially curious to know what his business is with you."

She squinted at the man. "Are you for real?"

"As real as you're gonna get, babe."

"Listen, dude, as much as I appreciate you carrying my
monitor last night, that doesn't mean we're friends. You don't
have the right to question me on people I may or may not know."

"Fair enough, but friends or not, we're gonna have a little chat and you're gonna tell me what I wanna know."

"Oh?" She gave a nervous chuckle because, well, the man made her nervous with all that testosterone coming at her and her ovaries soaking it all up like greedy little sponges. "No, we're not."

"Yeah, we are." He got a smidgeon closer. "Outside, right now."

"Even if I wasn't working, you honestly think I'm going to go anywhere with you. Step foot outside this store the way you're acting—all *hooligan* like."

"Hooligan?" He seemed to ruminate over that like he'd never heard the word before.

"Helen says you have my phone?"

"I do."

"So, how about you give me it to me and you can be free and go and do whatever it is you like to do on a Saturday afternoon. I'll even say thank you."

"Not getting your phone until we chat."

"There's nothing to chat about," she said and held out her hand, palm up. "You absconded with my phone, now give."

It was his turn to snicker and cock an eyebrow, but he made no move to hand it over.

"You're holding it ransom?" she asked.

"You coming outside or what?"

"I choose what. Look, I realize being rude comes naturally to you, but since *I'm* not rude or a jerk and *I* don't want to waste any more of *your* time why don't you just give me my phone already."

His mouth curved very slightly upward. "Is this what you consider not being rude? Running your mouth off with someone who went out of their way to do you a favor."

"You're the one who kept my phone and I didn't ask you to bring it to me. I was planning to pick it up on my way home."

"Well, now you don't have to, ergo, I did you a favor."

"Ergo?" She couldn't help chuckling again. "Do you even know what *ergo* means?"

"Yeah, babe—I know how to use a dictionary."

"Stop calling me 'babe.' How did you know where I worked—should I be worried you're a stalker?"

"The only thing you should worry about is telling me what you're doing with Vasily Melnikov."

"Like I said, none of your business."

"Are you fucking him?"

What?

"Seriously?"

"Yeah, seriously."

Holy hell—what?

"I suggest if you want this to go your way, tell me what I wanna know. That way we both get what we want. Or I walk away with your phone."

Terra placed her hands on her hips and leaned forward, getting in his face. "Which part of 'none of your business' are you not getting?"

"So that's how it's going to be." A crooked smile that was far more attractive in all that sexy stubble than she was comfortable with split his face, showing gorgeous white teeth. "Works for me. You can pick up your phone on your way home."

Then the jerk walked away. Terra's jaw dropped.

Oh, fucking shit!

He played her!

The asshole totally played her and what was worse, he was enjoying it. She stamped her foot, wincing at the needles shooting through her toes.

"Wait…come back," she called to the closing store door and his very broad, retreating shoulders. The jerk's legs were much longer than hers and he moved fast. He snapped on his helmet while he walked, then swung a shapely thigh over that Harley.

Passers-by gave him a wide berth, avoiding its rumbling power as he started the engine.

She reached him just as he inched it off its kickstand. When she put her hand on his leather-clad arm, he lifted the visor with his other, turned to face her and winked. Then he flipped it back and rolled into the traffic.

Dammit!

Not for a long time after he roared away did her double-crossing, bitch of a treasonous heart slow down. It wouldn't surprise her one bit if he was laughing behind that helmet.

CHAPTER SIX

Saturday late afternoon

Zander pulled the Harley under the carport and killed the engine. He blew out a painful breath when he dismounted as he was still hard. He'd woken up hard and at this rate, he'd die hard. Not even kick-boxing the shit out of a hundred-pound bag at the gym had lessened his frustration.

Damn woman. What was her thing?

He could still see her doing a slow, sexy duet with Dannie which he simultaneously loved and hated considering the way the asshole looked at her. Or that cute little sneer when she got up close and personal with her mic, crooning her version of "Black Velvet." His dick, the horny bastard, had enjoyed it even more.

Dannie had been less than pleased when he'd called him.

"Yo," he'd yawned into the phone. "How did we do last night?"

"Better than average thanks to your girl."

"Yeah, Terra's got a voice. You got another gig for us?"

"Maybe, but that's not why I'm calling."

"You're calling about Ruby. Man, the girl…"

"Forget Ruby, I need Terra's address."

"What?"

"I have her phone."

"What the fuck are you doing with her phone?" He could imagine the dude jolting straight up in bed.

"She forgot it."

"She forgot it—where?"

If he was a bigger dick than he already was, he'd have let Dannie think it had been at his apartment, but he didn't fuck with people's heads, even with douches like him. Often the consequences weren't pretty, and he liked to avoid consequences.

"At the bar," he said, since it was half true.

"Ah…yeah. She's always doing shit like that. The woman would lose her ass if it wasn't attached."

"Give me her address so I can return it."

"Dude, you're kidding right?"

"Nope."

"Man…I can't. She'd kill me— she's not happy with me right now and I'm trying to smooth things between us, not make them worse. Besides, she's probably not at home."

His stomach had tightened at the thought she might be in some other dude's bed. "Where would she be if not at home?"

"She works Saturdays, so my guess would be there."

Work—after a grueling gig like that?

"And work would be where?"

"Give her phone to me." Dannie's voice had hardened a bit. "I'll get it to her."

"I'm already on my bike and she needs it now. Not when you finally get your ass out of bed."

"Fuck." He'd heard a long sigh and then a *thump*. He had pictured Dannie tapping his phone on his forehead and grinned.

"Tell me where she works, and I'll give you another gig."

"Two."

"Fine—two." He'd have gone for three.

"Provocative on California, a few blocks from St Mary's Cathedral."

"What the fuck is Provocative?"

"One of those high-end lingerie stores. Man, don't tell her I told you—like I said, she'll kill me."

Well, shit—the woman sold lingerie, which would explain the sexy bra she'd worn. The fantasies that inspired almost broke his face he grinned so hard on the ride to the store after googling the address. Then because kismet, karma or coincidence, of all the panty-selling joints in the city—Vasily-fucking-Melnikov.

Clearly the man's street instincts were still decent as he'd tossed Zander a narrow-eyed glance that lasted longer than it should have. Granted he'd still had his helmet on, but Vasily didn't stop to follow up. That could prove to be his mistake. What disturbed him more was that perhaps the rumors were true. He'd stepped into the power gap his older brother Dean had vacated when he went to prison.

But what was his interest in her? The woman had declined to answer his question and that bothered him more than it should.

"I'm a fucking chump," he mumbled to himself as he made his way carefully up the stairs to his office. Stairs he'd usually take two and a time, but his jeans still felt too tight.

Inside, he removed both their phones from his pocket, placed them on his desk, then tossed the jacket onto Chuck's derelict brown leather couch. Someday he'd get around to remodeling this office. But it was the last of the man he'd considered the closest thing to a father's decorating skills and perhaps that explained his procrastination.

He dropped into his desk chair and scraped his hands over his face. Those eyes…Jesus. A man could fucking drown in those.

She was so damn pretty.

Even prettier in daylight and not in the wholesome, girl-next-door kind of way, but in a dangerous, grab you by the dick, edgy kind of way. He closed his eyes and envisioned her as he she had been on stage, her skin damp and glistening and the tiny bling in her nose catching the light.

Then his phone dinged. The caller ID caused him to deflate a little.

Heather: *Need some action baby. Didn't get any last night.*

Yeah—well neither did he.

Zander: *Sorry, can't. Busy.*

Heather: *Too busy for me?*

Zander: *Work.*

Heather: *Work my ass which by the way looks incredible right now.*

Zander: *I'll text you.*

Heather: *You blowing me off?*

Yeah—he kind of was.

Zander: *Sorry.*

Heather: *Sorry???* A moment later a photo of her shapely ass in skimpy white panties popped on his screen. *This will make you sorry.* He shook his head. It was a nice ass, but it wasn't the one he was interested in. One he hoped would show up very soon.

Zander: *Later, babe. Gotta work.*

Heather: *Fuck you Zannie.*

Whatever, although if he thought about it, he *was* fucked. He couldn't get Terra out of his head. How was her jean-clad ass bent over her equipment sexier than Heather's almost naked one? Didn't make sense, yet there it was.

He rose from his desk and headed back down to the bar to deliver instructions. Something he had to do in person as Barney never checked his texts when he worked. And the old man chose to work all the time.

"Barney," he called over Zeppelin's "Whole Lotta Love" when he reached the server station.

"What?" Barney looked up from pouring a couple of cosmopolitans.

"Remember Terra from the band last night?"

"Pretty redhead with the killer voice?"

"Send her to my office if she shows."

"Right."

"And if Heather shows do *not* send her to my office."

Barney smirked then shook his head.

Allowing women up to his office had become part of Barney's job description. But it was seldom he'd ordered the old man to block one.

"Finally getting a clue—that woman's the devil," Barney said. "By the way you need to order more whiskey."

"There was a full case last I looked."

"I just cracked the seal on one. That leaves two bottles."

He squinted at the old man, as he didn't remember pouring that many whiskey orders last night. Not enough to almost kill a case anyway. Mostly beer and wine because it had been that kind of crowd. But the bar had made bank regardless.

The woman *could* pull a crowd and for that reason her band could have as many gigs as she asked for. How the hell she hadn't been discovered yet was beyond him. Though he didn't actively promote the bands, he knew talent-seekers sometimes frequented his bar and a few had been discovered here as his line-up was good. Even eighties cover bands like hers.

Good bands equaled good crowds. That was the extent of his business philosophy.

Back inside his office, he planted his ass into his desk chair. "Let's get to know you a little better, babe," he mumbled, reaching for her phone, then leaned back and stuck his boots up on the old cherry-wood desk, crossing his ankles.

Smart girl had a passcode on her phone, but he could still read the first two lines of each text. It had buzzed all day and he'd checked them as they came in.

Mom: *Need to move bad juju*

Dr. Rodham SI: *Terra, please call me as soon as you get…*

Lucas: *Yo, dude you kicked ass last night.*

Reminder: *Your hair appointment with Shelley is scheduled for...*

Dannie: *Tee, I'm an idiot. Call me before you go to sleep.*

Dannie: *Let's talk okay? Miss you. X*

Dannie: *You're still pissed.*

Dannie: *Fuck. Guess I've got some ass-kissing to do.*

The last ones from Dannie bugged him. What was their deal—more than band-mates? He'd definitely gotten that vibe the way he'd looked at her, like he'd fucked up in a big way, and the way he'd held her after their beef before the gig. But then there was that thing with Ruby implying Dannie was her man.

Christ—relationships.

Too many damn feelings involved and way to messy—which is why he avoided them. Dropping his legs, he leaned forward to type on his keyboard and there was no way he should be as happy as he was when it popped—Obsessed's Facebook page.

Ironic, he thought, as he had a disconcerting feeling *he* was becoming obsessed. One by one, he scrolled through the photos, mostly regular iPhone pictures, but some more professional looking. The most recent, though not many, were of Ruby. As he got further in, they changed to Terra.

Then he saw it.

All his blood left his brain and went south. She held the mic close to her mouth like she was in the middle of a song. Her head tilted back just a little, eyes closed, but her lips were parted enough to make a man believe she was in the middle of an orgasm.

He groaned as if he hurt physically.

Fuck. Him.

He wanted to be responsible for that look. And after staring at it, he wasn't sure what he wouldn't do to get there. He downloaded the picture onto his computer and emailed it to himself, then saved it onto his phone. He wondered how many other dumbasses had done exactly that? But more importantly, how many *had* put that look on her face? The thought did not make him happy. She'd called him a stalker and he was beginning to think she might not be wrong.

Her phone buzzed again. *Terra, Dr. Rodham from SI. Please call me, it's important. Your …*

Who was this Dr. Rodham and what the hell was SI? He was an intelligent man with access to Google. Easy enough to figure out and despite every instinct telling him to leave it, he did it anyway.

The Sunrise Institute: Cutting-edge opioid addiction specialists with an address in Mill Valley, in the north Bay.

What the fuck?

She was an addict?

He slumped back into his leather desk chair as if all the air had been sucked out of him. Like a mule had booted him in the guts. Then he scrubbed both hands through his hair.

It made no sense.

He'd seen her have a shot and a beer and if she was recovering, she shouldn't touch anything. His head fell back, and he closed his eyes.

Damn!

He could not go through that again—with anyone. Even for a casual fuck and there was something about this woman that tugged at him—wouldn't leave him alone. If she got beneath his skin, he had a distinct feeling he'd be in deep shit.

But he didn't do addicts.

Period.

He pushed to his feet, disappointment washing over him like a cold shower. Barney would handle returning her phone. In his rush to get downstairs, pulled his office door open harder than normal and barreled forward—straight into *her*.

"Hey, watch it," she called out.

Their legs tangled, and he lost his balance. She gripped his T-shirt but her backward momentum took her down, and him with her. Her phone went flying as he instinctively wrapped one arm around her waist, while his other went to the back of her head.

"Oh crap, I can't..." she cried. The rest cut off when he shoved her face into his armpit.

It took strength, but he controlled the fall. His knees hit the concrete. A jolt shot up his thighs, reverberating through his spine, then his arms connected with the hard surface, then his head. White orbs of light popped behind his eyelids as pain exploded in his skull. It came in waves and he lost sense of time, breathing through it until it dissipated. At some point he became aware his lips touched warm skin and a beating pulse in her throat that fluttered like a frightened bird. When his vision cleared, he noticed a dark freckle just below her ear and, despite the blow, he had an urge to lick and suck on it.

And she smelled good.

He inhaled.

Flowery and clean and...warm. Exactly how she'd smelled last night and nothing like the sour, rancid smell of an addict coming down.

Adrenaline coursing through his veins heightening his relief and the situation was so absurd it made him chuckle.

"What's so funny?" she asked, her voice a little breathy.

"I'm between your legs."

"That's not funny at all— get off me."

"Woman, I just saved your head from cracking like a coconut at the expense of my own. Give me a minute."

To ensure he hadn't bumped it harder than he thought, that the electric buzz vibrating through his body wasn't caused by some wicked hallucination, or damage to his brain, he looked down—past the soft mound of her breast inches from his face to the length of her body.

Her legs were hitched at the knees. The excuse of a skirt had dropped back exposing a creamy strip of skin between her thigh-high stocking and the edge of her panties. They were black with a lacy trim around the legs.

Hot. As. Fuck.

"Are you okay?" That husky voice came out just a little bit huskier and his spine tingled, his balls tightened. Naked, raw need seared through his veins.

"I will be as soon as the stars stop exploding behind my eyeballs." They had, but she didn't know that, and he wanted draw this out as long as he could.

"Okay, um…while you're waiting, I need you to move a little." Terra squirmed beneath him. Her central heat against his thigh with nothing but a thin layer of silky fabric and his jeans almost made his brain circuits misfire. "You're squashing me."

Zander hissed.

"Babe," he grunted, clamping down his desire to rub his cock against her. "Don't move."

"What?"

"Don't. Move."

Color spread across her cheeks. "Ohmigod…okay…um, maybe just a little to the side…"

"Woman," he growled between clenched teeth. "I said don't move."

He saw it in her eyes, the way her lids fluttered, her pupils dilated.

"The thing is…you're um…"

In her sweet spot—exactly where he wanted to be. Exactly where he needed to be—and would kill to be. He lowered his head until his lips were parallel to her ear, blasting her with his breath.

"In the perfect place."

She shivered.

Fuck!

Her face angled towards him, their eyes locking. He could see the little patterns in the blue, the same color as the hydrangeas his grandmother grew on their balcony. But he also saw something else—something that called to him. That same weird connection, that buzzing he'd experienced last night in the bar when he'd looked in her eyes. His heart pounded, sending more blood to his cock. Something in his brain adjusted and fell into place. Like a missing puzzle piece finally being discovered.

In that moment, he'd never wanted a woman more.

She saw it too. He read it in her eyes just before she blinked, then turned her head and broke the connection. His arm was still beneath her and he felt her heart, beating as fast and strong as his.

"I need you to get off me," she said.

Christ—he knew he should, but he couldn't make himself move, except for the tip of his nose—which he ran across the curve of her shoulder and up her neck. There was a dark freckle, just below her ear that he couldn't resist, and he sucked on it.

"I believe you're lying," he muttered, hoping like fuck she was.

Her flush brightened, but she pushed against him. "If you think for one second I'm gonna let you fuck me on this floor, you better up your meds."

"Babe!" A stupid grin spread over his lips. "That implies that you'll fuck me somewhere else. I have a couch in my office."

"What?" The pretty brows snapped together. "Ohmigod, you're so full of it."

"I'm full of a lot of things—some of which I'm happy to give you, but I'll settle for a kiss."

"Dream on, buddy, and how many times do I have to tell you —I'm not your babe. Get that *thing* off me."

He looked her straight in the eye. "Problem is I can't."

"What do you mean you can't?"

"You're lying on my arm."

"Oh."

She turned even pinker and it should have been impossible, but he found her to be even more adorable.

What the fuck was wrong with him?

"Sorry," she said, arching her back slightly, pushing her chest against him. That did another number on his blood pressure, but he reined it in, inhaling slowly, getting one last sniff of her. Then he slid his arm out from underneath her waist and used it to push himself up.

When he stood, he offered a hand to help her, even though it shook slightly. And because he was such a fucking a gentleman, he did his best to keep his eyes off her legs, 'cause if he didn't... well. Though out of his peripheral he could still see that alluring strip of naked skin at the apex of her thighs.

She was going to kill him—unless his case of blue balls finished him off first.

It didn't surprise him she didn't take his hand. What did was when she shifted onto her knees and started crawling, allowing him a prime view of her ass barely covered in those hot little panties. He expelled a frustrated breath, raising his eyes to the ceiling.

"Woman," he growled. "What the hell are you doing?" Did she not get how close he was to losing his shit?

"What does it look like?" she said over her shoulder, looking for all intents and purposes like she just fell off the sexy train. "I'm getting my phone."

Right. He closed his eyes.

That damn phone.

He'd forgotten all about it.

CHAPTER SEVEN

Saturday evening

"**W**oman!"

His voice—though in all honesty it sounded more like a lion doing its *lord of the savannah* thing—rumbled through her, setting her nerve endings crackling. As if they needed any more electricity.

When she turned her head, she had to look up—way, *way* up. Past those long, hard thighs, narrow hips and holy hell—the man had a package. A very *large* package that made her uterus purr, *Come to mama*. It looked every bit as happy and unapologetic as she'd felt between her legs. She forced herself to keep going, taking in that washboard stomach, that broad, strong chest, the hollow between his collarbones until she reached his eyes.

Those beautiful, liquid, *blazing* eyes. *They* certainly did not look happy. For whatever reason she seemed to have that effect on him.

She ripped her gaze away and kept crawling to her phone.

The device survived unmolested, thanks to the cute little plastic dragonfly cover—unlike her stockings.

"Oh…shit," she exclaimed. They were fifty percent silk, high-end and even with her employee discount, pricey.

"There's a problem?"

"Yes, I got a problem—these." She made a sweeping gesture at her knees. He offered his hand again, but she ignored it and pulled herself up using the metal railing. The man was too hazardous to touch. "They're not the kind you get at Walmart," she said, smoothing her skirt. "I need them to boost my sales quota. Sell by example, so to speak."

"Does it work?"

She nodded and tucked a few curls behind her ear.

"Of course it fucking works," he mumbled, his voice rough. "Makes your legs look hot."

"You owe me a new pair."

"Babe, as much as I enjoyed that sex kitten act, I didn't make you crawl to your phone."

"Well, excuse me," she said, planting a hand on her hip. "How the hell was I supposed to know you wouldn't make a go for it. Specially after that little stunt you pulled."

"Which one? Saving your head from cracking." He caught her eyes. "Or getting you this close?" He leaned in, showing her his thumb and index finger a millimeter apart.

Her breath caught—heat spread through her core at his reminder. She *had* been close—which only proved once again, as if there had ever been any doubt, she was on God's shit list.

The asshole smiled. A really sexy, slow smile, making him look smugger than a vagina in a dildo factory.

"Thank you for saving my head," she said, looking at his dark, stubbly chin instead of meeting his gaze. "But you still owe me a new pair."

Zander tilted his head, which did nothing to lessen the mischief in his eyes. "I'll make you a deal."

"Oh"—she rolled her eyes—"this should be good."

"I'll buy you two pairs, long as I get to see you in them—naked."

Despite herself, and before she could stop it, an image flashed in her mind and she was definitely naked—and so was he.

Zander chuckled. "You're picturing it, aren't you?" He leaned in again. "Yourself naked—*me* naked."

She huffed and curved a brow. "I'm picturing something, only it involves a sharp, pointy weapon."

It was really rather irritating how accurately he could read her, and how beautiful he was when he laughed. The kind of beautiful that should be illegal on a man. But she was over men, wasn't she? She turned her back on him and took a step down the stairs. There was one upside—she hadn't thought of Dannie and his cheating ways since she'd been in his presence—until now. Surprisingly, it didn't hurt as much.

He stepped in front of her, one step below, stopping her progress.

"Where are you going, babe?" he asked, so close they were mere inches apart.

"Home, where else?"

"I haven't finished with you."

"Sucks for you then, doesn't it?"

"Stay."

"What for?"

"Well for one, I've got a pantry full of wine that needs drinking. I was hoping you could help me with that. How about we start there."

Holy hell, wine and him—bad combination. But even so, she considered it—for half a second.

"How about we don't start at all," she said on a sigh. "I've had a long day, my feet are killing me and besides the hot date I've got with a bubble bath, I've got phone calls to make."

He held her eyes for a long moment, and something flickered

through them. But he stepped out of her way, holding out his arm, suggesting she should pass. It was then she saw the deep scratches in his skin and before she thought to stop herself, she reached out and grabbed his wrist.

"You're injured."

Those dark brows came together as he looked at his arm, as if he was surprised to find he was.

"So I am," he muttered and pushed up his sleeve further, revealing more scratches—and a name inked into his bicep

Ginny.

A small tendril of jealousy unfurled in her gut—startling her as there should be absolutely no reason for her to feel anything, let alone *that*. She was just getting over a man. So, who was this woman?

Girlfriend?

Wife?

The love of his fucking life?

And how many other names were so beautifully inked onto his body? Suddenly it was vitally important for her to find out—to know more about him. Crack whatever code made this man tick.

"Does your boss keep a first aid kit in that office?"

The hard lines on his face smoothed out and softened. "Come again?"

"A first aid kit?" she repeated slowly. "So I can clean those scratches for you."

"No, babe." His lips quirked. "The first part."

"Your boss—you know, like the big *Kahuna*." She did a little shoulder shimmy.

He snort-grinned.

Given she was just a few inches away from his lips, she couldn't help but notice how perfect they were, even when they were spread wide, showing off his perfect teeth.

"Or you can let it get all nasty and fester," she said softly, flicking her gaze back up to meet his, putting a little flirt in them. Suddenly his were no longer snarky—they were warm and golden like the California sunshine.

He waited a beat, his gaze still locked on hers. "Upstairs." He used his chin to point at another flight of stairs she hadn't paid attention to before.

"Excuse me?"

"There's a first aid kit upstairs."

"Oh." Her fingers slipped off his arm and she noticed the action left a rash of goosebumps in their wake.

He inhaled long and deep then murmured, "After you."

This was treacherous but for whatever reason she no longer cared. Logic told her she was playing with fire without an extinguisher—that she should be running down the stairs, not leading him up to...wherever. Yet she didn't feel unsafe. He'd sacrificed skin protecting her head and could have pressed the issue when he was on her.

She almost giggled.

Pressed.

The least she could do was take care of his injuries. What kind of horrible person would she be if she didn't?

"What is this?" she asked when they got to the top of the landing and spied another door painted brick red. "An infirmary?"

He remained quiet, but he exuded a kind of suppressed energy that electrified the air between them. After opening the door, he waved her in.

She'd imagined a dingy utility closet packed with toilet paper and cleaning supplies. Or maybe an off-limits staff bathroom overflowing with bleach to hide urine smells.

Instead, she walked into a beautifully furnished, open-plan apartment with cushioned bay windows and two large, glass patio doors. They offered stunning views of the city and the Bay Bridge. And it smelled clean.

It became immediately apparent that the space was rustic by design and not from neglect. She stepped onto an oversized rug, rich in ocher colors, lying on dark wood floors.

"Who lives here?" It was impossible to keep the wonder out of her voice as she surveyed warm earth-tone walls decorated with unframed abstract art.

"The boss," he answered, shutting the door and leading her into the homey space to a granite breakfast bar. It was long, mottled beige with coffee colored veins running through it and uncluttered, separating the kitchen from the living room. He slid out a padded bar chair and patted it. "Take a seat."

Then he ambled to the far side of the room flipping light switches as he went and vanished through a hallway.

Then it hit her.

Holy hell—*he* was the boss!

Terra palmed her face—her eyes popping wide. *This* was the guy Ruby had probably performed a Hoover act on to get them the gigs.

Her stomach dipped, as this was yet another, much more compelling reason to stay away from him, and therefore, she needed to go. Any man big enough to ride an ass-kicking Harley and who owned a rowdy bar was capable of taking care of a few scrapes. She swiveled her chair and slipped off to make a getaway before he came back.

The painting stopped her—it was that stunning.

She hadn't notice it when she came in because it had been behind her, but the way it dominated the room, strategically placed for maximum effect, spoke volumes. It was of a woman, gorgeous, with lush, wavy dark hair swept to the side, full lips and amber eyes. It was so breathtaking in its beauty and simplicity, she gasped.

And it looked familiar.

She was certain she'd seen other works in the gallery across the street by the same artist. He had a style, distinctive and easily recognizable.

"You like it?" Zander asked from behind her, making her jump. She'd been so drawn in by it—by the woman—she wasn't aware she'd moved closer and hadn't heard him come back.

"It's…extraordinary." Her face angled to look at him. "But I can't find a signature—who is the artist?"

He shrugged. "Just some obscure, anonymous artist."

Her gaze slid to his for a moment. "You're being facetious. Who owns a painting like that and doesn't know who painted it?"

"Facetious is my middle name, babe."

"Whoever he is, I think he's a genius."

"What makes you think it's a he?" His tone struck her as odd, causing her to look back at him.

"I don't know—just a feeling, I guess. It's uncomplicated. Women tend to over-complicate things."

He stared at her. Then something shuttered in his eyes and he looked away.

"I'm curious about the woman," she said, trying a different tactic—trying to sound nonchalant while keeping her gaze on his retreating back. "Do you know her?"

Again, he lifted a shoulder, and she got the message. Whoever she was, she meant more to him than he acted but he wasn't willing to talk about. Perhaps this *Ginny*, who was so beautifully scrolled into his skin. That thing in her stomach with the prickly little tendrils grew a few more inches.

The more she looked at him, the more intriguing and interesting he got. He wore all that thick, dark, wavy hair brushed away from his face—like he needed a haircut three months ago. But it looked good on him. And the way he moved was powerful, yet smooth and easy.

Lordy.

Men like him however, came all wrapped up in sexy packages but disguised something else—trouble. And had women twisting themselves into pretty little bows. Definitely not worth the heartache.

Zander placed a blue bag with a white cross on the counter and unzipped it. "Knock yourself out," he invited.

She glanced at the bag, then at him, mentally bracing herself while she removed the silver, celtic-knot ring from her thumb and placed it on the counter next to the bag. Then she washed her hands at his sink, before selecting a small pair of surgical scissors and got to work.

He had long, slender fingers, but they were hard and rough and smelled soapy. It mattered somehow that he cleaned himself before she touched him.

A small chip in her armor fell with each piece of torn skin she cut from his knuckles. As she swabbed his forearms, she tried not to focus on the veins standing out against his muscles or the soft touch of his breath on her hair, the warmth radiating from his body as he sat for her.

She worked quickly—dabbing antiseptic over the scrapes, wrapping his arm. After checking her work, she was satisfied and oddly reluctant to break the connection.

"That's going to hurt. You should take something for that." She sterilized the scissors again in alcohol then zipped up the first aid bag.

"I've had worse." His gaze stayed focused on her. "You've done this before."

Yeah, she had.

"You had training?"

"I'm not a nurse if that's what you're asking." Although she wouldn't admit to him how many times she'd taken care of her mother when she'd injured herself during a high. Even sewing a few stitches once after a gig when Rebecca sliced herself on broken glass. "I hope you're up to date with your tetanus shots?" she asked, only half-joking. She expected him to smile back but he didn't.

Instead, he studied her with an intensity that unnerved her. "Who's Dr. Rodham?" He threw at her, catching her off guard and the air left her lungs as if he'd stolen it.

"Did you answer my phone?" she snapped.

"Just saw the texts on your screen, babe." His tone was quiet—determined, but not angry. Almost like he had a personal stake in her answer, which she did not understand at all.

"Oh, please, help yourself," she said, waving a hand. "Feel free to read my texts. Why don't I just give you the code to my phone so can delve even *further* into my life?"

While she collected her purse, he positioned himself in front of her, blocking her path to the door. "Who is he?"

"None of your damn business."

"Not the answer I'm looking for."

"That's the answer you're getting. What is it with you and men I may or may not know?"

He didn't respond to that, just stared unrelentingly.

She sucked in a breath, glaring at him through her lashes, realizing he wasn't going to let it go. And that the man didn't respect other people's boundaries. "He's just a doctor."

"Bullshit."

"Oh, come on! You want to tell me you haven't googled him already?"

"I have. Is he yours?"

She shook her head. "No, he's not mine."

"Then whose?"

"You have some morbid fascination about me? You want to pick my life apart, scrutinize who I hang with, who I don't?"

"Maybe I just find you interesting."

Those golden-brown eyes trained on her and something about the way he looked at her compelled her. She blinked, not knowing what to make of that knowledge. With her recent experience in men, she was reluctant to trust her instincts. Reluctant to trust him.

"If you really have to know, he's treating someone I love." That was all he was going to get—not one nugget more. "Now, I'm going before you can lay another ambush on me."

She made a start towards the door but didn't get very far as he'd stepped in front of her, causing her to walk into warm, well-defined, and definitely male muscle.

"I'm gonna ask you to expand a little more on that," he said, gripping her hips, keeping her way too close to his body.

"And I'm gonna ask you to let me go."

"Why?'

"Because players play and the only thing I suspect you're *interested* in is recreating between my legs."

"And this is a bad thing because?"

He had her there and she cursed herself for bringing it up. With the man-drought that was her current reality, there were perhaps a thousand reasons why recreating with him wouldn't be so bad. The fluttering in her stomach and the heat between her legs concurred. But nope—she could not afford a man like him. It would be *her* that got burned.

"Men like you are always bad ideas, and I've had enough bad ideas to last me a while, thank you very much."

"Okay, then answer me this. What's your deal with Melnikov?"

"What's your deal with manhandling me?"

"Jesus, woman, you always answer a question with a question?"

She glowered at him. "Do you?"

While he glowered back, her phone buzzed breaking the tension that had grown thicker that the San Francisco fog.

"I'm gonna to need to get that."

He sighed, let his hands drop then took a step back, leaving a strange, cold absence in his wake. When she dragged her eyes from his and glanced at her caller ID, her eyes widened, dread flooding her system.

There was no good reason her mother's doctor should be calling at seven forty-five on a Saturday evening. For a second, she considered not answering because whatever it was, she didn't want to know. But the nagging feeling she'd had ever since yesterday necessitated she did.

"Hey, Dr. Rodham." she answered, her voice sounding small and uncertain, even to herself.

"Terra." She heard him clear his throat which only deepened her anxiety. "I've been trying to reach you all day."

"You have? I'm sorry but I didn't have my phone."

"I'm afraid I have very bad news. Are you sitting down?"

Sitting down?

Oh...no.

"God, just tell me," she whispered, closing her eyes. "What's she done now?"

"Your mother... Rebecca went missing sometime this afternoon."

"What do you mean missing?"

"We didn't realize until she didn't show up for dinner. The staff checked her room and she wasn't there. Then we did an extensive search of the property and someone found her about an hour ago. The police are here now."

"Is she all right?"

"Terra...she overdosed."

No.

Nononono!

"I'm sorry Terra, she's gone. Your mother is dead."

"No!" Her breath caught in her throat. "You're lying."

"I'm so sorry."

"It can't be true," she said, shaking her head and struggling to find air. "No." It had to be some terrible misunderstanding, some mistake. "You're wrong. Somebody somewhere fucked up badly and it's...it's a case of mistaken identity...not...not her."

"Terra..."

"No…um…I'll call you tomorrow…in the morning, when this is all sorted out. When…when they've figured out it's not her."

"Terra, it's her. I identified her myself."

"Oh God," she whimpered, swaying. "Oh…God, no!" Then she hung up and stared at the screen for a few seconds before placing her phone like a robot into one of the side pockets of her purse.

"It's not true," she whispered. "It can't be."

Her mother had been getting better. How could she overdose in a *rehab facility*?

"Babe?"

A cold sweat broke out on her forehead as blood drained from her head. The world turned fuzzy, the lines around his edges blurred, then her legs buckled. Fortunately, Zander caught her under her arms before she collapsed into his carpet.

"Jesus, woman," he muttered against her ear. "What the hell just happened?"

Her breath faltered. "It's not true." It came out strangled as she clutched at his shirt, trying to regain her footing but the messages from her brain weren't making it to her legs.

"Okay—let's get you sitting down." Those big, warm arms scooped her up and while he carried her the short distance, she buried her face into his chest, seeking something warm—something alive. He lowered her onto his couch, parted her knees then helped her place her head between her them allowing the blood to flow to her brain. He sank into a squat in front of her, supporting himself with one hand on the couch next to her, his other rubbed a spot on her back making little circles. It felt good —and real. Something to cling to.

"I take it that wasn't good news."

The tightness in her throat prevented her from speaking, but she didn't want to acknowledge it, or say it out loud, because that would make it true. But her mind kept spinning—how could she be dead?

Zander heaved a sigh, then his hand left her back as he got to his feet. "Don't move, babe, you need a drink. I'm gonna get you one. Whiskey?"

She missed his hand, missed the comfort it afforded her as he stepped away—to an antique cabinet filled with bottles of all kinds of liquor and exquisite glasses that burst with rainbow prisms as they caught the light.

"Ice?" His eyebrows came together, creating two parallel furrows between them.

Again, she shook her head and clutched herself with one arm around her waist, swiping a tear from her cheek with a thumb.

"Okay, no ice." Zander poured two generous servings and carried them back to her.

Her hand shook as she accepted it, and curled both hands around the glass, her fingers pressing into the grooves of the cut crystal while she sipped. The welcome burn slaked down her throat, warming her from the inside.

It can't be true, her mind kept chanting. A memory sprung to mind of her as a child, playing at the beach one summer, building sandcastles and moats with her little red bucket while her mother played guitar, singing softly with the breeze blowing in her long auburn hair. It struck her that was the last time they went to the ocean together. Now they never would again. A sob bubbled up.

"You wanna help me out here and tell me what happened?"

"It's too much," she whispered.

"Too much to tell or too much to deal with?"

"Both." Her gaze lifted to meet his. "I don't know what to do." Her lip trembled, she bit down on it as she placed her glass on the coffee table next to him, spilling a small amount of whiskey on her hand. She sucked it from the mound below her thumb.

"What do you mean, babe?"

As the whiskey crawled through her bloodstream, it worked its magic. Years of resolve, of holding life together for herself and her mother surfaced enough for shock to release its grip. "I have to go."

"Wait." Zander rose with her, putting his hand on her upper arm. "I don't know what it is you don't know what to do about. Whatever it is, let me help you."

She stood in front of him, staring at him while her thoughts tumbled in her head. "Even if you mean that," she answered, her voice cracking. "And even if you wanted to, you can't."

"I don't say anything I don't mean. But just out curiosity why do you think I can't?"

"It's too late."

"For what?"

She shook her head again.

"Woman, throw me a bone here—I'm trying to help." This time his voice was softer, kinder—and she didn't know why, but she wanted to believe him. Wanted to trust him. She still had a debt to pay to the Russian and before she could curb her runaway mouth, she blurted, "You got five thousand dollars I could borrow?"

He tensed and drew in a harsh breath through his nose. "You serious—this about money?"

She wiped another tear from her cheek, not caring particularly for his tone. But she couldn't blame him. What kind of person asks another they've known for a minute for a loan?

"What do you need it for?"

"Well, you see Zander, as of five minutes ago, I have a funeral to pay for." Then as an afterthought, she mumbled, "Among other things."

"Fuck, I'm sorry," he said softly, his face registering his shock. "Who died?"

"My mother."

CHAPTER EIGHT

Still Saturday evening

His stomach twisted as it all connected.

Dr. Rodham, the opioid specialist, treated her *mother*.

Zander stared at her for a long second before the familiar cold prickling began in his neck. Therefore, he didn't stop her when she slipped past him, her footsteps sounding on the wooden floor. The tiny squeak he'd forgotten to WD40 when his door opened, the lock engaging when it shut.

The flashbacks weren't common anymore but when he did get them, he'd learned how to manage—most of the time. He braced and shut his eyes before the images overwhelmed him. *His* mother, dead and cold on the floor, her face kicked to shit by a pair of bloody, size-twelve boots.

A shudder reverberated through his body, his muscles seizing, hardening his face. He squeezed his fists until his knuckles paled, his nails digging into his palms, the pain helping him to focus.

Ten...nine...he swallowed and sucked in air. Eight...seven...

six…so many years, yet that fucked-up day still encoded into his brain was as clear as a mountain pond. The metallic stench of drying blood crusted on the floor, soaking into the carpet. A memory he kept locked tight in a dark vault deep in his mind.

Another breath—he scrunched his nostrils…three…two…one. Sweat trickling down his neck, dampened his hair—yet he shivered. Ironic how witnessing Terra's tragedy had turned the key in that vault and unlocked his own.

With massive will, he directed his thoughts away from his mother and focused on the image of Terra's face—tried to remember the exact pattern of the faint cluster of freckles on her nose, that particular rose gold of her hair. There were so many different colors in the individual strands, only someone with a trained eye would notice.

He came back slowly, breathing short and hard, the vertigo began to fade. Her scent still touched the empty space around him and he cast his gaze at the door, as if expecting her to reappear like some apparition he could conjure if he willed it hard enough.

He wiped sweat from his brow, reached for his glass on the coffee table and slugged the remaining whiskey in one gulp—welcoming the fire in his throat—preferring it over the one in his chest.

Well, wasn't that just fucking groovy.

The woman had brought it on, but she'd also taken him out of it.

Chuck, that stubborn bastard's words rumbled into his head as if they'd driven in on his shit-kicking Harley. *When she walks through your door and boots your sorry ass awake son, you better pay attention.*

Well, he was awake, and he was paying attention, but he hadn't expected it to cut him open. He needed air—and to ride.

Clear his head.

He pulled his phone from his back pocket and sent Nicky a

text. *Help Barney close. Taking the night off.* Then he grabbed his jacket and helmet from the coat closet in the hallway and five minutes later he rolled the Harley off its kickstand and rumbled out the parking lot behind his bar. Other than between a woman's legs, his bike was his favorite place to be—the only place he could shut his head off.

Except for now.

She looked so goddamn lost it made his chest hurt. He rubbed it with his palm as he sat at a light, waiting for it to change. When it did, he let instinct guide him out of the city, heading south on Highway One. Along the western seaboard until he hit the artsy little fishing town of Half Moon Bay. The Harley growled into to a parking lot along the beach and he found a secluded spot. Far enough away from a couple rocking a Jeep Cherokee, hell-bent, it seemed, on conceiving the next genera-tion of young Americans. Unfortunately, when he took his helmet off and the ocean breeze dropped, the grunts and whim-pers traveled across the gravel. It made him wonder what little noises Terra would make when he got his hands on her. Was she wild like her hair, and loud? Would she throw her head back...*fuck!*

He was here to *stop* thinking—*stop* obsessing over a woman he'd only known existed for little more than twenty-four hours and to think about another woman. One he tried never to think of until he had to.

Alexandra Milan—his mother.

And Christ, it hurt. It sliced, it mangled, it fucking *crushed*.

How could he reconcile a woman who was alive and so beau-tiful, and who he wanted, with a woman who was dead, who'd abandoned him when he was eleven?

You gotta face it to heal it, baby, Ginny had said when he'd refused to talk to that shrink she'd arranged for him. But he couldn't face it. The unmitigated violence of that day that even now he still relived.

This was where they'd scattered her ashes. On this beach, one summer afternoon so long ago.

"Fuck, Mom," he whispered, staring at the water. Must have kept his eyeballs open too long because the damn salt breeze made them sting. "Why didn't you listen to me? Why'd didn't you pick me? You might still be here."

He cleared his throat and wiped the wet from his eyes with the edges of his palm.

They'd let her go. Taking turns dipping into that vase, letting the wind take her. A little oval thing, iridescent and shiny that changed colors when the light shifted. His grandmother let him pick it and he'd chosen it because it reminded him of rainbows.

We'll find our rainbow, Zee I promise.

A promise his mother never kept.

Instead he'd found a hell no eleven-year-old kid should have to endure—and he'd hated her for it.

"I tried, Mom. I really did but I couldn't help you. That asshole took you from me. You're free now. Find your rainbow."

And maybe one day, he'd find his.

He took a long breath, tightened his jaw and set his attention on the waves, finding the elusive colors the moonlight caught as they pounded the shore. Like his art instructor taught him.

Thank fuck for his art. It helped him more than that shrink ever did and without it, and in spite of Chuck and Ginny, he'd be dead. Trolling the mean as fuck streets, gangbanging or just in general, looking for his demise—anything other than remembering where he came from.

He sat for a long while with his arms draped over his spread knees, boots digging into the sand until he felt that easing in his chest. Until he could breathe comfortably again. Then he lay back and stared at Orion's Belt.

All things aside, it was a perfect night.

A long time later, he returned to his bike and shook the tiny granules from his hair. The Jeep in the parking lot was long gone, leaving him alone. After he swung a thigh over and fixed his helmet strap, he flexed his forearm muscles. The sting as his leathers scraped against his bandaged skin reminding him of her again.

You got five thousand dollars I could borrow?

Was she playing him—did she think him an easy mark?

His gut and that lost, ravaged look in her eyes that spoke to an old part of him—one he'd thought he'd buried—told him she didn't. But he had a way to find out.

The Harley roared to life and he headed back to the city. Instead of going home he ended up in a neighborhood not his own. Judging by the two police cruisers parked outside The Flour Barrel, rumors of the relationship between cops and doughnuts couldn't be denied.

Zander rolled to a stop behind a black and white outside the bakery, tucked away behind a consignment jewelry store. It would be easy to miss if a person had no sense of smell.

He cut the engine and swept his eyes around, searching for anything that looked hostile now that Vasily was back in town. Who knew what that fucker was up to? He noted nothing, just the normal drunken human traffic passing by late on a Saturday night. No loitering, suspicious-looking assholes standing in seedy, urine-soaked alcoves selling narcotics. Nor desperate, beaten down hookers selling themselves.

It wasn't that kind of neighborhood. Probably thanks to the constant police cruisers, but more likely due to its residents. One whose expertise he intended to take advantage of.

The Flour Barrel bustled despite it being after midnight. Situated less than a block away from a rowdy Irish pub pretty much guaranteed a steady business of late-night sugar junkies.

Zander pushed open the door, breathed in the vanilla and baked goods' scents, getting a minor, contact sugar high.

His eyes connected with a brunette sitting alone in a red Naugahyde booth. She smiled and held his eyes for a moment

then dropped her dark head to stare at her chocolate-filled crois-
sant. *Cute*, he thought as he walked to the counter. But for some
reason tonight cute wasn't cutting it.

A skinny, anemic-looking kid of college age and indetermi-
nate sex took his order of a coffee and a chocolate eclair.

"Carmine here?" Zander asked, searching the premises.

The kid turned and eyed him for a moment before shaking
his head. "Working."

"He expected to check in anytime soon?"

"Tomorrow morning."

Zander wrote his name on a white napkin and passed it
across the red Formica counter.

"I'll send him a text, but make sure he gets that."

The kid touched his black beanie with two fingers and rang
him up. Then slid the paper napkin under the cash drawer of the
register.

With his coffee and eclair in hand, Zander found a vacant
booth and slipped in. The brunette was heading towards the door
and threw a shy glance at him. He held her eyes again, proving to
himself he still could until hers fluttered and she looked away.

Any other night he would have pursued it. Followed her sweet
little ass out, got her number and maybe more. But tonight, it
seemed he'd suddenly developed a discriminating preference for
strawberry blondes. With eyes the color of hydrangeas.

He shook his head and looked at his eclair.

He was fucked.

CHAPTER NINE

Sunday morning

"Take as much time off as you need, Terra," said Anna, her boss.

"I just need a couple days, you know…to sort out things out. I've already talked to the police this morning, but I have to go north tomorrow… to pick up her things." She hugged her phone to her ear and took a sip of her coffee. It was her second cup and the caffeine still hadn't kicked in. Her mother's text message rolled around in her head all night and she'd been unable to sleep. *Need to move bad juju.* What had she meant, and did it have anything to do with Vasily showing up yesterday?

"Honey, you haven't taken any vacation this year. You've been working so hard. Now is a good time and believe me, death can be a messy affair. Just take it and grieve. I'm not putting you on the schedule for the next two weeks."

Shit. This wasn't what she needed.

"Anna, please. I need to work."

"It's paid time, Terra."

It may be paid, but she didn't make commission on vacation. How had her situation gone from shit to shittier with one simple phone call? She slapped her palm to her forehead.

Really, God?

"Let me know if there's anything else I can do for you."

Let her work! But she knew Anna well enough to know arguing would be useless. She'd only dig her heels in thinking she was helping instead of fucking her financially even more.

"Okay...thanks, I will." Though she knew she wouldn't.

She hung up and stared at the Navajo rug on her wall, unable to focus on the geometric patterns. Her eyes were too blurry. But she knew them by heart. Rebecca had acquired it at an estate sale years ago in Arizona from a snow bird who didn't realize it was genuine. Neither did her mom who bought it because it was pretty and cheap. It spent a short time in Iris while they travelled across country, then decorated the floor of their apartment in Seattle until a friend recognized it for what it was. Terra took it from Rebecca before she could sell it to score heroin.

Fucking heroin.

She wondered if whomever developed it first ever knew of the damage it would do to countless humans or the pain and misery it caused to those left behind—those who had to deal with the aftermath.

Assholes.

She blew her nose and made her next call. Since she had no money left, she needed to cancel her appointment with Shelly. Her haircut would have to wait, and she left a message on Shelley's cell to that end. And after that, one on Dr. Rodham's letting him know she'd see him the following day. She'd tried several times to reach him, but every call went straight to voicemail which only served to increase her frustration.

Need to move bad juju.

Did Rebecca mean she needed to move from the rehab center? If so—why? Had she been in danger and the overdose was really something else, and again, was any of this connected to Vasily's visit?

Why *had* he shown up exactly when her mother went missing?

She took a shower. Standing with her forehead against the tiles, the hot water sluicing over her body and her mind swirling with a million questions, she cried.

Not one bit of it made sense.

After a while she dressed, silently singing "Zombie" to herself. Because that's how she felt—like a fucking zombie. And even though she had no appetite, she had to eat. Just as she was cracking eggs to scramble, a thump at her front door had her head jerking and her heart jumping into her throat.

Holy hell!

Somebody was trying to break into her apartment!

Shit!

Adrenaline shot through her system achieving in a second what the caffeine failed to do all morning. She spun around. Her naked toe caught in the bottom of her wide-legged yoga pants and she flailed, almost tripping. As she stumbled forward, her knee slammed into the cabinets.

Fucking *fuck*!

Fighting tears of pain and clutching her leg, she hopped on one leg, yanking open a drawer, looking for a weapon. Her meat mallet! Thanks to the cute salesman at Crate and Barrel for talking her into buying it.

The doorknob jerked.

Jesus—was it the Russian?

Well he wasn't getting any of her digits without a fight. She waited three heart-pounding beats, then sucked in a deep breath and with meat mallet in hand, she limped to the front door.

It jerked again and before she lost what was left of her courage, she took a quick peek through the brass peephole.

Nothing.

Other than the red bottle brush tree with its blanket of needles decorating the sidewalk like some red-carpet affair.

It yanked again. She jumped.

Then sucked in a shaky breath and tried again. Her assailant was either very short or on their knees—perhaps picking the lock?

Oh...God!

She strained the edges of the view finder until she saw it. The wide, butt end of a stocky dog pulling towards the street. Each time he moved, so did her door.

Her knees almost buckled in relief. She'd seen that mutt before, lying flat on its stomach, legs sprawled wide on a fluffy doggy-bed tucked away in a corner of Shelley's salon.

An almost hysterical giggle bubbled up as she unlocked the door, boosted by relief and adrenaline.

"Hey dog," she half-called, giggling and pulling the door inward as much as his leash allowed her.

At her voice, the English bulldog turned.

"Give me some slack, buddy, so I can open the door."

The dog dipped that broad, wrinkled head and sneezed, after which it shook that same broad head, spraying droplets of drool in a wide arc before swaggering towards her on legs too short for his body. His tongue hung out the side of an unfortunate under-bite and glinted in the muted sunlight as he panted.

Once she had the door open enough to step outside, she got a good look at the mutt. He was blonde, had a stub for a tail and he was as wide as he was short.

"My God, how did you get so ugly?"

He raised red-rimmed, watery eyes, met her gaze and blinked.

Twice.

Something inside her stomach went *plop*—the damn dog was smiling. How the hell? Especially this one, with those jowls hanging halfway to the ground?

"Hey!" She dropped to her haunches and rubbed his folded ears, grinning back. "What're you doing here?"

His entire body waggled, not just what was left of his nubby tail. Suddenly, and despite his dental incongruity, he wasn't so ugly anymore. That wrinkled, earnest face morphed into something ridiculously charming—and cute.

"Where's your mamma?" Terra unhooked the brown leather leash from her doorknob. It was attached to one of those cliché silver spiky collars you'd expect to see on a guard dog, and she let him take the lead. He tugged hard, and she almost lost her grip on his leash.

"Oh shit, you little bugger, slow down. I've never had a dog so gimme a break here."

Strangely the dog seemed to understand and slowed his stride as she followed him down the street past several parked cars.

Shelley De Luca lifted a leg and kicked the door of a blue Mini Coupe closed while juggling her purse, a white pastry box and a bottle of something bubbly and light peach in color.

"Hey." She leaned forward and gave Terra a hug, the cold bottle brushing against the middle of her back. "See you found Truman."

Truman—that was his name.

"He almost gave me heart failure. I thought someone was trying to break down my door."

"Oh God—sorry!" She lifted the bottle and pastry box. "The little bastard is all muscle and strong when he decides to be, and I couldn't handle him and this at the same time without risking dropping anything." She hefted the box labeled *The Flour Barrel* and bottle up a bit. "I brought these for you."

"Not that I'm not grateful, but why?"

"I was at my uncle Billy's bakery when I heard your message. The way you sounded, I figured something really bad had happened. I thought what kind of person am I if I didn't bring you doughnuts and Bellini?"

Buh-what?

"I don't even know what that is."

"Bellini? It's an Italian thing. We'll pop it in a sec and you'll find out. But first I need to look at you." Shelley stepped back, her face changed. "God, girl, you alright?"

That hit her in the chest and despite her best efforts, Terra's face crumpled.

"You've been crying?"

Terra nodded.

"Oh shit, honey—what's going on?"

"My mom died." Her voice broke on the sob.

Shelley gasped. "Oh, no!" She put the box of doughnuts and the bottle on the sidewalk, pointed at Truman and ordered him to sit and stay. Then wrapped her arms around Terra and pulled her in. "God, I'm so sorry."

Terra dropped her head onto Shelley's slim shoulder and clung to her. "You took time out of your day," she sniffed. "To check on me?"

"Of course, you didn't sound good. Why wouldn't I?"

She'd always wanted a sibling. Helen was the closest thing to one, though she hadn't yet told her about her mom. Knowing Helen, she'd want to take the day off work and rush over—and she needed her commissions almost as much as Terra. But if she did have a sibling, this is how she would imagine it would feel.

She sobbed, and Shelley held her until she stopped and then for a little bit longer.

"Come on," she said after a while and took her hand. "Let's get you inside before Truman eats the doughnuts. Trust me on this, we do *not* want that to happen."

❦

"*T*hree thousand dollars?" That peachy champagne buzz and doughnut-induced sugar high fizzled and crashed.

"Yes, ma'am," said the man on the other end of the phone. His tone was as dead as the people he provided services for. "That includes one of our unique cremation urns."

How unique could their urns be if they were mass produced enough to be included in their services?

"There's nothing cheaper? I mean, what if I supply my own urn?" She searched for the least used Kleenex on her coffee table. The box was empty, and she'd have to break out the toilet paper next.

"The non-ceremonial cremation is the cheapest service we provide," the man droned, "as do most funeral homes. And the urn comes with it. There's no discount if you provide your own."

Awesome.

"You accept credit cards?"

Perhaps if she wore a really short skirt and showed a glimpse of her best bra she could get one of those personal bankers to up her credit limit. Or open up another one. Or she could consider robbing a bank. Her sexy Pirates of the Caribbean Halloween costume still hung in her closet. With a dreadlock wig and lots of makeup, she might be able to pull it off.

"Yes, ma'am, we do."

"Okay. I need to think about it. Thank you." She jabbed the red button on her phone and closed her eyes. Then tapped her phone on her forehead. Her next paycheck, plus the advance she'd asked Anna for would cover a deposit on a funeral and some of the expenses.

That was it.

Definitely not the next payment to Vasily—or rather, cigarette-man—or who-the-fuck-ever. She wasn't even sure, on top of everything, she could make the minimum payment on her credit card. And she had other bills to pay if she wanted to keep the lights on and her internet connection. Not to mention the inconvenient matter of having to feed herself—occasionally.

She eyed the last remaining doughnuts on her coffee table. Perhaps she could freeze them in case things got really bad.

Wait.

Hadn't there been *four* doughnuts on the plate the last time she looked?

"Did you steal a doughnut, buddy?"

Truman lifted his head off her lap. The dog held her gaze, then blinked slowly. A telltale white powdery substance transferred from his jowls onto her yoga pants.

"Shit…okay, just don't tell your mamma. She won't let me babysit again."

To which Truman farted.

Terra's eyebrows rose a moment before it hit her. "Oh my GOD!" She jumped off the couch and staggered back a few feet. "What the hell was that?"

Truman scrambled after her, unsuccessfully—as he nose-planted onto her carpet. The bottom half of him splayed and got stuck up against the edge of the couch. He shook his butt, maneuvering himself until he plopped onto his side. When he regained his footing, he hung his head looking straight at the carpet. Terra half-gagged, half-laughed at his clumsiness, then picked up a cushion, swinging it in a wide arc to fan the area.

"Good lord, Truman! Remind me never to leave unattended doughnuts around you again," she said and opened her windows wider. "Or any food for that matter."

She should've heeded Shelley's warning before she left to run errands. "Truman is good for the soul," she'd said. "Just don't feed him, even if he begs."

Well, she'd learned the hard way. The little bastard wasn't a beggar—*he was thief*!

While Terra swung cushions, Truman busied himself with an

inspection of her apartment, seemingly fascinated with a spot on her wall. He sniffed at it repeatedly.

"Please tell me you're not going to pee on my wall."

The dog looked at her, then at her front door.

Ah!

Toilet time.

After he'd completed his business outside, and her apartment was sufficiently aired inside, they returned to their spots on the couch. Truman made endless circles next to her in one direction, then the other until he found the perfect position and she continued with her funeral home search with not much better results.

"You got eight thousand dollars I can borrow?" She asked the dog, scratching his ears. "Five to pay off the Russian and three for the funeral?"

He wrinkled that fleshy brow and snorted.

"How about five hundred?"

This time he whined. "Yeah," she sighed and dropped her head back to stare at her ceiling. "I didn't think so, buddy, but thanks anyway. I'm up a creek and none of the guys in the band have the money either."

Which was true—they all had regular paying daytime gigs, student loans and rent to pay, just like her. They couldn't help even if they wanted to.

Helen would.

Helen would take a high interest advance on her credit card, be Will Turner to her Jack Sparrow and help hijack an armored car. Which was exactly why she would *not* ask Helen.

The only break was they hadn't released her mom's body yet. According to a Detective Fetzer from the Mill Valley Police Department the autopsy hadn't been performed yet due to too many bodies in the morgue and too few medical examiners to perform them. Therefore, giving her a few extra days to get her crap sorted. Regardless, her choices were limited, and she was out of options.

Let me help you.

Zander's words popped into her head. *Had* he meant it? Probably not if you took into consideration the look on his face when she'd asked him rather spontaneously for a loan.

But there was *something* between them. A pull she couldn't afford, but one she couldn't deny either.

What would it make her if she played on that attraction? A whore, like her mother? Could she live with herself—look herself in the eyes in the mirror every morning if did? Desperate people do desperate things, but the question was—exactly how desperate was she?

A long, exhausted sigh escaped her. She'd sell some valuables before she did that.

She had the Navajo rug, her Gucci purse and some jewelry that wasn't worth much.

Jewelry?

Holy hell! She examined her thumb and noted her missing ring.

Where the…?

Oh…crap!

She'd left it on Zander's counter.

CHAPTER TEN

Monday

It was almost noon when she arrived at the Sunrise Institute. The property was peppered with tall redwoods and bordered the edge of Muir Woods in the hills north of San Francisco. As Iris puttered to a stop outside the repurposed and restored Victorian mansion, Terra wondered for the millionth time how her mother managed to get admitted as an inpatient. When she'd asked Rebecca, she'd shrugged it off—said *she knew someone who knew someone* but wouldn't answer the question.

She'd finally stopped asking, figuring if Rebecca wanted her to know, she would. Trudging up the stairs, she announced herself to the lady manning a large, vintage mahogany reception desk situated to the right of the main door. The woman eyed her wearily then picked up a phone and pushed a few buttons. While she waited, she took in the ornate wrought iron and wood banister decorating a central staircase that led to the inpatient bedrooms. Where her mother's room was.

"Terra." Dr. Rodham's fancy Stanford School of Medicine voice carried across the large cream-bordered-with-blue marble floor tiles. He wore loose-fitting beige linen pants and a Hawaiian short-sleeved button-down, giving the impression he was on vacation instead of the executive of a rehab facility. "I'm glad you came. I've spent most of the morning thinking about you." He took her offered hand in both of his. "How are you doing?"

"I was doing fine, up until this second," she croaked out and forced back the tears. "Being here just makes it that much more real."

There was a long pause, while Dr. Rodham expelled a breath and let her hands go. Then he scrubbed his own through his graying beard. "Why don't we talk in the sunroom. It's quite lovely and we'll be alone as all the patients are at lunch."

He led her to a room off to the side of the building, with floor-to-ceiling windows decorated with an abundance of pink and purple fuchsias, cascading ferns on pedestals and potted dragon plants.

As she took a seat in a wicker chair with a dark blue cushion, he sat next to her and asked, "What can I do to help?"

"Well, I'm not sure yet, but you, um…you said she went missing? That nobody noticed until she didn't show for dinner? Is that normal? I mean, aren't they monitored most of the time?"

"They are, very closely when they first get here and throughout the detox period. But Rebecca had been an inpatient for, what, two months now?"

Terra nodded as she remembered the exact day she'd brought her mother here, and helped check her in. It was the same day she'd discovered Ruby's mouth attached to Danny's dick when she walked into her bedroom several hours later. Apparently, they hadn't expected her home so soon.

Not the most fun day she'd ever had.

"Once they have reached a certain point in treatment," he

continued, "they have a little more freedom to wander the grounds. We give them jobs to encourage a sense of purpose and Rebecca enjoyed working in the vegetable gardens. Said it gave her peace, growing things."

"Yeah, we never had a garden. At most, all we could afford was a small apartment with a little balcony or a patio, but she loved to putter." She pulled in her lips at the memory then pressed the back of her hand to her mouth, thinking of the tomatoes Rebecca had tried and failed to grow in Seattle. "I'd been trying to reach her for a couple days. She sent me a strange text that made no sense and I was worried…"

"You thought she might have broken treatment?"

She nodded and dabbed at her eyes. "It's been known to happen. I mean, this wasn't her first time in rehab, and I guess I've just learned to expect disappointment—but good lord, I wasn't prepared for this."

"You should know we do random urine tests, and at her last one—the day before she died, she was clean."

"Well, I suppose that's good to know. I've spent a long time on the phone with the cops, but they have no real answers yet. I mean, how did she get the fix?"

"Yes, it's very early still, and I'm not sure what the police have as they haven't given me details yet either, but *we're* doing our own internal investigation, of course. It's very troubling that someone was able to bring in drugs. Our staff have all been thoroughly vetted with extensive background checks."

Perhaps another patient then—though she couldn't see how. Rebecca and all her possessions had been searched by the staff when she'd first checked in and she assumed that was standard procedure with all new patients.

"I know you know this already, Terra," Dr. Rodham went on. "But if addicts are going to get better, they have to want it enough, and they have to learn to say no."

"I understand that." She stopped to blow her nose with a

Kleenex. "It's just that I really thought this time was different, you know. That she'd make it. Especially after our last therapy session together—she just seemed so ready."

"She made a lot of progress and I honestly don't know what changed—or when."

"What about at the other group sessions? How did she seem then?"

"Determined like she was when you were here, but sometimes they aren't always honest."

Terra brought her hand to her forehead and closed her eyes. "None of this makes any sense. I didn't have my phone on Saturday, and I was going to call from work, but the day was crazy and I…do you think if I…?"

"Terra—stop!" His voice got firmer as he cut her off. "Listen to me. It's not your fault. Addiction isn't just physical, it's also psychological. Rebecca's problems were deep insecurities that began before you were born. They had nothing to do with you."

"We both know that's not true. They began *because* I was born."

"I'm not going to let you put that on yourself. She made her choices."

"She didn't have to have me, and I could have done more to help her."

"But she did have you. She *chose* to keep you, remember that. And there isn't a person I know who could've done more, and besides, it wasn't up to you. It was up to her." Another long sigh escaped him as he pinched his eyes underneath those John Lennon glasses. "I don't want to speculate until I know more or until we get the full autopsy results from the medical examiner, but you may want to prepare yourself that sometimes despite outside appearances, the internal struggle can often be too much. Sometimes addicts just give up."

"Give up?"

She stared at him for a long time while she processed that. So long, Dr. Rodham said, "I probably shouldn't have said that."

"But you did," she said, getting to her feet. "You think she OD'd on purpose?"

"Only Rebecca knew for sure. I'm truly sorry. I wish it were different, that you weren't left with this."

"Give up?"

Suddenly, the sunroom, though open and airy, felt like those tall, glass walls were closing in on her. She walked to the glass door and stepped through into the sunshine, gulping the warm, August air.

"I can't believe she'd do something like that without saying goodbye. I mean, Mom made stupid choices, but she wasn't fundamentally selfish. What aren't you telling me?"

"Sometimes when people are desperate enough, they do desperate things."

Fuck—she understood that, as she'd had that very same thought just yesterday—but still.

"I don't believe it." She shook her head. "She would've found a way. It doesn't feel right." Her stomach dropped, and her chest felt tight when she said, "Did she leave a note?"

"Perhaps she wrote something in a letter," Dr. Rodham said.

Her eyebrows jumped. "Letter?"

"I encourage my patients to keep a journal—old school with a notebook and a pen, or alternatively as in Rebecca's case—to write letters to their family or the people they believe they may have wronged. Writing the words helps them process unresolved traumas in a safe way."

"I haven't received any letters from her." But then again, come to think of it, she hadn't checked her mail lately either. Too many bills she couldn't afford to pay. "Are there any upstairs, in her room?"

Dr. Rodham grimaced. "Whatever letters she hasn't mailed, if there were any, are currently in the hands of the police. I'm assuming they need them for evidence."

"Evidence of what—suicide?"

"She may have written something that can help them reach a conclusion. Look Terra, you're in shock. This has been terrible for you. I suggest when you get back to the city, take it easy for a few days while they do their investigation. Let it settle, allow yourself to grieve and we'll talk again after you've had some rest."

Rest?

She almost laughed. She couldn't afford to rest even though she'd been forced too, thanks to Anna.

The lump in her throat was back, making it tight and her voice come out thick. "I don't know what to do next."

"Talk to someone. Get some counseling."

"Um…"

"Please—promise me. There are support groups I could steer you to. People who've been through what you're going through. This is too much for you to handle alone."

"Okay," she mumbled, although she wasn't sure how she was going to swing it even if she wanted to.

"Here's the key to her room," he said retrieving a simple, brass key attached to white plastic tab with the facilities logo and a number on it from his linen pants' pocket. "You remember where it is?"

She nodded, accepting it from him.

"I'll leave you to it then—give you privacy to sort her things, but if you need me, I'll be in my office."

"Wait—before you go, I have one more question."

"Go ahead."

"Who is…was paying for her treatment?"

Dr. Rodham blinked, then he got that dear in the headlights look, his eyes wide behind his round glasses. "I…uh…I can't discuss that with you, I'm sorry."

What?

"Why not? I'm her next of kin, surely patient confidentiality no longer applies? I only want to know who I have to thank for trying to help her."

"We—meaning your mom and I signed a non-disclosure agreement and that isn't invalidated by her death."

An NDA?

Who would want to keep that secret—and why? One of her clients? She stared at Dr. Rodham until he broke the contact and looked away.

"I'm sorry," he mumbled and shook his head.

She clutched the key in her hand and watched him walk away, willing him to stop and tell her—but he did not turn back.

When he disappeared around the corner, she let out a short blast of air. Then she threaded her fingers through her hair and pulled it off her face.

An NDA?

She examined the tiny pebbles in the graveled pathway for a long time before she walked towards Iris to retrieve a box to pack Rebecca's things in. After which she made her way up that ornate staircase and set about clearing her mother's room.

CHAPTER ELEVEN

Tuesday

"This is what I could gather in forty-eight hours." Carmine Niccoterra pushed the hardcopy of his report across the wood table to Zander. He pulled his dark curls off his face and secured them at the back of his head with a hairband. "If you weren't such an impatient fucker, I'd have more."

Lynyrd Skynyrd's "Free Bird" played over the speakers, courtesy of Barney, who was restocking the top shelves behind the bar. They'd just opened and except for Zeke, a regular, sitting silently and nursing a rum and coke, it was just them.

Zander eyed his friend. "You all right? Looks like you've had better days."

"My current case is killing me. I'm gonna need like a year off to recover when it's done." Carmine's light-green eyes looked haunted and there were dark circles beneath them that he'd never seen before.

"I appreciate you doing this. I wouldn't ask if I didn't feel it was important."

"I know that." Carmine nodded. "Which is why I'm doing it."

"Give me the basics," Zander said and took a sip of his beer, pleased to note it tasted good—not too sweet or heavy.

Carmine did the same. The man didn't grimace, in fact his head cocked to the side as he savored the new brew.

Maybe he should order more from the rep.

"In a nutshell," Carmine said, placing his glass on the table, then pushing back in his seat, "Only one person has OD'd at the Sunrise Institute in recent days. Rebecca Miller, your girl's mother. Turns out she was one of Dean Melnikov's girls."

Zander's gazed snapped to his friends. Say what?

"One of the few," Carmine continued, "who weren't taken into custody the night the Feds raided the asshole's operation."

"Are you saying her mother is…was a hooker?"

Carmine nodded. "She didn't work The Farm—was more of a private clientele kind of girl. High end, every move controlled by Dean."

"What do you mean by 'the farm'?"

"Dean had several brothels operating out of houses all over the city. One, much more exclusive, was located in Napa on a vineyard up in the hills. They called it The Farm. He held parties, and I use the word *party* loosely. More like orgies. Johns forked out truck-loads of green for the privilege to partake—invitation only. No limits on the women, or how they used them. They could do whatever the fuck they wanted. Lots of drugs, booze and sick shit." Carmine rubbed his temples as if he had a headache. "Rebecca landed in a different category—more exclusive for select johns only." He removed a couple glossy five-by-eight photos from the folder and tossed them onto the table. "Woman was gorgeous."

Zander studied them, fingering the edges, amazed at Carmine's ability to find shit out about people. There was no denying it. Rebecca Miller *was* gorgeous. He could have been looking at a photo of Terra, except for her being older and thinner with straight, darker hair, more on the auburn side. One was a regular studio shot with her head turned slightly to the side. Beautiful, but posed. The other was her looking over her shoulder, the wind in her hair on a street in the city.

Stunning.

Knowing she was gone, that the world now missed that beauty and Terra missed her mother, hurt him more than he wanted to admit.

"What's her story?"

Carmine sucked in air and let it out on a long sigh. "My source says she was basically a slave. Dean kept her in an apartment where she serviced very wealthy, very powerful men. Controlled her through her heroin habit. Then Dean went down, ended up in prison and Vasily shows up out of the wide blue yonder and takes over. That's all I know for now about her mother."

Fuck.

It was even worse than he thought.

"What about Terra?"

"I took a look into her finances like you asked. She earns decent money, mostly commission. Up until about two months ago, had a little over fifteen thousand dollars in savings. One big withdrawal was made, then ever since there's been weekly ATM withdrawals totaling five hundred dollars and now, she's cleaned out. Financially, she's in a hole."

Hence the request for a loan.

Zander worked his jaw while he pondered what the withdrawals were for.

"My new dude in training, Brady showed Vasily's photo to a co-worker of Terra's. Said she'd only seen him once, this last Saturday. Must have been when you saw him, but says another man, one who looks like he belongs in prison—her words—shows up every Saturday and your girl doesn't look happy to see him. Only stays a minute—my guess just long enough for a handover."

"You mean the five hundred dollars every week goes to that fuck?"

"I'm working on getting an ID, but it should be noted he sports a tat on his neck—some kind of cross or the hilt of a knife."

A ripple of unease ran through Zander and tickled something in his subconscious, but he pushed it aside—for now.

"What was Terra paying for— her mother's habit?"

Carmine shook his head. "Not sure yet—could also be some kind of protection money now that Dean's gone."

"Any way you can find out?"

"Intend to."

"Why rehab now?" Zander asked, scratching the stubble on his jaw.

"Indeed—and why a private facility? Private costs a bucket load but I'd venture a guess that's not where Terra's money is going. Five hundred a week would not cut it. Anyway, she'd be paying the facility directly, not through a middle man who may or may not be working for Vasily." Carmine took another sip of his beer. "This is good shit." He tipped his glass.

Zander nodded. Yep, he definitely needed to order more from the rep.

"You wanna keep going? Giving you my friends and family rate."

"Do it," Zander ordered. "I wanna know who is paying for rehab. Also, who is this dude that shows up every Saturday?"

"I'm thinking it's safe to say he's part of Melnikov's organization, but the question is—which one? Dean or Vasily? I'll know more when I get an ID. But whatever the deal is with Terra," Carmine said, "and if it is at Vasily's behest you gotta reckon this probably isn't about cash. Besides now running Dean's stable of women, I don't know how else he makes his money, but he's not lacking for any."

"Yeah—I'd really like to know what he's been doing the last ten years." Zander scraped his hands over his face, then let out a long, drawn-out sigh. Then the two men sat in silence for a few moments sipping on their beer until Zander broke it. "Let's hope this anonymous fucker belongs to Vasily and not Dean."

"There's a difference?"

"Vasily is younger, but smarter and less likely to do anything stupid. The man is cold enough to freeze vodka, therefore his men would be less likely to do anything stupid."

"Never met him but you would know. You never talk about them." Carmine's brows creased.

"Never had occasion to."

"You in the mood for sharing? Could use the intel."

Zander looked across the bar. Barney hung freshly washed wine glasses in a rack above the bar. "The old man, Dmitri, had an unhealthy interest in my mother. Came around often and a lot of times he brought his sons."

"Ah! Fun times?"

"Not so much—Dean is a hothead and liked to fight."

"I'm aware."

"Especially liked to fight with me."

"Fuck."

"Vasily is like his old man. No emotion, every move calculated and one of the few who could control Dean. Had a way of calming him down. Would just look at him, say a few words in Russian and boom—problem solved."

"That's fucking scary."

"Uh-huh. You sure Rebecca's death is an OD?"

"No."

Zander grunted.

"Because I'm a forward-thinking individual, I asked a cop

friend of mine to look into the medical examiner's report. They're doing a full workup, including toxicology."

For the first time that day Zander smiled.

"Full disclosure," Carmine went on. "You should know, I've a personal interest in your case."

Zander's head cocked. "Why is that?"

"Two reasons. First, your girl is a friend of Shelley De Luca who is a friend of mine. Actually, Shelley's more like family. And the second is—your girl is a tenant of Shelley's man who also happens to be a friend of mine."

"And that is?"

"Gianni Cadora."

The hairs on the back of Zander's neck stood to attention. "Jesus—coincidence?" Gianni Cadora, he knew was head of what was left of the Italian mafia in San Francisco, though the rumor mill had him going mostly legit, having transferred his assets into real-estate in and around the city.

"Only if you don't consider that Terra lives in the unit that Gianni's younger brother happened to get himself killed in because of a deal gone bad."

That made him sit up. "Killed by whom?"

"One guess."

"Shit—Dean?"

"Bingo," Carmine said. "And Dean had an obsession from hell with Shelley De Luca prior to her becoming Gianni's woman."

"And now Vasily has developed an interest in Terra."

"And both brothers are connected to her mother." Carmine nodded while sucking on his beer. "That would be one helluva coincidence. Good thing I don't believe in them."

Christ.

"Your girl is in deep."

"Yeah."

"Question is how deep."

"That's what I need you to find out."

"How deep do you want me to go?" Carmine asked.

"As deep as it takes you."

ta

*Z*ander stared at the bottle of whiskey, running his thumb over the label, feeling the indentations of the imprinted ink.

Crack.

The woman was like crack.

One hit hooked his ass and he had a nasty suspicion it was only gonna get worse. He never allowed them into his head yet from that moment she'd smiled over her shoulder, ass in the air, she'd found a gap, slipped in and now he couldn't fucking get her out of his skull.

It did his head in.

"Zander."

And her mother—Jesus! He didn't even know the woman, but his heart twisted thinking what Terra was dealing with. None of it his business and why the fuck he made it his business was reason enough he was gonna need therapy.

"*Zander!*" Barney's rough voice broke through.

"What?" He cast his eyes to the old man.

"For fuck sake, son, get your head outta your ass."

Zander snorted. Normally he wouldn't take shit from his staff, but Barney wasn't staff. Barney was almost family. Ancient as those sequoia trees and just as rugged. He had been part of the bar longer than Zander had been alive. Probably die here too.

"Trouble at the door," Barney grumbled. "Heather's having a hissy fit, giving our new boy Pete a hard time."

Heather.

He dropped his head and let out a sigh. Pulled the last bottle of whisky from the crate, stacked it on the shelf under the bar. Next time he was ordering something cheaper. This shit wasn't as cost effective as it ought to be. He should recheck the inventory logs against the sales logs. Perhaps he'd made a mistake.

Or someone was skimming.

He did not want to think it was his staff, especially Nicky. The woman had a kid to support—but fuck!

"Fine." He rose from a squat and dusted his hands on a bar towel, then tossed it back under the counter. "I'll deal."

The problem with these women, you fucked them one time too often they got entitlement issues. Clearly time to *un*-entitle her ass. Though, if he was honest, he hated this kind of showdown, which is why he never allowed it to get to the entitlement stage.

Heather was persistent if nothing else, but the woman just wasn't doing it for him anymore.

The crowd parted as he approached. Her voice cut above the music and the noise, grating on his nerves. Then he caught sight of her and groaned.

The last couple of times he'd seen her, she had a hyper kind of a buzz happening that bordered on nasty. Might go a long way to explaining him losing interest, but this was more than that. This was plastered.

He nodded at a member of the band setting up and gave a two-finger side wave to a couple sitting at a corner table before he got to the door.

"I said, get out of my way, asshole." Heather wobbled on a pair of sparkly stripper heels that rivaled the famous Coit Tower.

"Name is Pete, ma'am."

Zander approved of his bouncer's temerity. He was new and young, but loyal and determined to learn and follow the rules. He stood blocking Heather's way, with his considerable arms folded.

"Donchou ma'am me. When Zannie hears you won't let me in, he'll be *pisshed*." She poked her finger an inch from his face then used her fake boobs as battering rams, trying but failing to budge Pete.

"You are drunk. Policy is"—Pete leaned forward a little forcing *her* to lean back—"we don't let *drunk* people past the door."

She took a step back, almost losing her balance, and would have, had the person she stumbled into not steadied her.

"Polishy, my ass, and I'm not *drunk*. Get him—you'll see."

Pete widened his stance and held his ground.

Good man.

He'd taken a liking to the kid, sorta like an annoying younger brother—without the annoying part.

"Got it, Pete." He didn't like to interject when his staff did their jobs, but Heather's issues with him weren't Pete's problem. And he needed to have words with her anyway, but she was further gone than he'd thought. He could practically smell the booze on her breath from five feet away. He sighed.

"Zannie!" Heather swiveled and threw out her arms as she took a step towards him. An ankle twisted, causing her to lurch. He caught her around her waist, which resulted in her face-planting into his shoulder.

"There you are," she mumbled into his armpit, lobbing her arms around his neck, getting a handful of his hair to hold onto. He grimaced at the sting and gripped her wrist. "Let go of my hair, babe."

"Sush pretty hair. Wanna run my fingersh through it."

While she clung, he stuck a hand in the back pocket of his jeans to retrieve his phone—thumbed in his pass-code and pulled up the app he'd downloaded specifically for times like these, then handed Pete his phone.

"Getting you an Uber," Zander said to Heather, gripping her wrists to ease the pressure on his hair. Gimme your address."

"No." Heather tipped her platinum head back and grunted into his face. "No Oober." That's when he noticed her eyes had that glassy, unfocused look that made him suspect something else other than booze was going on. He despised drugs of any kind, but the reality was, he encountered it daily in his world. "Wanna pardy with you." She stamped her foot, her stripper heel catching the edge of his toe.

He grunted. "Address, babe. I'll come with you."

"We'll pardy at my housh?"

He didn't answer, but Heather mumbled an address in Laurel Heights and Pete keyed it in.

"Deal with the door," he said, retrieving his phone. "I've got this."

Tightening his hold on Heather's waist, he waited for her to find her feet. "C'mon, babe, let's get you fresh air."

"Don't want fresh air." She dropped an arm from his neck to grab his crotch, but he caught her hand before she got a handful. "Les go upshtairs."

"Nope." He adjusted his arm around her waist and guided her towards the door. "You're going home."

"Want more of this." Heather cackled in the back of her throat and made a second go at his crotch. This time she got a fistful. Zander felt his balls retract, and as he wrestled her fingers off him, he felt something else—a tingling at the base of his spine which had nothing to do with Heather's hand.

He looked up and his heart stopped. His breath left his body, every muscle froze then his mind went blank—except for one thought.

Her.

In his bar.

Watching him!

Pete, that little asshole, leaned in and cloaked her in a bear hug that lifted her off her feet. His lizard brain processed she hugged him back—clung to him like he was her lifeboat. It made his whole body get tight.

Heather felt it move through him, even in her wasted state. Her head lolled, and she stared at him with a belligerent gleam in her eyes. Then she returned to the side and saw who he was looking at.

More like ogling at.

Drooling at.

Whatever.

The woman was crazy-ass-fucking beautiful—made him lose his breath.

"Whosshe?" Heather demanded, throwing out an arm in Terra's general direction, hitting a man walking by in the shoulder.

"Hey," the dude called, steadying his beer, giving Heather a wild-eyed stare.

"Sorry," Zander said and reined in Heather's arm.

"Who the fuckisshee?"

"C'mon, babe, shut it," he said close to her ear. "Don't do this."

"She one of 'em?" Heather twisted in Zander's arms, her voice getting louder. Loud enough that Terra pulled away from Pete and turned to face him.

Their eyes locked.

It was several moments before he realized he'd gone blank again. Unable to process anything, except for the chemistry or pheromones or what-the-fuck-ever buzzing between them, setting his synapses to rapid fire.

She broke it when her eyes dropped to Heather, gave an almost imperceptible head-shake and by the time they got to his again—the way they changed from sad curiosity to something that looked a whole lot like disappointment, he knew it was going to shit.

"You fuckin' him?" Heather's voice got hoarse and broke a bit as she yelled at Terra. A small crowd had gathered, mostly people coming in but curious at the side-show nonetheless. Heather jerked, and if he hadn't already had an arm tight around her waist, she would've launched.

"*Mine.*"

Jesus.

This wasn't going to shit—it was already there.

"Donchou forgeddit." She jerked again, harder this time.

He'd had enough.

"Shut it!" he growled in Heather's ear and moving fast, he grabbed her wrists, bringing them behind her back. Clasping them together with one hand, the other on the back of her neck, he marched her stripper heels and too-short skirt towards the front door.

A few people clapped, which he didn't particularly love. Out of his peripheral, he caught that Terra wasn't one of them, though he didn't have much time to think about that, as right then Heather chose to heave.

He aimed her at the sidewalk. They made it to the storm drain, between two parked cars and far enough from the line of people outside before she projectiled. Rather there, he figured, than into the little potted palm trees outside the bar's doors. They were a bitch to clean and had seen enough vomit in their long lives.

He held her hair away from her face, with one arm wrapped around her waist while she hurled, turning his face from the stench, struggling to keep it locked down himself. It seemed to last forever but in reality, was probably less than a minute.

When she finished, he realized he had another problem— nothing to wipe her mouth, not even a grungy bar towel that would normally be stuck in his back pocket.

He called Pete, but it went straight to voicemail. Probably too busy getting it on with Terra. His nostrils flared. He was gonna have to have words with the kid, reminding him to keep his phone on.

However, words or not, it didn't help his current situation. It would have to be his shirt.

Shit.

He liked his shirt.

Heather stayed doubled over, ass tucked into his crotch, dry heaving. Her palms were planted loosely on the trunk of a Ford Focus. If he let her go, she'd collapse. Therefore, it would have to be done one-handed.

Adjusting his hold on Heather, he loosened a couple buttons, and keeping his face up-wind of the stench, reached behind his neck to tug on the collar.

The skin on his arm tingled, raising the hairs to full mast. He didn't even have to turn his head to know. But he slid his gaze to his left and encountered Terra's glinting in the street lights. A rushing started in his stomach, expanded and moved up into his chest.

It was simple.

He wanted her.

He wanted *in* her, something fucking fierce—so much, just the thought made him start to get hard. But his reality was, he had another woman's ass pressed against his crotch.

Terra broke eye contact, and while she dug in her purse he worked his jaw and fought with his dick. Didn't need Heather thinking it was for her.

"You here with someone?" he grunted out, much gruffer than he intended since that disappointed look was still present in her eyes.

"Not at the moment," she said with her head still down.

What the hell did that mean—she was out cruising for dick? He didn't fucking love that—unless it was *his* dick. In which case he was all for it.

"What are you doing out on your own?"

She stilled, then her head cocked to the side. "Sorry…what?"

The woman had to know she had a dangerous fucker after her ass, though he had to be careful. She didn't know he'd looked into her life. It wouldn't do to chase the woman away before he even got started.

"You shouldn't be out on your own, Freckle. The city's a dangerous place for a woman alone."

"Freckle?" she asked, raising a brow.

"You have one on your neck—where I kissed you." He was pleased to note, he'd marked her and would have touched the spot, except his available arm couldn't reach her, so instead he touched the same spot on his own. "Right there."

Her eyelids fluttered. "Yeah, thanks for the hickey, by the way," she snarked.

He almost smiled.

"And who says I'm on my own?"

A quick survey of the street and the bar doors told what he wanted to know. No dude shooting him the evil *get away from my woman* eye. "I don't see you with anyone."

"Maybe I'm meeting someone and they're just not here yet."

He almost growled, regretting he'd brought it up. Not relishing that he was gonna be leaving with Heather and unavailable to cock-block some prick wanting in her pants.

"Yeah? And who's this dumbass?" Zander watched her eyes get wide and he could have sworn she blushed, but it was hard to tell under the city lights.

"None of your business."

"Simple question, Freckle. Not much of a man if he's making you wait."

"Oh, for fuck's sake—I'm not meeting anyone, I'm here for a different reason. My ring, for example. I left it on your counter— but the better question is, do you need help with her?" She indicated Heather with a flick of her wrist. "But since you're such a dick, I'm thinking I might not ask anymore."

"You're calling me a dick?"

"Yeah, I'm calling you a dick, *you dick*."

"Zan*nie*." Heather groaned. Terra's eyes dropped to her, then came back to his, rolled them and shook her head. She began to walk away, and he knew he'd fucked up, he had one shot to fix it.

"You got something you wanna tell me about?"

"Nope."

"So, what's with the attitude calling me a dick?"

"It's not me with the attitude, *Zannie*. Good luck with your *girlfriend*."

Jesus, he was an idiot.

Of course, she'd think Heather was his girlfriend. If their positions were reversed, after the move he pulled on her on his landing outside his office, he'd think himself a dick.

"She's not my girlfriend," he called after her, desperate for her to know. Yet desperate not to sound desperate, which he seemed to be failing miserably at.

"Yeah—whatever," she called back. Then she stopped and turned, facing him with her head tilted slightly—like what she had to ask next mattered a whole fucking lot. "Let me ask you a question, Zander."

"Shoot."

"Does *she* know that?"

He didn't get to answer because Heather blew again. All over the back of the Ford, splattering on his jeans and his shoes.

Christ—how much more did the woman have in her?

"You got anything in your purse I could use."

"You mean like a Kleenex?"

"Kleenex would be good."

He watched her take a deep breath and dip into her purse, relief torpedoing through his body. He didn't stop and ask himself why he didn't care what her reasons were to stay, just that she did.

"Zannie," Heather groaned again. "World's shpinning."

"Okay, babe." He hitched her up, keeping his arm around her waist, but with the back of her head resting against his chest. "I got you."

"Hold her steady," Terra said, her tone soft.

His eyes snapped to hers.

"I'll wipe her face. Keep her head up."

"No need, Freckle." He had to clear his throat, it got so tight. "I got it."

"You'd be guessing—probably smear her face and nobody needs that. Just keep her hair out of the way."

"You did this for your mom?" he asked softly, cupping his palm against Heather's forehead, keeping her head against his chest while Terra wiped the vomit and saliva from the corners of her mouth. She nodded but that nod carried the weight of so much sadness. He wanted to drop Heather where he stood and pull the woman into his arms, kiss that sadness off her face. While he contemplated that, a Toyota Prius with the Uber logo on the back window pulled up next to him. The window slid down, and the driver's head popped through. "You Zander?"

He grunted and adjusted Heather, preparing to guide her to the car. The driver indicated with his chin at Heather "She coming with?"

Zander said nothing but kept his arm around Heather while he opened the door.

"Better not puke in my car, man."

"I'll take care of you if she does." Though he doubted—correction, he hoped—Heather had nothing left in her *to* puke.

"That's what they all say," the driver muttered. "Just keep the damn windows open."

Zander situated Heather, snapping her seatbelt before the driver could change his mind and cancel on him. He walked around and just before he pulled the handle to open his door, Terra's eyes caught his over the roof.

"Stick around," he said, holding her gaze for a good deal longer than was necessary and hoped like fuck she would. Even if it was just to get her ring back.

CHAPTER TWELVE

Tuesday evening

*S*tick around.

Yeah—whatever. Terra disposed of the soiled Kleenex in a city garbage can then turned in time to watch the Prius turn the corner. She continued to stare long after the car disappeared, unwilling to acknowledge that thorny tendril of jealousy had grown into a full-blown vine.

No man...*no man* had a right to look that good with so little effort. Sex practically oozed from his pores, made her want to lick him with her eyeballs. She'd caught a glimpse of a flat, six-packed stomach as his shirt rose up when he lifted his arm to grab his collar.

And what the hell was that look about?

She swallowed. The intensity in those golden-brown eyes as he looked across the car made her ovaries spasm.

But he hadn't answered her question. He'd definitely given her the impression he was single, but after that scene with that woman—she was no longer sure, regardless of what he proclaimed.

It didn't matter because something had become unequivocally clear: in her delicate state, the man was nuclear—too dangerous to be around. Single or not. Though in all honesty what he did for that woman was so far from a dick move it could almost be categorized as sweet.

She eyed the bar's doors and the line of people still wanting to get in, debating if she should stay. She'd only come for her ring, but Pete caught her eye over the head of a couple, waved and beckoned at her. Because sitting at home and crying didn't appeal either, she ambled over. Perhaps one drink while the handsome jerk was gone, then *she'd* be gone before he came back.

Pete's face split into a huge grin when he saw her coming back. "You sure I don't need to pay?" she asked when he refused to take her money.

"Get yourself inside and try to enjoy yourself." He took her offered wrist and stamped it, leaving a motorcycle wheel inked on her skin.

"Thanks, Petey." She laid a kiss on his cheek. "I'll see you later." She weaved her way through the crowd towards the bar, trying to catch a groove as Debbie Harry belted "Heart of Glass" over the speakers.

As she got closer to the stage, a voice called, "Yo, carrot top." Normally she'd ignore comments like that because she wasn't *exactly* a carrot top, but there was one person who called her that. It broke through her funk and made her giggle.

Rory Jones—the lead singer of a bunch of rowdy alternative rockers and an old friend. He'd tried to date her before Dannie, and then several times during, making no effort to hide it either.

"Hey, you sexy thing," he said, hopping off the stage and grinning, then pulling her into a hug.

"Ohmigod," Terra called. "I can't believe you guys are playing tonight. I didn't think this would be your scene."

"Are you kidding? Look at the ceiling. There are wagon wheels for chandeliers. All weirdos are welcome."

That was true. There *were* wagon wheels on the ceiling, along with motorcycle rims, handlebars and several large-screen televisions mounted on the walls.

"This place is banging, babe, and so are you." He snuck an arm around her waist and kissed her on the side of her neck.

She didn't mind too much, or take him too seriously. She'd known Rory a long time and although he'd tried to get in her pants, she wasn't the only one. It was just who he was: a gigantic flirt and hot in that long-haired, unintentional Keith Urban kind of way—minus the accent.

He kissed her in the exact same spot Zander had. It was warm and sweet, but barely registered on her flutter scale.

"What the fuck is this?" He pulled back, his gaze focused on her hickey. "You got a new dude?"

Jeez—the grapevine in this city!

"Um…"

"Is he here tonight?"

"No new dude, just someone got a little frisky. Kinda like you."

"I'll beat his ass."

Terra laughed, because she figured he was more than half joking. But she couldn't help wondering if he'd say the same thing if he knew he was talking about duking it out with Zander?

Probably—because he was Rory.

Not that the sexy jerk *would* duke it out over her, but she had a hard time picturing Rory winning. He was big and hard-bodied, but it was the kind of hard that came from hours in the gym with a personal trainer. He didn't have the street-tough that Zander exuded, setting her girly parts zinging with a single look.

Rory drove a Lexus. Zander manhandled a Harley.

Yep.

No!

She didn't need to go there, getting all hot and well...*zingly*. Especially since he was probably this very minute putting his girlfriend or whatever the hell she was to bed.

"Hey." Rory's voice brought her back. "You wanna sing? We could do a duet."

"No...no." She waved a hand at him. "I don't think so."

"Oh c'mon, we could smoke 'em with a hot, raunchy booty-call number. Get 'em all riled up and send 'em home horny. It'll send the booze sales soaring and make the big dude happy." He tapped his forehead with his index finger in an *I'm thinking here* gesture. "Which means we'll get another gig."

"Well, when you put it like that." She flicked her eyes towards the stage. "Won't they mind?"

"Hell, no." His brows came together. "Why would they care if you sing? You'll make us look good."

"Yo Terra," On cue, Ben, the drummer, called from the stage and saluted her with his drumsticks. "Gonna sing with us?"

She waved back and smiled. Singing with them would be fun, and a distraction. Keeping her mind off her mom and her money problems and—well, *him* and whatever he was doing to take care of *her*.

"Okay!" She took a deep breath and said, "Let me see your set list."

They went back and forth a few times before they settled on a couple that weren't on the list, but pretty standard songs every musician worth their guitar pick should know. Just in time, as Ben drummed off a *badum badum badum bum bum bum tshhhh*— every band's call to instruments.

Rory winked and said, "Get yourself a beer and put it on my tab. I'll call you when it's time. Wanna warm this lot up first." A chin jut indicated he was talking about the crowd.

"Okay." She grinned, grateful she didn't have to fork out money for a drink, just a tip. The night may have started out crap, but things just got better. She watched Rory jog up the stage stairs in well-fitting, ripped jeans. When he took his guitar off its stand, he winked.

Why couldn't she get interested in that? Even for a fling. He was a good guy with a tour-bus full of talent, a singing voice that made a girl's nipples get happy. And he came from a good family, had a serious job and a bunch of money.

Holy shit. *He had money!*

Her eyes went wide.

Why hadn't she thought of it sooner? Maybe she should consider asking Rory for a loan. She'd already decided to nix the idea of asking the handsome jerk as anything to do with him after what she'd witness was a non-starter.

Win, win, right?

Right.

So how come it didn't *feel* right?

"Hey, cupcake." Barney, the ponytailed geezer behind the bar greeted her, a lopsided grin splitting his craggy face. For some reason, she really liked him. If she'd had a grandfather, she'd want him to look like him—with that cool-ass silver goatee and mischievous blueish eyes.

"Hey Barney! You a permanent fixture here?" She angled into a spot next to the server station and rested on her elbows.

"Pretty much."

"Your boss ever give you time off?"

"He does. I just don't take it. Ain't got nothing to go home to, so may as well spend my time here, getting paid. What are you drinking?"

"Beer please, on Rory's tab." Terra pointed to an amber ale on tap. "No special woman waiting for you at home?"

"Nope—never had one."

"What?" Terra's eyes narrowed. "I have a hard time believing that?"

He cocked a bushy brow.

"Come on—how does a handsome dude like you swing that? What little woman let you get away?"

"You're full of shit." He chuckled and shook his head as he pulled the lever. "Cute, but full of shit."

He slid her glass over and muttered, "On the house," then pulled quarter of one for himself. They touched tips and a little of hers sloshed onto the polished wood.

"That's sweet, but seriously, Rory said to put it on his tab."

Barney shook his head, then reached for a cloth to wipe the spilled beer.

"Bar is buying."

"I promise I won't tell him."

"Zander can kiss my wrinkled ass, but *I promise* he won't mind." He caught her eyes. "Sometimes he acts like an asshole but deep down he's a good man."

"Yeah?"

Where was he anyway? She couldn't help her stupid eyes from sweeping the room. Where the hell did that woman live—across the Bay Bridge? Barney opened his mouth to say something but right then Rory's band launched into a cover of "Love Song" by The Cure, making conversation pretty much impossible. Barney shrugged then leaned across the server station to take an order from Nicky, the sultry, dark-haired cocktail waitress Terra had met the last time she was here.

When Barney retreated to fill her order, she noticed Nicky scrutinizing her and she smiled. Nicky gave a grin in return.

A seat opened up and Terra snagged it, watching the crowd head off to the dance floor while she sipped her beer and ran through the songs she was going to sing in her head. It was towards the end of the first set, when a spot between her shoulder blades tickled—like someone's eyes were on her. Jerking her head to the side, she scanned the room but couldn't find anyone paying particular interest in her.

There were people hidden behind others, but her attention kept coming back to a corner. She squinted but the lighting wasn't great and before she could reflect further, Rory called her up.

Hoots and hollers came from the floor as she slid off her chair and a wolf-whistle she suspected came from behind the bar. She chuckled, some of her unease dissipating. Barney was nothing if not enthusiastic.

"Terra, get yourself on stage," Rory crooned. "Let's give 'em a show." Which caused even louder hoots and her pulse to quicken. If there was one thing she knew how to do, it was *give 'em a show*. But no matter how many times she'd done it, she still got nervous.

One of the guys moved his stand next to Rory's and adjusted the height to suit her then whispered "knock 'em dead" in her ear. She grinned and tapped the mic with a fingernail to verify it was on. Using a hand to shield her eyes, she surveyed the floor and drawled into the mic, "Hey, you all."

Movement seemed to slow, then still as she made eye contact with several people—the ominous presence in the dark corner forgotten. When a hush fell across the room she knew she had them. Behind her Ben counted off the beat. She looked at Rory who nodded and hit a chord on his guitar. Terra gripped the mic, pulling it closer, then shut her eyes, swaying a little while she waited for her note.

CHAPTER THIRTEEN

Late Tuesday evening

$\mathcal{H}$eather had vomited again. Fortunately for the Uber dude not in his car—but unfortunately for Zander, as he carried her to her apartment. Therefore, he had the driver drop him off at the back door and tipped him a fifty.

He unfolded out of the Prius and as his head cleared the roof, he stopped short. Then found himself grinning because squeezed between his Harley and his truck, sat Terra's van.

The sight of that ugly death trap in his carport was like a present under the Christmas tree. He'd asked her to stick around, but didn't expect she would. Her showing up was a gift and he'd mishandled it. Not a mistake he intended to make again.

He entered the keyless entry code and considered for half a second going straight through to the bar. But stinking of puke wasn't good for business any way you looked at it.

Half way up the stairs to his apartment, his phone rang with a number he didn't recognize.

"Yo," he said, pulling his apartment keys from his pocket.

"Zander." A woman's voice, slow and wrecked. "It's Ruby."

He slowed his steps. After not calling him back that first night, he didn't expect to hear from her and probably only one reason she'd be calling. She wanted something.

"Rube, you okay? You sound messed up."

"I am messed up. Just not like you think."

"Where are you?"

There was a long pause before she said, "Seattle."

He glanced at the area code displayed on his screen and it wasn't Seattle. Four-one-five meant San Francisco. But he could hear a lot of traffic noise, which definitely meant *a* city.

"Who's phone you using?"

"A…friend's."

"What can I do for you, Rube?"

"Have you seen Dannie?"

He sighed. Really? "I saw him at the gig. You know, the one you didn't show for."

"Yeah, well, things got a little…hot."

"What do you mean by 'hot'?"

She ignored that, asking instead, "Did Terra come back?"

"Uh-huh." Where the hell was this going?

"Good…I knew she would."

"Rube, babe, not to be rude, but I'm kinda in the middle of something." Like needing to get his ass in the shower, ten minutes ago. "Is there a point to this call?" He unlocked his apartment door, dropped his keys in a bowl on the credenza next to it and undid his shirt buttons one-handed.

"I want you to give her a message for me."

"Why don't you call and tell her yourself?"

Off came his shoes. He dumped them and his shirt in the laundry basket to cover the smell. He'd deal with them later.

"I…I can't face her."

"You won't be facing her babe, you're on the other end of the phone."

"I haven't been a good friend, Zander."

"Why is that?"

"I fucked her man—I fucked Dannie right under her nose and she walked in on us while I was blowing him."

"Jesus."

He felt slightly sick—and conflicted.

On the one hand, he couldn't be happier Terra was single, thanks to Ruby, but on the other…he hated they put that kind of hurt on her.

"Exactly, so you see my predicament." The traffic noise seemed to be getting louder along with wind noise. Where the fuck was she—and who's phone was she using?

"Yeah, and that sucks you did that to her, babe, but in my experience, people appreciate it when you apologize to their face. Not some half-assed message through a third party."

His jeans landed on top of his shoes and he closed the lid of his hamper.

"I get that."

"Then do it, Rube. Shit like that goes a long way. I don't have her number, but I can text you Dannie's. Get it from him." Fuck if he was going to be some message boy.

"Zander, please, it isn't like that. It's more complicated. I did her a favor as far as Dannie is concerned but…if you could just tell her I'm really sorry about her mom." Her voice broke after sorry and came out as a whisper.

Fuck.

He knew Ruby well enough to know the woman didn't care very much about others and had little remorse about anything, so this was big.

"You knew her mom?"

"Yeah."

Then he thought of something.

"Who's your dealer, Rube?"

"Zander, please, just tell her."

"Who do you get your smack from? Speak, otherwise I got shit to do." Somewhere in the background he heard the sound of a car horn passing at high speed. "Jesus, where are you?"

"It doesn't really matter where I am."

"It matters to me." He softened his tone—because, honey and flies and all that. But she remained quiet, and he sighed. "Fine, just tell me who your dealer is then."

"One of Dean's men."

The wind noise coming from her side was bad and he thought he misheard. "You mean Vas?"

"I mean Dean…Vas doesn't deal. He never has."

What? That was news to him, but it made sense. Back then Vasily had never shown an interest in his father's businesses—the heroin trade and running girls—like Dean, so maybe that hadn't changed. But what the fuck did he do to make money?

"Then who, Rube?"

"Like I said, one of Dean's assholes."

Zander rolled his eyes, beginning to lose patience. "I need a name."

"He goes by Boris. He's a bad dude, Zander. He scares me and not a lot of people scare me."

More car horns—and this time more than one.

"Are you in danger—fuck you sound like you're in the middle of the freeway"

There was a sigh, then a silence that lasted long enough he thought she'd nodded off.

"I'm not on the freeway. I'm okay," she said finally and so softly he almost didn't hear it over the wind. "Don't let him get to Terra."

"What does he have to do with Terra?"

"He has a thing for her mother."

Zander expelled air—the woman was high as a helium balloon on the fly. "Ruby, what is going on?"

"Will you tell her?"

"I'll tell her if you tell me what's going on."

"Just tell her."

Shit.

"You're a good man, Zander. Despite all the…bad blood and shit you think about yourself. I just need you to know that."

It was his turn to be silent as he processed.

"You hear me?" she asked, her words getting slower.

"I hear you."

"Good."

Then she hung up. He stood naked in his bathroom and stared at his phone before he tried calling back. It went straight to voicemail—not Ruby's, though a woman's voice with no name. Probably another junkie.

But whatever *that* was, he didn't like it, but there wasn't much he could do about if the woman didn't want to be found. But that little tidbit she gave him? He shot a text to Carmine.

What do you know about a dude called Boris? Works for Dean.

May as well make use of the retainer he'd slapped down to cover expenses. Despite Carmine's *friends and family* rate, the man didn't come cheap.

Then he hit the shower and shampooed the crap out of his hair. After he put on clean jeans and a shirt, he headed back down and entered through the side door, in time to hear the band calling Terra's name.

Damn if his heart didn't jump.

Again, he was impressed at how she took the stage and wondered if that was what attracted him so much. Her confidence up there, flaunting her stuff and giving every straight man in the house a boner, of which he wasn't a big fan.

Or was it her mix of sweet and spice? He couldn't say. He liked all of it and if he was honest, he'd liked it from that first moment he saw her ass out in the air in his alley.

What didn't impress him, was how Rory looked at her or how

she smiled back. They leaned into each other while he said something into her hair.

Fuck—she was here for that motherfucker?

He found himself blowing out air, ass planted to the bar at the
server station, arms folded and trying to keep a lock on that ugly
thing in his gut.

Terra reached for the mic. Her tight, pink T-shirt rode up a
couple inches showing a glimpse of that smooth, slightly rounded
belly and what he felt in his crotch wasn't ugly at all.

People stopped moving, everything went still, and the air felt
thick. When he looked around, every person in the joint's eyes
were on her, including Barney and Nicky standing two feet away
from him.

Terra began to sing, and her voice moved *through* him. A little
husky and a lot sexy as she put her own sinful spin on "Bobby
McGee". He'd never liked the song up until that second. The skin
on his entire body puckered, a shiver moved up his spine and he
had a funny feeling it was going to become one of his favorites.

Then he caught Nicky watching him with a smirk on her face.

"What?" he mouthed at her. She pulled in her lips as if trying
not to laugh and shook her head. Mouthed "nothing" then went
back to watching Terra.

Nothing—his ass!

Because life was a bitch, his back pocket chose that moment
to vibrate. He pulled his phone from his pocket and checked the
ID: Carmine.

For a moment he considered sending it to voicemail, but the
song was almost over. Privacy had always been big on his list of
priorities, his own and his patrons, therefore he'd resisted, but
now he was glad he'd entered the modern age and installed
cameras. The tiny red light in the corner of room confirmed it
was indeed recording. They may prove to be more advantageous
than just catching whiskey thieves.

As he answered the call, a prickle on the back of his neck

started that instinct told came from someone watching him. And not the good kind of watching, like a chick checking him out. This was darker, gave him the creeps. He pivoted looking for the source, but nothing.

"Yo," he said to Carmine, still surveilling his bar, making his way through the swinging doors. "Give me a minute to get somewhere quiet." As he headed through the passageway to the alley door, he rubbed the skin at the back of his neck. Pushing the door open, the cool air felt good as he asked, "What you got?"

"Boris is the name of the dude who ran my uncle over like a dog and participated in a kidnapping. He went off radar after that and we think he left the country 'cause none of us could find him. Lucky for him because otherwise the dude is dead. But Boris is also a pretty common Russian name. Why do you ask?"

"Apparently a dude named Boris dealt smack to a friend of mine and had a thing for Rebecca. Just wondering if it's connected."

"I'll check it out but, and this is the real reason I'm calling, I just heard from my contact at the medical examiner's office."

Zander's stomach dipped.

"Go on."

"Before I start, let me just say Rebecca Miller snorted heroin —she did not inject. There were no old track marks on either arm or anywhere on her body. Which makes the fresh one on her forearm extremely suspicious. Compound that with the bruising around the entry point, indicates the needle was shoved in with force."

Zander closed his eyes and took a deep breath.

"Her body was in bad shape. Scratches and bruising on her wrists, the middle of her back, and her cheek bone was cracked."

"Is there a theory of what happened?"

"A staff member found her at the bottom of a hill in a wooded area just inside the border of the Sunrise Institute. Cops initially assumed she'd gotten high, lost her footing and fell."

"But?"

"They took a second look because of the lack of track marks on her and did a full work up. Toxicology showed a dose higher than it would take to OD—much higher."

Shit.

He heard Carmine release a long breath and he knew he hadn't heard the worst.

"The theory is, she was either pushed or fell before being shot up. Pine needles and gravel were trapped in her clothing, skin and hair suggesting she slid or rolled before she came to a stop. It's a pretty steep incline, so that doesn't surprise me. But the pattern of bruising tells an interesting story. It seems she was held face down, probably with a foot in the middle of her back. One arm pulled behind her and the needle shoved in. Her left shoulder was dislocated. That could have happened in the fall or she fought really hard."

"What makes them think she didn't shoot up before she fell or was pushed."

"One, no syringe has been found. Two, the needle mark was in her left arm, and since Rebecca was left handed, she would've injected into her right."

He wanted to throw up. He sat his butt on the concrete stairs with his back against the door, squeezing his eyes with his thumb and fingers. It was a while before he spoke again. "Woman had no chance."

"Nope."

"Why?"

"Million-dollar question, but I did some more digging. Rebecca had an interesting clientele."

He sighed and braced himself. "Yeah?"

"Haven't confirmed it yet, but one of them is rumored to be a United States congressman."

CHAPTER FOURTEEN

Even later Tuesday evening

God, she loved to sing.

And hamming it up on stage with someone she had chemistry with, even better. She and Rory had it in spades. Pity it didn't translate into real life off the stage.

They finished the set with a raucous cover of "Mony Mony" with the crowd on their feet, arms in the air, echoing her each time she pointed at them. It was exhilarating and nuts—the endorphins coursing through her system got her more than a little high.

"You killed it." Rory wrapped an arm around her neck, pulled her in and squeezed hard. "I wanna make out with you so bad right now, but I better watch myself. I may end up asking you to marry me."

She had to laugh. "Shut up. The way you go through women, you're never getting married."

"Shh, don't tell my family. But hey, now that I've got you, I've been meaning to ask you. I wanna do a video with you."

A video?

"I've got some original stuff, you know? Some songs I want to record, a couple duets and I think you'd be perfect." He wiped sweat from his brow with a small white towel he kept on his guitar stand then ran it over the neck of his instrument. "Don't know if we'll make any money, but it would be great exposure."

Holy hell! She'd give her eyeteeth to do a video.

"I'd have to talk to Dannie and the guys," she said, trying to keep the excitement out of her voice. "See how they feel before I commit to anything."

"Dannie?" He stopped what he was doing and squinted at her. "Terra, you don't need his permission."

"Maybe not, but as a courtesy I'd still talk to him—to them."

"After the way he treated you?" He held her eyes for a long beat then scratched his cheek. "Shit—I don't mean to be a dick, but what they did wasn't cool."

"You referring to Dannie and Ruby or the guys?"

"Whatever, but listen, if you ever want to leave them, you could join us. Girl, you're too good for them. Did you see what you did tonight?" He flung an arm out to the dance floor. "Without rehearsing? You have an instinct…a something that most musicians would kill their grandmothers for. And *we'd* kill to have you."

She stared at him. "Rory, that's the nicest compliment anyone has paid me regarding music."

"That's because it's true and you deserve it."

"But I'm sticking with them for now."

"Of course you are, but a man's gotta try, right?"

"You wouldn't be you if you didn't."

"Want a beer?"

"Thanks." She shook her head and looked over the heads mulling around, still not seeing Zander. "But I think I'm going to hit the ladies', then I'm heading home."

"Let me know if you change your mind," he said as they hugged. "And about the video."

She promised, then left the stage, pushing through the throng of people. As always when she got to the bathroom, there was a line. Being buzzed with the endorphins coursing through her system, she was too angsty to stand in line. Singing was *her* addiction and if everyone got high like she did doing it, people like the Russians would be out of business.

Too bad it hadn't been enough for her mom.

God—*Mom!*

She gasped like she'd been stabbed as it hit her again.

Beautiful, talented and beyond messed-up Mom.

Funny thing about endorphins—they could turn on you faster than a shitty ex-friend could steal your man.

Dead.

Forever.

Her vision blurred. Crying in front of everyone was not gonna happen. And it was easier to head out to the alley than escaping through the front where she'd have to pass Petey. Therefore, she pushed through the swinging doors into the back passageway and made it outside before it ripped from her. Her breath hitched as she leaned her butt against the wall with her chin down, arms wrapping around her stomach. And let it out.

After a minute she found the last two Kleenex from the pack she kept in her purse, wiped her eyes and blew her nose. Then pulled it all back in—like she always did.

The muted sounds of the band's cover of Green Day's "Boulevard of Broken Dreams" pulsed through the wall, reminding her life chugged on, and so must she.

Exhaustion hugged her like a shroud, her legs felt like lead and not having slept much the last few nights didn't help.

Strike that.

Not having slept *at all* the last few nights didn't help. Which would explain why a big, black Harley with silver-studded saddlebags parked in front of Iris didn't register.

"What the hell—really?"

She recognized his bike from the day he came to the store, and earlier, she remembered parking *next* to it.

"Stick around, huh? Well, guess what, buddy, that's my choice, not yours and right now I'm not in the mood to stick around."

She chewed on her lower lip while circling the bike. It didn't take a genius to know she couldn't handle it by herself even if she wasn't exhausted. That thing would topple and crush her.

She took a deep breath. This was why they invented Uber. She'd deal with Iris tomorrow.

She met the driver half a block from Chuck's, away from the cigarette smokers and a couple all tangled up in each other making out in an alcove. And it seemed only a few moments after she'd climbed inside that the driver called, "Hey lady?"

"What," she answered, snapping her eyes open.

"We're here."

"Oh, God…sorry."

She crawled out, entered a tip into the app and gave him five stars. The filmy night air clung to her as she yawned up the stairs of the Victorian to her front door. Maybe tonight she'd finally get some sleep as God knew she wasn't able to nap during the day. The unit next door was undergoing a remodel and the noise from the compressor, the sanding and pounding on the other side of the walls was enough to wake the dead.

As she stuck her key in her front door the hair on her arms stood to attention. Then she shivered—not the kind of shiver you got when you forgot to wear a jacket on a cool night. But the shiver you got when that primal part of your intuition, the one that kept our ancestors alive, prickled. Like when you sensed someone's eyes on you. Like she had at the bar.

Get inside, that primal voice screamed.

Terra turned her head slowly to check the street. The red tail lights of the Uber car cut a path through the soft light cast by the street lamps. Everything looked normal, yet she *felt* it. It was there and set her heart beating double-time and sweat broke out on the back of her neck.

Get. Inside!

She turned the key and got inside.

CHAPTER FIFTEEN

Wednesday afternoon

erra took yet another photo of the Navajo rug with her iPhone—one of many. They were all fine. It was just her way of keeping herself busy and her mind off the lack of progress the police seem to be making.

As Detective Fetzer explained, these things had life of their own, and moved at their own pace. There was nothing she could do to force it.

It was also her way of delaying posting the ad she'd created because it hurt her to sell the thing. The geometric patterns and earthy tones represented a better, carefree time but she no longer had a choice.

Same applied to her Gucci bag, though with less sentimentality. She sighed at the memory of Helen talking her into buying it one crazy, champagne-buzzed afternoon at Neiman's when she'd still had the money to splurge. Before Rebecca told her she'd stolen the heroin.

She'd met them one block up from Provocative. Cigarette

man had stood leaning against the wall of a parking garage, cleaning his fingernails with the tip of a pocket-knife watching with hooded eyes while her mother shivered, eyes red rimmed from crying and explained she'd stolen the drugs.

"I'm sorry, baby," Rebecca had stammered. "I'm so sorry."

"You pay, or Mr. Melnikov not happy," he'd said with his lip curling in his snarly Russian way. "Bad things happen."

Therefore, she'd emptied out her savings. There never had been any question—she loved her mother and it was only money.

Now she had neither.

She'd start with the purse. Put it up for auction and if she got her asking price, maybe a miracle would happen, and she wouldn't have to sell the rug.

Of the few possessions her mother had taken to rehab, none were valuable enough to sell. Some books, the matching celtic-knot rings they'd bought together at an arts-and-wine street-fair. Rebecca had lost so much weight her ring no longer fit which was why it wasn't on her when she died.

She slipped it onto the middle finger of her left hand.

Then there was the beaten-up guitar that Rebecca guarded so preciously—the one Terra learned to play on until she was old enough to have her own. And finally, a framed photo of the them on stage together with her mom's band when she was nine. She still remembered that day so clearly. Rebecca was a fan of the Indigo Girls and at an open-air festival in Seattle one summer, called Terra on stage. They sang "Closer to Fine" and it was her first taste of performing live. As it turned out—they were a big hit.

Just as she took another photo of the rug, her phone buzzed.

Helen: *How are you?*

Terra: *Okay, better I guess. I need help getting Iris back.*

Helen: *Where's Iris?*

Terra: *Stuck behind a Harley in a parking lot at Chuck's.*

Helen: *What the hell?*

Terra: *My thoughts exactly.*

Helen: *I'll pick you up after work.*

&.

"*O*h, brother," Helen muttered when she pulled her little fire-engine red Fiat behind the Harley still blocking Iris. "You weren't kidding."

"Shit," Terra mumbled, her margarita-induced courage fizzling. After Helen had picked her up and insisted she was *starving* they'd hit a nearby Mexican joint for a quick dinner and drinks (Helen's treat) before driving into Zander's Alley. "I swear that thing looks even bigger than it did last night."

"Dammit, I didn't want to do this but we're gonna need help." Helen tapped her iPhone screen a couple times.

"Who are you calling?"

"My brother."

"Helen, don't! Zander will probably fire him."

"Not if he doesn't know."

"What if there's cameras—did you think of that?"

"Shit. I didn't think of that. But I'm calling him anyway. He'll know if there are."

They sat quietly while Helen's phone rang several times.

"Yo, big sis. What's happening?"

"You at work?" Which was a silly question really as they stared at Petey's blue Jeep Wrangler tucked into one of the parking spaces reserved for staff.

"Yeah?"

Helen smiled. "We need you out back, in the parking lot."

"What parking lot?"

"The parking lot behind Chuck's."

"Wait...why do you need me there?" Petey's tone turned suspicious. "What are you up to?"

Helen rolled her eyes. "Why do you automatically think I'm

up to something? Good God, maybe I just want to talk to you, little bro?"

"Because I know you, Helen. What's happening in the parking lot?"

"Nothing."

"Nothing my ass!"

"Okay, never mind. I'll talk to you later."

"Don't never mind…"

Helen hung up and held up two fingers. "Two minutes," she said with a wicked smile on her face.

It took less. About one minute and forty-five seconds later, Petey burst through the back door and marched to where they stood next to the Harley.

"What the fuck?" he growled and held his hands in the air. "I'm supposed to be at the door, what do you want?"

"That." Helen pointed to Zander's bike.

"Oh, *hell* no, I'm not touching that."

"Come *on*, Petey."

"I like my job and my legs unbroken, thank you."

"He can't break your legs, little brother."

"It's okay," Terra interjected. A full-on war between the Resnick siblings though often entertaining, wasn't her intention.

"Don't be such a pussy," Helen goaded.

"Call me whatever you want, the answer is still no."

"Guys, it's fine," Terra tried interjecting again.

"It's not fine, Tee. What kind of little brother abandons a girl's best girl in her hour of need?"

"'Hour of need'—Jesus!" Pete turned to her. "Terra, I love you, but I love my life more. I can't do it."

"Don't worry about it," she said. "It really is fine. I'll ask Zander to move it."

"See?" He turned back to his sister, eyebrows to the sky. "At least *she's* reasonable."

"Helen, go home, honey," Terra said. "You've been working all day. I've got it from here."

Her friend clasped her wrists and stepped back. "Unlike someone else in our presence." She slid her eyes to her brother. "*I'm* not going to abandon you in your *hour of need*."

"Don't be so dramatic," Petey grumbled. "Always with the fucking drama."

"Shut up, Petey."

"Actually," Terra stepped in between the two with her back to Petey and put her hands on Helen's shoulders. "I'd prefer to do this alone."

"Wait...what?" Helen's pretty brown eyes got wide. "Terra...no."

"Honey, I'm fine...just go home."

"No."

"Yes."

"*No!*"

"Helen! Let me do this. I wanna do it alone"

Helen sighed, then said softly, "You're sure you're not just saying that?"

"I'm sure." Terra pulled her in to a hug. "I love you and thanks for dinner and the ride."

"Anytime, TeeTee. Just don't let that man cast any voodoo spells on you."

While Helen did a three-point turn in her car, which sounded far more butch than it looked, Terra and Pete crossed the parking lot. As Petey entered the combination and held the door open for her, Helen gave a little goodbye toot on her horn.

"The big dude's upstairs," Petey said. "You want me to come up with you?"

"No, but thank you, really. Get back to the door, Pete. I don't want you fired because of me."

He nodded. "Call if you need me."

"I will," she stated, though she knew she wouldn't. After

placing a kiss on his cheek, she waited until he'd disappeared through the door marked *Private.* When she heard it latch, she sighed.

Okay, this was *not* the plan. Therefore, it was good she'd taken the time to shower and fluff up her hair—and had the foresight to wear a cute blousy top and her sexiest jeans to dinner. The pair, according to Helen, that made her butt look super curvy and hot.

Even so, it was a long climb up those stairs. Because she wasn't in the least bit excited to see him—just a lot afraid he might not be alone. There wasn't a single reason she needed to know how many women he had. Or what they looked like. Well, she knew what *one* looked like, but preferred not to dwell on it.

While she stood outside his office door, she noticed for the first time another door down the hall. It was easy to miss as it was painted the same cream color as the walls.

Maybe another apartment?

After no answer, she forced herself up the other flight of stairs where she stood with her fist poised for several seconds before she dropped it.

Then she knocked to the rhythm of the words *stick-a-round— stick-a-round.*

Why they kept bouncing around her head was beyond her.

She waited long enough for her to envision what he might be doing if he wasn't alone.

Stick-a-round—stick-a-round.

Okay, so the jerk wasn't home—or he was busy. She did not want to think about what—or who—he was busy with. Turning on her heel she made it halfway to the stairs when the door opened.

"Yo, Freckle," he called. "Where are you going?"

She paused and bit her lip. "I thought you weren't here," she said to the stairwell. "I was going to check the bar."

"You got my message."

When she finally turned, his shirt was halfway buttoned and

untucked and his hair was damp, like he'd just stepped out of the shower. Holy hell—now she had to think of him all naked and soapy, water sluicing through all the valleys between his muscles.

She swallowed. "Message?"

"The reason you're here, babe."

"If you mean by message your Harley blocking Iris, yes I got your message."

"Good—then come inside."

"I'm not coming inside...there with you. Can move your bike, please?"

"Nope."

"Why not?"

"Don't want to."

Her brows snapped together. "What?"

"We need to have a conversation."

She shook her head. Talking would be bad and spending any more time with this man wasn't an option. Just being in his space caused her panties to melt, he was that hot. Especially as her head was now filled with pictures of him naked, soaping himself, those hands on his body, on his...

She swallowed again.

"What if I don't want to have a conversation with you?"

"See, I figured that already." He straightened his considerable height and moved closer. "Which is why I blocked you."

"Okay, I get it." She shouldn't let him get closer, he smelled too good, but for some reason, she couldn't make herself back up. "You want me to apologize." Her head tipped. "I'm sorry I parked in your spot."

Their eyes caught. It was a mistake as his had turned warm, like melted caramel and crinkly in the corners. Then he chuckled.

God!

Like the man wasn't sexy enough.

"That's a new one," he said.

She dragged her gaze away from his, focusing on the dip in his throat instead.

"A new one what?"

"You, apologizing."

"Yeah…well, that's me—a surprise a minute."

"I'm beginning to see that." He was still grinning. "But that's not why I blocked you. Come inside. You look like you could use some wine."

Wine?

God…yes.

God no!

"I don't want to come in. I just want my ring and for you to move your bike."

"Freckle, I'm gonna say it again. We need to have a conversation."

"Fine—we can talk here." She folded her arms, not that it did her any good. It certainly didn't insulate her from all that was him, all that energy, caged up in that god-like body.

"I'm not talking here when I have a couch for you to put your sweet, tired little ass on."

He hadn't shaved recently, which made him all dark and *Dangerous*—with a big, fat upper-case D.

"Is this another one of your surprises?"

"What?"

"You, being indecisive."

"Uh…"

"Wine's not gonna pour itself, woman. You got three seconds to make up your mind."

"Or what?"

"Or I'm gonna make it for you."

See.

That's why she couldn't have wine with him.

"Are you always so…aaah!"

He took her by the shoulders, spun her round and marched her into his apartment.

"What are you doing, you big jerk?" she cried when he nudged the door shut with his foot. "You said I had three seconds."

"You were about to make the wrong decision."

"You don't know that."

"Woman, I can read you like a spreadsheet. You were about to run down those stairs and that's not happening until we talk."

He could read her—good lord!

Did that mean he knew she'd been thinking of him naked and soapy in the shower?

"Well, there's no need to go all caveman."

"No need for you to be so stubborn."

"I am not stubborn, and you can take those *caveman* lips and kiss my ass."

For some reason he found that funny. "Works for me, Freckle."

"Don't call me Freckle and move your damn bike. Or I'll bull-doze it."

"With what?"

"Iris…she's indestructible and anyway, what's one more dent?"

His eyes sparked then narrowed. "Woman, you go near my bike with that van, I will not be responsible…"

"Now *you*"—she jabbed a finger in his chest— "have three seconds to decide."

While he sucked in air through his nose, emitting a low growl, she took a sideways step and hustled to the front door. "You're taking too long," she called.

But she'd miscalculated and Zander's arm snaked around her waist and used her momentum to lift her like he would a small child. Then he dumped her like a crate of beer on the couch. She landed on her back and then he was on top, straddling her with his long, hard legs.

Luckily, her arms were still free, and she flailed them, landing a few blows catching him on the side of his jaw and shoulder. They may as well have been little feather slaps for all the good they did her as he caught and pinned her hands on either side of her head. With his pelvis pressed against hers and using his feet to trap her shins, she had nowhere to go.

"I said we need to talk." His voice was a low rumble and it vibrated all the way through her.

"And *I* said I don't want to talk. Get *off* me."

She bucked her hips, but it did no good. The couch, being comfortable and wide, was soft and didn't allow much leverage and the man wasn't only heavy, he was strong.

"That means," he said slowly as he lowered himself and rested his weight on his elbows, still keeping her wrists trapped. "You're going to listen."

They were both breathing hard. Her chest rose and fell, while his breath fanned her hair. His body, solid and warm, felt way too good.

"Look at me."

"No." She didn't dare. Having his gaze burn into hers, working its magic would be treacherous. Consequently, she focused on that amazing painting of the woman on his wall.

"Freckle, *look* at me." His voice got lower and softer and sexier as he gave her wrists a gentle squeeze.

"Go to hell," she said and hefted her hips in another buck.

It became immediately apparent she should not have done that.

How did this keep happening?

"Already been to hell, babe. I'm trying not to go back, though you're making it really fucking difficult. Especially when you do shit like that with your hips."

She blinked and after a moment slid her eyes to his, not sure what she'd find.

They were anything but hard and even more gorgeous close up, like little slivers of gold sprinkled on a bed of maple leaves.

"You've got yourself a problem," he said.

Yeah—she did.

Several, but he was the most burning at the moment and the way he looked at her wasn't helping her solve that problem. To be more specific, it wasn't helping to stop the heat spreading through her body. She swallowed. "Exactly which problem are you referring to?" She whispered. Please God, don't let him say the one between her legs.

"You have more than one?"

"Don't you?"

There was a whole lot of warmth in his eyes when he shook his head. "Babe...you've been a problem since the moment I met you. And right about now I'm having an even bigger problem focusing. So yeah, when you put it like that, I guess that means I have more than one."

"Perhaps if you got off me, you'd have one less?"

"The way I see it, if I got off you, I'd have two more. Very blue ones."

She giggled—because that was the effect he had on her. Intoxicating and infuriating and the combination of the two made her stupid. Though that stupidity quickly turned into something much hotter when that softness in his eyes flared. He lowered his head to touch his lips against her neck and that delicious stubble scraped right where he'd marked her before. His nose roved down the line to the crook in her shoulder and to her dismay, she couldn't stop a hiss escaping her lips, or the shiver running through her. Even worse—she couldn't stop him from noticing.

"Jesus, Freckle," his breath razed against her skin, which had broken out in goosebumps. And not just on her neck. All across her chest and of course her nipples, those horny little bitches poked right through her top. "*That* is not helping any of my problems."

Or hers for that matter.

Suddenly she wanted things from him. Things she knew were detrimental but lying under him with his hard body on hers, something even harder between her legs, she had stopped caring.

His mouth moved along her jaw, taking little nips along the way. Desire ran wild and free. When his tongue touched the corner of her mouth, sparks fired through her nerve endings.

Her body reacted and before she could take her next breath, she turned into his kiss and his mouth captured and consumed hers.

He kissed her hard, like he was starving, like she was the only women left alive and the survival of the human race depended on it. He tasted a little like whiskey and freedom and delicious man.

He'd let go of her wrists, slid a hand under her head into her curls and gripped a fistful, holding her head exactly where he wanted it. The other slid under her top, along her side and came to rest on the curve of her breast while he ground his hips against her. Her insides rolled and flipped—her inner muscles quivered, her toes curled. Circuits in her brain shorted and her heart pounded so hard she swore she heard it everywhere—the steady thump bouncing off the walls.

Zander stilled, and it was most unfortunate.

Then she realized it wasn't her heart.

Someone banged on the door.

"You're shitting me." He groaned long and low, breathing hard against her lips.

"Zander!" Barney's distinct gravelly voice yelled from the other side of his door.

Zander turned his head and growled at the door, "Go the fuck away."

"We've got a riot downstairs, son."

He tensed, those dark brows came together, separated by two little vertical lines. His body slumped, and he dropped his head onto her shoulder for a second before pushing himself upright on his arms. Then he took a deep breath and climbed off her.

"Apparently there's a riot downstairs," he grumbled in a voice that had gotten a lot huskier.

The absence of his body heat left her cold, nonetheless, she took a little satisfaction when he adjusted his jeans on the way to the door.

"You never heard of using the phone?" Zander yanked it open and barked at Barney.

"I did, smart ass. You didn't answer. I've already called the cops, but you need to get down there—fast."

Terra swung her legs over the edge of the couch, realigning her top as she watched him run his fingers through his long hair.

"Where the fuck is my phone?" He muttered, patting his back pocket and looking around before spotting it on the kitchen bar. Glancing at the screen he scowled and shook his head before shoving it into his back pocket.

He focused his gaze on her. "Don't move," he ordered. "Help yourself to anything. Wine in the fridge, coffee or whatever you want, babe, just don't fucking move. Stay—till I get back."

She blinked but wasn't going to promise anything in case sanity prevailed, so she said nothing.

His eyes narrowed, but not in an angry way—more like a resigned way.

"Stay," he said softly one more time, then closed the door behind him.

Terra collapsed back on that huge, plush couch and flung her arm over her face, blowing out air. That dull, needy ache between her legs...well...it fucking *ached*. It pulsed and throbbed and *tingled*. She took in a breath, squeezing her legs together and while she waited for it to dissipate, she scrunched her nose and bit her lip.

"What am I doing?" Terra asked the woman in the painting. "I'm not one of *those* women."

Lies.

She most definitely had become one of those women. Who the hell was she kidding? But she was so not going to sit in his apartment and wait.

Nope.

Getting to her feet, she hooked her purse off the floor and started searching for her keys. It was odd, but she felt like the woman was staring at her and from that angle, she seemed to be smirking.

"Bet you've seen some shit from that little perch," Terra said, and held up a palm. "But you can keep it to yourself, thank you very much, because I don't want to know."

Then she remembered.

"Oh shit!"

She didn't even have to wonder why it took her so long, because it was simple. There was no blood left in her brain—it was all still in her clit.

He hadn't moved his bike!

She clattered down the stairs and pushed through the private door, then the swinging doors which led to the bar. She'd seen her fair share of bar fights. They were usually drunken idiots aiming their fists at each other and more often than not, missing. But sometimes they were more, and this was of the second variety.

The floor was littered with upturned tables and glasses. A woman had her legs wrapped around a tall, bald man's waist. One arm circled his neck while she swung a beer bottle at Petey's head. He ducked while trying to dislodge her from the man's back. It didn't work until he tickled her. The woman howled and dropped the bottle which bounced off the wood floor and rolled under a table. While Pete unwrapped the woman from the man's torso, Terra noticed Zander kicking ass—literally.

He had his boot on some dude's oversize, jeans-clad rear and sent him out the front door onto the sidewalk. Where he would have collided into the crowd waiting outside had they not seen him coming and parted like the Red Sea. The ejected dude kept running without bothering to turn around.

This might have been because two police cruisers pulled up, sirens wailing, lights flashing, dispersing the crowd. Four uniformed cops jumped out wielding batons and Zander stepped aside to let them in.

Alrighty then.

Things were under control. Cops had arrived, everybody was safe. Time for action.

To that end, she scanned the bar and saw a candidate— someone she knew in passing and had seen at gigs before.

"Hey, Johnny," she said as she approached him, smiling her best smile. "I've got a problem, I was hoping you could help me." No point in wasting time as she'd had very little to spare.

"What's your problem, Terra."

"My problem is outside, in the alley." Before he could get any wrong ideas about her intentions, she quickly asked. "Have you ever ridden a motorcycle?"

"Uh…yeah?"

"Good. That will help."

"Why's that good and why does it help?" Johnny's eyes narrowed with suspicion.

"I need help moving a bike."

"Wait." His eyes went wide as his head move back. "You're asking me to touch another man's bike?"

"He's blocking me in. I need to leave and…" She shrugged.

"Fuck, Terra, I don't wanna touch another man's bike. It's like touching his wife."

"Trust me, this dude doesn't have a wife and that's actually, like, why I'm asking you. Because you see…" *Shit, she was going to hell, moving up one more spot on God's shit list.* "He's my friend and he's with a girl he just met, and I don't want to blow his chances to score. He's so into her and the guy hasn't been laid in months.

So… if you do this for me, you're actually really doing it for him? You know, bro-code—the anti-cock-block and…all that?"

"Fuck," Johnny mumbled and stared at her, clearly conflicted.

"Please?"

"What the hell—we're all dying anyway. May as well help some lucky asshole die happy."

"Exactly."

"But I'd like to live as long as I can so don't tell your friend I helped you."

"He'll never know." Well, she *hoped* Zander would never know but she'd never established whether or not there were cameras in the back. "But if he does, I'll take responsibility and I'll buy you a drink next time I see you."

Johnny sighed, then shook his head like he doubted his own sanity but kept going regardless.

Yeah.

She was definitely going to hell.

CHAPTER SIXTEEN

Wednesday evening

"Tell the police what happened, Pete," Zander said. He toggled the mouse and found the approximate time-stamp when the fight started in the video footage. Carmine hooked it up so he could control it from his computer and view it on a sixty-inch TV mounted on the wall of his office.

He wanted back in his apartment. He wanted to continue *thirty minutes ago* what he started with Terra on his couch, and he wanted to finish it in his bed. This was taking too damn long, but something didn't feel right.

"Yeah, well," Pete said as he faced the shrewd Asian-American cop whose name-tag read Lee. "I didn't see how it started because I had my eye on the door. But those two fuckers weren't here long. Maybe five minutes before all hell broke loose."

Five minutes? Zander's brow furrowed.

"Were they drunk—high?" the cop asked.

"Couldn't really tell, but we don't allow people in who are messed up." He glanced at Zander. "Bar policy. I'm new, but usually by that time of night, most people out partying have at least a buzz happening." Pete gripped his chin between his thumb and index finger. "Probably should've figured something was up."

"Not your fault, kid," Zander stated.

"Have you seen them before? Are they regulars?" Lee asked.

"I saw the older dude last night, but not the other one. But then again, like I said, I'm new."

Lee swiveled his head towards Zander and raised a brow.

"Can't say until I've seen the tape," Zander said as he split the screen so he could check the street view at the same time as the inside. He scrolled to the little triangle on his screen that indicated *start* and clicked.

At first, he saw nothing out of the ordinary. People milled in front of the bar, the band was halfway through a rendition of the Black Crowes "Hard to Handle" and the humans on the dance floor gyrated, some sloppier than others.

"There!" Pete pointed a finger to two men entering. Both were lean and dressed in button-down shirts and jeans. Easily passing for regular dudes just out on the town cruising for whatever they were cruising for.

The first man, somewhere in his middle thirties, didn't raise any alarms. It was the taller man that caught Zander's attention immediately.

"That's the dude who was here last night," Pete confirmed of the older man.

He looked to be upwards of fifty with light, thinning hair, rugged Eastern European features and a tattoo Zander couldn't make out on the side of his neck. That was when the first prickle started at the base of his spine.

They paid the cover and received the little motorcycle wheel stamp on their wrists. Neither hit the bar for drinks. Instead, they took opposite corners in the back and seemed to be assessing the crowd, like they were looking for someone.

After a few minutes, one took a position close to a table. More specifically behind an individual standing by a crowded table and soon after, the second man did the same. About fifteen seconds later, according to the time on tape, they nodded to each other, and in a coordinated movement, shoved their targeted individual into someone sitting at the table. Hard enough for them to topple. After which they pointed fingers at random people, clearly accusing them of causing the fight.

Before anyone realized what had happened, they stepped aside and walked to the exit.

As chaos ensued, the two men passed Pete rushing to the brawl and slipped out the front door. The older one smirked and raised his middle finger.

Fucker.

Zander switched his focus to the camera facing outside and watched them walking across the street. Then they hopped into the back of a large sketchy white panel van.

For some reason, the hairs on the back of his neck stood and his eyes went to the ceiling.

"I gotta check something," he said to no one in particular as his heart began to thump harder than normal. He exited, leaving Lee in charge of the mouse and Pete in charge of his office.

Through the window in the stairwell that faced his parking lot, the empty spot where Terra's van used to be stuck out like a crater. Suddenly the air felt as flat as a can of soda that had lost its fizz.

Fucking hell.

How did she move his bike? No way she could have done it on her own. That burning thing in his gut, kinda like indigestion yet much worse, mushroomed up his chest. He'd have to fully explore *that* feeling at a different time, because right now he needed to know one thing. Hopefully the tape in his office could tell him.

"Terra anywhere on that footage?" he asked Pete, when he re-entered his office.

His bouncer stood behind Lee with his arms folded. Pete's head jerked towards him at his tone. "Why are you asking?"

He took his own position behind the cop, who was seated in Zander's office chair while he worked the mouse, rewinding then watching certain parts of the video. When his bouncer continued to stare at him he snapped. "Pete, answer the question."

"Uh...didn't see her on tape," he answered. "Saw her earlier this evening but not after the fight started."

"That's because she was upstairs with me when the fight started."

"So then why are you asking if she's on tape?"

Zander narrowed his eyes but ignored Pete keeping his eyes on the video. Then they saw her.

"Looks like she hung for a few minutes chatting with that dude," Pete said. "I've seen him a few times but don't know his name."

"His name is Johnny." Zander watched her put her hand on his arm and lean in. Again, that heartburn thing that hadn't completely gone away flared, because sure as shit he knew what the woman was up to when he followed her out the back.

Why the fuck was she touching another dude's arm when he'd asked her to *stay the fuck on his couch*. Had she merely taken advantage of the situation to make her getaway, or had she organized it?

He didn't like either option.

"Right." He hardened his jaw and turned to Lee. "I think we're done here."

The cop examined him. "Assuming we identify and find these characters, are you wanting to press charges?"

Zander shook his head. "We're done." He had a pretty fucking good idea who these men belonged to.

Lee nodded then stood. "Gonna need it for an insurance claim."

"I won't."

"Right! Less paperwork for me." Lee smirked. "Don't know who this Terra is but I suggest don't piss her off next time."

Zander glared at the cop. "The fuck that's supposed to mean?"

The cop didn't even flinch. "Found it's much easier not to get a woman mad at you." He tipped his chin to the monitor. "Less expensive too."

"Wait," Pete spoke up, looking between the two men. "Are you saying Terra had those dudes start the fight?"

"You seem to know her." Zander worked his jaw. "You tell me."

"Nah, man." Pete shook his head slowly. "That's not like her."

"How would you know, Pete?"

"Because I know her, Zander. No fucking way would she do something like that."

"Better question is," Zander countered, "exactly how *well* do you know her?"

Pete's eyes hardened a bit. "I've known Terra a long time. She works with my sister, Helen, and they're best friends."

It clicked—the other pretty redhead at Provocative.

Fuck, now he felt like a dick. And as he had that bit of information, he could see the family resemblance, except Pete's hair was dark brown and wavy, not straight and auburn.

"And?" Zander prompted with a chin lift.

"And nothing. Driven those two nuts when they've decided to go on a wild one. Like when my sister's ex dumped her or when Dannie—Terra's limp-dick-piece-of-shit-ex dumped her for a skanky ho. Fucking idiot—like seriously, man, the dude's whacked."

Zander's shoulders relaxed a bit and he almost smiled. He agreed whole-fucking-heartedly with Pete's assessment of Dannie and his respect for the kid grew a little. To that end, he nodded, acknowledging the fact.

"Terra's cool, man."

That was still to be determined. And he didn't want to believe it, but the facts were, the woman had been there both times at least one of those pricks were.

The cop was watching the exchange and Zander turned to him. "Can we wrap this up? I've got shit to do."

"Fine." The cop shrugged. "Let me know if you change your mind."

Zander accepted the cop's card, and after everyone left his office, he sat in his chair and rewound the tape until he found Terra again. He watched her leave, followed by Johnny, the man she'd talked to, until he lost camera view. His fist clenched until he saw the man reenter through the front door nine minutes later, alone.

Only then did he breathe easier, assured the asshole didn't go home with her.

Good, he thought as he collected his truck's keys. He wouldn't have to kill him.

CHAPTER SEVENTEEN

Very late Wednesday night

It felt like a lifetime since she'd slept as she parked Iris and cut the engine. Terra dropped her head on the steering wheel. If it didn't get so cold at night, she could fall sleep right then in Iris. It wouldn't be the first time.

She focused on the stillness around her. Other than the normal night noises, she didn't sense creepy vibes like the night before and she relaxed a little. Which meant her brain replayed what happened on the sexy jerk's couch like some A-roll movie footage.

Holy hell—the man could kiss.

There may have been a riot in the bar, but it compared poorly to the one between her legs. Their chemistry was undeniable.

But she couldn't afford to take him seriously.

Not that it mattered. Men like him didn't suffer blue balls and he probably had another woman already lined up. What did they call it for women anyway? *Pink ball? Nasty nub? Terrible tingles?*

She rolled her eyes at herself because she was *hilarious* and stuck her key into the deadbolt and turned the lock.

After she shut the door, there was no time to process a big looming shadow appearing from inside her kitchen. He shoved her against the wall—cutting off her squeal by covering her mouth and chin, pushing up against her nose. His other forearm crossed against her chest between her breasts, palm curled around her shoulder.

"Hello, Terra," Vasily said softly.

Her brain screamed fight but the rest of her wasn't getting that memo, especially as he now had his body flush against hers.

"Don't scream," he breathed close to her ear, then pulled back to look her in the eye. "Blink if you understand me."

She blinked rapidly. Vasily's eyes narrowed and held hers for several seconds before the pressure on her mouth relented. "I'm not going to hurt you, but that doesn't apply if you scream. We good?" he asked.

No, she was absolutely *not* good. How could she be good with a fucking Russian mob boss pinning her against a wall, but she nodded as much as his grip on her face would allow.

"What are you...?" She stopped as it used up her oxygen and her breath felt hot against his hand.

"Doing here?" he finished for her, like it was the most natural thing in the world for him to be pressing his body against her and the wall in her hallway. "Obviously I've come to see you."

She threw a wet sideways glance at her lock. How had she missed him breaking in? But the lock was undamaged. And the knowledge that it was undamaged freaked her more than if he'd broken down her door with a pickaxe. He'd gotten to her so easily and she'd sensed nothing.

Not one tiny thing.

"You need to speak to your landlord," he said, taking note of where her eyes went. "They aren't as secure as you need them to be. Took me less than two minutes and there's much nastier characters out there than me."

Yeah.

She'd get on that, first thing in the morning. *If she lived.*

He turned his head to the side a little, studying her before he spoke. "I'm going to remove my hand now. Behave or this won't end well for you. Understand?"

Again, she nodded and swallowed, feeling the pulse in her throat throb so hard she thought it might burst through her skin.

Vasily removed his hand from her face and pressed his palm to the wall beside her head. His arm and the rest of his body remained in place. And just to remind her how much Zander fucked with her head, she couldn't help comparing his body to Vasily's, which was also hard, but leaner.

"You don't seem happy to see me."

Uh...no.

"I'm not sure why you're here." She blinked a tear away and it ran down her cheek. "I don't have your money...I mean I'm still working on it...I haven't had a chance...to get it...yet."

"Not everything is about money, Terra," he murmured softly.

His cologne was subtle and woodsy, his shampoo not unpleasant. That too fucked with her because it should've been unpleasant. She should've hated it, found it oppressive, especially when she became aware he was hard—his erection digging into her lower stomach, and coupled with all that focused ruthlessness, her fear notched higher. The longer he pressed against her, the harder her heart thumped and the more fear, she was sure, showed in her eyes.

"Please...don't rape me."

Vasily's head moved back a few inches, then he glanced down, comprehension glittering in his eyes. One corner of his mouth moved ever so slightly, but not enough to qualify as a smile. "It's a simple matter of biology, out of my control. But I don't force women. I won't deny, now that you've mentioned it, I'm enjoying the feel of your body against mine. You're very beautiful and I wouldn't be a man otherwise."

Oh...God.

He brought his face closer, sniffed her neck, though without actually touching her. "You smell good too." He said it in a way that suggested he was surprised she smelled good. "But I'm here for a different reason, one not quite so pleasant." He pulled his face away and waited till she looked up. "Where is it?"

"What?" She whispered, confusion wrinkling her brow. "Where is what?"

Suddenly that free hand moved from the wall, laid flat on her breastbone, then slid up her throat, circling around it like a warm, deadly scarf.

She whimpered.

If he squeezed, she'd be done—dead in minutes.

"Don't make me get crass, Terra, or repeat myself. One thing I hate, is repeating myself. Where *is it?*"

"Please..." she begged as his fingers tightened. Not enough to cut off her air supply or leave a bruise, but enough to communicate he was gravely serious.

"I swear," her breath hitched. "I'm telling the truth. I don't know what you mean."

He continued to stare into her eyes, then slowly the pressure on her throat lessened. His hand stayed in place, as did the one across her chest, keeping her pinned. Her legs buckled, however the force of his strength and weight pressed against her kept her from sliding down the wall. "All right," he muttered, expelling a long sigh. The top half of him leaned back. "I believe you. But I need to ask you some questions and you're going to answer them."

"Can you take your hand off my throat please?"

"When I'm satisfied." He shook his head and adjusted his position against her. "Rebecca mention a shipment to you?"

"A shipment?" The furrows in her brow deepened. *Holy hell, what had her mother done?* "What kind of shipment?"

"You don't need to know the details, just tell me if she did." His gaze hardened again as he studied hers. "Hmm?" He prodded when she just stared at him.

"No, she never said anything to me about a shipment."

He got closer and leaned forward, his eyes glittering. "You've got one chance to tell the truth and I'm guessing you know I'm not a man you want to lie too."

Fuck yes, she knew that. "I'm not lying. I swear I don't know anything about it. I only know about the bag she stole which you know I've been paying for. Whatever my mother did...*if* she did anything, I had nothing to do with it."

"What about messages, like a text? Anything strange she might have sent you?"

"No..."

Oh shit.

Need to move bad juju.

He saw it before she could hide it and tightened his hold around her throat a bit as a reminder.

"What?"

"A text...I didn't understand it. I got it the day she died, and she said something about bad juju."

His eyes narrowed, reading hers for a long while. Then he gave a short nod. "Give me your phone."

"It's in my purse, you're going to have to let me go so I can..."

He hooked his thumb under her purse strap and slipped it off her shoulder then took a slow step back. When he found her phone, he ordered, "Pass code."

"Let me..."

"Pass code." His tone was short and hard and did not leave room for argument.

She gave it to him.

Vasily tapped the numbers and scrolled through her texts,

pausing a long time on her mother's, then closed the app but did not return her phone. Instead he dropped it back into her purse and tossed *that* onto a chair in her living room—way out of reach. Then he stood peering at her for a few moments, though not really seeing her, like he was deep in thought.

A small amount of relief washed through her, but not enough to soften the knowledge he could still reach out and squeeze his rather large hand around her neck and kill her. And she certainly wasn't going to give him any reason to do it again.

"Okay…we're good for now," he said, causing her shoulders to slump. But, before she had time to step outside of his space, he slipped a hand into her hair gripping it gently at the back of her neck. Making her think he'd lied about being done, that he'd changed his mind about raping her. His other smoothed across her cheek, cupping it and running his thumb under her eye, swiping the remaining tears from her skin.

"Get some sleep."

With her feet stuck to the floor, she held her breath, not daring to move or to provoke as one semi-strangle a night was enough.

Vasily tugged at her hair, lifting her face to his and bringing his lips close. They hovered above a spot on the corner of her mouth before he kissed her, letting his lips linger, but making no attempt to take more. It was strangely possessive and provocative, like he was testing her.

He pulled away slowly, still holding her eyes. His had gone back to ice. "Make sure you turn the deadbolt behind me and watch who you open doors for."

The pressure in her hair relented as he coiled a lock around a finger, pulled and let it go, watching it bounce back. "I'll be in touch." Then he was gone.

As soon as the door clicked shut, she threw the deadbolt and gathered her hair at the back of her head, covering her face with her elbows. The wall was rough and cold against her skin as she slid down onto her bottom, because her legs couldn't hold her anymore.

Shit.

Shit, shit…*shit*.

Shipment? What fucking shipment? What the fuck did Rebecca do?

The cool tile bit through her jeans and into her ass as she pulled her legs up and wrapped her arms around legs with her forehead on her knees.

When the weight of his words sunk in, her teeth began to chatter as her body continued to shake.

What did she do?

CHAPTER EIGHTEEN

Five minutes later

What was her deal?

Or perhaps he should be asking himself what was *his* deal with *her*?

He didn't chase women!

Yet here he was, in his truck, fingers clenched around the steering wheel compelled like a dog to a bitch in heat. His damn head needed examining.

"In a quarter of a mile, turn left onto California Street," Siri announced.

He approached the turn, then took the left, then the next. As he rounded the corner his truck headlights hit the windshield of an oncoming low-slung Mercedes. The same Mercedes he'd seen parked outside Provocative.

And yep, would you look at that—seated behind that sleek windshield sat that smug son of an asshole.

It did not improve his mood.

In fact, he considered making a U-turn and chasing the motherfucker, blocking him off, pulling him out by his fancy button-down collar and pounding the smug right out of him.

But he needed to look the woman in the eyes and hear it from her. Clarify this shit.

Vasily could wait.

"Arrived. Destination is on the right."

He pulled the truck onto her driveway behind that ridiculous van, blocking half the sidewalk. Then he stepped out and studied the old two-story Victorian. There was scaffolding on the side, indicating construction was under way. Her unit was number Two, on the left, ground floor.

The pulse in his forehead throbbed when he jogged up the steps and approached her door. Maybe he was overreacting. Shit, he knew he was, but he needed to know. He wouldn't sleep until he did.

He rapped on the door and waited, tapping a foot on the concrete. After several seconds and no answer, he tried again a little harder. A moment later he heard a groan coming from just the other side of the wood. He put his ear to the door and tried the knob—locked, of course, and he wasn't sure if he was relieved or pissed.

"Woman?"

"Go *away*," she grumbled, exhaustion overriding the bitchiness in her tone.

"I'm not going away—open the door."

"I've had enough of bossy assholes for one night."

"Not leaving until I know you're okay. Open up."

"Like I'm gonna do that when you're grouching at me through my door."

"Then we're gonna be here all night and you should know I'm not opposed to waking your neighbors."

"God, you're so obnoxious. You just happened to be passing by in the middle of the night?" she asked, her voice sounding thick and tight. "Or are you stalking me too?"

Shit.

The woman had a point. Though *he* wouldn't label it stalking. More like due diligence.

"And by the way, how do you know where I live?"

"Friends in low places. I asked you to stay put."

"And I asked you to move your Harley, so I guess we're even."

He looked up at the overhead light above her door, to the moths circling the bulb, drawing the parallel of their inevitable destruction to his own inability to stay away from this woman. She was his light bulb. Was anything ever gonna be easy with her? Did he want it to be?

"We need to talk," he said to her peephole. "That wasn't a line I used to get you into my apartment."

"Talk about what?" The rawness in her husky voice tugged at him and if she didn't open her door soon, he wasn't sure he wouldn't grab a few tools from his truck and open it himself.

"That little runner you pulled for starters."

"Oh what—like you've never had a girl change her mind before?" He heard the lock disengage, then her door swung open and she stood with her hands on her hips. His voice got stuck in his throat and he had to swallow past it. Even in the dim hallway light shining behind her, he could see she was mess.

A gorgeous mess, but a mess.

That hair all mussed up like she'd run her hands through it and that black shit smudged beneath her eyes and fuck, he wanted to pull her into his arms and just hold her, but he couldn't let that get in the way. Not until her knew her game.

"I'm sorry about your bike. I realize it's sacrilegious to have one dude touch another dude's bike, and I own that. But I needed to go."

"Why?" he asked, getting it together enough to take a step inside before the woman shut the door on his ass. She closed it behind him and a whiff of her flowery scent touched him. Suddenly he knew, despite his earlier dissatisfaction of chasing her across town, he would do so again. In less time it took for a clock to tick. He took another step closer, tilted her chin with his finger and looked her straight in the eye.

"Did you play me?" he asked, his voice coming out gruffer than he needed—but dammit, this *woman*. She made his head explode.

"What?"

"Did you. Play me?"

She scowled and pulled her head back as far as the wall would allow. "No, I didn't play you. Why would you ask me something like that?"

"You're not being straight, and I don't like games."

"Ohmigod, I don't have the energy for games."

"I saw him leave. Are. You. Fucking him?"

"Take your hand off me, you big ass"—she slapped his fingers from her chin—"and use your eyes. Do I even remotely look like a woman who has just been fucked?"

She didn't, but that didn't make her any less fuckable in his mind.

"What was he doing here, and don't tell me it's none of my business?"

"It isn't."

"Woman!" he growled.

Christ, she was gonna kill him—make his brain stroke out.

"Fine! He thinks I know something about something, but I don't know anything. At least not about what he's thinking I might know."

"So, you want me to believe it's a coincidence his men were in my bar, both nights you just happened to be there, fucking with my customers, starting fights?"

"Yes, it's a coincidence. Who do you think I am—Shakira? I don't have that kind of power and anyway, how do you figure they were his men and how do you know they were there both nights?"

"I know."

"How?"

"Did you organize that riot?"

"What—no," she yelled. "I wasn't even there. I was upstairs with you—remember?"

Yeah, he remembered—his balls still hurt with want for her. "What was he doing here?"

"I already told you, he thinks I know something that I don't."

"You expect me to believe that."

"I do because when I got home he was *in* my apartment. I know I locked my door because I always lock my door. I'm kind of freakish like that, but I didn't invite him."

The picture that made inside his head, caused the muscles in his gut to tighten, his blood to curdle. Made him to want to punch something and Melnikov's face being unavailable, he forced himself to relax and reached to his side and with deliberate control turned the lock on her door instead.

"Did he hurt you?" he asked.

She shook her head. "He just scared me." That cute little nose wrinkled as she rubbed her arms. Which made him feel like a shit. He didn't need her scared of *him*. To that end, he took a deep breath through his nose and calmed his ass down.

Then he asked softly, "You okay?"

She tipped her chin to look at him but didn't answer.

"Freckle?"

"You know, it's really annoying you keep calling me that."

"What's annoying is you not answering me."

"Are you always this objectionable?"

"Usually much worse," he said, one corner of his mouth kinking up. "This is me toning it down—for you."

"Careful you don't hurt yourself."

He snorted, then grinned. "I'll keep that in mind. You're dead on your feet, woman. When was the last time you slept?"

Her eyes moistened and she angled away from him. "I can't

sleep. This thing with my mom…and Vasily breaking in to my apartment. And during the day there's construction…the noise…and…I think someone's watching me."

An unpleasant shiver shot down his spine and he remembered what Ruby said. *Keep Boris away.* He tilted his head to see in her eyes better and noted the fear clouding them. "Who do you think is watching you?"

"I don't know, but I don't think it's Vasily. It's someone else."

"How do you know this?"

"I felt it."

"I mean how do you know it's not Vasily watching you?"

"I can't explain it. I just know."

"You gotta give me more than that, Freckle."

"Okay…the other night when I was at the bar and when I came home I sensed it. My hair stood on end, you know? Like someone breathing down your neck, only not in a good way."

"Doesn't mean it wasn't Vasily."

"No, it doesn't. Except when I got home tonight, I didn't feel *him.* He was *inside* my apartment and even when I stuck the key in my door I didn't feel him."

None of what she said sat well with him, but for reasons he couldn't explain, he particularly didn't like her associating any kind of *feelings* with that fucker. But what if she was right—and somebody other than Vasily was watching her? *Somebody like this Boris asshole.*

"Pack a bag."

"What?"

"I said pack a bag, Freckle."

"Why?"

"You wanna sleep, you're coming home with me."

She eyed him for a long while, then came to a decision and packed a bag.

*H*e'd only been gone a few minutes.

To check all was good with the bar, the alarms were set and the surveillance cameras on. It wasn't that he didn't trust his staff, he was just kinda anal like that.

When he reentered his apartment, Terra lay on her side on his sofa with her hands clasped together as if in prayer next to her head. Those juicy lips slightly parted. The woman was dead to the world.

He sat on his coffee table opposite her, resting his elbows on his knees with his hands hanging between them—debating the cons of moving her to his bed and the need to ensure she didn't freak the shit out when she woke. His living room being something she was somewhat familiar with, but his bedroom—not so much. Though he planned on changing that as soon as humanly fucking possible.

She surprised him—for once doing what she was told. Packed a bag and sat her exquisite self in his truck without any argument, which meant she was way more spooked than she admitted. As if the haunted look in her eyes weren't enough of a clue. He didn't question it. Didn't care anymore if she was using him or what her motives were. She was here.

He wanted her in his bed, tangled up in his sheets. Where he could smell her and watch her while she slept and wake up to that wild beauty. And in a perfect fantasy she'd roll over, put her hands on him and start something.

Jesus—just the thought made him get hard. He cleared his throat and stood to loosen the building pressure in his jeans.

"C'mon, Freckle." He dragged his knuckles softly against her cheek, then because he couldn't stop, her lips. "Let's get your pretty self to bed."

He waited a moment, and when she didn't stir, he took a deep breath and slid his arms under her and lifted. She looked pale—from exhaustion no doubt—and that light cluster of freckles stood out on the lower bridge of her nose. As he adjusted her, she gave a sweet little snore, smacking her lips against his neck. The resulting grin cracking his face was only surpassed by his chuckle.

It was fucking adorable.

"Shit," he mumbled. "Gonna turn into a sappy little punk-bitch if I don't watch my ass, woman. What the hell kind of magic you got?" As he carried her, the irony wasn't lost on him that this was the second time he'd put a woman to bed in as many days and hadn't fucked either of them.

"Just gonna put you on top of the covers, babe. Leave your clothes on. As much as I wanna see you naked, I guess tonight's not gonna be that night."

He lowered her onto his king-sized bed, unzipped those sexy sandals and slipped them off her feet. And damn him if he didn't sit there on the edge of his bed and stare at her cute little pink-tipped toes. He'd never been a foot man, but those chubby little digits he could get into.

Zander dropped his head and shook it.

Torture.

He had one shot and he wasn't going to fuck it up. "I'm gonna go and keep myself busy—get a little therapy while you sleep."

He pulled the comforter over, cocooning her by tucking the ends under. After turning the dimmer on his light to low, he left his bedroom.

With his phone in his pocket, the front door locked behind him, he walked down the stairs— made a left and continued down the hall past his office to the door on the far end of the landing.

It had been months since he'd crossed this threshold. Months since he'd had the inclination or even the desire. Yet now, the more he thought about it, the more compelled he became.

He moved over the venerable, blue, paint-stained rug covering the scratched oak floor. Weaving between several naked easels, he reached the windows and threw them open, allowing fresh air to infiltrate the stuffiness.

This was his sanctuary.

Where he regained his sanity by painting and where he had lived when Ginny and Chuck occupied the apartment upstairs. A fully functional studio unit with a bathroom and a kitchen and a faded old futon he used to call a bed. Now it served as a decrepit couch adorned by two crumpled pillows and a tartan throw Ginny had absconded with from Scotland.

The only occupants nowadays were the ones he painted onto canvas with acrylics and his agent sold in galleries at ridiculous prices to snobby art elitists. Or the occasional movie star, and an obscenely wealthy Silicon Valley entrepreneur whose wife insisted she would *just die* if she didn't have an original *A.M.* portrait of herself.

Who was he to argue?

The bar did well but this was how he made his real money, though he hadn't taken a commission recently by choice. He still had no clue how, but over the years he'd become a name—albeit a mysterious one.

Alekzander Milan.

He used his initials to sign his paintings because he liked the anonymity. Fame, unlike for some of his subjects, wasn't his thing. He'd never wanted anyone scratching too deep, uncovering shit about his past that needed to stay deep-sixed. Shit he especially wanted to keep from the woman upstairs.

After he refused to talk to his shrink, Ginny bullied him into taking art classes and thank fuck she did. It saved him after his mother died.

And here was the only place he allowed *her* to be. His paintings of her covered with old fabric remnants adorned the walls with expressions he'd tried to remember other than her last.

Bitch...she dead. Come with me.

He winced, then shook the memory from his head—her last day before it dug in and took traction.

Once in a while, like on the anniversary of her death, he'd uncover one painting to refresh his memory and honor hers, but he couldn't let her stare at him too long.

It hurt too damn much.

Still.

To that end, tonight she remained covered.

Terra's face was already imprinted, but to be sure he pulled up the picture he'd downloaded onto his phone. Found a canvas and pencils in the desk drawer he kept in the corner and sharpened them with a knife. Satisfied, he parked himself in front of his easel and began to draw. Occasionally referring to the photo, pinching his fingers, then spreading them on his phone screen to enlarge her lips. He examined the plump little cushions and grooves because those had to be perfect.

Only when the first orange light of dawn cracked the edge of the bay and the city skyline, and he was content with the lines of her face, he stepped away. Then lay back on the futon with one arm across his torso, the other crooked above his head. He fell asleep with her image painted on the inside of his closed eyelids.

Until hours later, the water flowing through the pipes upstairs woke him and tortured him some more.

Damn woman was naked in his shower.

CHAPTER NINETEEN

Thursday morning

 ell, she'd found the coffee.

Stashed in a stainless-steel container that looked remarkably like a miniature beer keg. Now all she had to do was figure out how the coffee maker worked. Terra stood with her hands on her hips and squinted at the fancy machine sitting on the kitchen counter.

She knew how to use the one-cup-at-a-time thingy her boss kept in the break room and her own twenty-dollar Mr. Coffee she'd bought at Target. But this thing had a display panel, nobs, dials *and* its own grinder attached on top. Fit to launch a frigging rocket.

Any man who owned one of these took his morning beverage seriously. A check mark in the *For* column of her newly constructed *For and Against* list.

Where the hell was the sexy jerk anyway? Although she should probably stop calling him a jerk. Thanks to him bringing her here, she'd finally gotten some sleep. But she'd woken up ages ago, fully clothed, wrapped up like a burrito in his comforter which smelled deliciously like him, and he was MIA.

Check mark in the *Against* column.

What kind of man collects a woman in the middle of the night, brings her to his apartment then, when she falls asleep, leaves for places unknown?

No signs of pillows or blankets indicating he slept on that huge couch either. She'd done a thorough walk-through of his apartment and discovered a large patio, a metal fire escape that led to the roof and a well-stocked pantry off the kitchen. No other bedrooms, and no Zander.

If the thing with Dannie and Ruby hadn't happened, she probably wouldn't have thought of it—but it had, and she did. Perhaps he'd gone to that Heather person.

It hurt her brain. Was is it too much to ask for a note? At least that way she knew where she stood.

Hey Freckle...gone to get my rocks off. Be right back.

Or.

Babe...sticking it to one of my regulars. She did a little shoulder shimmy as she silently mouthed the words, *Make yourself at home.*

Sure as hell didn't stick it to her.

Maybe she'd misread him. Maybe he just wasn't that into her. But he hadn't kissed her like he wasn't into her.

Okay.

That kiss.

A big and definite *FOR.*

But none of this solved her current problem—how to operate that space-age coffee machine.

She tapped a foot and scrunched her nose.

Fuckit!

It required more brain cells than she had functioning at this time. There had to be a coffee shop or something nearby. Just as she reached for her purse on the kitchen bar, the latch on the front door clicked, sending her pulse jumping. Zander entered, glistening with water droplets and dressed in nothing but a pair of black sweatpants and a towel draped around his neck.

He'd showered?

Where?

Shit—she didn't want to know where.

He'd also shaved, and how that made him hotter was beyond her. Thanks to the missing stubble, a little cleft in the middle of his chin had become visible.

Strange—there seemed to be an epidemic of dented chins lately.

His eyes found her in the kitchen. One side of his mouth lifted in a crooked smile—and holy fucking hell—the man was *cut*. Like he worked out two-hours-a-day cut. Broad, powerful shoulders, and other than the scrapes on those sculpted arms from when he caught her on the landing outside his office, he was perfect.

A little quiver began in her stomach at the memory. And that quiver intensified along with her heartbeat when her gaze roamed over the hard planes and valleys of his muscles. Down, until she paused on the defined, flat V in his torso.

She followed a couple veins and they disappeared into those sweatpants riding low on lean hips. They jogged even lower when he dropped his phone into the pocket.

She swallowed.

"Freckle." He grinned that pantie-melting grin then ruffled the towel through his hair. "Get your beauty sleep?"

Didn't matter he was off-the-charts hot or he stood there looking all sexy and *clean*, he so wasn't getting off that easy. She sent him a glare, which contained enough buck-shot to drop a bison.

He didn't even flinch. In fact, his smile broadened. And when those damn muscles in his arms flexed, causing the scrolled letters inked on his arm to roll, a little squeak in the back of her throat threatened and almost escaped.

Somehow, she kept it silent but couldn't do anything about her cheeks pinking up. Especially when she noticed another tattoo on his left hip. Done in that tribal style that she couldn't quite make out, but sure as heck wanted to find out.

"Um," she mumbled, ripping her gaze away and pointing to his coffee-maker. "That *thing* is beyond my expertise."

The jerk chuckled. "She's crabby without her coffee. Noted."

She was crabby all right, but not for the reasons he thought, as that needy ache between her legs attested.

"If you'll give me a minute to change, I'll hook you up."

She cleared her throat and despite her efforts to keep her eyes off that tat, they dropped down anyway.

Giant mistake.

Zander's movements from toweling his hair slowed, then his arms dropped, and he focused on her.

Really focused on her.

Like his predator radar pinged and she'd marked herself as prey. That broad, perfect chest rose as he took a breath and seemed to hold it for a long moment. As he let the air out of his lungs, he closed his eyes.

"Then again," he said when he opened them again, "I should probably hook you up before I change."

Her eyes widened. Since she still didn't know where he'd showered, he should definitely *not* hook her up before he changed.

He was almost *naked*. And since her brain got stuck on naked, she couldn't mount a protest.

His gaze never left hers while he tossed the towel onto a stool at the breakfast bar before he stalked into the kitchen. If her heart beat any faster it would burst, and she was pretty sure he could see it pounding through her skinny-ribbed, peach tank.

"No, no…it's fine, don't let me stop you from changing." She cursed her voice because it came out too breathy and she had to tilt her head when he stopped in front of her. One of his very muscular, very warm arms curled around her waist holding her against him while he walked her a step closer to the counter—like they were dancing. Then he leaned in to remove the coffee pot from its launch pad. It forced her to lean back and her palms went wrap around his neck to steady herself. His skin was hot and smooth, slightly damp and he smelled of soap and all kinds of interesting things started to happen in her lower belly to join what was happening between her legs.

"I can wait for you to change."

"See now," he murmured against her ear, and those interesting things got even more interesting. "It wouldn't be good manners if I made you wait any longer than you already have."

"You don't strike me as a good manners kind of guy."

"Freckle." His brow furrowed but she saw the glint of amusement in his eyes. "You hurt my feelings."

"A big, tough man like you has feelings?"

"Don't wanna shock you, but I've got all kinds of feelings. Some of those I'm feeling right now."

"Uh…"

"Let me show you, babe, how the *thing* works. So next time I'm not around you'll know what to do."

Next time?

"Getting a little ahead of yourself, aren't you? What makes you think there's going to be a next time."

He eased back, still holding her, keeping her slightly off-balance and flipped the lever on the faucet, holding the pot under it. When it reached the halfway mark, he set it on the counter, and placed his hands on her upper arms.

"Well, first we gotta have a *first* time. Then we'll definitely have a next time." He turned her, so her back was snug against his front. "Water goes in here," he said and poured it into the canister.

His breath fanned her ear and made her nipples tighten. Then he touched a button on the coffee-maker with an index finger. A flap yawned open.

"Coffee goes in here."

That same finger came back to move her hair off her shoulder and trace a slow line along the curve of her shoulder, setting off tiny explosions beneath her skin. It kept moving, and continued on a path over her elbow, her forearm until his fingers entwined with hers. He had the hands of a carpenter, but the roughness felt good against her skin.

He felt good against her skin.

So good, the air sparked around them. He pushed gently against her, until she was trapped against the counter, and though he was already hard, he got harder as he nestled in the groove between her butt cheeks. When he released her hand to scoop coffee out of the bag, she detected his movements were slow and measured, and they shook a little when he dumped it into the filter. Good to know it wasn't just her.

"Set it to regular," he continued, his voice softer and even more husky. "Flip this switch"—he touched his lips to her nape— "and you're good to go."

She drew in an unsteady breath, as she was more than good to go. So good it felt like there were Pop Rocks under her skin. But before she lost control, or anything that couldn't be stopped started, one tiny matter needed clarifying.

Her head tilted up and to the side, and when he caught her eye, she was struck by those long, curly lashes most woman would commit homicide for. "Where did you sleep last night?" she asked.

"Babe," he whispered. The hard muscles in his stomach tensed against her back, like she'd caught him by surprise.

A dark, familiar pit in her stomach, crawling with disappointment opened. She tore her gaze from his and looked at the gurgling coffee pot instead. He exhaled—the heat of his breath on her skin was intense, and she wanted more of that. A lot more.

But sloppy seconds, she was not.

She had no rights, no claim to tell him what to do, but she did, have a choice. Stiffening her spine, she pushed at him. The arm around her waist tightened, while his free hand slid up the side of her neck, into her hair, tugging her head gently.

"This is a bad idea, Zander," she said, gasping slightly when he nipped the tendon in her neck. "I think I'm just gonna get my things and go."

"I'm gonna have to disagree," he said, his voice unsteady. "I think this is a very *good* idea. I know you feel it, babe—this chemistry between us. It's fucking explosive."

He had that right and *holy hell*, this was hard. She closed her eyes before twisting in his arms.

"Look, you've been super-generous...sweet even, but I'm not like your other women. I don't operate that way."

"Operate which way?"

"You know...hit and runs. One-night stands, or in this case, morning."

"Who said anything about *one*? The way I see it, if I get you off enough, maybe you'll wanna stay for longer than one."

Okay, her head almost exploded—if he got her off *enough*?

"Just out of curiosity, what would you consider getting a woman off enough to be?"

"Well, that depends on how much you want. Because I'll give you as much as you need...and then I'm gonna give you more, before I take some for myself."

She munched on her bottom lip as she thought about him *taking for himself*. "This is all very tempting...*you're* very tempting, but I'm in a delicate place. I just got out of a relationship and the way *I* see it, I need to guard myself. Besides, you still didn't answer my question which makes me think..."

"Downstairs."

"Downstairs...what? In your office?"

He shook his head. "Not in my office. I have another apartment next to my office."

She remembered the door down the hall. "And that's where you showered?"

"Yep"

She pulled back to see him better. "Seriously?"

"You don't believe me?" An eyebrow curved up.

"Due to a recent and not so great experience with my ex and an exfriend, I'm a little skeptical of men at the moment."

"Yeah—okay, I'll give you that. But in my defense, I'm not your idiot of an ex."

"I realize that, but why would you have two apartments? Who lives in the other one?"

"Just a few ghosts."

"Ghosts…?"

His mouth took hers. As she opened to protest, he dove in deeper, his tongue mingling with hers. Those rough hands cradled her face and it took less than a moment for her body to concede, even if her mind didn't.

He tasted so good—fresh and minty—she stopped fighting. She wanted him—wanted this, whatever this was. And he was right—their chemistry was explosive. It would be stupid and horrible to deny herself something nature obviously intended for them. So, ignoring her brain, she listened to her body and kissed him.

He dipped, and gripping her under her butt, lifted. Her legs instinctively wrapped around his waist and she circled her arms around his neck, clinging to him as he carried her to his room.

Then putting a knee on the bed to steady himself, he laid her down then he paused, as if expecting her to change her mind. Every muscle in his body taut and defined. She skimmed her palms over his shoulders, testing the texture and warmth, before they slid into his hair.

"Just to be clear," he spoke as if it hurt him, "if you're gonna stop me, now is a good time because in about five seconds it's gonna be too late."

"I'm not stopping you," she whispered.

"Thank fuck," he growled, pulling her higher up the bed, then crawled between her thighs. He took her mouth again. This time he didn't hold back and devoured her like he couldn't get enough.

"Need you naked, woman," he said when he came up for air. And removed her tank, tossing it across the room. His gaze lingering when they hit on the lacy material of her peach-colored bra. "Christ, woman…you're beautiful. Tell me you're wearing matching panties."

"Not exactly," she teased, looking at him through her lashes. "They're not panties…I'm wearing a thong."

His gaze flared and fixed on hers for a long second, then his fingers curled around the edges of her yoga pants and slid them down to her pubic bone. Catching one of the thong straps between his teeth, he held it in place while he pulled her pants down further.

She squirmed beneath him. She couldn't help it, she needed him. Had needed him since the day on the landing outside his office.

"This stays"—he fingered her thong—"for now."

But her yoga pants didn't. They joined the tank, along with his sweats in a growing pile on the floor.

She was ecstatic to discover the man didn't only have a beautiful face—he was beautiful *everywhere.* His cock, thick and hard, stood tall and proud and her heart beat impossibly faster as he maneuvered between her legs. Before he pushed the tiny triangle of lacy material aside, he ran his nose over the little patch and pulled in a long breath, inhaling her scent. It was rude and primitive and unbelievably hot.

Terra threw her head back, arching her spine as he emitted a low, feral growl a second before he clamped his mouth over her.

Her fingers gripped his hair as he took her higher until she deto-nated on his tongue.

Before she had time to recover or catch her breath, while her body reeled, he did it again. She couldn't tell if it was one long orgasm or two different ones. When she trembled with the inten-sity, when she thought it was too much she might just die, he moved back, slid the thong off, caressing and kissing her legs on the way down.

"These are mine now." His voice was gruff and deep. "I'm keeping them."

He could have whatever he wanted—there wasn't a single cell left in her to protest. From the dresser next to his bed he produced a condom and ripped the foil with his teeth, his eyes blazing and locked on hers. He rolled it on, stroking himself, his hands shaking, his breathing, ragged and harsh. It made her want more. Even if it killed her.

Zander lowered himself and supporting his weight on his elbows, he filled her. She knew he held back—she could tell by the tightness in his jaw and stomach— giving her time to adjust to his size. He was big, and gorgeous and he looked at her like she was the fucking Mona Lisa. Until she moved her hips, urging him deeper. Then he began to move. Slow at first, keeping his eyes on her, moving them over her face, her breasts and to where they connected.

"So fucking beautiful," he muttered again as he took her mouth. Then angled his hip which hit her just right, and she let out a moan against his lips. It unleashed him. His strokes got faster, deeper, *wilder*. He adjusted her thigh, pulling it up close to his side, giving them both more. It was only seconds before she felt herself flying, like she was out of her body, yet still connected —to everything. This time when she crashed over, he came with her. He held her head and pushed his face into her neck shud-dering his release before he collapsed on her, crushing her with his weight, before he slid off onto his side next to her.

Their legs remained tangled, his arm across her chest, slick with sweat, their hearts beating against each other. It took a while for their breathing to slow and even out.

Terra turned her head and took in the pile of clothing on the floor. One thought entered her mind. The only one she could process.

A definitive and absolute fucking *FOR*.

CHAPTER TWENTY

Thursday around noon

Zander lay on his side—his lips connected to her shoulder, keeping his eyes shut while he waited for that emotion storming through his chest to go away. Except the longer he waited, the stronger it got. He was gonna embarrass himself.

"Gonna deal with the condom, babe," he managed without his voice breaking.

"'Kay," Terra mumbled, rolling her head to look at him, with a smile so sweet he almost lost it.

Somehow, he didn't as he untangled his leg from hers, and strutted to the bathroom. Yet, when he turned to shut the door, he couldn't stop himself from taking her in, lying on his bed, those curls like a halo all fanned out looking so fucking lovely it made his heart stop.

Like she belonged.

He hardly had the door shut and the condom knotted when

he couldn't anymore and sat on the edge of the massive oval tub, letting his eyeballs leak.

He'd heard of this happening to people after sex.

Shit, Chuck admitted he cried the first time with Ginny.

But besides getting off, he'd never felt anything other than mild affection for any of the women he fucked. He took them in his office, made sure they got as much out of it as he did. Sometimes more. Then he kissed them goodbye and that was that.

Never in his home, never in his bed—and never had he felt anything like this.

Told you, son. Chuck's gravelly laugh echoed in his head. *Now you're awake.*

He allowed himself five more seconds, cleared his throat and rose to snatch toilet paper from its fancy little brushed-nickel holder. After blowing his nose he washed his face, flinching at the icy water. Then he cowboyed the fuck up.

When he left the bathroom, Terra had shifted to a sitting position with the sheet covering her body while she stared at her phone. His brain took snapshots and stored them for later use. He wanted to paint her, looking exactly like that. But when she looked up, instead of a smile, she had a frown on her face.

"Shit, babe, what's up?"

"The medical examiner has released my mom's body, and the cops want to talk to me again. Apparently, they have an update and…more questions."

"Well," he said, and sat facing her, smoothing a curl behind her ear. "They're just gonna have to wait until I've fed and plied your beautiful ass with coffee."

A small smile touched her mouth. "You have a fixation on my ass."

He smirked and was about to pull her into a kiss when his phone, still tucked in his sweats pocket, vibrated. He sighed but leaned over and snagged it off the floor.

Carmine: *Need to talk. ASAP.*

Shit.

This couldn't be good.

୧∙

L ater Thursday afternoon

D etective Fetzer, who sat to Zander's left on the short part of his L-shaped couch took a big slug of coffee, then placed his mug back on the table in front of him. Zander noted the dark circles beneath the man's tired, brown eyes, and figured the cop was working Rebecca's case full throttle. When he looked up, he imparted in a tone that suggested he'd done this too often. "Were you aware, Terra, your mother was pregnant?"

"What?" Terra's jaw dropped as her hand slid across the fabric of Zander's couch, sought his and gripped it. Her fingers felt icy in his warm ones. "Did you say pregnant?"

Zander swallowed and caught Carmine's eyes. He sat on one of the stools at the breakfast bar, arms folded and jaw set in a way Zander recognized. He was just as surprised which was confirmed by his raised eyebrows. Suddenly, the toast and omelet he'd made for brunch felt like a brick in his stomach.

"I take it that by your reaction, you were not."

"Are you sure you're talking about *my* mom?"

"She was twelve weeks according to the medical report," the cop continued.

"Pregnant...ohmigod." Terra covered her mouth, then turned to look at Zander.

"Babe," he said softly, not knowing what else to say.

She blinked several times, then turned back to the cop. "Do you know what the sex of the baby was?"

The cop cleared his throat, then said softly, "A little boy."

She sucked in a sharp breath and held it for a long moment. "A baby brother." Her voice broke on a whisper as tears rolled unchecked down her cheeks.

Zander didn't think she realized she held his hand, but he hoped like hell he could give her what she needed.

Fuck, Ginny, he tore his gaze from Terra and pleaded to the painting on his wall. *Could use a little help.*

Ginny stared back at him, looking equally puzzled.

While Terra swiped the tears with her thumb, Zander left her briefly to retrieve a roll of paper towels from his kitchen, then tore off a sheet and handed it to her.

"Thank you," she murmured when she took it from him. "That must be why she finally chose to go to rehab," Terra said, seemingly to no one in particular. "But if she went because she was pregnant, why...why would she OD if she knew...why would she do that?"

Fetzer glanced at Zander as he took his seat next to Terra again. The cop leaned forward and rested his elbows on his knees. "We don't believe she OD'd. In fact, we've ruled your mother's death a homicide."

Her head jerked up.

"The evidence seems to point to someone forcing a fix on her."

"Forcing...ohmigod! Who would want to do that —and why?"

"That's what we're trying to find out and we're looking at this from all different angles."

"Homicide," she whispered, then her gaze shifted from the cop to Zander and then to Carmine. "I don't know if that makes me feel better or worse."

Carmine got to his feet, walked across the room and took a seat next to Fetzer. "Were you expecting it to be something other than a homicide?"

"Something her doctor said—that sometimes addicts just give up."

The cop tapped his pen on his knee and referred to his notebook. "Do you have any knowledge of your mother seeing someone outside of her regular clients? We've ordered DNA testing on the baby, but it would help and save time if we could narrow it down."

"You mean like a relationship? I doubt it. I'm pretty sure she would've told me if she was."

"Were you close with her?"

"We were getting to be again. The last few years have been... difficult. I had to disconnect in order to...you know...stay sane." That last part came out in a whisper. "But we used to be—very."

A sharp, all-too familiar pain sliced across Zander's chest. He'd had to disconnect from his own mother after *that* day— when Ginny found him, covered in blood.

He squeezed Terra's hand, but this time it was him seeking comfort. He did not want to remember, not now. And he forced it to the back of his mind—forced himself to focus *her.*

"What did Rebecca do before she became a...call girl?" Fetzer continued, looking slightly uncomfortable.

"It's okay," she said, putting him out of his misery. "You can call it what it is."

"Right....go on."

"We sang."

Fetzer's head tilted. "Can you elaborate on that—give me a little history on your mom."

Terra closed her eyes and let out a long sigh, as if she were searching for the right words. "Mom was kind of a gypsy. She had a really hard start in life. My grandparents died when she was very young, and she was raised in foster care. For...um, various reasons she never stayed with a family for long, but she mentioned once the last one was the worst."

"When you say *the worst*, what do you mean?"

"She never actually said the words out loud—most likely to spare me—but I believe she was raped, and that resulted in me."

Zander tensed, every damn muscle locking up, he and saw Carmine do the same. Their eyes caught and there was a long moment of silence. Even the cop seemed shocked.

It was Carmine who recovered first. "Do you know the name of this family?"

"Not their last name. She wouldn't talk about them. It hurt her too much and because it hurt her, I didn't push it. She only ever referred to them as Tom and Jerry—like the cartoon. That's all I know. Anyway, she didn't trust the system, so she left and never finished high school."

"What happened after that?" the cop asked.

She met someone—the man I knew as my dad and he helped her run away. They formed a band and travelled. Apparently, she was on stage when she went into labor." Terra turned to Zander, her eyes shimmering. "I was born in Iris on the way to the hospital."

Something developed in his gut, moved up his chest and wrapped around his heart. He decided right then he'd never disrespect her car again.

"Tell me more about this man your mom met. Is he still around?"

She shook her head. "His name was Ethan Miller, and he died when I was maybe four. After that we spent a lot of time on the road, always moving to some new place until I had to start school, then we settled in Seattle." She gave a sad half-chuckle, half-sob. "It was the nineties and Mom had a thing for Eddie Vedder."

"Is that when she started using?" Fetzer asked.

"No," she said and reached for a fresh paper towel from the roll on his coffee table. "She liked to have fun, drank a little too much sometimes, but she never did drugs."

"So, what changed?"

"About five years ago she tripped over a mic cord and fell off stage— hurt her back really bad. She was in pain and had no health insurance. One of the guys in the band scored oxy, you know to help her out, and I guess she liked it a little too much."

"And at some point, oxy turned into heroin?" Carmine asked.

Terra nodded. "Sad to say it's easier and cheaper to score. After a while, she couldn't hold it together anymore. The band got her into rehab, but it didn't stick so they fired her. At that point we'd moved to San Francisco and she charmed her new dealer into letting us live with him."

"Dealer got a name?" Zander asked.

"Andrei, he had a big scar on his face." She made a slashing gesture with her finger. "I think he's dead now too."

Not that Boris fuck, he thought. Thank fuck.

"I hated him—he gave me the creeps and we fought about him a lot, but she wouldn't listen. I guess at that point heroin was more important."

Zander felt his chest go tight. He understood that feeling far too well.

"That's how she met her pimp—through him, and I couldn't deal anymore. I already had a job and as soon as I graduated from high school, I took Iris and moved out—shared a room with a friend, Lu, my drummer."

"By pimp you mean Dean Melnikov?" This was asked by Carmine and her gaze moved to him.

"Yeah—she worked with him for a while, then something happened, and Dean went to prison. Vasily took over." The pressure on Zander's hand increased but when he looked over, Terra's eyes were on Fetzer. "Do you think he killed her?"

"We don't know that." Fetzer answered. "But as I said, we're looking at all angles—all possibilities. Have you met any of her clients?"

"Never met, no. I saw her with one from a distance in the elevator of the Fairmont Hotel a few months ago. He looked familiar, but I couldn't place him and when I asked her about him she brushed it off. Just told me he was nobody important—just a man with a lot of money. I let it go because, like I mentioned I had to disconnect— otherwise, I'd have gone insane. I couldn't think about what my mother did with these men or why she was doing it."

"Familiar how?" Fetzer asked.

"I honestly don't know. Just a face I've seen somewhere—maybe on TV."

"You mean like an actor?"

"Or a politician." Carmine's brow furrowed.

"Politician?" Terra focused on Carmine again. Something about how she looked at him made Zander's skin prickle. He caught Carmine's eye again and knew exactly what he was thinking.

Congressman.

"Would you recognize this person if you saw him again?"

"If I saw a photo I might."

Fetzer sat up straighter. "We'll get working on that. In the meantime, I'm very sorry for your loss, Terra."

She ran her fingers through her hair and sniffed. "Thank you."

Zander hooked an arm around her neck and pulled her in, burying her head in his shoulder. This comforting thing was new so when she relaxed against him, put her arms around his waist, the warmth that swelled up surprised him—made him feel...protective.

Fetzer passed his card to her, and she took it as he laid a kiss on the top of her head. Everyone stood, except Terra who brought up her legs and curled in a ball with her chin on her knees.

"If you think of anything I should know, please call me," Fetzer said, his gaze ping-ponging between them.

"Okay," she mumbled and gave a short nod.

Zander showed him to the door, they shook hands and the

Mill Valley cop left. Carmine, however, stood back with his arms folded. When Zander caught his eye, he ticked his head to the side indicating he wanted a private powwow. Zander nodded then walked back to his couch and dropped into a squat.

"Freckle." He waited until he had her attention.

"She tried so hard," she whispered.

"I know, babe."

Then her control slipped, and she started to cry. "Why didn't she tell me she was pregnant.?"

"Babe"—he took her face between his palms—"don't do this to yourself."

"I should've known. She should've told me."

He rocked from his squat to drop to his knees. She reached for him, sliding her arms around his waist and cradled her head against his chest. Until she pulled away, wiping her face with the back of her hand.

"I'm sorry...I don't mean to be so needy."

"Nothing wrong with you being needy, babe. But I gotta get Carmine something from my office. Will you be all right for a minute? If not, I can..."

Her hand came to his face. It felt warmer than before and stopped him mid-sentence. "I've been doing this a long time, Zander. I'm not going to break."

He sucked in a breath, feeling more helpless than he should. "Maybe you wanna call your girls? Have them come over?" Though if he was honest, he wanted her to himself—just for a little bit longer.

"Why are you being so nice?"

"Nice?"

"Don't get me wrong—I like you being nice. It's just that..."

Shit, he was coming on too strong.

"I'm not used to..."

Moving too fucking fast.

"Used to what, Freckle?"

"I'm not used to anyone taking care of me."

That appalled him for more reasons he cared to admit. *Fucking idiot piece of shit ex, Dannie.* Pete was right. Asshole didn't know what he had. More than ever he wanted to kick his ass, but then again if he hadn't cheated on her, she wouldn't be here with him. But he didn't express any of that to her.

"That sucks, babe. When your girls get here, raid my booze cabinet and if you want something else, I'll get it from downstairs."

"No. No girls right now. I'm fine. I just…need a little time to process," she said and reached for another sheet from the paper towel roll, ripped it and dabbed at the moisture pooling in her eyes.

"You sure?"

"Go." She waved him away. "I'm gonna ugly cry and I'd rather do that alone."

Zander watched her blink the tears from her eyes and kissed her forehead. A lump the size of a marble formed in his throat and he fought it while he led Carmine downstairs. Leaving her was harder than it should've been. But he didn't know what else he could do other than what he already was.

In his office and once he'd shut his door, Carmine said, "Heard you had some trouble in your bar last night."

"I did."

"Also heard you have surveillance," he smirked.

Zander smirked back. "I do."

"Mind if I take a look?"

Zander tipped his chin at Carmine, "Have at it." He pulled up the footage on his computer from the fight and gave him a moment to watch it.

"Shit—that one." Carmine pointed to the taller of the two men and Zander froze the screen. "See that tattoo on his neck? Shaped like a cross."

Zander looked closer and nodded.

"Not familiar with that but I'm thinking this dude is one of Dean's men."

Zander's head jerked. "Not Vasily's?"

"Well, since Dean's in prison, I guess by default he's Vasily's man now. Either way, he looks like a dangerous fucker."

"Think this dangerous fucker could be Boris?"

Carmine's eyes narrowed, and he again scrutinized the taller man. "Don't know. The intel on that fuck is limited but here's something about him that twists my ball hairs. Rewind it to when they come in."

As Zander did so, he remembered what Terra had told him—how she'd felt she was being watched. What if she was right and it hadn't been at Vasily's direction? What if these fuckers had a different agenda?

"I'm not liking this, bro."

"Can't say I do either. Why your bar?"

"Yeah," Zander exhaled. "Doesn't feel random and my door dude, Pete says the older fuck was there two nights in a row. Both nights Terra was here."

"Shit—can I get a copy of that?"

Zander stuck a new thumb drive into his computer and when the transfer completed, he handed it over. As Carmine stuck it in his pocket, the man's phone rang.

He glanced at the screen. "Gotta take this, it's about the other case I'm working."

While he spoke, Zander studied the older man's face. Mid-fifties, rugged, scruffy and Eastern European for sure. Then he focused on the tat. Most of it was hidden but what he could see was the twisted handle of what he assumed was a dagger pointing down.

Fuck!

He zoomed in.

Jesus! He'd seen one exactly like that before.

I kill you.

No—no, you can't take him. DON'T TAKE HIM!

Zander sucked in a sharp breath and squeezed his eyes shut. It hit him hard—much harder than before.

He leaned forward, placed both hands flat on his desk and braced himself. And dropped his head. His world rotated like he'd had too much to drink. Then his vision got blurry and...red.

"Milan?"

Zander sucked in another breath.

"Fucking hell, Milan?" Carmine's voice sounded distant and disconnected like he was in another room.

"Ungh." Zander collapsed into his desk chair and covered his eyes with his palms.

"What the hell, man? You okay?"

He couldn't speak because he couldn't unclench his teeth.

Blood.

Christ, the smell.

"Breathe," Carmine ordered. "Just fucking breathe."

Zander did exactly that. Pulled one in, wrinkling his nose at the imaginary smell, trying not to let the stink gas his head, before he let it out. Then another in, and another one out.

"Shit...dude, you look like you've been through combat."

Thing was, he wouldn't describe it as combat. It was close, but he couldn't tell Carmine—he couldn't tell anyone. The only people who knew what happened that day were dead. Zander closed his eyes and fought to even his breathing. He could still picture it—the double-edged blade—the ornate hilt and little curlicue scrolls.

"Talk to me, Milan."

"That tat," he ground out.

"That tat remind you of something...or someone?"

A sheen of sweat accumulated on Zander's brow and he wiped it away with his sleeve. Then he opened his eyes and blinked.

Carmine stared at him. "What happened to you?"

Zander cleared his throat. "Just a dizzy spell."

Carmine's eyes narrowed. "Don't insult me, man. I know what PTSD looks like. And unless I'm mistaken…"

"Forget it." Zander grumbled. "It's over."

"Really?" Carmine cocked an eyebrow. "Then why do you look like a raw doughnut? You're whiter than those invoices on your desk. Who do you know has a tat like that?"

The man's eyes bored into his and he figured, what the hell. The asshole was dead, couldn't hurt him anymore. "Dmitri Melnikov."

He watched his friend take it in, mull it around. "He beat you?"

Zander worked his jaw at the memory. That part was safe enough to admit to. He nodded. "Not just me."

"Your mother?"

"All of us, Dean and Vasily too—saw their bruises often enough."

"Exactly how much time did you spend with them?"

"A lot."

"You see much of them after Dmitri disappeared?"

"Not up close. Mostly Dean—occasionally around town, but I avoided him. Vasily went off radar. Didn't see that fucker for ten years."

"They ever find Dmitri's body?"

Zander shook his head and was relieved when Carmine's phone rang again. The man sighed and scrubbed a hand through his dark curls while he checked the caller ID. "Got a situation with the job I'm doing. Don't want to leave your ugly ass but since you got a little color back, and you've got that beautiful woman up there to take care of, I gotta get back to work. But we aren't done talking about this. I'll catch you later, Milan."

Zander tipped his chin at his friend and waited for his door to close. He pulled in air through his nose, counted backwards until the calm settled over him. Then steeled himself and clicked on the start button.

What was he missing?

What purpose did that fight serve other than to annoy and cause him damage? A distraction maybe—but from what—or rather from whom? It didn't feel like Vasily's style. Whatever it was, it wasn't coming to him. He leaned back in his chair and closed his eyes—let his mind wonder to when he was ten. Dmitri kicked them out of his mother's apartment—sent them to shoot hoops on a middle school basketball court half a block away.

Though the brothers were taller and older, Dean by three years and Vasily by one, Zander was faster and outscored them both. Dean hadn't liked it. His temper manifested in rougher than necessary shoulder bumps and blocks, knocking Zander on his ass more than once until he'd had enough and fought back. He'd plowed his head into Dean's stomach, straddled and pummeled the shit out of his ribs. He took a bunch of blows himself and ended up with a bloody lip and a black eye. But it was Vasily who broke it up—pulling Zander off Dean. "Don't be a bully, *brat*. Don't be like *him*."

Fucking assholes.

He moved on, checking the surveillance for any sign of his whiskey thief and while he did that, his phone buzzed in his pocket. He dug it out. When he saw the ID, he dropped his head and groaned.

Heather: *I HAVE to see you.*

Fuck.

Not what he needed with Terra upstairs. *Can't. How's your head?*

Heather: *Not hungover anymore if that's what you mean.*

Zander: *Yep.*

Heather: *Want to say sorry.*

Zander: *No need.*

Heather: *And thank you in person for getting me home.*

He knew from past experience what thanking him in person meant and it didn't appeal. *Appreciate it...though not necessary.*

Heather: *Necessary to me! Calling dibs tonight.*

The muscles in his jaw worked while his thumb moved over the keyboard. *No, babe.* He didn't need another shit show inside his bar. *With someone.* He didn't wait for the bouncing dots indicating a response. As far as he was concerned this conversation was over. He shut his computer down and stood to head upstairs, dropping his phone in his sweats pocket. Then it buzzed again.

Heather: *The bitch from the other night?*

Okay, now he really was done.

Heather: *You're still with her?*

Zander sighed then shook his head. *Don't do that. Not cool.* Jealousy bored him, and the moment any of them went there, he cut them loose. But lately he'd had a touch of his own and had to remind himself it didn't feel good.

Heather: *What's not cool is you blowing me off again! For her? Seriously?*

Zander: *Talk later. Gotta go.*

Heather: *Want to talk now.*

Zander: *Later. Turning my phone off.*

Then he shut *that* down and locked the office door. This thing with Terra, whatever the hell it was, scared him. Worse, he had no notion where it was headed. But what he did know was he didn't want to fuck it up before he could figure it out. Heather was a complication he didn't need. Time to cut her loose but not via text.

He opened his apartment door and checked the couch. Terra wasn't where he'd left her. It made his heart skip. He stilled and closed his eyes, trying to catch her vibe. It was quiet, but not the quiet of complete emptiness.

His bedroom.

A current of something hummed through him as he made his way down the hall. Relief? Warmth?

Yeah…the woman made him feel warm—cozy as a fucking kitten.

She lay on her side with her back to the door with a paper towel balled up in one of her hands and he made a mental note to buy some tissues for her.

The oriental rug he'd received in payment for one of his paintings from an importer who'd made a bad bet and had suddenly gotten cash-poor hushed any noise his shoes made as he approached.

She didn't move, except for a small hitch in her chest as it rose and fell in her sleep. He stood staring, taking in the dip in her waist and the smooth curve of her hip until her breath hitched again.

"Babe?" He asked softly. "You awake?"

When no response came, he parked himself on the edge of his bed and toed off his shoes, then his socks. After which he grabbed the collar of his T-shirt and pulled it over his head, dropping it on the floor. He lifted the comforter and saw, though she'd taken off her yoga pants, she still wore panties and the tank. He slid in behind her.

When he tucked himself up against her body with his legs nestled in the bend of hers she still didn't wake. He slipped an arm around her waist, letting all that soft, feminine warmth infuse him. It felt natural and good. As he breathed in her scent, she wiggled her ass closer to him and he tensed. The woman was crying in her sleep. Now was not the time to get hard. Not that he was opposed to having her again. In fact, he was all for it, but…shit. Even he wasn't that much of a dick.

Once she settled, and he was sure she was still out, he let the tension leave his muscles. This cuddling thing felt nice—maybe too nice.

He had to watch himself. All this was so far out of his normal experience, his normal routine, and way beyond just getting laid.

The woman was so different, so beautiful and so much more than he was used to.

Maybe much more than he deserved.

Christ.

He closed his eyes and hoped like fuck he'd never have to tell her the truth. About what he really was.

CHAPTER 21

Thursday evening

*E*ven though they weren't touching, Terra felt him before she opened her eyes. It was getting dark, but thanks to the ambient city lights and the orange glow of the rising full moon she could see him clearly.

He lay on his back. The forearm closest to her rested on his naked stomach, while the other was thrown behind his head with his face turned slightly towards her. This gave her a chance to check him out. Those ridiculously thick lashes on any other man would look girly, but on him…just sexy.

And that bottom lip, full yet firm and skilled in a way that made her stomach flutter. She wanted to suck on it for hours.

The thing about death—it reminded one to live. And she wanted to feel something other than overwhelming grief, something good—even if it was just for a moment. A little shiver ran through her at the memory of where that lip and his tongue had already been. The back-arching, toe-curling pleasure his mouth had brought her. A warm flood started between her legs while her fingers itched to roam the bulges on his arm, the scrolled ink, then down the warm skin on his chest.

But she didn't want to wake him just yet. She wanted to take him in, memorize every little character on his face. Like the horizontal scar in the crease of his chin. And the slight bump in the bridge of his nose, suggesting it had been broken. Instead of detracting from his face, those little flaws made him more interesting, harder. Less pretty, yet more beautiful.

Just looking at him turned her on. Made her want to explore. He was so solid, so strong and so...man.

She crept closer. Enough to touch her lips to his skin. And to slip her hand under the comforter. Letting it trail across the hard, flat plane of his lower torso, smiling when he twitched in his sleep.

His breathing stayed even and deep, until her fingers ran into his happy trail. As her fingers pursued the fine hairs, getting closer to her prize, she glanced up, noting his eyes were still closed but those lips had parted.

Terra had never been timid in bed. Neither was she particularly bold, but something about this man, about his warrior body and the strength harnessed in those muscles, joggled her hormones. Made her want to be wild and creative.

Live in the moment.

She inched the comforter down to the edge of his sweats and centered her gaze on that tribal tat she'd been dying to check out.

Ha!

A Harley—of course it was.

It suited him. Bold and fierce and beautifully inked in rich black. Definitely kiss-worthy and definitely dangerous.

And this thing with him couldn't last.

It just couldn't. She'd be a fool to think otherwise but she'd also be a fool to waste it. The tip of her tongue touched the flame shooting from the Harley's exhaust, then she brought her lips to his flesh and breathed out. Zander's skin erupted with goose-bumps and tasted just a little bit salty.

It wasn't enough. She needed more and pulled the comforter down further, then as smoothly as she could, straddled his thighs and hooked her fingers round the edge of his sweats, dragging them lower. Much to her delight, he went commando. His cock, already well on its way to being thick and hard, sprang free.

Terra looked across his body and her eyes caught his. They were still sleepy, but those gold flecks blazed.

"You got something in mind, Freckle?" he asked, his voice lazy with sleep, yet with a hint of gruff. "Or you gonna torture me and just keep staring at my cock?"

"I got a lot in mind," she whispered. "I hope you're up for it."

"It's an established fact I'm up for it, babe. But do me a favor?"

"What's that?"

"Take your top off."

She held his eyes. The growing intensity in his caused her to become suddenly shy yet filled her with power at the same time. *In the moment,* she reminded herself.

She crossed her arms around her waist and slowly brought them up, teasing off her tank. He seemed not to move, not even to breathe while he watched her.

"And your bra," he murmured in voice that had gotten a lot rougher. She took it as a good sign. An even better one was the bump in his throat dancing when he swallowed.

"I think I might need a little help with that." She moved forward using his broad chest for leverage and allowing the satin of her panties to drag slowly across his cock.

He went taut and sucked in air in a long, sharp hiss. "Easy, woman...you're gonna make me blow before you even get started."

"Unhook me," she whispered in his ear, letting her hair fall to one side. It fell in a wild, curly curtain across his shoulder.

He undid the tiny hooks on the back strap of her bra and

while he did, she lay soft nips and kisses on his neck. Then he slipped the straps off her arms, freeing her breasts and capturing a nipple with his lips. It sent an electric jolt through her and it was her turn to hiss.

Zander nuzzled, scraping her skin with his new stubble, making her prickle all over. He secured her by wrapping his arms around her and rolled them over. Now on top, he went to town on her tits until she wriggled and arched her back from the sensations rocking through her. Somehow, through all this, he shifted and stripped her panties and kicked off his sweats. Before she could think, he clasped those big hands around her waist and took them both to the headboard. He arranged a pillow and reached over to the side table, groping in the drawer for a condom. When he found one, he tossed it onto the dresser.

"Straddle me," he commanded after he'd straightened, resting his back against the headboard.

She obeyed, keeping most of her weight on her knees and holding onto his shoulders. He slid his hands up her thighs, her hips, her waist, cupping then dragging his thumbs over her breasts. Up, over her collar bones, her neck until he entangled his fingers in her hair brought her mouth to his in a long, deep, slow kiss.

She broke it and not because she needed air. But because she had other plans for where she wanted her lips.

"This is my show," she murmured holding his eyes. They flared bright at her words.

"Knock yourself out, Freckle. Can't wait to see what you got for me."

She made a path, starting at his jaw, then down his corded neck, his pecs, grazing his skin with her teeth. By the time she got to his six pack, his grip in her hair tightened his abs jerked with each little nip.

God, he was so strong, and everything about him was hard and warm and he smelled so good.

When she drew him in her mouth, circling her tongue around his tip, he was solid as concrete, and she knew it was because of her. The way he held her hair back, so he could watch. The way his eyes glazed, and his breath caught each time she took him deeper told her so. But she also knew, like before, this was dangerous, assuming she might have more power than she actually did. For the moment she didn't care.

Zander allowed her another minute of play until he pressed his head back and released a low, primal groan. Then his grip tightened in her hair, stilling her head. "Freckle," he growled, "gotta stop you there."

There was no time to mount a protest, and she did want to protest as she wasn't ready to stop. But as he tackled her sideways and rolled her onto her back, she had no choice.

"I wasn't done," she said.

He positioned himself over her, elbow on either side of her head and one knee between her thighs. "You were done," he murmured against her lips. "Because if you weren't done—I'd be done. And I'm not done. You get me?"

"I get you," she said on a gasp as he moved his head, all that new roughness grazing her skin. "But it still isn't fair."

"Can't let you be in control." He slid a rough palm over the tender skin of her inner arm. "Not when you're naked." There was an edge in his voice. But it was a good edge. It sent a thrill through her that started in her toes. And hummed up through her legs while he continued to move down her belly. And over her thighs until finally, he pushed them apart. The hum turned to a purr. She squirmed and gripped the sheets behind her head, looking for an anchor when he dipped his face between her thighs.

The first one hit her so fast it had to be some record. While she recaptured her breath, he worshipped the area around her bellybutton and her hip bones, sucking and kissing the skin on her inner thighs, before he started on her again. Somewhere in the middle of her second, before she came down, before she caught her breath, before she could think to open her eyes, she felt the touch of cool air as he lifted off her. The foil packaging ripped and not long after that he was back.

Like before, it started slow, but intense and hungry. As if he wanted to savor every second yet couldn't at the same time. It built quickly into something heel-digging and delicious. And it was just minutes before she got there again, and he got there right along with her. Together they rode it, during which her nails dug into his back and he cradled her head like he never meant to let her go. Like they were glued to one another.

Dangerous.

When at last she had the strength to move, she shifted onto her side and found him looking at her, his eyes warm and satisfied.

"Hungry?" he asked.

"Starved."

"You eat meat?"

She started to giggle—*did she eat meat.*

"Zander, I think it's an established fact I eat meat."

&a.

*H*alf an hour later, barefoot and dressed in one of Zander's white work T-shirts with *Chuck's* written in red on the back, Terra quartered small ripe tomatoes on a wooden cutting board. She added them to the sliced cucumbers, red onions and black olives already in the clear glass bowl.

"Babe," Zander said as he spiced and peppered the steaks with a large wooden grinder. "Pick out a bottle of wine from the pantry." The fork he held pointed to the door off the kitchen she'd poked her head through this morning.

"Anything in particular?"

"Whatever you want."

Now that she was in it, the pantry was a lot larger that she'd originally noticed. Like a dyslexic, she stared at the bottles lined up on an impressive mahogany wine rack attached to the wall, not really seeing them. There were so many, at least a hundred, and she didn't know where to start.

Her neurons seemed to be due to the multiple orgasms she'd received. Because of it, or maybe in spite of it, she couldn't help worrying.

Worried she liked this too much.

Worried it wasn't going to stop at like. It absolutely and unequivocally *had* to stop at like.

The man was addictive and it scared the panties off her. But she also wanted to enjoy the reprieve it gave her. Plenty of time to think about all the death surrounding her later.

This was all so normal, cooking dinner together—the things couples did. But as far as she could tell, Zander was not a *couple* kind of man and her situation was *not* normal.

Wine, wine and more fucking wine.

She pursed her lips and blew out air as she squinted at a label. *Chateau* something or other 1989! Yikes—not that one.

Joseph Phelps Insignia? Didn't know that one either but it also sounded expensive.

"You got any plonk in here?" She called. "Like something I'd recognize?"

"Just pick one, babe. It doesn't matter what. They're all good."

"Just pick one, he says," she mumbled. Fine. She raised her eyes to the ceiling, wrapped her fingers around a bottle and pulled it from the rack. She shut the pantry door and flipped off the light.

"Champagne?" Zander cocked a brow at the bottle she placed on the granite next to his upside-down phone. "We're celebrating?"

She glanced at the bottle.

Crap!

Those were the kind of thoughts she didn't need to put in his head. "Uh…I like bubbles."

His lips stretched into a smile. "She likes plonk and she likes bubbles. Check."

"You're making a list?"

"Don't need a list." He tapped his forehead with a long index finger. "It's all up here. Dig in the fridge. There should be a cold bottle in there somewhere."

Then to her relief, he opened the oven door and stabbed the baking potatoes with the fork, testing their readiness. After which he turned a knob to a burner that supported a cast-iron skillet. It made a series of clicks and burst into a small flame.

In the fridge, she found crumbled feta cheese, a vinaigrette salad dressing and, indeed, a cold bottle of Champagne.

Bollinger.

Pink Bollinger.

If it were her fridge, it would have been a bottle from the fifteen-dollar-and-under shelf. "This okay to drink?" She held it out for him.

His brows came together. "Champagne doesn't usually expire, babe."

"No, I meant it's pricey. Would you prefer I pick something else?"

"Rule number two. If it's in my fridge—or my pantry—it's okay to drink. Stick the other bottle in there too."

"Rule number two? What's rule number one?"

"You're naked, you don't get to be in control."

"I'm not sure I like rule number one," she muttered as she switched the bottle with the other one on the counter. "I think it needs debating."

"We can debate all night long," he said grinning. "In fact, I look forward to you trying to convince me otherwise, but the rule isn't going to change."

She flashed him a flirty look. "Hmm—we'll see about that."

Rules and lists.

Yeah, this felt different—but a rabbit-hole no less. *Don't get used to it*, she chanted silently. *Do not get used to it.*

His phone vibrated once. Or rather, it vibrated again. The thing had boogied with the granite at least twice since they'd been in the kitchen. He'd placed the steaks on the heated pan and perhaps didn't hear it over the sizzle. Since it faced down, she couldn't see the caller ID, but she was tempted to hand it to him.

That thorny tendril in her stomach tickled the base of her spine and woke her female intuition.

Had to be a woman if he was ignoring it.

No other reason he wouldn't pick up in front of her.

Oh, come on!

She gave herself a mental eye-roll. It's not like she didn't know about them. But instead of making her feel good she had all his attention, it made her uncomfortable.

"Question for you, Freckle."

Her eyes snapped from his phone to his and noticed his narrowed a tad. The exact look she wanted to avoid so she added a little extra sunshine into her tone. "Yeah?"

"How did your mom get into that expensive rehab center? The Sunrise Institute is a private facility and if she had no money of her own, who's paying?"

"I wish I knew," she said and tore her gaze from him, busying herself opening cabinet doors until she found two champagne flutes. She didn't need him thinking she was jealous because she assumed that was another woman texting him.

"It's something that's never made sense to me. Last time she got treatment it was from a state-funded clinic. So, it's not lost on me someone took a big risk."

"Obviously someone who cared about her." His eyes were still probing when she pretended to examine the flutes. "Maybe cared about the baby too."

The baby!

That hit her in the stomach. How could you miss something you didn't even know you had?

"Any ideas who this person might be?"

"You're suggesting whoever paid for rehab might be the father?" she asked.

"It's a possibility, right?"

"Well, the thing is, Mom *and* her doctor signed an NDA, so I may never know who paid unless that individual comes forward."

"A nondisclosure agreement?" Perplexity brought his eyebrows together. "That's odd."

No shit.

There was a moment while he seemed to turn this around in his head. Then he asked, "And what about this Dr. Rodham—how did she find him?"

"That I don't know either. Mom had all this sorted out before I drove her there. Somebody helped her...I just don't know who. When I asked, she wouldn't name names—figured she'd tell me when she was ready. I didn't push it because I was just happy she was going, and didn't want to do anything to jeopardize that. I understand now it was because of the NDA, but yeah—it's a really good question."

Terra's fingers tightened around the flutes, and before she snapped the stems, she placed them on the granite counter. "There's something I haven't told you."

His head cocked to the side as he studied her. "What's that?"

"Vasily says there's a missing shipment of something, I'm assuming drugs...and that she may have something to do with it being missing."

"Jesus, why would he think that?"

"She sent me a text saying something about moving stuff and I have no clue what she was talking about. But that's what he asked me about when he showed up in my apartment."

Again, his eyes narrowed as he turned to face her fully. Tension vibrated off him and she couldn't blame him. He'd put himself in danger by offering for her to stay at his apartment, even after his bar got trashed, maybe because of her.

His phone vibrated again. Terra sighed and looked at him. "Would you please get that?"

"Nope." He made a popping sound on the "p" and advanced on her.

"It's fine, Zander. I won't think it's rude. Just get it already."

"Babe, I said no." When he closed the few feet, he placed his hands on her hips and pushed her slowly against the counter.

"Why not?" She tipped her head back.

"Don't want to."

"Again, why not?"

"Are you always this persistent?"

"Are you always this evasive?"

"Only when I wanna focus my attention on the person in front of me instead of on a gadget."

"Except a person on the other side of that gadget wants your focused attention."

"Babe," he murmured, tilting her head with his thumbs.

"What?" she murmured back.

"Shut up." Strange how just the timbre of his voice could send ripples through her. While she contemplated this, he captured her bottom lip between his teeth, then kissed her. Heat swept through her. It wasn't fair, this effect he had on her. How easily he could distract her, and she had no will to stop him.

"Is that another one of your rules?" Terra breathed, squirming her hips against him.

"Kissing you?" The roughness in his voice reflected his own need, in case she couldn't already tell by the solidness between them.

"No...kissing me to shut me up."

"It wasn't, but I'll gladly add it. My dick seems to like kissing you. And I like to indulge my dick."

He nipped her on that spot below her ear and uttered a low

growl before he pushed away from her and put some distance between them. "But it's going to have to wait because unfortunately, the steaks can't."

The gas clicked off and he set the meat aside on a platter to rest. While she recaptured her breath, she added the feta cheese to the salad and tossed it, she glanced at his phone again and something struck her. What was his agenda?

"Can I ask you something?"

"Always."

"Why are you helping me?"

He paused then took his time in answering her but when he did, his voice was soft, and measured. "I fucked up something a long time ago. Maybe I'm just trying to balance shit out—right a few wrongs."

"What happened?"

"Not right now, babe. Not before we eat."

She sighed and set the salad aside, deciding to let it go for the moment and popped the champagne. After she caught the fizz in a flute, she dumped ice from the fridge ice-maker into a silver bucket Zander produced from a cabinet above his head.

"You have nice stuff," she said, sticking in the bottle and jiggling it until it was decently submerged in the ice.

"I can't take much credit. Most of it's my grandmother's."

"Oh...I thought maybe...I don't mean to pry, but you know the woman on your arm? I thought it was hers?"

He stopped what he was doing to consider her, then he smiled. A crooked, lazy, *sexy* smile that set her panties ablaze.

"The woman on my arm *is* my grandmother, Freckle. She shared this apartment with her man, Chuck. That's her." He took her shoulders and turned her, then pointed to that fabulous painting on his wall. "Tickles the shit out of me you like her portrait."

❧

𝒯erra lay back facing Zander in his massive tub coated in fragrant bubbles sipping on icy champagne. One of her heels rested on his chest as he kneaded and massaged the pads of her toes and feet. This did all kinds of intimate things in intimate places.

"Tell me about her," she asked a little huskily and as a matter of distraction. Who knew feet were so damn sensual?

Zander's gaze lifted from examining her pink toenails to hers and she noted it looked a little heated.

"Tell you about who, babe?"

"Your grandmother. Ginny—is that short for Virginia?"

His hard stomach muscles twitched as he let out a little chuff. "Virginia Mary Milan. Took no shit and left no prisoners kind of woman."

"With exquisite taste it seems."

"For material things. When it came to men, who'd have thunk her and Chuck would ever get together."

"Why is that?"

"When she met him, the bar was a titty-slash-biker bar and a front for running dope."

"Holy hell!" Her eyebrows jumped. "Chuck was a biker?"

"Not just *a* biker, babe. A big, badass, outlaw, one-percenter, nomad biker."

Terra giggled and shook her head. "I don't even know what that means."

"It means the man was scary as fuck and did business with even scarier fucks. Hard as nails, but around Ginny"—he chuffed again and shook his head—"he was like a newborn puppy. After he met her, he stopped allowing the bar to be used as a front for trafficking heroin."

Terra took a sip of champagne, savoring the bubbles then said, "Sounds like she's an amazing woman."

"She was."

Zander took one of those little toes into his mouth and nibbled on the soft pad. Good God, if he kept that up, she might just have an orgasm right there in the tub.

"Was?"

"She's gone. They both are. She went first, five years ago and it almost killed him. Got cervical cancer—took her so fast that by the time she was diagnosed, it was too late. Only time I ever saw him cry. Then he got sick not too long after that and died within a couple years of her. I think he just didn't want to live without her."

"That's so sad. Sounds like they really loved each other. You must miss them very much."

He nodded.

How did they meet?" she asked, after swallowing another sip.

He tensed and stopped nibbling, which could only be described as unfortunate. Then he took in a deep breath and exhaled it slowly, blowing on her toes. "They met because of my mom." His tone got suddenly quiet and carried a heaviness that spoke of old pain.

"Oh?" Terra mumbled, wondering if she'd opened a keg of bad beer.

"She'd been in some kind of fucked-up relationship with Dmitri Melnikov, Vasily's dad, for years."

"Ohmigod…are you serious?" she said, her mouth dropping open.

"Deadly, though I'm not even sure you can call it a relationship. The asshole was obsessed with her. I knew that even then—as a kid. Watched her every move, controlled what she wore, who she saw, who she spoke to—everything."

Zander placed the foot he held back in the tub and switched it out with her other, cupping it in his palm.

"Ginny hated it," he went on. "Hated *him*. But my mom"—he blew out a breath—"she couldn't see it. I remember them arguing about him. Ginny kind of stepped away, figuring my mom was an adult—she had to make her own decisions and they didn't talk for a while. Until he got her hooked on smack."

Terra's chest tightened and ached as she listened—picturing Zander as a small child being in the middle of that—having to witness it. It was bad enough as an adult to deal with a parent's addiction.

"He'd beat her," he said, then stopped as he worked his throat for a bit. When he spoke again, the sadness in his tone was unmistakable. "He'd give her *medicine* as he called it—for the pain. But by the time she wised up it was too fucking late."

"Zander," Terra whispered.

"When she finally pulled it together and tried to leave, he'd beat her more, then give her more, and since he controlled her fixes—he controlled her."

"Oh, God…I'm so sorry."

Zander reached for his glass resting on the edge of the tub and drained it of champagne. He took his time refilling both their glasses. Terra got the impression he was searching for his own control and gave him the moment.

"At the time," he continued after he placed the bottle back in the bucket. "Dmitri did business with the motorcycle club Chuck was associated with. He used the MC to distribute and to transport the drugs up the west coast. A couple of the brothers were truck drivers and hid the shit in their loads. After Ginny figured out what was really happening—discovered my mother was an addict—she blew into the bar and confronted Chuck. According to him, he'd never met a woman with bigger balls and fell in love with her on the spot. There's a whole lot more to that story but I'm not going to get into it right now."

"No wonder you inked her into your skin."

"She saved me," he said softly. "They both did, after my mom died." The lines around his eyes became more pronounced and after a moment, he exhaled. It was then she realized he'd been holding his breath. "This"—he indicated the Harley on his hip

—"is for him. He had no kids of his own, but kept me close, out of trouble for the most part. When the cancer got to be too much for him to ride, he gave me his bike and then the deed to the bar."

"How did your mother die?" Terra asked, though her throat had gotten tight and it was difficult to speak. "Did she OD?"

"No, Freckle—she didn't OD." He scraped a hand over his face, then pinched the bridge of his nose. "She died because that piece of shit beat her one time too many."

She stared at him, stunned, horrified and sad, all at once.

"There wasn't a fucking thing I could do to help her…to stop him before it was too late."

Zander shut his eyes, working his Adam's apple. Terra moved over until she was kneeling before him, then slid her hands up his hard torso to his face.

"What could you have done?" she whispered. "You were a child."

"I tried, Freckle…it wasn't enough."

"Zander…" She cupped his jaw with one hand and smoothed his hair back with the fingers of her other.

When he opened his eyes, they were tortured.

"I'm so sorry you went through that. I can't imagine what it must have been like."

He nodded, then his arms came around her and pulled her, so she straddled his lap. She laid a gentle kiss on his temple, then one on his cheekbone, working her way to his lips. They were meant to soothe, but when she got to the corner of his mouth she lingered.

"Long time ago." His voice was low and a little gravelly as he angled his face, so it was slanted. An invitation for her to take more.

She did. Her teeth caught his lip and bit softly. Zander groaned into her mouth and something hard between her legs rose up and rubbed up against her.

"I like this comforting thing, Freckle. Especially with your nipple so close to my mouth." At which he shifted his head and took it in his mouth. It immediately got hard as a nut and sent electricity buzzing through her lower belly—making her throb in delightful places. "I'm also kinda interested in what I can do to those adorable little toes of yours."

"Like what," she breathed, and wondered as he attacked her other nipple if it could be any more pleasurable than what he was already doing to her.

"Like I'm wondering if I can make you come by sucking on *them*. I'm sure as fuck gonna try."

Which he did—and she did.

CHAPTER 22

Friday

"You did what?" Helen shrieked. Terra jerked the phone from her ear so hard she almost sent it flying.

Jeez.

"I said I spent the last two nights here and I think I'm going to be here longer than anticipated."

"Ohmigod, I think I'm going to faint. This is all my fault." Helen's heavy breathing rasped in Terra's ear.

"Helen, stop, it's not your fault."

"I knew I shouldn't have left you there by yourself. Oh—my—God, I'm gonna kill Petey."

"Don't blame him either. He only did what I asked him to do."

"Shit, no wonder you didn't answer when I called. You were busy getting it on with *that dude*. Oh shit, I gotta sit down. This is *sooo* not good. Tell me you didn't do him?"

"Uh…"

"Holy hell, Tee!" Helen yelled again. Terra could picture her with one hand on her head, her eyes and jaw open wide. *"Tell me you didn't do him."*

"Um…" Terra plonked onto the couch, then flopped backwards, because yeah—she did do him. Thank the music Gods Zander had left ten minutes ago and wasn't witnessing this call.

"Petey swears this Zander dude has a magic penis and there's all these women that come to the bar, stand in line and take numbers. That's not you, right?"

"What…Jeez, no, I'm not taking numbers. I think Petey's exaggerating slightly."

"Slightly? My brother wants to be like him. Which in Petey-speak really means the man's a dog. Hot as Krakatoa, yes, I'll give you that."

Kraka…what?

"But a D.O.G., Terra, and from what I saw when he came to Provocative I can only concur. Although, in my defense, I didn't know it was him at the time."

"Helen."

"Oh, this is horrible. I mean, really Miller, if you had an itch couldn't you have done Rory instead? He's hot as hell too and a whole lot safer. I mean I would do him…"

"Helen!"

"What?"

"Shut up."

"Terra, I can't believe…"

"Please, Resnick, not today." Lordy, she loved Helen. Would stop a bullet for Helen—but dammit, sometimes!

"Okay…okay. I'm shutting up. But that doesn't mean I'm not worried about you. I know you, Terra Miller. When you sleep with a guy, you fall in love. And you don't just fall in love, you fall in *looove*. And this Zander dude is so not the guy to fall in *looove* with and I consider it my job as your best friend…no strike that, I consider it my *duty* to…"

"Helen."

"What?"

"*Shut up!*"

"Okay…okay, I'm really shutting up now. I'll be there in an hour to pick you up but we're gonna need tequila for later. I can't process any of this and go funeral shopping without knowing there's tequila at the end of it all."

Oh, God.

Terra rolled her eyes up looked at the ceiling. Nothing good could or almost ever did come from Helen and tequila.

"Forget the tequila, Zander said we could drink his. But you need to pick up Shelley on the way. She wants to come with, and she has my new key."

"Why does Shelley have your *new* key?"

"I had to have my locks changed and she's my landlady, remember? Or rather her man is my landlady. I mean my landlord…"

"Wait…why did you have to have your locks changed?"

"Uh…there was an incident at my apartment a couple nights ago."

"What kind of incident?"

Shit.

She did not want to freak Helen out because Helen was the Queen of freak-outs and all kinds of mayhem often ensued should one occur. "Honey, it's not important. It's been dealt with."

"Terra…what kind of incident?"

"Sweetie…"

"Oh…shit, you're in a situation and you can't tell me. Say 'mango margaritas' if you are."

"Not saying that because there's no need."

"Okay…cool. But really, we should have a code word in case one of us is ever in a situation, like being shackled to some dude's headboard, or something. I think we should go with…"

"Good lord…Helen, you're a nut. I am not in a situation *or* shackled to Zander's headboard." Though if she was completely honest with herself, she might not mind. Helen could be right about the magic penis part after experiencing what he did with just her *toes*.

"Oh...okay you're not in a situation, but you still sound a little funny. What's wrong? I mean, I know your mom just passed, but this seems like it's more than that." Helen's voice had dropped low. "Talk to me, babe."

Terra leaned forward and cupped her forehead with her palm then swallowed down the lump in her throat. "She was pregnant."

She heard Helen gasp, then whisper, "What?"

"With a little boy." Her voice cracked.

There was a long silence before Helen spoke again. "Oh...no, Tee. That's so sad, knowing what I know about you wanting a sibling."

"I didn't think it could get much worse and there's a whole lot more, but I'll tell you the rest later."

"Okay honey, I'll be there as soon as I can, and I'll pick up Shelley, but we have to get tequila. I'm sorry, but I'm not drinking that Zander dude's tequila. Probably got some kind of magic penis voodoo-sauce in it. Don't you dare drink any either, okay?"

"Okay."

"Love you, babe. See you soon."

Terra dropped her phone on the couch and reached for the almost-empty box of Kleenex. She wiped her eyes and blew her nose. Then picked up the remote to Zander's giant wall-mounted TV screen looking for something mindless that didn't require her to use more than a few brain cells—more for background distraction. Living in the city, one got used to the noise, and Zander's apartment, though beautiful and homey, was quiet and not her own. It made her feel alone. She clicked through the channels endlessly, until finally, frustrated, she settled on the news.

A familiar female reporter from Channel 5 interviewed a

group of surfers under the Golden Gate Bridge at Fort Point. Behind them, in an area blocked off by yellow crime-scene tape sat a parked van.

The victim is believed to have either fallen or jumped from the bridge and according to one surfer, seemed to have had track marks on her arms, although that is unsubstantiated at this time...

Huh, Terra scratched her head, wondering who the poor soul was. It seemed to be a particularly bad week for addicts and something that had burned inside her since the official ruling on her mom came back popped to the forefront.

At the bottom of her purse she found the Provocative card Vasily wrote his number on and flipped it over several times before punching the digits. It rang several times and she was about to hang up before he answered.

"Good afternoon, Terra."

She almost dropped her phone again. How had he known it was her? She never gave him her number, but then again, she suspected he knew more about her (some of it imparted by her mother, the rest she didn't want to contemplate) than she did of him.

"Are you calling to chit-chat," Vasily asked in a tone a quarter-notch above cold. "Or do you have information for me?"

"I don't know anything about your shipment, if that's what you're asking."

"I suspected as much, so therefore chit-chat."

"I don't chit-chat." *Especially not with him.*

"Hmm—that's probably disappointing for some men as it doesn't make for a good dinner date."

"Oh?" Was that humor she detected? She imagined not and shook her head as she'd yet to see a real smile from him. "Well, then it's a good thing I don't usually date. I'm calling to ask if you know anything about Mom's death."

"To the point—I like that in a woman, and no, I don't know any more than you, I suspect."

She couldn't decide if she felt disappointment herself—or disbelief. "The police have ruled it a homicide."

"I had heard, yes."

"How did you hear?"

"I imagine you're an intelligent woman, you know who I am and that I have my sources."

"Do you know why she's dead, Vasily? Is it to do with this missing shipment of yours?"

"It's not my shipment, Terra, but it could be part of why she's dead, I'll give you that."

Not his shipment?

She stood and paced the floor beneath that amazing painting of Zander's grandmother—Ginny. She looked up into her eyes, gaining strength from the serenity in hers, knowing a teeny bit of what she went through with Zander's mother.

"If not your shipment, then whose? And why are *you* so interested if Mom knew anything about it?"

"I can't answer that."

"You can't or won't?"

"Pick one."

"Fine," she took a breath, "then answer this—was it your men that trashed Zander's bar two nights ago?"

There was a long moment of silence before he said, "I have no idea what you are talking about."

"Zander's convinced two of your men started a fight for no reason in his bar—that it might have something to do with me. Why would they do that?"

"Milan is wrong."

"Really? I guess they must be going rogue then, but I can't imagine a man like you would allow your men to go rogue or do anything without your knowledge. So, I'm going to ask you this —are you watching me?"

"What are you talking about, Terra?"

"You're having me followed."

"*I'm* not having you followed."

"Then who is? The same people who killed Mom and my baby brother?" That's when her voice broke, but she fought hard to keep control. She did not want to show weakness—not to him.

She heard his sharp intake of air. "Jesus—she was pregnant?"

She covered her phone with her hand while she cleared her throat, then brought it back up to her ear. "Don't even begin to pretend you didn't know."

He was quiet for a long moment and when he finally did answer, there was gruff in his tone she'd never in her weirdest dreams believed she'd hear from him. "I didn't, Terra, and I have...had no interest in harming your mother, or *you*, for that matter."

"So, I guess you just broke into my apartment, scared the crap out of me by threatening to strangle me for shits and giggles because you had no interest in harming me?"

"There were reasons for doing so, which I'm not going to discuss right now. You've enlightened me with some very interesting information and now, based on what you've told me, I have work to do. Stay safe, Terra."

With that, he hung up.

Her jaw dropped, and she stared blinking at her phone for a long time.

Stay safe.

Holy hell—was that a veiled threat even though he had just said he had no interest in harming her? Could she afford to take him at his word?

She threw open the patio doors and walked out, her heart thumping hard. Two seagulls sat on the railing of Zander's patio and as she approached, they took flight, screeching their protest. When she got to the edge, she pulled her shawl closer and tighter around her arms against the breeze, staring down at the cars and people hustling below.

Threat or not, either way she'd just poked a hornet's nest. Problem was, she didn't know if she was ready for the resulting swarm.

CHAPTER 23

Friday early afternoon

Zander's phone buzzed, and he checked the incoming message as he held the back door wide for Carmine.

Heather: *What the fuck, Zander? Nothing?*

He'd deleted the nude photos she'd sent him when Terra took a moment after dinner to use the bathroom the previous night. But they kept coming. There were more this morning and now, another one, even after he'd told her to stop.

He was done—and blocked her number. Though he wasn't sure it would do any good. The woman would probably show up in person instead. At that point, they'd have to have words.

He tipped his chin at Carmine as he cleared the threshold, before he shut and relocked the door. Then led him to a corner table next to the stage.

It was still too early to open, Barney wasn't due for another hour, and the place was eerily quiet. It was moments like this when he missed Chuck, feeling the man's presence like he was still standing behind that bar.

"Your girl okay?"

Zander threw him a glance. "The baby, man—that's really fucked with her."

"Understandable. Keep an eye out. She doesn't know it, but she's in shock. Can come back in strange ways."

"Noted. What you got for me?"

Carmine tossed the red manila folder onto the round table, pulled a chair then sat with his legs stretched out, ankles crossed.

"Went back as far as I could with the information we got from Terra yesterday, and it wasn't easy. Rebecca Shanahan Miller had one shitshow of an early start. Her parents were murdered in Portland, Oregon in nineteen eighty. Shot execution style in their station wagon while four-year-old Becky sat strapped in her car seat. Left there, either on purpose or whoever killed them didn't see her. Neighbors found her the following morning freezing cold and starving. I found some microfiches of old newspaper articles. Speculation at the time was it was an IRA hit. They're in the file, and when the time is right, if she doesn't already, I thought your girl might want to know."

Zander picked up the file and leafed through, studying the grainy black-and-white photos of the couple. Seemed Rebecca looked like her daddy.

"IRA as in Irish Republican Army?"

"Parents were fresh off the boat from Northern Ireland when Rebecca was born in Portland. No family could be located either there or in the US, so she got shoved into the system."

Jesus.

Zander's heart ached for this woman.

"According to her records, she...was a *difficult* child. Prone to night terrors and 'freak-outs' as one foster parent wrote in a report. As a result, never lasted with any particular family."

"How do you get these records—aren't they sealed?"

"Not unless the kid's adopted—she wasn't."

Zander grunted. "Carry on."

"School records, and there were multiple from different states, indicate little Becky was bright, yet intense. Loner, which isn't any wonder considering she never had any chance to make lasting friendships." Carmine paused, then pinched the bridge of his nose. "I gotta tell you, Milan, this woman is breaking my heart."

Zander cleared his throat and nodded.

"She had one quality that stood out. Girl could sing. Sang in every choir in every school she attended. Then in April of nineteen ninety-four disappeared—eight months before her eighteenth birthday. According to the foster family she up and left with no explanation. Never to be heard from or seen again."

"Who is this family?"

"A doctor and his wife from San Diego, Thomas and Jeraldine Madden."

Jesus—Tom and Jerry.

"They had one son, Thomas aka Junior. Details are in the file." Carmine pointed to the manila folder. "Cops did the standard half-assed search until her eighteenth birthday, then dropped it."

"If Rebecca was raped as Terra mentioned, the timeline fits."

"It does indeed and I wanna dig deeper into this family."

Zander nodded. "Appreciate it."

"Moving on to your bar bandits. Don't have much info yet but, the older one is from Moscow. According to my source, he apparently dealt heroin to the wrong oligarch's daughter. And guess what…goes by the name of…"

"Boris."

"Indeed."

A pounding at the front door interrupted them and they looked at each other.

"Expecting someone?" Carmine asked with one eyebrow cocked.

"Could be for Terra."

"Hello?" A female voice called. "Anyone inside?"

Zander walked to the main door and cracked it. Two women and a mutt stared at him. The early afternoon sun shone in his eyes, so he couldn't see their faces clearly. "Not open yet, babe."

"Obviously, since the doors are still locked," one said, tossing straight auburn hair over her shoulder. "We're not here to drink. Well, not in the bar anyway. We're here to pick up Terra."

"In that case, come in." He stepped aside.

"I'm Helen." The petite redhead squared her shoulders and checked him out with a suspicious squint to her eyes. "I'm Terra's best friend and I'm also Petey's big sister. Just so you know, Mr. Magic Ding-Dong, I've got the four-one-one on you."

Magic ding...what?

"That's my girl you've got under your roof and if you so much as put a crinkle in one of those pretty little curls, I know people." She held up a finger and got a little closer. "People who are *connected*."

"Oh, God, Helen," the brunette mumbled behind her. "Nobody says *connected* anymore. Besides, give the man a chance, we don't even know him."

Zander's gaze swiveled to her. He barely had time to notice how attractive she was because his attention swung to the dog. It swaggered into his bar, swinging it's tailless behind with the attitude of a mafia don.

Ugliest damn thing he'd ever seen.

It approached a chair, sniffed its leg, took its time tilting its head to look up at him. Then it grunted, as if giving its approval.

Zander froze.

Damn mutt better not lift its leg and piss on his chair.

"Excuse Helen," the brunette continued. "She's a natural redhead, therefore fiery and a tad over-protective. I'm Shelley De Luca."

Zander dragged his eyes from the dog back to hers. When she stuck out her hand it was small and cool, but her grip was firm.

"I'm guessing you must be Zander," she said, then pointed to the mutt when he let her hand go. "That handsome fellow is Truman. You can relax, he's house-trained. Which means, lucky for you he won't pee on your furniture—unless you piss him off, that is. Then all bets are off because that little bastard carries a grudge and has a mind of his own, which not even I can change sometimes."

Zander wondered if she really meant the dog, or if it wasn't some coded message meant specifically for him. He grinned. Message received. "I'll try not to do that."

"Good." She smiled in return, flashing white teeth. "Then we'll get along just fine."

"This way." He ticked his head towards the swinging doors.

As the women entered, Carmine rose from the table and approached them. "I know those curls," Shelley called as she squinted into the dimness. "What the hell are you doing here, Carmine Niccoterra?"

Zander glanced at the table they had been sitting at and noted the man had stashed the file out of sight.

A smile stretched across Carmine's face, green eyes twinkling as he stepped forward and embraced Shelley in a big bear hug.

"Is it a coincidence you know each other?" Shelley asked, swinging a hand between them when he let her go. "Or are you working?"

"I'm helping Zander with his security system," Carmine answered. "I installed surveillance cameras in the bar and we're smoothing out the wrinkles."

Shelley's eyes narrowed, indicating she wasn't quite buying it. "That's all?"

Zander made a mental note never to underestimate the woman. Not that he knew her, but she apparently was savvy and for all intents and purposes *was* connected, being a daughter, in the truest sense of the word, of the Italian mafia.

"Join us for a drink?" Carmine asked Shelley, though his gaze had shifted to Helen. It was subtle, but Zander swore the man stood taller. He'd seen Carmine get his flirt on numerous times, but there was something different about it.

"Maybe some other time," Shelley answered. Her eyes followed Carmine's, then bit her lip as she noticed it too. "We're here for Terra, but we all should do dinner. You haven't seen Gianni in a while, and I miss Billy."

"Sounds like a plan," Carmine said, then switched his attention back to Helen.

"Whassup?" He grinned the kind of grin Zander assumed would have most single women dropping their panties and heading straight to his bed. Some of the married ones too.

To the mouthy redhead's credit, she seemed unaffected, and cocked an eyebrow.

"Whassup witchou," she answered with a little shoulder dip that offered a whole lot of attitude but no smile in return.

"You got a name?" Carmine's eyes twinkled at the challenge and his smile stretched even wider.

"Nope—you may as well stop right there, buddy. I don't do men."

Carmine's smiled absconded and his jaw dropped a quarter inch. Zander almost burst a blood vessel holding back a laugh. He'd bet real dollars the reaction wasn't anything his friend had experienced from a spicy little redhead before.

"What a coincidence," Carmine said recovering quickly. "Neither do I."

"Well, aren't you special." She again flicked her hair back with a dainty hand and turned to Zander. "Point us to my girl, would you? I need to make assurances."

"Through that door"—he indicated the double swinging doors —"up the stairs, third floor."

He folded his arms, stood back and watched Carmine's gaze follow the women and the mutt's progress as they left. Shelley turned back mouthing a silent *ooh* at them. Then her shoulders shook in silent laughter as she disappeared through the swinging door.

"Shit." Carmine finally turned to Zander. "That's unfortunate. I feel like I've grown horns."

"Only the one in your pants."

Carmine smirked.

Zander let the laugh loose. "Dude, your face."

"Fuck you, Milan." Carmine flipped him the middle finger, which only made Zander laugh harder. "I'm guessing you've never been burned like that before."

"Again, *fuck you*, Milan." Though this time he said it with a chuckle.

Zander allowed himself a few more seconds before he reeled it in and when they took their seats again, he asked, "Shelley know what you do?"

"My uncle Billy is like a dad to her, so she knows more than most."

"That could be a problem for me."

"Time to lay it out for your girl. I suggest sooner rather than later. My experience is women don't like it when they find out you investigated them—just saying."

Zander grunted, wondering exactly how many women his friend had investigated for his own personal curiosity. "You got any more info in that file on Boris?"

"Here's the thing." Carmine shifted in his seat and leaned forward. "My source says there are rumors that since Dean is out of commission, not everyone is ecstatic Vasily took over. A few feel he hasn't earned it—that he's in power only because he's a Melnikov."

"That can't be good."

"A civil war is brewing, and people are gonna die."

Zander's spine straightened.

"This man," Carmine's tone hardened as he pointed to the hardcopy of the screenshot Zander took of the man who caused the fight in his bar. "This fucker is *the* Boris who ran my uncle over with a station wagon, and the man at the center of what's about to be a hostile take-over. And we're not the only one who wants him. Gianni Cadora, Shelley's man, has a vested interest in his whereabouts as well."

Zander didn't like any of what he heard. His breathing got shallower and for the first time in a long while, real fear crept through him.

"I need you to find someone."

"Who's that?"

"Her name is Ruby Baker. She's gone AWOL, but we need to talk to her. The only info I have is *her* phone number, and one that doesn't belong to her." He searched his cell for the unfamiliar number Ruby called from the other night, found it, copied it and Ruby's, then sent them to Carmine's phone.

The man's phone buzzed as it received them. "Why do we need to talk to her?"

"The name of her dealer is also Boris. She called me and gave me a warning: keep him away from Terra. I don't know about you, but my spine is tingling, and I gotta tell you, I'm not liking how his name keeps cropping up."

"Jesus…me neither. This could be worse than we think."

CHAPTER 24

Later Friday afternoon

"Give me a non-hottie over a hottie any day," Helen stated to no one in particular. They had returned from picking up Iris and Terra's Gucci purse via visiting funeral homes and a deli owned by Helen's cousin—where they'd purchased goodies to whip up an antipasto plate.

"Since when?" Terra asked, noting Helen seemed unusually preoccupied while she tilted her face to allow Shelley to apply a clay mask with a brush. She reached across the wrought iron table and angled the clear glass pitcher to refill their mango margaritas. "Wasn't more than a few hours ago you said you'd do Rory because he was hotter than hell."

"I'd still do Rory. Good grief, I'm not dead. Hot men are good for certain things, but those certain things always lead to trouble with an upper-case T. And ever since…well, *you know*,"—she rolled her pretty russet colored eyes—"I'm so over hot men."

"Ever since what?" Shelley paused from rinsing the brush in a small bowl. She had another matching, larger bowl for dipping and rinsing washcloths to wipe their faces once the clay had dried.

"Helen had a really bad break-up and swore off men, but its relative." Terra explained, grateful her friends were occupying her head space with things other than police investigations and funerals. "It all depends on her definition of 'man'. Turns out, her ex had a cocaine habit bad enough to rival an eighties porn star. And"—she held a finger in the air—"get this. He forged her signature on a check and cashed it for two thousand dollars to pay his dealer. Then he dumped her. I mean who does that?"

"Yeah…that's not a man." Shelley agreed. "Only low-life losers with eighties' porn star cocaine habits do that."

"Give me one like Truman," Helen said, reaching down to scratch the dog's ears.

"You're talking about my dog, Truman?" Shelley smirked.

"Yeah, if he were a man, he'd be perfect. He's loyal, funny and nothing but love, and if I were a female dog, I'd be all over that."

"Honey, I hate to break it to you, but Truman's got no balls."

"He doesn't need to have *balls* to have balls. Non-hot men just seem to try harder, that's all I'm saying, which by default makes them hot."

"I hear you, and nine months ago, I would have agreed. I had a series of bad relationships with hot men—then Gianni. That's all *I'm* saying."

"Well, there's always the exception to the rule and I suppose your man is one of them, though I've never seen your man, so I can't really concur. But take that over-the-top hot dude downstairs."

"Which over-the-top hot dude downstairs?" Terra asked. "Zander?"

"No." Helen shook her head. "The other one."

"She means Carmine," Shelley answered, mixing up a fresh batch of her special pore-cleansing goop to plaster on Terra's face.

"Carmine is downstairs?" And yeah, she'd have to agree—the man was over-the-top hot with those yummy Italian genes, broad shoulders and sparkling green eyes, but in her mind Zander topped even him off. Especially now she knew he had a talent *bar none* in the bedroom *and* in the bath tub.

"Men like him have entitlement issues," Helen continued, testing her mask with an index finger. "They think that no woman can say no to them or *should* say no to them."

"I didn't get that impression."

"When did *you* meet him?" Helen asked, raising her eyebrows and putting a crack in the mask.

"Yesterday, when the cop came to interview me about Mom and the baby."

"Carmine came *with* the cop?" Shelley's head tilted as she paused mixing her goop.

"I don't know if they came together but they were there at the same time."

"Hmm," Shelley hummed and furrowed her brow. "Interesting."

"Why's that interesting?" Terra asked.

"Oh—nothing, don't worry about it, just my skeptical brain working overtime," Shelley answered. "He said he's working on Zander's security system."

"Yeah, Zander said that's why he was here yesterday, too. How do you know him?"

"You've heard me talk about Billy?" Shelley asked. "The man who's like a dad to me?"

"Uh huh."

"Well, Carmine's his nephew. He owns a bakery, but he also does other things."

"Do those other things involve dangerous shit?" Helen smirked. "Because he sure looks *dangerous* as shit to me. With all that…dark, curly hair…and stubble and…stuff."

"Oh boy." Shelley giggled and pointed at Helen. "*You* are curious. Though nobody would have guessed the way you dissed him downstairs."

"What? "Terra took a long sip from her margarita and made a rolling gesture with her hand. "This I gotta hear—go on."

"The man asked if I had a name."

"And?"

"She told him she didn't do men."

"Ohmigod!" Terra burst out laughing. "He thinks you're a lesbian?"

"That was the intention."

"Why?"

"I dunno—he just had that look. You know, the one where they wanna crawl between your legs, and I'm so not going there anymore."

"Okay, so on a scale of one to ten, Rory being a seven and a half, where do you rate him?"

"I'd say Rory's an eight and a half, but I'd have to put *him* at a nine point five."

"Good lord, that definitely puts him in panty-dropper class. Even as a *lesbian*"—she made quotation marks with her fingers —"I bet you wouldn't mind."

"That's the problem," Helen squealed. "I wouldn't. But he's the kind of guy it would lead to the aforementioned upper-case T as in trouble. *That* I cannot afford, so best to avoid any chance of it happening. Now, since he thinks I swing the other way, it's no longer an option, so problem solved."

"Don't count on it, honey," Shelley said. "I know Carmine and he's full-blood Italian. You just made it more interesting." Shelley's eyes got wide as she snapped her fingers and pointed both at Helen. "He could help you get your money back from your coked-out wanna-be porn star ex."

"What? How?"

"He knows people." Shelley leaned forward, and stage whispered, "People who are *connected.*"

"Oh…you're making fun of me."

"Just a teeny bit. But really, Carmine *is* connected. He knows people."

Terra's phone chimed with an incoming email. "Hey," she exclaimed after snatching it off the table and checking it. "I got a hit on my purse."

"What do you mean 'hit'?" Shelley asked.

"I'm selling it."

"You're selling your purse?" Helen's voice pitched higher than normal. "That's why you had me bring it here?"

"I have to."

"Why do you have to?"

"I just have to, babe."

"Tee?" Helen's tone got sober. "I need you to tell me why you *have* to sell your purse?"

Shit. What harm could it do now? She'd been quiet about it for so long and look where it got her. Besides, it didn't feel right keeping it from Helen anymore. She blew out a raspberry. "My mom had some money issues with some really bad people and I have to resolve them."

"Like what?"

"Like she stole heroin from her pimp." *And possibly a shipment of whatever.*

"You mean like a baggie?"

"No, babe, I mean like a *big* bag." She held her hands about a foot apart.

Helen jerked straight up, spilling some of her margarita onto her foot. "Holy hell, Tee!"

"Now I've got this Russian dude on my ass."

"Why didn't you tell me?"

"Because you just went through something like that with Cody. I didn't want to pile on. Anyway, I've been paying him off and I've got nothing left, so I have to sell my purse."

"You've got nothing left? I can't believe you've kept this from me. You know I'd help you. And what the hell does this man of yours have to say about all of this?"

"I don't believe we're in the 'he's my man' phase but regardless, he doesn't know I'm selling them."

"Them?"

Terra screwed up her face and chewed on her lower lip. "I may have to sell my rug too."

Helen's jaw dropped in a gasp. "Not your Navajo rug?"

"Yes…my Navajo rug."

"The rug notwithstanding, but your purse, Terra? It's a fucking Dionysus. You can't sell that!"

"I don't even know what a Dionysus purse looks like," Shelley said, cutting in, her tone very serious. "But before you say anymore, I gotta know exactly what you mean by *this Russian dude*. Because Terra, whatever it is, and if you're saying what I think you're saying, you've gotta take this very seriously."

When Terra's gaze came back to Shelley, she had turned a few shades paler. Truman's folded ears twitched as he looked up, then forgoing licking spilled margarita off Helen's foot, he grunted and waddled over to sit by Shelley.

Terra eyed Shelley, an unpleasant sensation growing in her chest. "If you could read between the lines, what would you think I'm saying?"

Shelly gnawed at her thumbnail with her eyes closed for a moment before she spoke. "I never told you, but I was kidnapped recently."

Terra's head jutted forward, her mouth dropping open.

"Wait, did you say kidnapped?" Helen asked.

Shelley placed the bowl and brush on the table and dropped into a chair. Truman moved closer and rested his jowls on her sandaled foot.

"I don't want to get into details because it's still fresh and I don't really wanna relive what happened, but one of those bad relationships I told you I had? Turns out *my* ex wasn't only psycho, he was Russian mob."

"Oh shit," Helen mumbled.

"So, trust me, when I say take this seriously. A couple of his goons snatched me. Broke through security, drugged Gianni's dogs, drugged *me* and drove my ass in a stanky, oil-stained van to Tahoe."

"Shelley…" Terra whispered, leaning over and taking her hand.

"That over-the-top hot dude downstairs"—Shelley looked at Helen—"used his incredible skills and figured out where my ex held me. Then Gianni…"

Shelley closed her eyes and Terra watched her pull her lips in as she fought for control. When she spoke again, her voice broke. "Gianni saved me—but it was close. Honey, whatever you do, do not fuck with the Russians. I almost died."

Despite the sheltered patio and the afternoon sunshine, Terra felt chilled. "And the men that took you—what are their names?"

"Dean called one Boris."

Dean?

"Ohmigod, do you mean Dean Melnikov?"

Shelley seemed to stop breathing as she turned her head in her direction. "Do you know him, Terra?"

"Dean used to be my mother's pimp, but I've never met him. Only his brother, Vasily."

The afternoon air had become thick, almost palpable, as Terra remembered the creepy feeling she'd gotten a few nights ago when she felt she was being watched. Her heart pounded as blood whooshed in her ears. "What does this Boris person look like?"

"I don't know," Shelley whispered. "I never saw his face but the one thing that sticks out is he smelled of cigarettes."

The hairs on Terra's arms stood tall.

Cigarettes.

A lot of people smoked and smelled like cigarettes, but she knew it. She could feel it in the base of her skull—it was the same man who picked up the money every Saturday. The one who threatened to chop of her digits if she didn't pay.

A sharp pain resulted on her tongue filling her mouth with a metallic taste, and she took an icy sip from the remnants of her drink to wash the copper away. Though swallowing had suddenly become difficult and the alcohol stung her tongue.

"Fuck." Helen stood, looking dazed. The metal chair she vacated scraped across the patio floor, making a sharp, grating sound. She smoothed her skirt before grabbing the empty pitcher off the table and headed inside. "We're gonna need more margaritas."

CHAPTER 25

Friday afternoon

Zander hit the gym hard. Terra's girls were still out on the patio when he went upstairs to change from his jeans to sweatpants, and he didn't want to intrude.

Carmine's report had left him uneasy and frustrated, yet strangely focused. He pummeled on his favorite hundred-pound boxing bag, mixing up his routines with spinning elbows, jumping front kicks and enough roundhouses to turn his legs into lead.

Situated on the first floor of an old pre-war building two blocks away from the bar, it stank of sweat and dirty socks. He was pretty sure that some of the smudges on the wall were dried blood, in clear violation of all kinds of health codes.

The owner, Jack Mulroney, had been a friend of Chuck's and his biker brotherhood. They'd pressed weights, boxed and strategized before drinking beer and bourbon at the bar. A win–win relationship that carried to this day, though it was just the two of them now. The others being long dead or having moved on. It was exactly the kind of place Zander could be free, let loose and think without any of the frills or the distractions of a regular gym.

"Watch your footwork on your cross jabs, son," the old man puffed behind him. The surviving son of a father–son operation, he looked older than God and probably was. "Keep moving, vary your patterns, don't be predictable."

Zander adjusted his movements as the old man instructed and after Jack left, satisfied with his adjustments and after another series of brutal punch–kick combinations, he called it quits. As he didn't trust the plumbing, he never showered at the gym and today was no exception. He wiped the sweat from his face with a towel he pulled from his gym bag, zipped up his black hoodie with the Chuck's logo on it and stepped outside into the breeze. Just as he cracked the seal on a bottle of water, he heard her.

"Zannie."

"Fuck," he muttered. He turned to spot her, dressed in a shortish black skirt and a denim jacket with sheep skin around the collar leaning her back against the wall. Had she followed him?

"Yo." He paused and chugged some water, wondering how long she'd been waiting. "What you doing here? This isn't the best neighborhood for you to hang in."

"Waiting for you," she said, wobbling a little on her wedge-heeled booties as she fell into step next to him.

"I got that part."

"I took a long lunch because I wanted to talk to you. You're ignoring my texts."

It was then he realized he wasn't even sure what she did for a living. Paralegal or something of that nature.

"Yeah, those texts." Terra accidentally seeing them didn't sit well. In fact, it made his gut burn like he'd eaten an extra spicy pot of vindaloo curry—the kind known to kill a man and make a widow. "I'm gonna ask you to stop with the photos." He didn't mention he'd already blocked her number.

"Why? You never minded before."

That part was true—he hadn't. He was a man after all.

"You don't think I'm hot anymore?"

Yep.

"Things have changed. So, it's good we're having this conversation."

"Changed? In three days?"

More like eight—but who was counting.

"Zannie, I know I acted badly. I'm here to apologize and I thought you'd enjoy the pictures but maybe I'm overdoing it."

As she leaned in, getting too close, he smelled the booze on her breath and he recoiled slightly.

"Okay," she continued, "I admit I made a fool of myself and I shouldn't have acted like that. Not in your bar. I know we don't have a *relationship* relationship and I've never minded the other women before, and I don't know why I behaved like that and I wanna make up for it."

"Told you there's no need, babe. But I'm also telling you we're done."

"What?" Her eyes got big, exposing how bloodshot they were. "What do you mean, we're done?"

He made a circle motion with the bottle he held. "Us, whatever you wanna call what us was—it's over."

"No." Her voice pitched higher as she grabbed his arm. "Zannie, don't do that. Please...I really am sorry."

"It's not about what happened at my bar."

"Then what? Tell me so I can fix it."

"Look," he said, as he came to a stop at a corner one block from his building, joining a small crowd of people waiting to cross the street. He turned to face her. "Like I said, things have changed. There's something I wanna explore and if we're still fucking, it's not gonna work."

She let out air like she'd been gut-punched but it didn't stop her voice getting loud. "It's her, isn't it? The curly redhead? The one you blew me off for."

He didn't answer as he didn't see the point in escalating this further, not in front of a bunch of nosy assholes who'd looked up from their phones.

"What does she do?" Heather's tone became desperate and she reached for his arm. "She got a trick that gets you off? I can learn, you just gotta show me."

"Heather, stop."

"Or is it just me? You don't like *me* anymore?"

He looked down at her hand gripping him, her nails digging into his skin through the hoodie sleeve and took a deep breath.

He *had* blown her off, but he'd never lied or promised more than he'd given but it was clear now that she wanted more.

"It's not just you," he said as gently as he could.

Though her face had gone pale, the lines around her lips hardened. As she stood in front of him, the breeze whipped her platinum hair across her face. When she brushed it aside he noticed she was older than he'd always thought.

"Well, that's something I guess," she said, swallowing.

The light changed, and the throng of people started to move.

"I wish you the best, Zannie, but you're not the kind of man to stick to one woman. I've always understood that, and I've always accepted it." She released her hold on his forearm and slipped her arms around his neck, clinging to him as she lifted herself on her toes to kiss him. ·

He let her, only because he wasn't a dick, but kept his lips closed. When she pushed her tongue between his lips, he tasted the alcohol and stiffened, twisting his head enough to break it. Though she wouldn't let go until he wrapped his palms around her wrists and pulled her arms from his neck.

"We're done, Heather."

She stared at him, then shook her head. After she backed up a few steps, he saw something he didn't like slither across her face. Something territorial and ugly.

"I don't think so," she said before turning. He watched her walk away, the bad vibe sinking into his bones and growing with each step she took until she was out of sight. Then he waited a few beats longer just to make sure she didn't turn around, before jogging across the street, just as the red hand in the pedestrian light stopped flashing.

Five minutes later, back in his apartment, that sense of unease still hadn't left him, until he found Terra sitting alone on the balcony with her back to the open French doors, strumming a guitar, singing softly.

He leaned his shoulder against the door post and listened. There was something about her voice that gave him goosebumps every fucking time. A combination of raw and sweet that reached inside and tugged at his gut.

Had it really only been just over a week?

In some ways it felt like he'd known her longer, like she'd been on the edges of his life, just out of sight, waiting to cross over. And now she had, he couldn't imagine her not filling up his space. She fit. And he liked her sitting on his patio with her pretty, shiny curls lifting in the breeze against the backdrop of Ginny's hydrangeas.

He liked *her*.

He really fucking liked her.

She turned her head and caught him staring like a horny adolescent crushing on his girl.

"Freckle," he said, having to clear his throat. Then he came around, so she didn't have to twist her neck and pulled an iron chair in front of her.

"Zander." She smiled and bit her lip, then put the instrument aside. He took her hand and kissed the tips of her fingers on those little guitar calluses. It was a sad smile, and along with touching her skin, being so close, looking into those gorgeous eyes, it did things to his chest.

"What you up to, babe?"

"Learning a couple of songs. One I'm thinking about singing at my mom's memorial. The other is pretty cool—an oldie from a Dutch band from the seventies that Dannie discovered. It's called "Radar Love" and I have to know it for rehearsal tomorrow night."

She was gonna see Dannie tomorrow?

Fuck.

"You think that's a good idea?"

"Going to rehearsal?" Those perfect brows came together.

"Don't wanna scare you, babe, but there could be something to that feeling you had of being watched." Though he wasn't going to go into too much detail of what Carmine shared, he needed to stress, for his own sanity, the danger she was in. "I'm not letting you take chances."

"I'm aware, and I'm not taking chances. I'll be with my guys."

Her guys?

What the fuck.

He should be her guy. Singular. Period!

"I'm not going to stop living my life, Zander and if I want to be back in the band I have to commit."

"I understand that, but don't you think rehearsals should wait?"

"Wait? No!" Terra sat up straighter. "They can't wait! We have gigs."

"Babe, cancel it. I'll give you all the gigs you need."

"Zander, I'm not cancelling rehearsal."

"Woman." He fought to keep the gruff out of his voice and wasn't sure he did a decent job at succeeding. "Cancel it."

She yanked her hand, but he refused to let go, instead pulling her closer.

"No—and since when do you get to boss me around?"

Christ, she was pretty...the way her eyes flashed fire when she got all indignant and...*pretty.*

He smiled because he couldn't help himself. "Since I know what you taste like."

He brought her index finger to his mouth and sucked, curling his tongue around the digit. It tasted like fruit and salt, but they both knew it wasn't her fingers he referred to. He saw it in the way her eyes darkened, her pupils dilated, and her breathing quickened.

"And since I've been inside you and made you come, more than a dozen times."

"You're counting?" she whispered.

"Every single one."

"Why?"

He considered her question for a long time while his pulse beat in his throat. A fresh bead of sweat trickled down his neck that had nothing to do with his workout and everything to do with the woman in front of him. Then he answered, choosing his words carefully, hoping he didn't expose himself too bare. "I'm invested, woman."

Those pretty lashes fluttered, then she bit her lip.

"Invested in what?"

"In you...and your safety."

Uncertainty, or maybe skepticism, flickered through her gaze as she blinked at him. "That's sweet of you to worry about my safety, but I'm not cancelling."

He sighed and let it go—for now and only because of what he saw in her eyes.

Her hand came to his face and smoothed back a strand that fell across his face "I like your hair long."

He drew his mouth slowly over her finger, sucking before letting go of her hand. Reaching behind to pull his T-shirt over his head, he tossed it onto the table. He knew he wasn't bad-looking. Had been told often enough, but he'd never thought much about it other than it got him laid. However, her liking any tiny fucking thing about him made his heart beat like one of those techno-pop songs at a rave he once attended in his teens.

"Just forget to get it cut, Freckle, but I gotta admit I like that you like it."

"I do," she said softly. "Why don't you take a shower, I'll get dinner started."

"What's on the menu?"

"Grilled salmon, baby potatoes and asparagus."

His stomach rumbled at the thought. "Anything for dessert?"

She smiled again. This time it wasn't sad. This time it carried a hint of things they'd already done to each other, things that blew every fuse in his body.

"Just me," she said and blushed.

That he didn't just *feel* in his dick.

That made his dick rock solid.

On that note, he went and took his shower and had to fight to keep his hands off himself as the anticipation of *her* on the menu was almost more than he could take.

CHAPTER 26

Friday night...later

"Fuck," Zander grumbled, then let out a frustrated sigh. "I've gotta work tonight, babe." He thumbed a reply to a text, waited for the whoosh confirming it had sent, then stuck it back in his pocket. "Nicky's son is sick, so I'm gonna have to cover her shift."

"Oh, that's not good," Terra said, rinsing the remnants of leftover salmon from a platter at his double sink and passing it to Zander. "The little guy okay?"

As he stacked it along with the other dishes in the dishwasher, it struck her how easily he moved around the kitchen. Zander by nature was neat and organized. And best of all—he didn't leave her to do all the cleanup. Whereas Dannie, on the other hand "didn't do dishes" and considered the floor another shelf in the closet.

Another check mark in the *For* column.

"Just normal kid stuff, but it's definitely not good."

She watched him take a sip of the wine he'd opened to pair with the fish, then set the glass back on the counter.

"Specially as I was looking forward to enjoying my dessert." He grabbed her from behind, wrapping his arms around her waist, sucking softly on the delicate skin below her ear. His lips were cold from the chilled wine, but his tongue was hot and decadent. "Then I planned on repeating whatever we enjoyed."

She shivered as his stubble tickled but her nipples hardened, poking through her filmy blouse. "You've got sex on the brain."

"Fuck, yeah—you would too if you were me looking at you and judging by what's happening in your bra—so do you." He cleared his throat, then ran his hands down her waist—positioning them on her hips and moved her gently to the side, away from the sink.

"You say the sweetest things," she teased, while he retrieved a soap pod, placed it in the dishwasher drawer, shut it and turned it on. "I can't believe it was just a few days ago I thought you were a jerk."

He stopped moving, then angled his body slowly to focus on her. "What did you say?" His head tilted, his expression changing to that of a smoldering badass, the one she was sure he used to intimidate misbehaving customers into behaving.

Oh...God.

Instead of scaring her—it had the opposite effect, making her blood rush. "Yeah," she bit her lip, and peeked at him through her lashes. "You were one, giant...jerk."

His eyes widened for a split second. Then he advanced on her like a stalking cat, stepping into her space, he clutched a bunch of her curls and held her fast.

"You're in deep shit," he growled into her nape. Though his voice was gruff, it carried a hint of play. Her breathing stopped, and she didn't doubt for one moment he knew exactly what his voice did to her. That charge of alpha pheromones spoke to an ancient part of her DNA—turning her on something fierce.

"After I plied that sexy little mouth with wine. . ." He tugged her head back gently, exposing her neck.

Her skin erupted in goosebumps as he nipped her shoulder. "God!" She giggled and squirmed, wiggling herself against his hips. "You see? This is why you're a jerk. You don't play fair."

"Neither do you, babe," he chuckled. "Just so you know, I'm never gonna play fair when you move your ass like that," he said this grazing his chin over her skin and into the crook of her neck. "I'm just wondering what I'm gonna do to make you pay."

His available hand cupped her breast, toying with her nipple over her top, scraping his thumb over the tight nub.

A flush moved up her chest and neck, then she circled her hips, ground herself against him.

"Fuck." He hissed through his teeth, and when he spoke again his voice had gone husky. "I want you."

With that, he tugged her head back and dove in, taking her lips. That unmistakable chemistry ignited as his tongue plundered her mouth—demanding more until they were both panting, fighting for breath and fumbling with each other's clothes.

Her fingers shook while she undid his jeans' buttons and pulled the zip, allowing him to spring free. His eyes blazed as he pushed her jeans down past her knees, then yanked them from her ankles. He spun her around, and supporting her around the waist, he kicked her feet apart and stepped between them. Skating one palm up her spine till he reached the base of her neck to keep her in place on the counter, he positioned the other on her hip and entered her—hard.

They both gasped and froze while she adjusted. There was tension in his thighs as he held himself taut waiting for her signal. When she gave it, he began to move with some measure of control. But when she pushed herself back, giving herself completely to him—looking over her shoulder their eyes connecting, she watched him lose it.

Completely fucking lose it.

And something between them shifted—something monumental—she could feel it. Like two tectonic plates deep below the earth's surface. The resulting earthquake made her vulnerable and exposed, but she didn't care. The look in his eyes, that unfettered primal need—the same look she was sure he could read in hers—made her lose it too.

It was hard, and fast and dirty as hell. Her mouth dropped open, her eyes squeezed shut and she cried out as she detonated around him. A second later his body stiffened in response, then he groaned and fired into her.

A long moment later, when it was over, he collapsed on her, his heart thumping against her back, his breath rasping unevenly on her skin.

"Christ, baby," he said in a voice that was unsteady. "What the fuck was that?" His knuckles grazed her shoulder as he moved her hair away, then he laid kisses in the hollow between her shoulder blades.

In that moment, she knew he'd felt it too—that shift.

"I don't know."

"I've never lost it like that before. I have no control when it comes to you. My brains pretty much leak out my skull."

"Zander," she whispered. "We just did it without a condom."

He went tense. "Fuck…shit…Jesus, I'm sorry."

"I'm on birth control, so that end is covered."

"And I've never fucked without a condom so *that* end is covered too," he said as he pulled out slowly, then snagged a few paper towels from the roll sitting on its silver holder on the counter.

"I got tested," she murmured as she turned to face him. "After Dannie and Ruby—well, you know—and I'm clean."

"Never thought you weren't, Freckle"—he tilted her face and kissed the tip of her nose— "but thank you for telling me." Then he dropped to his knees and wiped between her legs. Doing it in a way that was sweet and tender—like a man taking care of his woman—and like he cared a whole lot.

"Ah…shit!" He grimaced, getting to his feet when he was done. "Ruby—I just remembered."

"What?"

"She had a message for you." He fastened his button then he reached down to snag her thong and jeans off the floor.

"She wanted me to tell you she was sorry about your mother."

Her eyes flicked to his face, wondering when he had spoken to her. "At least she's sorry for something."

While she pulled on her pants and adjusted her clothing, he dumped the soiled paper towels into the garbage.

"There's something else. I should've told you earlier, but I didn't want to spoil dinner. Shit has escalated."

"Escalated how?"

He moved back to stand in front of her, placing his hands on her hips and looking into her eyes. "Vasily has a challenger to head the Melnikov organization. A dude named Boris."

"Boris?" She blinked.

"You know that name?" he asked, one eyebrow forming a perfect arch.

"Shelley mentioned a man named Boris kidnapped her, and after everything she told me about him, I also think he's the man who I make a payment to every week." She pointed to the side of her neck. "He's got a tattoo right here…like a cross, or a dagger."

His fingers dug into her hips. "Jesus."

She stared at him as something dawned. "When I asked Vasily why his men started that fight in your bar, he acted like he was unaware. He said you had to be wrong. I accused his men of going rogue, but if he *does* have a challenger, maybe he *wasn't* aware."

"You talked to Vasily?" Two vertical lines formed above the bridge of his nose. "When?"

"I called him today."

She felt his thighs and torso tense between her legs a second before he pulled away. "You call him often?" His hands left her hips, dropping to his sides while he scanned her eyes.

She shook her head. "It's the first time I've talked to him on the phone."

The relaxed, post orgasmic expression had left his face, along with the softness in his eyes and voice. "You just happen to have his number?"

"He gave it to me."

"This is the man who broke into your apartment, Terra. Remember?"

"Of course, I remember…"

"So…what—everything's peachy between you now? You just called to gossip?"

"No!"

"Or is there something else I need to know about?"

"Ohmigod…I'm not fucking him if that's what you're asking. Don't be an ass."

"*I'm* being an ass?"

"What's the big deal, Zander?"

"The deal is, woman, we don't know what the fuck *his* deal is. You shouldn't be talking to him until we do."

Perhaps it was because her emotions were raw in light of the phenomenal sex they'd just had, but she bristled at his tone, her own body stiffening as she moved out of his space.

"I have to talk to him," she snapped. "I owe him money."

"How much?"

"It doesn't matter how much. I sold something and once the funds clear I'll have enough for this week's payment. But I'm gonna try to renegotiate with him because I also have rent and my mom's funeral to pay for."

He leaned in and cupped her face, ignoring her attempt to move his hands. "Freckle, stop."

"But…"

"Stop."

"Don't tell me to…"

"Stop."

She stopped and glared at him.

"How much do you owe?"

"Five thousand."

"For what?"

"My mom"—she stalled, then took a deep breath and let it out—"my mom stole heroin."

"Fuck." He said it like all the air escaped from his lungs. His hands left her face and he stepped back, scraping them through his hair. "Listen to me. You don't need to sell anything, and you don't need to pay him. What that asshole is doing is illegal as fuck and now your mom is no longer with us, he's got no leverage. He can't hurt her anymore."

"But he can hurt me."

"You think for one second I'm going to let him near enough to hurt you?"

"You don't understand. He told me bad things will happen if I don't…well, actually, it was this *Boris* character who said bad things will happen…but Shelley told me not to mess with the Russians and I just happen to agree with her. I don't want bad things to happen to me, Zander."

"Are you're not hearing me? *I'm* not gonna let bad things happen to you. Which is why *you're* gonna let me deal with Vasily and this Boris dude. It's also why you shouldn't go to rehearsal tomorrow. Not while you think you're being watched."

She let out an exasperated breath. "Is this another one of your rules?"

"If you want."

"I don't want! And it's not fair that you're the one making them all, telling me who I can or can't speak too or what I should be doing. I have a say in what's happening here."

"Of course you do, woman, but in the meantime, you're staying away from Vasily."

"Why?"

"Making yourself a bigger target than you already are isn't exactly a smart move." His eyes flashed…something—though she couldn't say what. He moved a step away, his jaw tightening and for all kinds of wrong reasons that rubbed her the wrong way.

"What do you mean target?" she asked, grabbing his arm, stopping him as he turned away from her.

"The man wants between your legs, and I don't like one fucking bit that he wants between your legs. You talking to him is only going to make him want that more."

"You don't know that! And even if he does, it's none of your business."

He growled at that, but she ignored it and carried on.

"You want to tell me you don't have women who want what's between *your* legs?"

"That's different."

What?

"Why's it different?"

"Because it just is, Freckle."

"Ohmigod!" She rolled her eyes. "That is the most sexist thing I've ever heard and I'm telling you right now this one-sided, double-standard bullshit is not going to work for me."

"What are you talking about?"

"How do you think I feel when I know you're hiding something? You won't check your texts in front of me. I'm not telling *you*, you can't talk to women." *Even though she really wanted to.* "What are they doing—sending nudies of themselves?"

It was just a flicker, a slight widening of his eyes but she caught it. The resulting punch to her solar plexus took her by surprise and left her breathless.

"Oh, good God!" Shock reflected in her voice. "They *are*, aren't they?"

She attempted to move past him, put some distance between them, but Zander stopped her. She slapped at his arms and shoved his chest before he caught her wrists and twisted them behind her back. Which brought him flush with her body.

"You don't need to worry about them, *that's* what's different."

"You have some nerve telling me what to do." She glared at him tilting her chin.

"They're nothing."

"I don't care what you…"

He trapped both her wrists in one hand, caught her at the back of her head with his other. Then he took her mouth and there was nothing gentle about it. This kiss was punishing and possessive. She tried to turn her head and push him away, but his grip was ironclad. Caught between being mad at him and wanting him madly didn't help and despite her fighting it, and the fact that they had literally just fucked like rabbits, sensations built. He let go of her wrist and slipped his hand under her blouse. He groaned into her mouth and the kiss turned deep and slow and greedy as he ate at her. Suddenly he broke away. Panting hard, he stared into her eyes, his dark and solemn, glazed yet tinged with anger…and jealousy?

"I deleted those photos," he said, his tone low and dangerous. "And I blocked her. You gonna delete Vasily's number?"

She stared up at him.

"No," she finally said.

He released his hold on her hair, clamped them around her shoulders and put her away.

"Right." His jaw spasmed. "Didn't fucking think so." With that, and without looking back, he stalked to his front door, opened it, and after stepping through, pulled it closed.

She stared after him, then collapsed back against the counter, covering her face with her hands.

What the hell just happened?

She blew a loose curl off her forehead and reached for her

glass, noticing her hands shook.

Okay—so he deleted them.

Deleted or not, it didn't mean she liked he got them. In fact, she hated it that he got them. It made her feel insecure and anxious, like the ugly girl in a room full beauty queens. She didn't need that right now.

Perhaps it was time to rethink her situation, step back for a moment and slow whatever was happening between them down. She had bigger problems to deal with.

She poured the last of the wine into her glass, grabbed Rebecca's guitar and stepped outside onto the patio, shivering slightly at the cool air. Music soothed her—usually. But as her fingers found the positions and she plucked at the strings, her mind couldn't connect. It wasn't reaching her.

Her brain was like a windmill. Each thought a color-coded flag zipping past. Her mother—Zander—Vasily—Boris—spinning around and around. They all morphed into one giant blur and she couldn't make sense out of any of them. Finally, frustrated, she went back inside and put the instrument aside before her head exploded.

She finished cleaning the kitchen, straightened the already pristine living room, and with nothing else left to do, decided to test the stackable washer-slash-dryer she'd discovered he had in that louvered closet located off the kitchen.

Since her clothes weren't enough for a load, she set about sorting Zander's, separating lights from darks in two neat little piles on the tiled floor. On top of the dark pile, lay the faded gray, many-times washed T-shirt he'd worn earlier.

It was still damp with his sweat when she held it to her face and drew him in. His deodorant, a faint, yet definite whiff of him, of his sweat—and a tinge of something not Zander-like.

Something heavier.

Perfume.

That T-shirt had been clean earlier.

She'd seen him take it neatly folded from his drawer. Therefore, some woman got close enough to lay her scent on him.

And he'd let her!

Her head filled with images of that Heather person, rubbing herself like a cat against Zander and him doing things to her like they just did in the kitchen.

Then images of Dannie and Ruby the day she'd caught them. That glassy, gleeful look Ruby had tossed her as she went to town on Dannie's cock.

The salmon and wine in her stomach churned, saliva pooled in her mouth and moments after that, she emptied the contents and then some into the toilet.

They were joined by her tears.

This wasn't going to work.

It was all too much, yet at the same time not enough.

That perfume didn't have to mean anything. There could be a perfectly innocent explanation. But she was a realist and had to consider that there may not. Especially in light of those nudies.

He's a D.O.G. Terra.

Yeah—it hurt to admit Helen may be right, that perhaps he was. He got one chance—*one chance* to convince her otherwise.

Maybe this was all her fault. Maybe she had read in too much in what he considered being *invested*. He hadn't promised anything, but he made her believe…what exactly?

That he cared?

She rinsed her mouth, washed her face, did the laundry, stuck it in the dryer and when that was done, folded. After putting his away, she put hers in her little suitcase that sat in the corner next to his dresser.

Then curled up on the couch and watched a Bridget Jones movie, which she'd normally find hilarious, but tonight just wasn't. Before it was over, she went to bed.

When she woke at 4:05 a.m. according to her phone, she was alone. And still alone when she fell asleep again at five.

CHAPTER 27

Saturday morning

Zander surfaced the moment she untangled herself from his leg, her warmth slipping away. His spread palm planed across the sheets to capture her before she left the bed, but she shifted out of range before he could reach her. He let out a sleepy sigh and watched her walk to the bathroom. More accurately, through one eye he watched her cute little pink-shorty-pajama-covered butt cheeks walk to the bathroom.

He smiled. The woman liked pink. Noted.

First up after she did her thing, he'd apologize for being an ass. Because she was right—he was an ass. He hadn't stopped thinking about it all night. The woman bent his head backwards so far it took hours of therapy to straighten it.

He'd kiss her, show her exactly how sorry he was until she accepted his apology—because, dammit, they had chemistry. Explosive, combustive, ball-shattering chemistry that blew his brain cells into the stratosphere and sent his jealousy quotient somewhere past Mars.

But it was more than that.

She was more than that.

The bathroom door opened but instead of heading toward him with those curved hips swaying, she veered right and left the room without looking at him.

Huh.

He didn't like that.

That needed fixing.

Should've been his first clue.

Stretching, he winced as his aching muscles creaked and reminded him to not overdo his workout. He kicked the comforter off and puttered naked into the bathroom and did *his* thing. After which he washed his hands and splashed water on his face. Then rifled through his draw for a clean pair of sweats, observing the T-shirt he wore yesterday neatly folded on top.

She'd done his laundry. Again, he smiled because *that* he liked. It felt right and sweet.

Terra stood in his kitchen holding a mug against her chest, staring at the coffee maker. The set of her mouth, the way she ignored him, suggested she was feeling a little less than sweet.

Should've been clue number two.

"Staring at it isn't gonna speed it up, babe?" he said, scraping his hair back from his face in an attempt to lighten the mood.

She looked up, catching his eyes, and damn him if he didn't feel frostbite in his balls.

Jesus, how badly *had* he fucked up?

He kept her in his sights as he approached her. "Something wrong?"

The mug connected with the counter making a loud thud, but she said nothing.

Yeah—something was wrong.

"Coffee is almost ready," she declared. "Would you like a cup?"

"Please."

"How do you take it?"

"Hot, blonde and sweet, just like you." That didn't get him the smile he was hoping for either—not even a lip twitch.

"I'm not blonde."

Fuck.

Sweet was definitely *not* on the agenda this morning. Neither, it seemed, was she.

"Strawberry blonde. Tomato, tomahto babe—you're much prettier than any blonde I know."

"Am I?" She poured milk into his cup, dumped two spoons of sugar into it and pushed it across the counter to him. Like she planned on keeping the granite between them. He ignored it and entered the kitchen, aiming straight for her. She sidestepped but he countered, planting a palm to her chest and pushing until he had her backed up against the fridge. He would have kept going but she stationed the milk between them like it was her personal bodyguard.

"You wanna clue me in to what's swirling around in that beautiful head? You still mad about last night?"

She made a little snort, rolling her eyes and that really needled him. Nevertheless, he kept it calm.

"What can I do to fix it, Freckle?"

"I'm not in the mood for talking right now."

Right.

"Give me the milk," he ordered.

She hesitated for a second, then made the correct choice and handed him the plastic gallon container. He immediately freed himself of it, setting it down on the counter.

"First—good morning." He connected with her body, relishing her warmth against his skin.

"Morning," she clipped, placing her hands flat on his chest with her fingers spread. They were cold from the milk container and full of tension, implicating it wasn't a good morning after all.

"Second, I think it's time to establish rule number three."

Her eyes flicked up, then sideways, but she remained quiet.

"We say good morning or good evening or whatever kind of greeting, there's gonna be a kiss along with that."

She didn't move and definitely did not offer her lips.

"Woman."

She glanced up and he wasn't excited about what he saw, figuring this went well beyond their argument last night.

A long breath escaped him. "Okay babe, you're gonna have to help me out." He pushed a loose curl behind her ear and didn't like how she flinched. "Something has crawled up your ass, but I can't read your mind."

"No, I suppose you can't."

"So, you wanna explain the attitude."

"*My* attitude?"

Okay, damn. Maybe he shouldn't have used *attitude*, but tiptoeing wasn't his forte and last he checked he still had his balls —even if they were frostbitten. "Yeah, babe—your attitude."

"Okay fine, I'll explain *my* attitude. I told you, before we started this I wasn't like your other women." She shoved against his chest, but he stayed put, barely rocking. "Move."

He didn't move. "I remember."

"I'm not interchangeable."

"What's that supposed to mean?"

"Please move away."

"Not until you explain."

"It means, where do you go at night, Zander?"

Fuck.

He realized his mistake. She'd been asleep when he checked in on her after the bar closed and still asleep when he climbed in next to her four hours later. But what the fuck did he know about the sleeping habits of women, since he never spent the night. He'd definitely classified himself as a wham-bam-thank-you-ma'am kind of man—until her. His chest squeezed tight as he didn't want to lie but he wasn't ready to share that part of himself.

Not yet.

He took a step back and rubbed the back of his neck. "Have I given you reason not to trust me? You think I'm creeping out at night and giving it to someone else while I have you in my bed?"

"I don't know." Those big blues came at him, so full of fire it burned right through him. "Are you?"

"You shitting me?"

She sucked in that bottom lip and chewed on it in a way that, despite him being pissed, did things to him.

"Babe, I've got another apartment downstairs and I do shit down there that I'm not ready to share."

"Why not—is it illegal?"

"Illegal? Fuck—really?"

"If it's not illegal, why can't you tell me?"

"It's personal and you either trust me or you don't."

"I want to."

"Then why can't you? You think I'd screw you over?"

"Well, that's the thing. It's been my experience with men lately, and I don't know you well enough to have reason to believe otherwise."

"Yeah, well I can say the same about you. I don't know you well enough to share what I do down there with you, yet."

"Fair enough, but when I'm in your apartment and you aren't in bed with me, I don't know where you are or who you're with or what you're doing to who you're with, it's a little disconcerting. I realize we're not in a relationship and this is just fucking to you because you're *that* guy."

Just fucking—that guy—*what?*

"You brought me here," she continued. "You told me to pack a bag. I did not show up at your door uninvited."

"Where the hell is this coming from?" He kinda had the feeling that no matter what he said, this was headed for a train wreck and he just had to brace himself for the impact.

"I know I have no right to question who you're with. God

knows it's my own fault for not getting to know you better first. Maybe…no, definitely, I shouldn't have given it up so easily or perhaps given it up at all. But I didn't think you'd treat me with so little respect."

"Respect?"

"Obviously those other women don't care, but I'm not *that* girl, so take that little nugget and add it to what you know about me."

"Babe, what the fuck are you talking about?"

"I did your laundry."

"Yeah…?"

"And I don't know where you were at four a.m."

"Okay…?"

"Or at five."

Fuck.

"God, you must think I'm stupid."

"What I think is you don't trust me."

"I could smell her," she yelled.

"What…?"

"On your T-shirt."

Shit.

Shit!

He closed his eyes to process. *Heather—when she kissed him.* When he opened them again—that fucking look on her face. Jesus, it hurt—and it pissed him off more.

"Like I said. You don't fucking trust me. It was nothing."

"So, there was someone."

"She's not *someone*."

"Then where did you go last night?"

"I was downstairs."

"What do you do in that apartment?"

"It's none of your business, Freckle."

"None of my business?" She gasped. "Okay—was she with you?"

"No, she wasn't with me. Ever heard of the benefit of the doubt?"

"I actually did give you the benefit of the doubt, didn't want to think it…but now…"

"But what? You got some fucked-up notion all men are your ex because of what Dannie did to you?"

"No…don't you fucking go there."

"You went there, didn't you? You fucking think I'm like him—can't keep my dick in my pants?"

Again…the look on her face and again and he couldn't stop his anger from notching higher.

"Don't put words in my mouth, Zander." Her voice dropped to just above a whisper. "I don't have the headspace to sort it all out, but you *have no idea* how much that hurt."

Shit.

He didn't understand it, but she may as well have slid a knife into his heart.

"I've had enough," he grunted and cut her off because he couldn't stand to hear her say it. How much fucking *feeling* she had for that piece-of-shit. That she put him in that same fucking class.

"I'm not listening to any more of this crap and just for your fucking information—maybe you don't realize what you just said —how much *that* fucking hurts."

"Zander, I was going to say—"

"It doesn't matter what you were going to say, woman. I'm done discussing this. When you're in a better *mood*, or open to fucking trusting me, we can talk about it then."

He should've felt some satisfaction when her eyes filled, or when her face crumpled, but the burn in his chest and the glass in his throat made it impossible. His almost cracked a tooth as he bit down so hard keeping it off his face, stalking out the kitchen, avoiding her eyes until he made it through his front door without slamming it.

It was when he entered his office, slamming *that* door that he couldn't hold it together anymore and he collapsed onto his couch, dropping his head against the backrest. He sat with his hands clenched in his hair staring at the ceiling, not giving a fuck while totally giving a fuck.

Train-fucking-wreck.

He'd made her cry.

Jesus, she pissed him off.

Because of her feelings for Dannie?

Or was it because she made *him* feel...?

Fuck.

She made him feel.

He swore he'd never feel again—that day on the beach he'd let his mother go.

Feeling fucking hurt.

But hurting Terra fucking hurt more and *he'd made her fucking cry.*

He let out a groan while he rubbed his face, then found the remote to his TV and turned it on. Tried and fucking failed to watch the basketball rerun of the Warriors vs Cavaliers final. All he saw were figures dribbling back and forth. He was so out of his depth with this woman, he'd never touch bottom—not without drowning.

Problem was—he *was* drowning—in her.

He just needed to process—calm his ass down and figure *them* out.

Fatigue began to ebb through his muscles, so he adjusted his position on the couch, shoved a pillow under him with his head on the arm rest. Then he closed his eyes, listening to the game while he focused on the progress he'd made on her painting. The blue of her eyes, with those pale little lines, those strawberry curls and that cluster of freckles on her nose. Even the little guitar calluses on her finger tips. He didn't mind them—in fact he loved them. They were *her*.

Finally, he relaxed and dozed off.

Christ, even his dreams were so real he could feel her hands traveling up his thighs, grazing over his dick, straddling him, like she did when she woke him in his bed.

Something landed on his face—by the feel of the fabric he guessed her T-shirt. Which meant she was topless, her gorgeous tits available and ripe for grabbing. It sent blood heading south.

Her hand dug into his sweats, clasped around him, squeezing his cock.

"Fuck, babe," he hissed, still half asleep, clasping her hips. Her hand aimed his tip at her hot, wet center. "That's one fucking way to forgive a man."

In the midst of all the sensations rolling through his body he began to wake up. One tiny part of his brain registered it smelled different.

Wrong.

Not like Terra.

Her hands were too soft!

He snatched one hand from her hip and pulled the T-shirt from his eyes and looked into...*Heather's.*

Jesus!

"Ohmigod!"

Holy mother of fuck—*that* was Terra's voice!

His eyes widened as he looked past Heather and locked his gaze with Terra—standing in his doorway, eyes too bright, shock written all over her face.

"You lying fucking prick." Her voice came out strangled and hoarse and caused his chest to implode.

He bolted upright. Absolute terror shot like icicles through his veins compounded with crippling pain as Heather grabbed his balls!

Ungh!

He froze, then grasped the bitch's wrist.

But he had a bigger problem.

"Christ, Freckle," he implored as she spun and stumbled from his view.

"Go fuck yourself, Zander," she yelled.

"No, no! Come back."

*Fucking no…*this can't be happening.

"TERRA!"

He tried to shove Heather off his lap, but the pressure between his legs sharpened.

"Get your hands off me," he snarled. "TERRA!"

Heather's smile was full of evil intent, and she reeked of booze, but she did not let go.

Zander positioned his thumbs over her eye sockets, and gritted out, "Let go or I'll pop your eyeballs from your skull." He increased the pressure until the bitch's self-preservation kicked in and she let go, moaning like a cow.

He pushed her off his lap. "Are you insane?" he grunted, cupping himself, fighting nausea and the impulse to kick the shit out of her for the damage she'd caused. "What the hell is wrong with you?"

Heather floundered backward, her legs buckling as she grasped onto her purse lying on the couch for balance. It skimmed across the leather, landing on her stomach and made a dense, glassy clunk that he was particularly familiar with.

His heart skipped, then he dove for the leather bag, yanking it from her hand. When he opened it, he discovered two bottles of unopened whiskey weighing the leather satchel down.

He stared at the bottles, then at her. "It's you?" He pulled them out. "You've been stealing from me?"

"Zannie, I…"

"How the hell did you get in?"

"Zannie…"

"Explain—before I toss you down the fucking stairs," he bit out, frustration fueling his temper.

"I…I saw you enter the code…I remembered it."

His shoulders slumped with relief it wasn't one of his staff, but it still didn't explain how she got through the privacy door.

"Get up." He tossed her T-shirt to her then wiped his hands on his pants.

Zannie...don't...I just..."

"You got a hearing problem?" He placed the bottles on his desk. "Get your ass off the floor and get dressed."

While she did so, he searched for her keys and found them tucked in the corner attached to a yellow fuzzy Pokémon toy and examined them until he spotted one he thought was a match. He compared it to his own.

Bingo.

"Who gave you a key?" He demanded, removing the offending one from her ring and dropping it into his sweats pocket.

"I...I took Barney's and..."

"And what? You're wasting my time, Heather."

"I had a copy made."

"Where?" He was gonna have to have words with the fucker as his key had 'do not duplicate' stamped on it.

"The locksmith down the street."

Fuck, he knew the asshole. He'd rekeyed his locks after Chuck signed over the deed as Zander had no clue who else had copies.

"You're done." He had what he needed, now he wanted her gone. "You step near my bar again—you cross that property line, I'll have the cops drag you to jail. Understood?"

Her eyes went wide. "You'd do that—to me?"

"Believe it."

Christ, if she weren't a woman. He sucked in so much air through his nose he was surprised there was any left in the office, then curled his fists tight until his fingers hurt.

"You have no proof," she whined. "You can't do that."

He glanced at his office door, his pulse pounding in his temple because *he did not have time for this*! "You're on video woman."

"What?" Her mouth dropped open exposing a wad of gum stuck between her teeth and cheek.

"Yeah…now get the fuck out of my building before I call the cops." Taking her upper arm, he directed her towards the bar entrance. "Get some help, woman."

"Help?"

"Rehab. You've got a problem, you're stealing booze." His grip on her arm tightened as he didn't need her tripping down his stairs and suing his ass. He also didn't need her on his property not knowing what else she'd do in his alley or carport and suing his ass. Her heels barely scraped the floor as he escorted her through the bar fast as he could and deposited her on the sidewalk.

"Get this and get it clear. I have cameras everywhere. You step so much as your little toe on my property again, your ass is arrested."

"Zannie, I'm…"

He didn't hear what she said next, as he slammed the door, double-checked he'd locked it then ran back through the bar and up the stairs two at a time, fear making his heart pound—his palms sweat.

He couldn't lose her.

They'd barely begun, and he *just couldn't fucking lose her*.

"Terra?"

His apartment door stood open and he knew it. Felt it in his bones—felt it in the emptiness; she'd gone. But he moved forward, checking the patio, his bedroom, then last, the bathroom.

Empty.

She'd done the dishes, tidied and made the bed. Her suitcase and guitar sat neatly tucked in a corner of his room along with that rug.

But no sign of her purse or her phone, which meant she hadn't come back up after she'd seen them. She'd bolted.

Despite her things still being in his room, there was something so final about that whole scene, even the air seemed vacant. The band around his chest tightened to the point he couldn't breathe. He rubbed his hand over his heart, but it didn't help, only seemed to increase the pressure. She was out there—a possible target and he needed to get to her.

Right-fucking-now!

After changing quickly into jeans, he slipped on shoes and as he grabbed his truck keys off his kitchen counter, his phone rang. He pulled it from his sweats pocket; Carmine.

"Yo," he said jogging down his stairs.

"Got bad news bro'… I found Ruby."

"How is that bad?"

"She's in the morgue."

"Holy shit—what?" He skidded to a stop on the landing outside his office. "How?"

"Her body was pulled from the bay—was all over the news apparently. Looks like the woman took a header off the Golden Gate Bridge."

Jesus!

He remembered her call—how wrecked she was, the traffic, and the wind. He'd bet what was left of his bruised testicles that's where she was when he spoke to her!

"It's been ruled a suicide," Carmine went on. "But here's where it gets weird. One of those numbers you gave me belongs to Rebecca Miller."

His heart started to pound.

"Shit, dude. She called me from Terra's mother's phone right before she jumped."

"Fuck."

"They find heroin in her system?" Zander asked.

"Yeah and taking into account the half-life of the drug, which is about six minutes, she'd just shot up before she jumped. It hadn't fully metabolized."

Jesus—what the fuck Ruby? What the hell did you do? But, as much as he wanted to, he couldn't waste time thinking about her.

"What the hell was she doing with Rebecca's phone?" Carmine interrupted his thoughts.

"I don't know, man, but I've got bigger fish right now, man. Terra's gone—she's out there without her car. And so is that fuck. I gotta find her."

There was a long beat of silence. "I'm not even gonna ask what happened, but what do you need from me?"

"Can you get me Helen's number and address in case she doesn't go home?"

Carmine agreed and after he hung up, it took him less than two seconds to decide. He scrolled down to a contact he hadn't called in over ten years.

Surprisingly, the man picked up immediately.

"Little *brat.* To what do I owe the pleasure?"

Zander's jaw spasmed. "We need to talk."

CHAPTER 28

Saturday

erra wiped the tears with her hoodie sleeve, dodging blurry humans. One clipped her shoulder, making her do a half spin and bump into a man as she hurried through the early lunch rush.

"Watch it!" he called.

"Sorry," she mumbled back.

Each breath split her chest. Bile burned the back of her throat and threatened to fill her mouth, causing her to swallow constantly.

Iris was parked behind the deli they'd visited yesterday. It belonged to Helen's cousin and she'd insisted Terra leave her there—in case Zander *accidentally* blocked her in again and she needed a quick getaway.

God, she loved Helen.

Iris sat at the far end of a small parking lot, and with each step closer her control slipped further. She unlocked the sliding door, crawled into the middle to the spot where her mother had given birth and used her foot to slide it shut again. Then found her fuzzy childhood blanket and teddy bear under the sideways bench and freed them from their Ziploc baggies. Hugging them to her chest, she curled into a tight ball and let go. Spasms starting in her torso tore through her body, while her phone buzzed repeatedly in her purse, until she reached for it and turned it off.

"Go to hell," she sobbed.

She cried until her head ached and her eyes scratched but then a weird calm came over her and she slept—the sleep of the exhausted, or perhaps the dead.

When she woke, her eyes were crusted and swollen. The sun had shifted enough to tell her it was mid-afternoon. This was further confirmed by her iPhone after she pulled it from her purse. It showed several text messages, multiple missed calls and two voicemails.

Babe let me explain. Just talk to me.

Terra it's not what you think.

Fuck, Freckle don't do this. Where are you please come back it's fucking dangerous out there.

And then the last—and most painful.

I thought she was you.

He thought that woman was her?

Lame.

He could go fuck himself and his crap explanation, consequently she ignored his voicemail. It was the second, however, that really messed with her. That one was from Vasily.

Today was Saturday.

Her thumb hovered over his name for several seconds before she shook her head. "Fuck you too. Kill me, do your worst, it'll be better than this. I don't give a shit anymore."

Food and a bath, then wine. In that order.

She pulled a bottle of water from her emergency stash under

the seat and drank. The remaining half, she splashed on her face then dried it off with the bottom of her hoodie.

After which she climbed into the front and stuck the key in the ignition. Her fingers shook as she started her van up. A grey squirrel sitting on a lopsided wooden fence eyed her, twitching its furry tail while it chewed on a Snickers bar.

"Where the hell did you get that? Wanna share?"

The critter stared at her.

"No? Well, fuck you too, but you better get moving, squirrel." Her voice cracked, still husky and thick from crying. "Don't want you to have a heart attack."

Terra gunned the engine and beeped her horn, but the rodent held its place, checking her out with an unmistakable *that's all you got?* look in its beady black eyes. It didn't even stop chewing.

Fine.

"It's your funeral." She sighed and stuck Iris into reverse, then slowly backed out.

Five…four…three…two…PAPOW!

The squirrel back-flipped.

Its bounty flew into the air as it scampered to maintain a hold on the fence. Once it got traction it shot like a bullet along the edge of the fence to disappear into a mound of overgrown morning glory.

"I warned you, you little shit." Iris clanked as she engaged the clutch and changed gear and made a mental note to get her into the shop before her transmission went out. "Fucking urban wildlife—you're cute but too jaded for your own good."

For half a second, she considered retrieving the Snickers bar, but since she didn't want to get rabies nixed that idea and drove down the parking lot, found a gap and eased into traffic. A long fifteen minutes later, after navigating on autopilot, she pulled into her driveway and pulled her parking brake.

Food, bath, wine. Food, bath, wine.

The keys rattled when she unlocked her door and as she

schlepped herself over the threshold her phone vibrated again. A quick glance told her it was neither Zander or Vasily.

It was Helen.

Later—she'd read her text later.

Food, bath, wine.

An odd grunt made her look up, straight into the wide, black eyes of the man who came to collect her money every Saturday.

Fuck!

There was no time to scream as something hit her in the forehead, just above her eye, splitting her skin. Lights burst in her frontal lobe, turning her vision gray. She rocked and dropped to her knees covering her face with one hand while the other searched for anything to steady herself. A hot weight pressed on her head, keeping her down, then something whizzed past her face. A moment later, her front door slammed. Then he hefted her under her armpits and dragged her, heels scraping across the floor. Terra twisted and kicked, and almost got free but his grip was too strong, and he moved too fast.

"No…NO!"

"Shut up," he grunted, dumping her onto the couch in a sitting position.

"Don't kill me."

"Be good girly."

"Please don't kill me."

"*Shut up!*"

"No…HEL…!"

His giant paw smashed her face—fingers and a thumb dug into her cheeks while his palm smothered her nose and mouth, cutting off her voice and air supply but the smell of cigarettes on his fingers made her gag. She bucked and flailed, landing a blow somewhere, because he grunted and her big toe hurt, but it wasn't enough. He pressed her head into the back of her couch, then used it as leverage to shift his position.

Pressure.

Oh God...*too much pressure*, her skull was going to pop. Absurdly she saw that scene from *Game of Thrones* when some dude's head exploded after another crushed it with his hands.

That couldn't happen to her.

She didn't want to die with the remnants of her head all over her couch.

She didn't want to die.

Period.

She screamed against his palm, used what strength she had to strain against it. But he tightened his grip on her face, until he maneuvered a shin and his weight onto the top of her thighs. Next, he reached behind his back and pulled a gun with a really long barrel putting it to the middle of her forehead. Somewhere it registered that long barrel was a silencer.

"Stop." Those black eyes were as wild and wide as his nostrils flared. "Don't want to kill."

She froze and blinked.

"Be good girly."

She blinked again and the pressure on her face relented, enough for her to suck in a series of quick, breaths through her nose. Cigarette man's dark eyes held hers. Keeping the gun joined to her head he got off her legs, extending his arm as he took a step back.

It was then she saw the huge square hole in her living room wall and a large, open suitcase. It was red, shiny and hard-shelled containing white brick sized objects. Inside that hole stood a stack of even more bricks about three feet high.

Oh, good fucking lord!

It suddenly became certain. "You're Boris," she whispered. "You kidnapped Shelley."

That was her mistake. The man's straight, thick eyebrows jumped, and he stared at her. Then the furrows in his face smoothed as his expression changed to resigned, his eyes went flat, and he let out a long, drawn-out sigh.

"Don't want to kill." His tone sounded almost sad and somehow that was far worse than if he'd yelled. Because she believed him, but knew he was going to do it anyway.

This was it.

Her life was over—the Millers were not destined to survive.

Boris cocked his head slightly to the left, straightened his aim at her forehead. She saw his breathing stop, his yellowed knuckle tighten and turn paler when he began to squeeze the trigger.

As she waited to be obliterated, for her existence to cease, instinct kicked in. She lunged forward and at that same moment, Zander happened.

He was in the air, one leg extended and her dying thought was —*he's flying.*

She heard an odd, high-pitched *phewt* as the bullet buzzed millimeters above her. Shards of drywall exploded outward and stung her scalp. In slow motion, she watched the gun spin and hit the ceiling. Boris, reeling back from the impact of Zander's kick, collapsed on her coffee table. Zander fell on top and their combined weight snapped it in two.

Chaos erupted, and she had the strange feeling she was floating above herself, looking down at the scuffle. The two men pinwheeled and rolled, there was grunting, and she was pretty sure she heard a growl or two, then it was over.

Boris emitted a sound like a bull getting its balls cut off as he lay on his stomach with his arms pulled high up behind him, trapped in Zander's hands, a knee pressed deep into the middle of his back between his shoulder blades.

Zander's chest heaved, a vein pumped in his neck, but his head stayed bowed with his hair draped in a wavy, dark curtain hiding his face. She stared, unblinking and unable to move. Several dozen heartbeats later and after she noticed his breathing had visibly stopped, he turned slowly, like he was afraid to look at her. Afraid of what he might see.

It showed when his gaze connected with hers—unmitigated fear.

She blinked.

His breath hitched as comprehension set, then those strong, warrior shoulders slumped as he released the air in his lungs.

"You're alive," he croaked and blinked as if he didn't believe his own eyes. "You're fucking alive."

Paralysis spread through her muscles as her mind and body hadn't yet reconnected. And then, if her shit day couldn't get any shittier, Vasily strolled in like they were having a fucking picnic. He too held a gun.

Everything came together and she jerked upright. "NO!" she screamed.

Zander's body tensed and went into fighting mode as his head swiveled to face the Russian. The two men stared at each other, then Vasily raised both hands in the air, and with his free hand slowly reached behind himself and pulled a pair of handcuffs from his jeans back pocket.

"Restrain him, *brat*. I've got this."

What...*what?*

Her eyes widened as she absorbed Zander accepting the cuffs and slapping them around Boris's wrists. When the locks clicked into place, keeping his eyes on Vasily, Zander pushed himself to his feet. The two men locked eyes again, both full of an intensity that made the air crackle and went beyond anything she understood.

Vasily gave a slight chin nod. Zander reciprocated a moment later with one of his own, then moved towards her.

Through the lens of everything that had been that day, everything that had been that week, her mother's murder, her baby brother's murder, Zander and that woman—it was too much.

All that gorgeous wavy hair fell over his face making him look wild and strong and so heartbreakingly beautiful, the tiny pieces of her heart shattered a little more. Those long legs bent, and he placed his hands on either side of her on the couch. Some emotion stormed through his eyes, but she chose not to guess what it was. She couldn't trust it anyway. Then he dropped to his knees and pulled her to him, wrapping her tight in his arms, the side of his head pressed to hers.

"Christ," he murmured into her hair. "I can't believe you're alive."

She didn't respond. Only allowed him to hold her, while she absorbed his warmth, his smell, because truthfully, she needed it herself. But when it became overwhelming, the tears threatened, and she pushed him away. He let go, reluctantly.

"You okay?" he asked, his voice cracking.

Terra nodded once, then looked away trying not to notice the glint of sweat on his skin, his ripped T-shirt, his strong, taut body or the bleeding cut on his cheek.

Instead, she saw that woman straddling him.

It overrode everything. Her eyes began to burn from the pressure of keeping the tears from falling.

"Freckle." His voice was soft and gravelly, yet every syllable of her name stabbed her heart. "Look at me."

She blinked even harder and kept her eyes off him, focusing on Vasily who spoke in Russian on his phone—one Ferragamo sole situated between Boris's shoulder blades—also watching her. When Zander reached out to touch her face, she jerked her head away.

"Don't."

"Babe…you're injured."

"No!"

He stilled, his hand midair while his breath fanned across her forehead. Even that was too much. She swallowed the goose egg in her throat.

"Look at me."

She couldn't—too many lies in his eyes.

"I know it's fucking cliché as hell," he said, "but I swear on Ginny's grave I thought she was you."

A pain sliced through her heart so violently it made her gasp.

"Listen to me...please."

"Fuck you, Zander," she managed. "Fuck you and your *invested* bullshit. It's all lies." Her hands went to his shoulders and she shoved hard. He rocked back but then caught himself by dropping an arm, planting his hand on the floor, preventing him from landing on his ass. She got unsteadily to her feet and wavered to her bedroom. Avoiding the red suitcase and the drugs, she dipped to pick up her phone and purse on the way as his eyes burned holes into her back.

Once her bedroom door was locked, she found several missed calls from Helen, and called her back.

"Can I stay with you for a few days?" She choked on a sob.

"Oh shit, babe, what's happened? I'm going out of my mind. Everyone is looking for you—where are you?"

"I'm at home."

"Ohmigod—you sound awful, are you okay?"

"No...there's a hole in my wall and...um...there's drugs...and a Russian on my floor..."

"Drugs? You don't do drugs. Sweetie, what are you talking about? You're not making sense."

"Um..."

"Where's Zander?"

"Helen..." She sniffed, then used her sleeve to wipe the wet from her cheek. It came away bloody. "I...uh...I don't want to talk about him."

"Fuck." There was a long, tense silence then Helen proclaimed, "I'm gonna kill him."

"No...don't..."

"I'm going to fucking kill him."

"Honey...please, I don't want to talk about him."

"Shit...okay. Listen to me—do not drive. You sound like you're in shock, so just hang in there. I'm coming to get you."

"Okay," she agreed, because she doubted she could drive anyway—she could barely walk, her legs were so wobbly.

"Do I need to bring my brother?"

"No." She stepped into her bathroom and grabbed some toilet paper. "Just you. Please."

"Okay, honey," Helen whispered. "I'll be there in twenty."

Helen hung up. She flipped the light switch and almost screamed at her reflection. The right side of her face was covered in blood with bits of drywall stuck in its stickiness and in her hair. She methodically picked out the shards and when she had most of them, undressed and stepped into the shower.

The hot water ran pink, washing away blood from the split above her eye and little wounds in her scalp. She didn't mind the sting. It was proof she was alive—broken and bruised, but still breathing. As she stood under the spray, that weird calm settled over her again.

One day she'd thank him for saving her head from exploding, but not today.

Nor tomorrow.

After dressing the cut with a butterfly bandage, she noticed the marks already forming where Boris's fingers had dug into her face—four on one side, one on the other.

She ran a wide-tooth comb through her hair, pulled on clean blue jeans and a long-sleeved Pearl Jam V-necked T-shirt. Packed a small bag, stuck her phone in her back pocket and opened her bedroom door.

The hum of low voices, testosterone and tension, filled her living room. The space pulsed with it. Three more large men had joined the party and crowded into her small living room. Gianni Cadora, her landlord and Shelley's man, and his cousin Marco. She'd seen his photo taped to a station mirror in the salon where she got her hair cut. Apparently, he was dating Shelley's partner, Cas. And Carmine.

"Babe," Zander said, noticing her first as his eyes seemed to be glued on her bedroom door. The hum of male conversation dimmed, then went silent. They stood circling Boris, whose legs had been wrapped in hot-pink duct tape she recognized came from her kitchen drawer.

All eyes came to her when she stepped out of her room. She was used to people watching her when she performed, but this was nothing like being on stage. She felt like a specimen in a petri dish, each man scrutinizing her as she picked up the remaining items that had spilled from her purse and slung the strap over her shoulder—avoiding eye contact with all of them.

"What the fuck did he do to your face?" Zander demanded, his voice strained and barely contained. This ratcheted the tension one more notch.

"Is that a handprint?" Vasily asked, eyes narrowing to slits.

Terra ignored them, but out of her peripheral she saw them look at each other. One growled a deep, feral iteration that set the hairs on her arms standing. Though she couldn't decide if it was directed at each other or at Boris—until Zander made a move.

"You motherfucker!"

"Whoa!" Carmine and Gianni jumped in his way, pushing him back by his shoulders—away from Boris. "Don't blame you for wanting to kick the shit out of him," Carmine said, "but not in front of her. She doesn't need to see that."

"He's right." Vasily's eyes had gone even colder. She didn't think it possible, but they were virtually Arctic. "Get her out of here, Milan. Let us deal with this."

Us?

What the hell did he mean *us*?

What had happened since she'd left the room—weren't they

all of different mafia factions and sworn enemies set on killing, or at the very least, maiming each other?

"What's going on?" she asked all of them in general as she checked out the drugs piled on her floor. "Did Zander call you?" she said, looking directly at Gianni who eyed her with weary consternation creasing his brow. "Did you know about this?"

"Carmine called us," he answered. "I'm sorry this happened to you."

"You're sorry?" she said, her voice getting louder. Then she turned to Vasily. "This is your shipment?"

"It's not my shipment, but yes, it's the one we were looking for."

"What the fuck is it doing in my apartment?"

Zander took her by the shoulders. "Freckle, you need to get out of here.

"What...no!" She attempted to shrug him off, and even though her anger fueled her, his grip remained steady. "Don't touch me. I need answers. Is this why my mother is dead?"

"We don't know that yet," Vasily answered calmly. "We're trying to figure this out."

"Then figure it out because I want answers. You fucking get them for me—you owe me that."

Again, Vasily nodded, then Zander directed her out the door. The fog had come in and it soothed the hot spots on her face while he steered her down the stairs, towards the street, staying silent. When they reached his truck he turned her, then pushed her gently against the cab, keeping his hands on her shoulders.

"Freckle...did he hurt you anywhere else?"

She shook her head avoiding his eyes.

"Baby, look at me."

Again, she shook her head.

"I'm gonna take you home with me."

"No."

"You can't stay here. Your door is busted, and this place is gonna be crawling in a few."

"I'm not going anywhere with you."

"We need to talk about what happened."

"No."

"Babe…"

"Shut up…I hate you."

"Don't fucking say that," he hissed, like she'd punched him. Then he pressed forward, their hips connecting. Suddenly her shoulders were free, but only for a second as he cupped the back of her head and hugged her tight to his chest. "Don't say that."

She struggled while his other arm went around her shoulders, his heart racing beneath her ear. "No," she mewled, her voice coming out thick and funny. "Let me go."

"Terra." The warmth of his whisper soaked into her curls, his body vibrating, his voice trembling. "I don't want to lose you—I *can't* lose you." He pulled her even closer to him and for a moment she allowed herself to go slack with her arms hanging loose by her sides.

"You're an asshole," she accused.

"I know…I am."

"The kind that makes a woman feel safe and makes her care and think you're a good guy, and worth taking a risk on. Then you take all of that…that could've been so beautiful and defile the shit out of it."

"Jesus." His voice broke. "It's not what you think."

"She was virtually naked, Zander, with her hand on your dick. You had *your* hands on *her* naked ass—her tits in your face and *it wasn't what I think?*"

"I know how it looked…"

"Don't…" Her voice cracked as she pushed his chest. "I can't…just stop."

"Freckle…don't do this."

"Let her go, Milan." Vasily stood about five feet behind them and she didn't know whether to thank him or curse him, his timing proving to be bitter-sweet.

Zander's body locked up solid, his arms becoming steely bands around her. "Fuck off, Melnikov," he said between clenched teeth.

"Not gonna do that, asshole, and she asked you to let her go."

From her view point, she saw Zander's Adam's apple bob in his throat as he swallowed, then he tugged on her hair tilting her head back. His eyes glittered—emotion burning in them as he stared down at her, the creases in his brow deepening.

"Please," she begged.

Those beautiful lashes flickered before his eyes closed, then he dropped his arms, but he didn't step away. She maneuvered herself from between him and the truck just as Helen pulled up next to them in her fiery little Fiat. She adjusted the strap of her overnight bag then made a move towards the car.

Zander caught her hand.

Her gaze slid to his and when she looked deep into his eyes, she read the sadness in them. And her heart shattered all over again.

"Fuck you," she said, pulling her fingers from his. "Goodbye, Zander."

Then she turned her back on him and walked to the car. As she yanked the door open, Van Halen's "Running With The Devil" spilled out and filled the street.

"You okay?" Helen asked, as Terra climbed into the seat.

"Drive," she said and buckled her seat belt, clinging to whatever held the tears at bay. They made it around the corner before she covered her face with her hands and lost it.

CHAPTER 29

Saturday afternoon

*Z*ander watched the Fiat growl around the corner, his chest on fire. Every breath seared his lungs, burning like a motherfucker. He sat his ass on the stairs, rested his elbows on his knees and dropped his head into his hands.

He had to fix this. It wasn't goodbye—not by a long shot.

"You're an idiot, Milan."

Jesus, he'd almost forgotten about the asshole. He lifted his head to see Vasily standing with his hands on his hips, staring at him.

"You still here—didn't I tell you to fuck off?"

"When have I ever listened to you, *brat*, and the only one fucking off is that beautiful girl. What the hell kind of stupid move did you pull to make her run? You hurt her like that, you don't deserve her."

His eyes snapped to the man—he wanted to kill him.

"Can't say I'm unhappy about it though. Leaves the path clear for me."

Over his bleeding, broken body. Zander bit down hard enough to pop a muscle in his jaw. "Stay away from her," he growled.

"Or what?"

"I'll rip your fucking throat out."

Vasily eyed him for a moment, smirked, then the dude *beckoned!* "Come at me, if it'll help."

He didn't hesitate, letting out a roar as he rushed him. Grappling Vasily around the waist with his head in the man's shoulder, they hit the sidewalk, arms tight around each other. Each man trying to get the upper hand, they rolled using their legs for leverage, constantly flipping each other. Until finally Zander had the stronger position. Vasily lay on his stomach, Zander on his back with his arm pinning Vasily in a headlock.

The Russian tapped out and grinned. "Gotten stronger, little *brat.*"

"Fuck you," he grunted, then released him and staggered to his feet. Using his sleeve to wipe his face, he noted it was ripped and came away covered in sweat and blood. His face stung, the scabs his forearm from his earlier injury had scraped off and burned like the bejesus. His heart pounded and he breathed hard, but he couldn't deny he felt better. The pain in his physical body only just surpassed the agony in his soul.

Vasily grinned as he got to his feet. Zander was satisfied to note there was a bloody scrape on his chin, his nose, also bleeding, jagged slightly off to the side and that fancy button-down was in tatters.

"You're still an aggravating little shit, Alek."

Alek!

The name shocked his sensibilities. It reverberated through him, triggered things he'd rather keep suppressed. No one called him that, except them.

Then Vasily took his nose between his thumb and index

finger and pulled until the cartilage crunched. "Ugh, fuck, that's better," he groaned when he let go.

It did seem straighter but was already beginning swell.

"It's been a long time," Vasily went on, "and I hate to say it but it's actually good to see you, little prick."

"That's still to be determined. What the hell are those drugs doing in her apartment?"

Zander watched the Russian suck in a deep breath, testing his nasal passages and being somewhat successful.

"In a nutshell," Vasily deadpanned, which had to be hard as fuck considering the pain he was probably in from his broken nose. "I'm gonna keep this simple because that's what your limited brain cells can accommodate."

Zander snorted. *Fucker.*

"That shipment went missing nine months ago. Our dear brother Dean, in all his diminished wisdom had a deal with Cadora's brother to deliver twenty kilos of coke which Cadora Junior failed to do."

"Half-brother, asshole."

"Half or not, Dean is still blood."

"Just because we share a sperm donor doesn't mean he's my family."

"You're wrong, Alek, we're all family, you'd be wise to remember that. But anyway"—Vasily ticked his head towards the apartment—"Cadora Junior hid it in there during a remodel then got his ass killed."

"And you've known about this shipment for how long?"

"A couple months. But Dean charged Boris with finding the coke when it went missing, which he was unsuccessful at—or so we thought. Come to find out that Boris had designs on taking over the business while Dean sat in prison. Apparently, he was waiting for the trial to be over, but the lawyers keep pushing the date out and Boris got impatient."

"So, his plan was to use the coke to finance his takeover?"

"Yep, he needed the money to bribe some of the men to side with him. Most of them are loyal though and didn't like what he was doing."

Zander's brows snapped together while he stared at Vasily. "And that's why Dean brought you in. To keep an eye on the fuck?"

Vasily sighed. "Yeah, not my choice in careers, but he's family and somebody other than that piece of crap in there needs to do it to keep the women safe."

"How fucking admirable."

"Fuck you, Alek. You don't know shit."

"Besides the coke being in her apartment, how else does this tie in with Terra?"

"That part is a little more complicated."

"Then uncomplicate it, motherfucker."

Vasily rolled his eyes. "Still the pain in the ass."

Zander grunted.

"After I took over, I changed the rules and made the girls off-limits—unless it was their choice and *only* their choice." Vasily surveyed the street then seemed to choose his words with care. "It wasn't Rebecca's."

"What are you saying?"

"Boris and a couple others took exception to my rules."

"Again, what do you mean?"

"Boris set her up. Left a large amount of smack lying around, knowing she'd take it. Then used it as leverage to fuck her. Told her it was my product, threatened to hurt Terra if she exposed him. *I* took exception to *that*."

Zander's blood pressure began to rise again. "That's fucking rape!"

"Can't disagree with you and besides being stupid, and impatient," Vasily continued, "Boris got greedy—figured it was also a way to make some more cash and since Rebecca had none, he targeted Terra and made her pay for the heroin."

Zander closed his eyes, regretting he hadn't pushed forward when he had the chance to leave his boot print on the prick's face. "He cleaned her out, man," he said. "She's got nothing left."

"She'll get it back."

"*With* fucking interest."

"With fucking interest," the Russian agreed.

"You knew this was going down today?"

Vasily sniffed then gave a reluctant shake of his head. "Had eyes on Boris for a while and noted that he had a once weekly visit to her store. Hadn't figured out why until I made a visit myself and asked her."

"He almost killed her, Vas," he rasped. He had a gun to her head—I saw his finger squeeze the fucking trigger."

"Well then, it's a good thing you got there first, isn't it, *brat*."

Jesus!

He got goosebumps at the thought of what would have happened if he was one second later.

"I had to play it through," Vasily explained. "I had no choice. Also had to be sure Terra wasn't playing me—that Rebecca hadn't disclosed the shipment's location to her before she died."

"Did Rebecca know?"

Vasily shrugged. "She sent Terra a text, but it was mostly nonsense. Something about moving bad juju."

Zander closed his eyes. He remembered seeing it on her phone.

When I think about it now," Vasily continued. "I think she was trying to tell Terra to move apartments, because of bad shit being *inside* and not moving the shit itself. Anyway, I had to investigate and wasn't sure who I could trust."

Zander stomach dropped. "That text was sent the day she died. If she knew, she must have found out right then, maybe right as she figured what was about to happen to her and tried to warn Terra. Whoever killed her took her phone."

Then fucking Ruby called him on it.

Coincidence?

They heard the white panel van long before it pulled up, double-parking next to his truck. Russian hip-hop poured from the windows. Vasily made a slicing gesture across his throat and the driver cut the engine and the music. Two men wearing dark blue overalls folded out. They looked at Vasily with somber expressions while he spoke to them in Russian. Apparently ordering them to stay put as they folded their arms and leaned against the sliding door. The senior dude took out a pack of cigarettes from a pocket in his shirt and lit one, dragged hard and let the smoke stream from his nostrils. Zander studied their faces but didn't recognize either one from the video of the fight.

"Why did Boris trash my bar?"

Vasily's eyes snapped to his. "I wasn't hip to that until Terra mentioned it. My guess is to make you think I ordered it—to cause bigger problems between us and keep me distracted from his real intentions which was getting the coke. But no mistake, he'll make restitution for that too."

"Understood."

He was about to turn to go back inside Terra's apartment when he took in the scaffolding on the side of the building, and it suddenly dawned.

"Fuck...the asshole wanted her to know she was being watched."

"What?" Vasily's eye twitched. "Why?"

"To scare her so she wouldn't want to be alone. He couldn't get the coke during the day because Cadora's workers were all over the place. And night time would be too risky because of the noise cutting through the drywall. Tenants would bitch and someone would check. He had to wait for the weekend. He just wasn't..." Zander stopped because his throat got suddenly tight as he thought of the pain on her face—why she ran. He cleared it and wondered what the fuck he was still doing here. "He wasn't counting on her coming back so soon."

Vasily eyed him, then he sighed and looked at his men. One of them said something to him and he acknowledged with a single nod.

"Time for you to get out of here, Alek," he said turning back to him. "You've done your piece and you don't want to part of what happens next."

Dude was wrong. He did want to be part of it. He wanted to hang the piece of trash on a butcher's hook, slice him open and lay his entrails for the rats to eat.

"Fucker needs to be put down," he gritted out

"He'll be taken care of. Every man in there has a stake, but first we need intel, and she needs answers."

For that reason, and that reason only, Zander acquiesced.

"Besides, you have another problem to sort."

Yeah—number one on his list.

"'Cause if you don't," Vasily drawled in that annoying way he had that made Zander want to deck him again. "I can't say I'm not gonna give it a shot."

"You so much as point your dick in her direction, I'll cut it off."

Vasily laughed.

Fucking *laughed!*

It wasn't a bad sound, as laughs go. It just happened to be something so foreign, having heard it so seldom as kids—their childhood was that fucked up. Even his two henchmen stopped and stared, their eyes bugging out of their faces, cigarettes halfway to their mouths.

"Careful, *brat,*" he said when he finally stopped. "You've got more of the old man in you than you'd like admit."

Shit.

He breathed out through his nose and looked at Terra's door. "He has the same tat in the same place." He didn't need to explain further. Vasily caught his meaning immediately.

"As Papa."

Zander cringed. He hated the sound of that word when it referred to Dmitri. And he never thought of him in those terms. That prick was not his father—merely the scum who'd blown his wad inside his mother, but he nodded anyway.

"Prison brotherhood thing—they served time together in Moscow, which is why Dean took him in. Speaking of the old man, I hear you were the last to see him alive."

His gut clenched and a chill moved through his veins. An image slithered into his head before he had a chance to black it out: Dmitri standing over her limp body on the floor.

Bitch, she dead. Come with me.

Then the asshole grabbing his arm, the scuffle as he fought to get to his mother. Somehow, Dmitri's knife ended up in *his* hand. And more blood.

"Yeah," his voice came out strained. "The day he killed my mother."

Vasily froze then trained those steely gray eyes on him, his complexion having turned a shade paler. "What happened?"

"He turned her brain into jelly."

A silence stretched between them filled by a dog barking at a mail truck in the distance. Neither broke eye contact and the longer that silence went on, the harder Vasily's face got.

"He did the same to mine. It's good he's dead." Then the dude turned on his heel and spat blood on the ground, making a circular motion with his hand in the air. His two men pushed back from the van, dropped their cigarettes, ground them out and followed Vasily up the stairs to Terra's apartment. He watched his half-brother and a moment before he closed the door of Terra's apartment, Vasily caught his eyes again—and nodded.

He knew that look.

It was a nod of respect, and in that moment he understood the man knew—he fucking *knew* what he'd done—but that was as far as it would go. They would never speak of it.

Zander climbed into his truck, cranked Bad Wolves' version of "Zombie" to almost unbearable levels because it was better than the noise in his head. Then he drove home. Instead of doing what he'd normally do, like kicking the shit out of a punching bag, he took a long shower and for the first time since Ginny died, drowned himself in a bottle of whiskey.

CHAPTER 30

Monday afternoon

"Sure you'll be okay?" Helen asked as she stared at the spot on the wall in Terra's living room where Boris had cut a hole. The same spot Truman had repeatedly sniffed. The drywall had been repaired, but it still needed sanding and painting and according to the note from the maintenance man, that would happen the following day. "I don't mind, Tee, in fact I'd really like it if you stayed with me a few more days while they finish fixing your walls."

"I'll be fine, sweetie," Terra answered as she emptied her over-full mailbox for the first time in a week and dumped the contents on her kitchen counter. "I love you for asking, but I have to get back to something close to normal. The smell of a little paint isn't going to kill me."

She had survived bigger things than that—like a gun to her head. It sort of put things into perspective. Life—or death for that matter— kept on keeping on whether she participated or not.

Case in point: at the previous evening's rehearsal, Dannie had learned from one of Ruby's friends and then shared with the rest of the band the news that Ruby had jumped from the Golden Gate Bridge. Despite what had gone down, it hit them all hard—even Terra. She'd cared for Ruby once and didn't wish her dead, especially not like that.

None of them could focus, therefore, rehearsal had been cut short.

On the positive side however, she had received texts from Zander and Vasily informing her she was safe—that Boris was no longer a problem. Neither of which she acknowledged.

"What do you think they did with him?" Helen asked.

"Who…Boris?"

"Uh huh."

"God, I don't know. I'm not sure I want to either," she said, sorting her bills from the junk mail.

"I hope they made him suffer," Helen said. "Chopped him into little bits and fed him to the sharks after what he did to you."

"Holy hell." Terra's mouth dropped open at Helen's statement. "Who knew you were so blood-thirsty. Remind me never to piss you off."

"Speaking of pissed, I may be boiling mad at him, but Zander saved your life, Tee. That takes up a lot of space in the redemption column and I know you're not ready…" She stopped as Terra had suddenly turned pale.

"Are you okay—what's wrong?"

Terra's hands shook as she showed Helen the pink envelope with a handwritten address. "It's from my mom," she whispered.

Helen gasped. "Oh, honey."

"It was mailed the day before she died." Her face crumpled as she held the envelope to her chest like it was the most precious thing ever. "It's been in my mailbox for a week."

"To be fair, Tee, you weren't here—don't be so hard on yourself."

Terra wiped a tear that had leaked with her thumb. "You're

right...It's just that her doctor said she may have written something. It wasn't Mom's thing, so I wasn't really expecting anything."

"Well, I'll let you read that in private. I've gotta get going anyway. Petey is setting me up on a blind date and I figured *what the hell*. Can't do any worse than Tinder."

"Good luck with that. Text me if you need a bail out."

"Yeah...codeword mango margaritas."

She snort-laughed as they hugged and after she closed the door behind Helen, she stared at the envelope for a long time, almost afraid to open it. She took a deep breath and walked to her couch, where she curled into the corner with her feet under her and began to read.

My beautiful girl

Strange, it's been so long since I've written anything other than music, and here I am holding a pen in my cramping hand. It's a gorgeous day, and for once I can really appreciate the beauty around me. Because for the first time in five years, I see clearly.

Let me set the scene a little. I'm sitting with my back against a gnarly old oak tree with the sun on my face. It's hot but it feels good to be out of the city fog. There's a blue butterfly on a rotted stump a few feet away and I'm wondering how the hell my legs got so skinny and so white. And where did all these freckles come from?

The counselors at this place tell me writing is good for recovery and I've got nothing to lose so I'm giving it a shot.

*You know most of my beginnings therefore I'll start at the part I never shared with you. But before I do, and in case I give you the wrong impression due to my terrible letter-writing skills, let me say this up front. I **never** regretted having you. **Never.** You, my love, are the* *beauty, the light and my anchor to this earth. That's why I named you Terra.*

So here goes.

It's April 1994, Kurt Cobain is dead, Courtney Love is reading his suicide note to a crowd of mourning fans and I've just confirmed after several tests I'm pregnant.

It wasn't a good week. In fact, it wasn't a good year. When I first arrived at that estate in that fancy-pants neighborhood in Southern California, I thought it was a joke. It had to be. This kind of stuff didn't happen to me. I got track housing in lower income burbs, with foster parents who were in it for the money—not this. The social worker had to be fucking with me, you know? I kept expecting her to start the car and yell "psyche" then drive away laughing her stupid underpaid head off. But she announced us through an intercom thingy and these gigantic iron gates with a crested "M" opened.

*We drove up a long driveway that never seemed to end with a monster dog chasing us until we got to this castle with the tallest front doors I'd ever seen other than on a church. I still didn't believe it. But she got out the car and walked me up the pathway. Two stories, gorgeous gardens, (yes, gardens, plural) with a view of the Pacific Ocean, a pool and tennis courts. **Tennis courts**, honey. What girl wouldn't want that? I thought I had to be dreaming.*

Anyway, they started off okay. Good-looking people with nary a hair out of place. They had an older son who I didn't meet right away as he was away at college. But when I did, I fell hard. Which was kind of sick because he was several years older and supposed to be my foster-brother. But he was gorgeous. Tall, curly blonde hair and the bluest eyes I've ever seen. Built like a swimmer, which he happened to be.

Tom and Jerrie (yeah—I wasn't joking) were an ambitious couple with hooks deep in San Diego society and designs on an even bigger house for their son. The Governor's Mansion and then The White House. You see, Jerrie came from a political family and, determined to carry on with tradition, groomed her son from day one. I made them look good on their resumé for when Junior made his run at the senate or whatever. No starting at the bottom for him. Junior was gone a lot, away at his Ivy League school most of the time and Tom worked long hours at his practice (he was a doctor) so I hardly ever saw him.

Which left me with Jerrie. I was her project. It was nice in the beginning, nothing I had experienced before. She meant to refine and pretty me up. I got my nails and hair done, and she bought me clothes. They weren't my style, but I didn't care. They were new. And best of all, I had my own room.

But everything was just for show. Jerrie was cold and often cruel. No love in that woman unless it was for her son. He was her world and she'd do anything to further his ambitions. Although I'm not so sure they were his ambitions. More like what she expected of him. Poor Tom Senior, no wonder he was gone most of the time.

After a while the social worker stopped checking in and Jerrie took less and less interest in me. I was left alone a lot. I wasn't allowed to have friends unless they were the daughters of her friends and none of those girls from that upper-crust society wanted much to do with Jerrie's "Foster Freak" as they called me. Though I'd never really had much time to develop real friendships with the other foster kids I got placed with, because we were all rotated out like a Ferris wheel, but they were kids like me, so we at least related. You learn early not to become attached to anyone.

So, living in this castle was lonely. I got driven to and from school every day by their gardener-slash-driver who mostly ignored me. The housekeeper kept her distance as well but looking back I believe they were instructed not to interact with me.

But they did have that dog. A big, muscular scary ass Rottweiler named Harold. I called him Harry and it took a while for him to trust me, but when he did, he became my only friend in that house. Thanks to stolen chunks of meat and a jar of Skippy. Never underestimate the power of peanut butter. Which made me wonder if he'd ever received any love from that fucked-up family either. Probably not, he was only there to fulfill a purpose, much like me.

My outlet was school and the choir unless I swam or banged a tennis ball up against the practice wall, which I did a lot. Eventually I got talking to a kid in the school band. He was a year ahead and kind of a loner like me, but we had music in common, so we were drawn to each other. His name was Ethan. Remember him? Tall, dark and kind of geeky? Maybe not, because you were very young when he died. He's the one who caught you when I popped you out. I still have this image in my head of him holding your tiny, waxy little body with the cord attached, you wailing like a banshee. You had good lungs even then. All this while Stevie, our drummer, drove like a bat out of hell with its tail on fire to the hospital, leaning on Iris's horn. That dinky horn. It still makes me laugh.

Anyway, Ethan and I talked a lot about forming a band like Nirvana. Only different 'cause neither of us wanted to do heroin, but funny how that worked out. It was difficult to rehearse as I wasn't allowed to see him outside of school. According to Jerrie, he "wasn't of our social circle," but we practiced at lunch or any other chance we had, and our harmonies were pretty good.

We were close but not romantically. Not then anyway. Besides Harry, he was the best thing in my life.

Junior graduated and after spending time in France and Spain learning to parlé Français and hablar Español, came home. Didn't pay much attention to me at first but that soon changed. I mentioned he was hot? Yeah, well, he was, and I crushed hard.

The weekend after Thanksgiving and my seventeenth birthday, Tom was off doing his Doctors Without Borders thing and Jerrie occupied with a charity in New York. So, it was just the two of us besides the housekeeper. He cornered me at breakfast one morning, and said, "Today's your birthday." I was beyond flattered he knew. He drove me to the mall in his sporty little red Porsche, gave me a hundred dollars in cash and let me loose.

Baby, I went nuts.

Spent most of it in the Gap and the rest in Victoria's Secret. A hundred bucks went a fair way in '93. After that he took me to dinner and treated me like a lady. Opened the car door for me, held my hand as

I got out and I thought life couldn't possibly get any better than it was in that moment. After dinner, he drove us home and popped a bottle of Champagne. The real stuff he'd selected from Tom's wine cellar and gave me my first sip of alcohol. Well, really it was more than a sip. I got tipsy. Then he took me by the hand, led me to my room and seduced me. He took my virginity in my bed.

I'm not gonna lie, I liked it. I was over the moon but I'm going to spare you the details. What I didn't realize at the time was I was just a gap-filler until his soon-to-be fiancée Emily (who I had no clue existed) came back from her six-month soiree in Paris for Christmas. Imagine my humiliation when Tom out of the blue announced their "union" at a big dinner shindig they held New Year's Eve.

I wanted to die, and I had no one to talk to. I couldn't reach Ethan. Remember back in those days we didn't have cell phones. Pagers were a thing, but he didn't have one. His parents were poorer than dirt and lived in a tiny little apartment on the wrong side of town.

The worst part, Junior didn't want to stop. I may have been young and stupid, but I wasn't into being used. Well, I wasn't then. So, I rebuffed him after the New Year's Eve party, but like his mother, he's one determined son of a bitch when he wants something.

On January the 5th, 1994, the rain came down like it was monsooning...is that a word? Anyway, we were alone in the house and he came to my room drunk, stinking of booze after partying with his frat boys. Again, I rebuffed him, but this time he got pissed. This is hard for me to write, and as I sit here, I'm hyperventilating. Even after all these years my fingers are shaking, so I'm going to stop for a moment.

Okay...I fought but he was so much bigger and stronger. He shoved me onto the bed, ripped my clothes off and stuffed my panties in my mouth, then held me by my neck while he raped me. He was nothing like he'd been before. Brutal and angry and cold. Kept repeating "this cunt is mine" over and over.

He hurt me, baby. Made me bleed and he didn't use a condom. The man I had crushed on and given my virginity to was nothing that I wanted. It lasted forever, then when it was over, he collapsed on me and passed out. I showered until the water got cold, but I couldn't get his smell off me. Then I slept in the bathroom with the door locked.

He was gone the next morning. Back to Paris with Emily and I didn't see him for three months. No one knew what he did to me since it was winter, I hid the bruises with scarves and turtlenecks. Ethan suspected something, and I eventually broke down and told him. It devastated him, and he cried with me. Then I missed my period and the next one and I knew I was in deep shit.

When I confronted Junior he laughed and thought I was joking. That I was trying to trap him into breaking off his engagement to Emily and force him to marry me. Said who the hell was going to believe a little piece of foster trash like me. He bought a pregnancy test and I took it in front of him. He turned white, then blamed me for not using birth control.

Then he told his mother and the real fun began. According to them there was only one option: get rid of the runt. I already loved you so there was no shot in hell I was going to comply, but I played along. Said I would do whatever they wanted. Jerrie made an appointment with one of Tom's doctor colleagues for the following week. I knew where the housekeeper kept the emergency grocery money, and I took it all. Packed whatever I could fit in my backpack and left that night. I wanted to take Harry, but I couldn't. Saying goodbye to that dog is one of the hardest things I've ever done.

I cried while I walked to the nearest public phone at a Seven Eleven and called Ethan. He and Stevie picked me up and we drove to Stevie's apartment in San Diego where I spent that night and the next couple months hiding out until Ethan graduated from high school.

It was pretty easy to hide back then, no internet, therefore no digital tracks, but my disappearance was all over the news for about a week. They were looking for a skinny, long-haired redhead. Not a pregnant Billy Idol look-alike. I must say, I always liked that look on me.

The whole "search" was quite pathetic really. Jerrie cried on TV, pleading for "whoever had me" to please bring me home and how much they missed me. Thing was, I left a note which they obviously never told the cops or the social workers about and used my disappearance to gin up sympathy for Junior's upcoming campaign. In fact, he made that his platform. Missing and exploited kids. What an asshole. Anyway, the hoopla died down after a bit, the cops determined I was just another runaway and didn't spend much energy on wasting resources on me.

That summer, Ethan scraped together enough to buy Iris, then we hit Interstate 5 and headed north with Stevie and a couple other guys. We got a gig in Portland and stayed until it got too cold, then drove back down south, through the desert into Arizona.

You came early, born on Labor Day weekend in Phoenix and the moment I laid eyes on you, I was so grateful I had made the right choice. You were beautiful and perfect and all mine. And a redhead. I have no real memory of my parents and never knew what happened to them. I remembered being told as a small child they were in heaven and as I held you, I knew it had to be true. I couldn't wrap my head around them abandoning me if they felt half the love for me that I felt for you.

Ethan especially adored you. I've never seen such wonder on another human's face when he held you screaming and kicking and so damn mad to be born in such an undignified way on that dirty carpet in Iris. He's the closest thing to a father you ever had. Changed your diapers, fed you so I could sleep and played his guitar and sang to you (the same guitar in the brown leather case I've had forever). Nobody could make you laugh like him and for a while things were great. We got married and we took his name. With regular gigs and jobs, we made decent money and could afford a small apartment.

Then on July 4th, 1998 after a gig, Ethan had a severe asthma attack. He'd forgotten to get a refill on his inhaler and thought he had a spare, but it was empty too. I called 911, and it was only minutes, but by the time the ambulance arrived it was too late. Ethan, my best friend, a third of my world and my rock died in my arms. It still hurts, baby. That hole never filled, and I've never loved any man since like I loved him.

Stevie blamed me. Things were never the same, so the band broke up. I had a little money saved and sold everything I could, then you and

I hit the road. We traveled down to the Gulf, followed the coast around the tip of Florida, camping at all the beaches on the way. I'd cry, strum Ethan's guitar and watch you play. You'd ask me why my eyes were wet, and I'd tell you it was from the sand. One day you said, "I don't want to go to the beach today, Mama." I asked why, and you said, "The sand makes your eyes hurt and I don't want your eyes to hurt anymore."

We left the next day. I'd thought about Nashville, but it really wasn't my thing. I was more of a West Coast girl, so we drove and drove listening to oldies like The Doors and CCR. Your favorite was "Midnight Special," and you'd do this cute little wiggle as you sang along with your curls blowing in the wind, getting in your face. God, I loved you. I always thought you were an old soul and channeled Joplin and occasionally Nina Simone with a much better voice than I ever had. Anyway, we finally settled in Seattle, because—Eddie Vedder.

Yeah—still.

The rest you know, so let me move on to after you moved out of Andrei's apartment.

As you're aware, I got in deep. I was angry. I felt you abandoned me, but then I was relieved you didn't have to see how low I went. Andrei introduced me to Dean and Dean introduced me to men. Lots of men. I never did The Farm, thank God. Dean thought I had potential as a "specialist" given my stage training and I could still sing and play the guitar. So instead of doing the orgies, I fulfilled men's fantasies in another way—role playing.

Then Dean got busted and some of his men got busted too. Vasily came in and sorted the chaos. He scared the crap out of me (and everyone else too) with that icy way he has, but he treated us well. He started to clean things up, got better security and vetted the men we did. He gave us girls hope, baby. He was distant but decent and so damn good-looking. Not like Dean who was a fucking psycho. But for all the vetting he did, there was always that one asshole. And life has a way of coming full circle, resurrecting your demons in the process.

My demon showed on April 31st 2018. Fucking Junior; the man who raped me and your sperm donor. It was like twenty-four years had *not passed. I recognized him immediately as the bastard looked the same. He **was** the same. There were profiles of us fantasy girls and apparently, he'd seen mine and decided he just had to reenact the night that gave me you.*

So, he raped me. Again. And by some weird cosmic fucked-up coincidence, I got pregnant again.

So yeah, honey this is me telling you, you're going to have a sibling. I didn't tell you earlier because I wasn't sure if the baby would survive, or if I would for that matter. Detox is a bitch by the way. But I've reached the three-month mark now. The ultrasound looks good and the heartbeat is normal.

The moment I figured I was pregnant, I realized I needed to get clean and not just for the baby. I remembered how much you always wanted a sibling. I figured finally I could give you one, and isn't it just hilarious that your little baby brother-slash-sister would be a full-blooded one?

Here's the bad part. I also figured I could use it to fuck Junior the way he had fucked me. I could never prove this baby is a product of rape, but by virtue of your birth, I could prove statutory rape because I'd been underage the first time. Although the statute of limitations has long passed, and I can't do anything legally, I could go public. The man does not deserve to hold office.

I told Vasily I wanted out and he arranged for me to come here and now I'm sitting in the sun, clean, pregnant, happy and with a purpose for the first time in years and life is good.

That's all I have for now, but this writing thing seems to work so I'll be doing it again soon and often.

Love you forever,

Mom and the little peanut

xx

. . .

*S*he read the letter twice. When she was done, and after she'd wiped her tears and blown her nose, she picked up her phone.

"Terra," Vasily answered. "Good to hear from you."

"I have something you need to see," she said.

CHAPTER 31

Wednesday

Terra laid her hands then her forehead alongside the wreath on Rebecca's casket. She'd held it together for the most part, even during the song, but the burn behind her eyes had become unbearable.

"Goodbye, Mama," she whispered. A fat tear rolled down the tip of her nose and dropped onto the varnish. "I love you. Have fun up there, but not too much. Don't need God kicking you out of heaven, because we both know the other place isn't any fun."

Another tear fell and joined the first. They shimmered down the wood, leaving a wet trail that briefly magnified the grain.

"And you, little brother—little Ethan, there's so much I want to say, but just know how much I wanted you, to hold you and smell your sweet baby smell. Take care of each other—keep Mama straight."

A hand slid up her back, then squeezed her shoulder. "You all right?" Lucas asked.

A sob escaped, but then she dabbed at her eyes with the fresh

Kleenex he offered. "I will be." He turned her into his arms and held her, with his temple pressed against hers, rocking while she cried.

"'Dancing in the Sky'—sweet choice of song," he muttered in her ear. "Your voice only broke twice and Dannie only fu… screwed up once on the bridge. Not that anyone noticed."

Terra let out a laugh-sob. "Yeah, we didn't have much time to rehearse. You know…with the Ruby thing."

"Dude, you had me bawling. By the time that last note faded, I looked around and there wasn't a dry eye in this place. Even the dog cried."

"Oh jeez, Terra," Shelley edged out of the second-row pew, her voice sounding a little nasally and joined them. Moving into their huddle, she dropped her forehead onto Terra's shoulder. "I had no idea the little bugger would howl like that."

They hugged until Terra pulled away to blow her nose. "It was cute," she croaked. "Mom loved dogs, so I'm guessing she didn't mind." Then she dropped to her haunches to rub Truman's ears.

"Truman De Luca, you are very handsome, and you can sing with me any time." The mutt responded with a shiver that shook droplets from his jowls. One landed on her black leather stiletto pumps.

"Oh, good lord," Shelley muttered and sank to her haunches too, using a complementary tissue she snatched from the end of a pew to wipe drool from Terra's shoe and then from his face. "I swear the older he gets, the more he oozes."

Truman snorted and lowered his head.

"It's okay, buddy, I'm just grateful you didn't fart."

That made Helen, Petey, Dannie and the rest of the band who had joined them burst out laughing.

"You all think it's funny?" Shelley smirked. "You haven't experienced one."

Still chuckling and while Brad Paisley crooned "When I Get Where I'm Going," they continued up the red carpeted aisle.

Several women who had introduced themselves to her prior to the memorial as coworkers of her mom offered sad smiles as she passed. They filled the third row, sniffling, careful not to smudge their already smudged eyes. Behind them stood Dr. Rodham. And Vasily—elegant in his Brooks Brothers suit, although somewhat beaten up. Those cool, gray eyes had bruising under them, as did his nose and there were scratches on his chin. When his gaze caught hers, she acknowledged him with a nod.

Receiving hugs and "I'm so sorrys" from people she didn't know, with Helen at her side, she struggled to keep her emotions in check. She really should have considered that Xanax Dannie had offered, but didn't want to slur during the tribute, therefore she'd declined.

The turnout had been much larger than she expected. The small church almost filled, except for the last couple rows, but of course there was one notable exception; Zander. She didn't know why his absence hurt so much. There had been a moment she thought she saw him, but she must have been mistaken, because he was nowhere to be seen.

Then again, there was no reason for him to be there.

As the line of mourners got shorter, Terra notice Dr. Rodham in a serious conversation with Vasily, which struck her as inter-esting. The Russian didn't seem the chatty type, but he listened, nodding occasionally until Dr. Rodham stepped forward to take his turn.

"Terra," he said, covering her hand with his. "Rebecca always said you could sing, and she was right. You have a beautiful voice."

She gave a small smile, as she was just about out of *thank yous.*

"I hope you'll consider my advice and reach out to some of the groups I referred you to. Their grief counselors are wonderful."

He held her eyes until she nodded and wondered if they could help deal with a different kind of grief. "When things calm down a bit, I'll think about it."

They chatted for a moment, then he patted her hand, and said goodbye. She watched as he headed down the stairs.

Vasily waited to be last. He approached as she stood in the vestibule between two giant vessels of fresh-cut irises and pink chrysanthemums. She'd splurged, since the money Boris took from her had been returned, in cash. Hand-delivered by one of Vasily's henchmen and with instructions not to deposit large amounts into her account at once. Something about suspicious activity reports and the IRS.

Fine—whatever. She was just happy she was no longer broke and pleasantly surprised by the larger than expected supply of fresh blooms, and made a mental note to thank the funeral director. Apparently, he'd under-promised and over-delivered.

Vasily stopped in front of her, then turned to Helen and focused all that silver-gray steel on her petite form.

"I need a moment of Terra's time," he said to her. "Would you mind?"

Helen moved closer to Terra and hooked her arm in hers. "Well, that's entirely up to Terra now, isn't it?"

"It's okay, honey," Terra interjected softly. "I need to talk to him. I'll be fine."

"Okay," Helen said, her gaze bouncing between them like a tennis ball. "If you're sure, I'll just…um…go talk to Rory and Shelley," Helen mumbled, throwing a *watch yourself* sideways glance at Vasily. On lesser men that look would have shrunk their testicles to raisins.

Vasily seemed slightly amused and shook his head, watching her friend's hips sway in her black sheath dress down the stairs before he turned back to look at her "Is she always that feisty, or is it just me?"

"Helen's like one of those miniature Yorkshire terriers—cute, fearless and totally overprotective."

He smirked.

"Thank you for returning my money, though it's more than what I paid to him."

"Call the difference interest and you're welcome."

"How can I help you, Vasily."

"Finally, you're calling me Vasily. It's good, we might be family one day."

"What?" She looked up, past his dove-gray silk tie that mirrored his eyes until she made contact, a little astounded. "What do you mean by that?"

He narrowed his eyes, then shook his head. "Never mind, poor joke. I wanted to apologize for how I treated you." He looked her dead in her eyes, and she noticed the bruising made them look more like shiny pewter, like the first time she'd met him at Provocative. "In your apartment."

"Those bruises have anything to do with you apologizing?"

He chuffed. "No, that's an entirely different matter altogether." Vasily stuck his hands in his pants pockets and looked down at his shoes. "I appreciate you coming to me first with the information in Rebecca's letter. That means a lot."

"She said you helped her, so I wanted to give you that courtesy. But you know I have to hand it over to the police."

"I would expect nothing less. I want justice for Rebecca, too."

"What are you going to do with the information?"

"Terra...for your own sake, those are questions you should not be asking me."

"Okay, but...um, I have to know. Did Boris kill her?"

"Perhaps now isn't the best time to discuss this."

"There's never going to be a good time to discuss this, but I need to move on. That starts today, but if there *are* questions—it's going to take a lot longer for me to work through this."

He looked out over her head towards the street, then pulled in air through his nose. Somewhere on the street a Harley started. The resulting shot to her heart almost stole her breath but she did her best to ignore it and not turn around. She'd probably never hear that sound again without it killing her in some small way.

"You don't need to protect me," she swallowed and went on. "You know Mom would want me to know."

His jaw ticked, then he nodded. "He was contracted, but he didn't do it himself."

"He didn't...wait...contracted?" Her brows snapped together. "Are you saying a hit was put on her?"

Vasily stood solid and stared at her solemnly. "He bribed another junkie with drugs to shoot her up."

Terra rocked back on her heels as the impact of his words hit her. "Why would someone want her dead?"

"It went horribly wrong. She wasn't supposed to die, just break treatment."

"I don't understand, what about the baby? I mean, didn't Boris know she was pregnant?"

"Cried like a little girl when he found out. But to be fair, none of us knew she was pregnant. He had a thing for her, but she didn't have one for him. And men like him don't like getting told 'no' which is why he took the contract. Figured if she broke treatment, he could control her again."

She gasped. He may as well have kicked her in the stomach, it hurt that much.

"God, that makes me so angry." She drew in a shaky breath and clenched her fists. "I just want to claw his eyes out and stomp on them."

Vasily said nothing, just watched her seethe. A rather big part of her wanted what Helen had suggested: that they chop him into bits and feed him to sharks. She put her hand to her forehead and took several deep breaths while she fought the tears.

"I'm sorry, Terra. I shouldn't have told you now."

"It's fine...but at least that part make sense. What about who paid for the contract—do we have a name?"

"It was handled through an anonymous third party. He doesn't know who paid him."

She rubbed her hands up her arms to try to dispel the anger. It wasn't working. "This might be a silly question, but do you keep records of their...um, activities. I mean, Mom gave an exact date of the rape even if she didn't give an exact name. She mentioned he held office and I've done some googling. There's a congressman, by the of name Thomas Madden Junior of California. Do you think this could be him? If it is, it's one hell of a motive."

"You're right...it is one hell of a motive. But this is where I'm asking you to trust me. Or at the very least trust the cops. When they get that letter, let them do their job. Don't be doing anything stupid that will ruin your life. But I promise you this, whatever happens, Rebecca will get justice one way or another."

It couldn't be called silence between them as it was filled with somber voices and passing cars—but it could be called a stillness as Terra caught the significance of his meaning.

"Will you be okay...after I hand the letter over?" Terra asked.

"Don't worry about me. Just take care of yourself."

"If you need more time, I can..."

"Terra, do what you need to do. Don't wait any longer than tomorrow."

"Okay." She let out a deep sigh and glanced at Dr. Rodham who was petting Truman and chatting up Shelley and Helen. Then something clicked, and it amazed her it took so long to make the connection.

"Ohmigod. It's you I have to thank, isn't it?"

His head tipped to the side to look at her. "For what?"

"Paying for rehab. Mom said you arranged it, but you did more, didn't you?"

One corner of his mouth tipped up, but he said nothing.

"Why?"

Something moved across his face and in his eyes and ended in him swallowing. "She reminded me of my mother."

"So, you and she never…"

"No."

Her face crumpled. "Thank you…for being her friend. I think deep down, despite all that scary badassness, you're a good man, Vasily Melnikov."

Again, something flittered across his face. Before she thought about it, she turned and put her arms around his waist. He hesitated then added his to her shoulder and cupped her head against his chest.

"No thanks needed," he murmured against her hair. "My family has done enough damage to women over the years and she deserved it. So do you. If you ever need anything, you pick up your phone and ask."

He smelled good. His cologne was expensive—but not overpowering. And he was warm and big—but not overbearing. Sexy in his own cool, *distant* way. This pimp—this mob boss, handsome and stylish in his thousand-dollar suit—was no doubt deadly to many, but now she realized, not to her.

They stepped apart and she hesitated to ask, but she needed to know.

"Was Zander involved in…whatever happened to Boris?"

He scrutinized her while she coiled a lock of hair around a finger, then shook his head. "He wanted to be, but he's clean."

"You sure?"

"As much as I'd like to make Milan look like a prick to you, I can't do that. That being said, what *is* the deal with you and him?"

"Nothing."

"You're full of shit."

Yep she was, but what's in the past is in the past. "There is no deal."

"Didn't look that way to me."

"I don't know what you think you saw, but whatever it was you're mistaken, and if there ever was anything, it's over."

"Terra, a man doesn't hold a woman the way he held you,

fighting to hang on if it's over. Whatever the fuck happened between you, he was just as unhappy."

Unhappy he got caught with another woman's hand on his dick—but whatever. It was no longer her concern.

Lies.

It *was* her concern because it hurt like a motherfucker.

The asshole had completely ruined her.

"Yeah," Vasily uttered without taking his gaze off her as he turned to leave. "You're full of shit."

CHAPTER 32

Friday night

Zander stared at Terra's face on his phone. *Finally*, the woman responded to his texts. Elation fizzed up like an uncorked bottle of champagne—almost making him dizzy.

Then he read it.

Can you give my guitar and things to Petey please.

What?

Absolutely fucking not.

The first words he'd heard from her and that's all he got, 'Give her guitar to Petey'? Give away the only leverage he had?

He slammed his palm on the bar causing Barney to look up from pouring a beer and glare at him. "You're pissing me off, son," he yelled across the bar. "Let Nicky take over. I don't need your grumpy sad-sack face behind my bar getting in my way."

He glared back at Barney who ignored him. That pissed him off more.

"Or breaking any more barstools."

His jaw tightened. "My barstools, old man, don't fucking forget it."

"Or what asshole, you gonna fire me?"

His nostrils flared but once he got past the desire to punch the old man's nose, once he got his fist to uncurl, fingers and thumbs to cooperate and stop crushing the shit out of his phone, he focused on the keyboard and typed a response.

Not giving them to Pete!! Stop being a pussy and get them yourself.

Before thinking it through he hit send, waited until it read delivered. Then, with deliberate care, lifted the server hatch, somehow managing to keep from slamming it down, though he very much wanted to. Except he didn't need *that* broken too.

What the hell was wrong with the woman?

Fuck!

What the hell was wrong with him—missing a woman who wanted nothing to do with him.

After spotting Nicky on the floor serving a table, he moved his way through the crowd and tapped her shoulder. She straightened, balancing a load of empties on her tray. Fortunately, the band was between songs, so he didn't have to yell. "Help Barney behind the bar. I'm going upstairs."

"He finally ejected your ass, huh?"

Christ!

He did not need this.

"You better watch *your* ass," he snapped, "before *I* eject *it.*"

Nicky's mouth dropped open, showing the tiny chip in her front tooth that could have looked ghetto, but on her, made her interesting. When she shut her mouth, her face hardened. "That's not cool, Zander."

He glared at her a few seconds longer, then relented and looked away.

Fine.

He'd give her that.

It's not like he'd follow through. He knew it. She knew it. He liked her and she'd proven her loyalty often enough.

"Yeah…okay." He worked his jaw. "Not cool." He surveyed the room, eyeing all the happy couples and the amped-up vibe in general. What the fuck did everyone have to be so fucking happy about?

"Finish up with them, then get behind the bar." He spun on his heel to do what everyone who should be minding their own damn business seemed to think he needed to be doing.

"Zander," she called, lifting the tray high to avoid a dude who put a new meaning on buzzed-walking. Or maybe it was buzzed-dancing; he couldn't tell.

"What?" he answered but didn't stop moving towards the private exit that led to his stairs.

"Dump that pride of yours."

Pride? He pushed through the doors and Nicky ducked in behind him. "What's that supposed to mean?"

"Just say you're sorry."

"I already apologized to you, Nicky."

"Oh," Nicky deadpanned. "Okay then. If that's what you want to call an apology but it's not me I'm talking about."

"Then what are you talking about? What's your problem?"

"My *problem* is, Zander," she said, tucking the tray to her side, "you're giving us all a headache with this grouchy bear act. Every night this week! You're gonna drive our customers away and I need the tips. I have a kid to support, remember?"

Jesus, what was it with his staff?

"You wanna bust my balls, go right the fuck ahead and say whatever it is you need to say."

Nicky got in his face. "*Untwist your testicles* and get your shit together. Whatever it is you need to do or need to say to *her* to make it right, go ahead and just say it already."

He folded his arms and prepared to square off with her. "You're going all sisterhood on me…picking a side?"

"No, dumbass…I'm on *your* side." She sighed then blew a

strand of stray dark hair out of her face. "Look, I've known you a long time. I've seen you with a lot of women. None of them lasted for more than five minutes. Heather, Denise, even that Missy who I thought may have had a skinny chance, but none of them lasted. And you've never looked at any of them like they meant something other than the next place to put your dick in, you know?"

"Yeah—so?"

"So, up until last week, somebody mentions Terra's name, you tried to hide it, but you go all goofy."

He unfolded his arms and looked to the side. Now he's a fucking Disney character?

"Goofy?"

"Goofy." She nodded. "Then, I don't know what changed but now, your face...your eyes...I see pain and misery and all kinds of unhappy."

Zander swallowed, because—yeah.

"You're hurting."

He looked away again and drew a sharp breath through his nose.

"But you're manifesting it as anger."

"When did you get your psychology degree?"

"No degree." Nicky put her free hand on his forearm and squeezed. "I'm just a mom who's seen her kid act out due to the shit his dad has pulled. I know you're not five, Zander, but I'm seeing the same in you. That night she sang with Rory, I watched you. You're different when you look at her. Your eyes get all soft, and your face relaxes, and you go all..."

Goofy.

"Nicky, make your point or get back behind that bar before I really do fire your ass."

"My point is, I don't think you've figured this out yet, because your ass is that dumb, and you are that ornery. But *you*, my friend, are falling in love with her and your heart is breaking."

He had to avert his eyes. Blink the wet away. A parade of goosebumps broke out on his skin, but he didn't have time to think about that because Nicky wasn't done.

"Not all of us get that shot. God knows, I probably won't trying to raise a kid alone. I don't know what the hell it is that put you in this mood this past week, but knowing *you* and what I know about you, seeing what I've seen on your face—it's too beautiful to waste. And if you blow this, if you allow your stupid punk-ass pride to get in the way of fixing whatever is wrong, Zander Milan, I'll be pissed at you forever. *That's* how much on your side I am."

He stared at Nicky, because, Christ, he couldn't do anything else. There was no chance to respond even if he wanted to, which quite frankly he wasn't able to. Nicky had pushed through the privacy door. The short concussion of music and her words left him stunned.

In love with her.

He felt it settle over him, then begin to sink in through his skin as he leaned his back against the wall, his heart pounding louder than the music.

Fuck, he was—and had been all along. Probably started the moment she smiled at him.

While he stood there, his limbs all liquid and his head spinning with Nicky's words, he checked to see if Terra had read his message.

She had. And the dots indicating she was responding bounced, then they disappeared. A few seconds later they started again, then again went missing.

Then...nothing.

Okay, he couldn't blame her. His text was rude. When it came to this woman, his control took a catapult off his patio, his frustration soared and whatever was left of his gray matter went *splat.*

He'd spent a week fuming, breaking shit, drinking more than

he should have because she hadn't returned his calls or answered any of his texts. Or given him an opening.

But now she had.

As he made his way up the stairs to his office, before he stuck the key in the lock, he hit her number. It rang twice but rolled to voicemail. His chest went tight that she rejected his call *again*, and his heart threatened to crawl out his throat while he listened to her voice on her message *again*. Almost hung up, then *did* hang up when the beep sounded.

Now who was the pussy?

The same one that arrived late to the funeral and sat in the back while she sang, her voice breaking and looking so damn *sad*. Then sat on his bike, watching her with Vasily when he should have been *with* her.

He rubbed his chest, then thumbed a new message. *We need to talk—please.*

And waited.

No response came.

The phone skidded across his desk. The propensity to kill something—anything—preferably Heather for fucking his life up, hadn't diminished. The remnants of the bar stool he'd executed after closing last night would also attest to such and his phone didn't deserve to be his next victim.

Zander dropped his head back and scraped his hands over his face, not surprised to find his cheeks wet.

He'd fucked this up.

Nicky was right.

Instead of expecting Terra to trust him—maybe he needed to get his head out his ass and trust *her*.

He turned to look out his office door at the parking lot where he could still envision her van. A tiny red light above the window caught his eye.

Fuck!

Maybe there *was* a way!

CHAPTER 33

Sunday

"You up for karaoke at Tony's tonight?" Helen asked. Tony's being Tony's Taqueria—a retro seventies Mexican joint run by a wannabe Steven Tyler. The music was groovy, the margaritas magical and the karaoke nights killer.

She glanced at the Provençal clock. Ten minutes to closing on her first day back. Was she up for an over-crowded albeit fun bar, faking a smile, waiting her turn to belt out Aretha's "Natural Woman" to a drunk hoard of Sunday night partiers? This while her heart tried to knit its threads together?

Probably not. She'd rather stab herself in the eye or reread Zander's text.

He'd called her a pussy.

Asshole.

Problem was, he happened to be right. She didn't have the lady balls to face him and get her stuff herself.

As fortune would have it, she was saved from answering

Helen as her attention was drawn to the jingling door and a private courier carrying a glossy box with a bow.

Back orders came by UPS, USPS or occasionally FedEx, but never by private courier. And never in shiny, pink boxes trimmed with gold.

"Well, what the hinky-hay is it?" Helen queried after finger-signing the messenger's iPad and studying the three-foot-by-three-foot-by-eight-inch packaging and handing it to Terra.

"Don't know. It doesn't look like anything I ordered for a customer…or for myself, for that matter."

"Well, open it. Let's find out."

"Who's it addressed to?"

Helen angled the package, so Terra could see the label. "You, Tee, it has your name on it." She pointed to the fancy font. "See?"

Terra did indeed see, and therefore couldn't ignore the little thrill prickling her spine. "Well, the box sure is pretty."

"Then open it already." Helen clenched her fingers and bounced on her toes. She hadn't lied when she'd told Vasily she was like a miniature Yorkshire terrier. Especially when she got excited.

Terra snickered and waved at the thing. "Knock yourself out."

To which Helen did not hold back and proceeded to knock herself out.

"It looks like a painting," she said after she'd stabbed the sealing tape with a letter opener and slit it to a point where she had the top of the box opened.

Painting?

She tilted her head. Who'd send her a painting?

Helen removed it from the box, then unwrapped the bubble wrap and placed it against the counter. They took a few steps back. Her pulse jumped into high gear and her breath caught.

Helen tilted her head first to one side, then to the other, scrunching her brows. "I don't get it. Is it one of those abstract things?"

"Flip it." It came out strangled, enough that Helen turned to look at her, then back at the painting, the back at her. "It's upside down," she clarified.

"Oh," Helen mumbled, keeping her lips pursed, but nevertheless took the few steps forward and flipped the painting. Then she returned to her place next to Terra. She studied it some more. Her head jutted forward. Her eyes got big, then she gasped.

"Holy hell, Tee." Her mouth hung open "That's you."

"Yeah," she whispered.

"It is fucking *gorgeous*."

"Yeah."

"Looks original."

"Uh huh."

"Who is A.M.?"

"Um…I…"

"There's no card. Who'd send something like this and send no card?"

"Um…uh."

"Terra, who is A.M.?"

"I think I've heard him described as an *obscure, anonymous* artist."

"Huh." Helen's nose twitched then she did this cute little circle thing with it, like she always did when she was puzzled. "Well, whoever the hell he is, he's hella talented."

"Yeah."

"That pose looks familiar."

"Mm hmm."

It should.

Helen had taken that photo and sent it to Dannie (before the dickhead stuck his nozzle into the Ruby Hoover). She remembered her words at the time. *Put it on the band's Facebook page. Every dude who sees that picture will get a boner and be a fan for life.* She had been embarrassed but it turns out Helen may not have been completely wrong. It was the most liked photo on the band's Facebook page, with the most comments—some a lot raunchier than others—and their following increased exponentially after it posted.

The shit she did for those guys.

"You got an admirer you never told me about?" Helen's eyes darted to hers.

"I think I'm gonna pass on karaoke."

"Okay…that's probably a good idea considering what you've been through, but honey, are you gonna answer my question?"

"Um…"

"Oh, for fuck's sake," Helen bounced again. "Just tell me. You're *killing* me."

"I don't know if I have a secret admirer, but I think I know who may have sent it."

"Who?"

"Zander."

"Are you serious?"

"Uh huh."

"Ohmigod, I'm going to faint."

ɛ੦

*A*fter they closed the store, they sat in Iris and googled A.M. Helen read from her phone screen affecting a fancy accent: *"The evocative and mysterious artist whose sensual, energetic depictions of rock stars, movie stars and CEOs' wives, with a finger on the pulse of the modern art movement is honest and trend-setting."*

"Ooh-la-la! Friends in high places, daahling."

Terra chuckled and slapped Helen's arm. "Shut up and read already."

"Their (as the artist's gender is unknown) latest piece of a prominent Bay Area musician sold for seventy thousand dollars at auction…"

Helen gasped then stared at her with her mouth gaping. "Seventy thousand dollars? Who is this dude?"

"What? Gimme that." She grabbed the phone from Helen and scrolled further down the Wikipedia page. It showed several of *their* works, but one was notably missing. "I've seen a couple of paintings by this artist, only one up close but it wasn't signed so I wasn't aware it was his."

"Why wasn't it signed?"

Terra scrunched her face, giving Helen a *fuck if I know* look.

"Okay, well where did you see it?"

"In Zander's apartment—it's of his grandmother and it's beautiful."

"You think Zander paid this dude to do a portrait of you?"

"I guess…right? I mean what else can it be?"

"That's a pretty expensive gift. Are you going to keep it?"

"Feels like a buy-off."

"I don't know, honey." Helen shook her head slowly. "Any man who's willing to pay for a portrait of a woman he had a thing with feels like something else—definitely not a buy-off. Have you considered he might have been telling the truth in his texts?"

"What? That he slept while that wench had her hand on his dick?"

"It's been known to happen."

"Why are you on his side all of a sudden?"

"Tee, I'm *always* on your side. But maybe you should listen to him."

"The only thing I should do is return that…that thing."

Helen tucked her hair behind her ears. "Ooh boy…okay. At the risk of getting my face chewed off, I'm gonna put this out there." She took Terra's hand in hers. "Babe, you've got *feelings* for this man."

Terra flinched and sucked in her cheeks.

"And considering what you've gone through with your mom and what you think happened with Zander…"

"Think?" Terra's head whipped to the side to stare at Helen. "I saw what I saw, Helen."

"I know, babe, but if you keep ignoring his messages and texts and don't hear him out, and there's one iota of truth in what he's trying to tell you, and you don't give him that chance, you'll regret it. Your heart's already been through the meat grinder—how much worse could it be to look him in the eye when he explains it?"

She contemplated that, and while she did, a tear rolled down her cheek. "I'm scared to trust him," she whispered. "Scared to believe him and then it turns out he's playing me. After Dannie and now him, I don't know if I can…"

"I know, sweetie. But I have a feeling you don't have much to be scared about. Just sleep on it before you do anything that can't be undone. Or better yet, come to Tony's, drink margaritas and watch me do a really bad rendition of 'Landslide.'"

Terra swiped the tear with the back of her hand then plugged in her phone to the only thing from this century in Iris—her stereo.

"Honey, your "Landslide" isn't half bad. Right up there with the Dixie Chicks' version. I couldn't do much better myself."

Helen snorted, opened the door and stuck a leg out of Iris. "You *liiieee* like a bad rug, Miller, but I love you anyway. See ya tomorrow."

"See ya." Terra blew a kiss and waited for Helen to shut the door and move out the way before she stuck Iris in reverse.

As she backed out, she watched Helen in the rearview mirror count off with her fingers. Five…four…three…two. On the PAPOW she threw a high kick that flashed her new ruffled, red boyfriend panties—a move she'd perfected as her high school cheerleading captain and she still had it.

"God bless yoga," Helen yelled after Terra, pumping phantom pompoms in the air. "*Whooo!*"

Terra chuckled for about five seconds before reality reemerged and it was back to the burn in her throat and lungs as CCR's "I Put A Spell On You" filled her car.

Helen had one thing right.

She would look him in the eye when she returned the painting. But she'd lied—she wasn't scared—she was terrified.

Terrified she'd lose her mind and make a fool of herself. Terrified that angsty feeling in her chest would never go away— that she'd *never* get over him. Go to her grave looking for a man who could come anywhere close to making her feel the things he made her feel.

And the sex…holy hell!

But such was life, right?

Well, fuck that.

She found a spot and parked Iris, then walked the one block to Chuck's. No bouncer guarded the door yet and as she entered her heart thumped in time to Ed Sheeran's "Thinking Out Loud." It was still early, but there were more than a few customers at the bar. Suddenly as the song's lyrics penetrated, her feckless courage suicided. *I'll just keep on making the same mistakes.* Stage fright slammed through her body, causing her legs to stop short.

Good God, what if he was with someone? What if he was with *her?* Oh…shit…big, big, *big* mistake. What the hell had she been thinking? She had to go—like *right now.* She spun a one-eighty, and was half way out the door before Barney spotted her.

"Yo, cupcake!" he called across the bar in his gravelly voice. Heads belonging to several bodies seated at tables raised half-mast from their drinks and turned to stare.

Her legs again froze, and she stared back, blinking rapidly, her mind spinning like a roulette wheel.

Why didn't she go to Tony's? She could be sucking on a margarita right now. And why didn't she send the painting back the same way it came—by courier?

"Get yourself over here."

A small whimper snuck past her lips, nevertheless she turned around. Barney may be old, but he'd dealt with ornery bikers and drug dealers back in the day. Challenging his ass-kicking abilities wasn't high on her list. So, she put one foot ahead of the other and headed towards him. Much slower and focusing on not tripping as she approached, feeling everyone's eyes on her.

"Take a seat." Barney indicated an empty spot at the end of the bar, though it should be noted it didn't come along with his usual smile.

"Oh, that's okay, I don't want anything. I'm only here to return something."

"Bullshit!" He pinned her with his stealthy eyes that she assumed had once been blue but now looked kind of slate and she realized there was no point arguing. "Sit your ass down and have a drink."

Okay.

She blew out air. Maybe liquid courage wasn't a bad idea. Considering how her insides quivered, alcoholic fortification may indeed have been in order.

"What are you having?" Barney raised overgrown eyebrows.

She mauled her lip. "A shot of tequila, please." May as well go for gold. Now that she had her money back, she could afford it.

He nodded, and while he selected from the top shelf, she placed the box with the painting on the bar but did not sit. She took a quick look around—no Zander.

Well, there was that.

Maybe he wasn't even here. She could drop the painting at his door or just leave it with Barney and make a quick getaway. Her mother's guitar, though sorely missed, could wait another week or so.

Barney slid the shot glass rimmed with salt in front of her with a wedge of lime. His rugged face gave nothing away, but his badass stance and folded arms did.

"How are you, Barney?"

"Had better weeks."

"Yeah…me too."

His expression softened. "Heard about your momma."

He had?

"This one's for her. Drink up."

Her fingers shook as she raised the glass, tilted her head back and slammed it, then took her anxiety out on the lime. When she'd sufficiently mangled the fruit, she dropped it into the glass and sucked the juice off her fingers. Reaching into her purse, she pulled out a twenty and placed it on the bar. Barney shook his head and pushed it back towards her.

"Take it, please." She blinked hard, not convinced the burn was all about the tequila. More like the vibe she was catching made her feel she wasn't welcome here anymore. "And could you give this to Zander?" The pink box joined the twenty on the bar. "Tell him I appreciate the thought, but I can't keep it."

"I think that's the kind of message you need to deliver yourself, cupcake. I like my ass employed."

Fuck.

Alrighty then.

Barney pushed the twenty back before reaching below the bar for something, then he walked to the end and exited via the server station. He indicated with his head she should follow him. Leaving the twenty on the bar, she did as she was ordered.

"Go on up," he said, unlocking the private door. "If he's not in his office, try the door down the hall—more likely in there."

Door down the hall.

Zander's *other* apartment. The one with all the ghosts and where he did whatever he didn't want to share with her.

"See you later, Barney." She turned before he could answer, unwilling to let him see the bright in her eyes or give him the opportunity to say *no, he wouldn't see her later*. She liked the old dude and his brusqueness hurt.

She pushed through the doors and sucked it up. This needed to be done and since she was here—no time like the fucking present, yeah?

Somebody needed to tell her legs that—since they didn't want to move.

His office door was ajar, and she knocked softly, keeping an ear out for anything that indicated he was *busy*. After no answer she pushed it further. No Zander.

Maybe she didn't need to see him.

Perhaps he'd left his apartment door unlocked like he sometimes did and if so, she could grab her stuff and get the hell out.

To hell with him and who the fuck cared if he called her a pussy again, because—well, she was. May as well own it.

Okay...so up the stairs she went...and knocked. Again, nothing so she tried the door...and would you look at that!

Almost dizzy from holding her breath she opened it slowly, poking her head through—no music or TV noises. She made a beeline to his room where her things still sat in the corner just as she'd left them.

What struck her was his unmade bed and she stopped and stared at it, unable to breathe, looking for signs of another body who may or may not have occupied it since she left. The second pillow, the one she'd used, lay perpendicular to his with an indentation in the middle.

She couldn't think about what that meant.

So she didn't.

Blacked it out and placed the fancy pink box up against the wall then went to grab her guitar, her rug and the little carry-on suitcase. Before she'd hooked her fingers around the collapsible handle, she felt it—the spine-tingling change in the air. Her skin began to prickle.

He leaned against his bedroom door frame with those strong arms folded. Wearing faded jeans and a black Henley with the sleeves pushed up exposing new scrapes on those ropey muscles, his eyes scorching into hers.

Seeing him again was utterly heartbreaking.

And as predicted, utterly terrifying.

"Hi." So little air was left in her lungs she was surprised her greeting was audible and it seemed to hang in the air between them for an eternity.

"'Hi?'" His voice, when he finally answered was low and guttural—and full of anger. "You sneak into my apartment without announcing yourself and that's all you got?"

She frowned, averting her eyes, because—yeah, she wasn't exactly on the high ground. But she didn't exactly expect anger. Mild irritation, annoyance she'd invaded his space and for ignoring him for almost a week, yes—but *this*—not so much.

"Your door was open, I knocked but you didn't answer and…I came to get my things…and…"

"And what?" he growled.

She swallowed, finding it almost too hard to the say the words. "Return the painting."

He took that in, eyes narrowing. "You want to return it?"

"I can't keep it."

He took a step closer. "You don't like it?"

"God, no—it's gorgeous, Zander, I know they're very expensive and it's a sweet gesture but…"

"Just fucking stop." He held up a palm and glared at her. "Sweet *gesture?*" Then he looked at the ceiling. "Jesus!"

"Well, it is…"

"What the fuck you want *me* to do with it?" he demanded, his voice beginning to rise. He was so built, so big, so intimidating and so delicious, those eyes smoldering with dark anger and intent.

"Burn it? Stick it in my shredder? *Piss on it?* 'Cause I can't fucking sell it. I'm not letting some asshole with a hard-on for you hang it above his bed and jerk off to your beautiful face every fucking night—not after I poured every ounce of my goddamn soul and my *motherfucking* heart into it."

What?

"And I can't hang it over my own bed, not if I wanna keep what's left of my fucked-up mind."

"Wait…what do you mean?"

"Or skin on my palms."

"You painted it?"

"Yes, I painted it. Who do you think painted it?"

Her eyes got wide. "*You* painted it?"

"Yeah, woman—that's what I was doing when I wasn't with you, when you thought I was fucking someone else—even though I *told you* I wasn't."

"Well, okay maybe not then," Her own voice began to rise. "But don't try to gaslight me, I know what I saw."

"Gaslight? What the hell does gaslight mean? What you saw wasn't what you thought you saw."

"Good God, Zander!" Her hands went into the air. "That's the very definition of gaslighting! Convincing someone that what they saw wasn't what they saw. *I know what I saw!*"

"And if you'd given me a chance to explain like I tried a million fucking times we could be past this already."

"Are you kidding? You seriously think after that stunt you pulled there is a *we*?"

"There's a *we* because there *is* a fucking we."

By now he was much closer. Her heart fluttered in her throat because the vibe between them had grown heavy. Much heavier than she could handle. Then he took another step, backing her into the space between his bed, his dresser and the wall.

"You're scaring me." Her breath caught in her throat as she stumbled over her guitar and tried to dodge right—but she'd left it too late.

"Scaring *you*?" His arm whipped out and blocked her. She dove for his bed, and he came up behind her as she tried to crawl away, getting tangled in his sheets. His palms wrapped around her ankles, scissoring her legs and forcing her to roll onto her back. Then he was on her, using his weight to trap her, he caught her hands above her head.

"You're the one who scares me," he ground out as he lay over her. "You fucking petrify me." The gold flecks in his eyes were blazing, making them more golden than she'd ever seen them. She twisted beneath him, seeking purchase to push away, but his body dwarfed hers.

"You think I'd stand for that shit? Look the other way like some oblivious bimbo while you bang every woman in your bar? I don't know what you think I am, but I've told you before, *I'm not them.*"

"What I think, woman, is you are a stubborn pain in my ass, and in my heart, and I wouldn't want you if you were them. *You* are the only woman I've fucked since I've met you."

"Bullshit."

"I don't want anyone else."

"Then what the hell was that?" she yelled in his face, bucking her hips trying to shift his weight.

"She fucking molested me," he yelled back. "Climbed on me naked while I slept and grabbed my dick. *That's* what that was."

"You're a fucking liar."

"I'm not lying," he said between clenched teeth. "I'm not."

"Get *off* me." She tried dislodging him again, but again, it did no good.

"What the fuck is it gonna take for you to believe me? You need proof…is that what you need? You wanna see the fucking video…'cause I've got it on video, woman. I was hoping I wouldn't need it…I was hoping you could see your way clear to trust me. But I'll show it to you if you can stomach it."

She stilled suddenly as his words soaked in.

"You have a camera in your office?"

"I have camera outside my office. But when my door is open, there's a clear shot to my couch."

"For real?"

Suddenly the fight seemed to drain from him. She saw it leave his eyes and be replaced with something else. "I thought she was you," he repeated, his voice low and raw with emotion. "There was no reason for anybody else to be in the building. It was too early and after you woke me in my bed with your hands and your mouth on me, why wouldn't I think it was you?"

They stared at each other until a sob bubbled up from deep within her. "I want to believe you...I really do." Tears leaked from the corner of her eyes and rolled down her cheeks.

"Oh, babe." His brow puckered. "Don't cry...shit, don't cry. You're breaking my heart even more than it already is. I don't want you hurt, and that I had any part in you getting hurt really fucking kills me."

He lowered his forehead onto her shoulder, resting his head as if it had suddenly become too heavy for his body. Like the weight of his thoughts were too much to bear.

"You almost died...Jesus." A violent shudder ran through his body that she felt all the way down deep in her soul—and suddenly she knew—even if she hadn't felt his tears on her skin, there was not one single shred of doubt—*she knew* he was telling the truth.

"I still can't process that," he said. "I shut my eyes and see that gun against your skull, and I can't...I just can't..."

Her breath hitched as she absorbed how his body shook, the wet on her skin and the agony in his voice. "Let go of my wrists, baby," she sniffled softly.

He froze for several moments before he lifted his head and angled it so she could see into his eyes. The rims were moist—the whites had turned pink and were tinged with anxiety and—hope. Then his fingers relaxed, and she slipped hers from his hold and smoothed them around his shoulders, pulling him close.

"I'm sorry," she whispered. "I'm so sorry, I should have listened."

His sucked in a quick breath, then he let it out in a short burst. "You believe me?"

She nodded, her face crumpling. "I do."

Another tear seeped from her lids. His own face relaxed, then he caught the tear with the tip of his tongue and licked it away, letting his lips linger. A surge of heat mixed with tenderness rushed through her.

"You called me baby," he said softly against her face. The warmth of his breath on her skin felt right—and good. "You've never called me that."

A small, wobbly smile tipped her mouth and she pulled back to see him better. "Will you forgive me?"

"Forgive *you*?"

She nodded. "For being an ass."

"Babe, there's nothing to forgive," he said, his voice rough and uneven. "I'm the one that's an ass." He kissed the spot on her nose where her freckles clustered. Then the corner of each eye before he took a shaky breath. "I wanna do this with you—you know—give this relationship thing a shot. I've wanted you from that first moment in my alley, even when I thought you were just a groupie trying to skirt the cover charge."

She gave a half-sob, half-laugh at the memory.

"But you've been in my thoughts every second of every day. The thought of losing you because of *her*"—he closed his eyes and swallowed—"or because that fuck killed you. I wanted to murder them both, but I took it out on everybody else. Nicky reamed my ass...Barney *ejected* my ass...I kicked the shit out of a barstool..."

She smoothed the hair from his face, and pulled him closer, kissing his temple.

"I'm falling in love with you, Freckle...I need you. And now that I've had one small taste of you, I don't want to face the world without you."

She stared at him, her lashes fluttering. "You're falling in love with me?" she asked with her heart in her mouth.

"I thought if you saw my painting, you'd see..." He stopped and expelled a breath. "See how I see you—how beautiful you are. And not just this." He ran the tips of his fingers over her cheek, down over her chin, her throat, then when he got to her heart, he paused. "But this too." Then, shifting his head, bringing his lips within a whisper of hers, he took one of her hands, turning it and pressing it against him, he used her fingers to squeeze him. He was solid, and big and just as she remembered, just as she'd dreamed about.

"This is what you do to me," he said, his voice low and gruff, full of need. "And will until my last breath."

She breathed in his Zander smell and made the first move—just a small one, but it was enough. Her mouth opened, he captured her lip and kissed her gently—like he was savoring the moment—her taste—*her*. Like she was precious.

Until it deepened and within moments, they were feasting and devouring each other.

"Christ, I missed you," he rasped against her lips. This caused an eruption of goosebumps over her entire body, her nipples tightening to the point of pain. But he pulled back to look into her eyes.

"Babe, I need inside you, like yesterday." The evidence of his need clutched in her greedy hand. She ran it over his erection, wanting it free and fumbled with his button and zip. He groaned and the muscles in his torso clenched, but he curled his fingers around hers and brought them to his lips.

"If we're going to do this," he said, "be in a relationship, we need to establish rule number four."

"What's rule number four?"

"Next time shit goes down, we talk it out, fight it out, whatever-the-fuck-it-out until we reach a resolution. No walking away from each other until we've done so—we clear?"

"As crystal," she breathed, anxious for him to continue.

"Good, because I don't know what tomorrow's gonna hand

us, Freckle. All I know is we have right now. And right now, I want you so bad, I'm gonna rip a hole in my jeans."

She giggled against his lips. "Perfect, because I think my panties are melting."

He emitted a low, feral growl that vibrated down her spine and landed between her legs. "Woman, you say shit like that to me, you better be prepared for what you gonna get." He slid his hands up her thighs until he hooked her panties.

"Is that a promise?" she asked, biting her lip.

"It's a fucking vow."

Then he proceeded to slide his hands down her thighs and gave her everything he vowed he would…and then, he vowed some more.

EPILOGUE

Labor Day weekend...three weeks later

"She belongs up here, Zander," Terra said, straightening the painting of Alexandra Milan situated between Ginny's and the one he'd painted of her, and stepped back.

"So do you." Zander curled his arm around the front of her chest, bringing her close against his body. "My women," he murmured into her hair as she nestled into him.

"Mm," she smiled. "All three of us."

He gave her a little squeeze.

"You all have the same eyes. I can't believe you didn't bring her up sooner."

"Wasn't ready, babe," he murmured as he caught her earlobe between his teeth and tugged gently.

She hissed softly. "And you're ready now...you're not doing it because I badgered you?"

She felt him nod, his stubble on her skin sending a delicious shiver down her spine. "Think I've finally forgiven myself."

Terra twisted her top half to look at him. "Forgiven *yourself*?"

"For a long time, I thought I couldn't forgive *her*. For not leaving him when I asked her to. I couldn't understand their fucked-up relationship or why she'd let him hurt us. But in the last few weeks, I've had a lot of time to reflect. I remember how he looked at her and I know on some level, beyond his obsession, in his own way he loved her. When he knew he was losing her, that made him feel weak and he'd do anything to keep her."

"Baby," she whispered.

"Meeting you" —his eyes softened, making the gold look molten—"has shown me we can't control who...or *how* we love. Or what *I'd* do to keep you. It's not a switch we flip and boom, it's over. I guess, what I'm trying to say is, it made me realize it wasn't just her I was angry at...it was both of us. That I also couldn't forgive myself for not being able to save her."

"You were a child, Zander. It wasn't your fault he killed her."

"You're right." He slid his hands down her sides, settled on her hips and turned her. Then he gripped her ass and held on. "It wasn't, but I never allowed myself to think about her because I had it jumbled in my head that no matter how hard I tried, she didn't love me enough to choose me, and that hurt."

"Baby." She wrapped around his neck and tilted her head to kiss the rough dent in his chin. "She loved you. How could she not? You have to know it was her addiction that chose him, not her."

"I know that now," he said, slanting his head to meet her mouth, nuzzling her lips. "Watching what you went through with your mom and dealing with the cops allowed some of those memories to come back and forced me to face my shit—and forced me to forgive us both. It was time to let it go and move on."

His phone buzzed in his pocket and he sighed before he stuck his hand in to retrieve it.

"What is it?" Terra asked when one eyebrow arched.

He passed the phone so she could see the text message.

Carmine: *Turn on the TV.*

Zander grabbed the remote from the coffee table and hit the power button. It didn't matter what channel he chose; it was on all of them.

"The FBI have arrested and taken into custody Thomas Madden Junior, a congressman from California in connection to a complicated murder-for-hire plot involving a pregnant prostitute that could be the storyline of a bestselling political thriller.

The victim, Rebecca Miller, who had checked into a rehab facility was initially believed to have overdosed on heroin. The case was first handled by the police, but after further investigation revealed a connection to organized crime and to the congressman, it was handed over to the FBI."

The hair on Terra's arms stood on end. Above a bright red banner stating "Breaking News" was a headshot of a man on the right side of the screen.

Terra gasped, as if she'd been punched in the stomach. "I still can't wrap my head around the idea that that man is my father. And I *saw* him with her in the elevator of the Fairmont the day he raped her...again."

"It is alleged that, in an elaborate scheme involving the congressman, a member of the Russian mafia was contracted to carry out this terrible deed for fear the identity of the child Ms. Miller carried could lead back to him, jeopardizing his reelection campaign. To further complicate the plot, it is alleged Ruby Baker, an addict known to Ms. Miller snuck onto the grounds of the rehab facility to ambush and inject her while she was on a hike. A needle, containing DNA evidence and Rebeca Miller's phone were found in a zip-lock bag by a maintenance worker at the spot where Ruby Baker ended her life by jumping from the Golden Gate Bridge.

A copy of the DNA results obtained by this network have confirmed the congressman is indeed the father of Rebecca Miller's child. There are reports of a letter that further verify these allegations, according to an unnamed source close to the investigation. Neither the congressman nor his wife could be reached for comment. Our next story..."

Holy hell!

Her legs threatened to buckle as she sobbed. "They got him."

"Yeah, babe, they got the fucker. His career is toast and he's gonna spend time in prison, being somebody's bitch."

Her heart pounded in her throat as Zander walked her back to the couch. Once she was seated, he left her for a moment to uncork a bottle of champagne he pulled from the fridge. Then snatched two glasses from the cabinet and a big, brown envelope off the counter. He brought them over. After handing her a filled glass, he joined her on the couch.

"First, here's to that asshole going down."

They tipped their glasses and took a sip.

"And second, I was gonna wrap this," he said, looking a little uncertain which was so unlike him. She found it charming, yet at the same time unnerving. "And give it to you tomorrow, for your birthday, but it feels right to do it now."

"What is it?" she asked, her brow wrinkling.

"Open it and find out, babe," he said, then handed her the envelope.

She studied his unease, before snuggling against his body. Lifting her face, she reached for his lips and gave him a soft, lingering kiss.

When he pulled away, she took another sip of champagne, and handed him her glass to hold.

Inside was a red manila folder.

As she opened it, the first things she saw were the two glossy five-by-eight photographs of her mother.

"Ohmigod," she whispered as she leafed through Carmine's official report, the newspaper cuttings and Rebecca's school records. "When did you do this?"

"Well, that's the thing," he murmured, then he leaned over and put their glasses on the table. "When you had just heard your mom had died and asked me if I could loan you five thousand dollars, I had to know why."

"So, you had Carmine do a background on me?"

"Yep." He swallowed hard, and she suddenly understood his uncertainty. "Are you angry?"

She let out a puff of air, then shook her head. "No, Zander," she said, and took his face between her hands. "I'm not angry with you—I'm in love with you." She blinked away a tear. "I understand why you did it and this is the best birthday present anyone could've ever given me."

His face broke out in a giant smile. "Fuck, for that alone it was worth it."

She looked at him, puzzled.

"You finally said it."

"Said what?"

"That you love me." He pulled her closer and held her tight to his chest. "Baby, you make so fucking happy it can't possibly get any better than this."

"Oh…yes, it can," she said, touching her lips to the corner of his mouth. "It can get a lot better. If you carry me to the bedroom, I'll show you just how much better it can get."

To which he did—and she did.

The End.

Thank you for reading.
If you enjoyed this story, please consider leaving a review, even if it's just one line. Thank you!

ALSO BY ANN HOWES

THE MARKER

The Bridge Series: Book One

The Marker
My Book

Follow Ann Howes at:
facebook.com/AuthorAnnHowes/
bookbub.com/profile/ann-howes
amazon.com/author/annhowes

UNTITLED

<<<<>>>>

Made in the USA
Monee, IL
28 October 2020